I0676154

KINGMAKER

A Brady James Novel

William J. Millman

SB

Sunset Beach Press

SB

Sunset Beach Press

This book is a work of fiction. Names, characters, places, and incidents either are products of the author's imagination or are used fictitiously. Any resemblance to actual events or locales or persons, living or dead, is entirely coincidental.

Copyright © 2012 by William J. Millman

All rights reserved, including the right to reproduce this book or portions thereof in any form whatsoever.

Manufactured in the United States of America

Cover photo: Colourbox

Library of Congress Control Number: 2012942379

ISBN: 978-0-9857918-0-3

For Mila. Always.

CHAPTER 1

October 14
Washington, DC

He liked being retired.

Not having to take phone calls at 2 a.m. from an editor wanting him to cover a double-homicide on Capitol Hill. Or having a weekend ruined by a bank heist out in the suburbs.

They say that a journalist's blood runs black with printer's ink. Brady James was perfectly content to fill his veins with Budweiser while watching the Redskins stumble through another season of hope misplaced. In fact, that was exactly what he was doing one Sunday afternoon in October when a knock on his apartment door brought the narrowed eyes and pinched lips that had sent many an editor scurrying for cover.

"Goddamn it!" he mumbled as he pushed himself up out of the stained, misshapen easy chair that had served as his base of operations for the past 7 months. "Who the hell comes knocking on a Sunday afternoon?"

"I'm coming, I'm coming!" he yelled as the tentative knock was replaced by the repeated buzz of his broken doorbell. "I'm not a goddamn sprinter…"

Brady knew that it was unlikely to be a friend, since he didn't have many of those and the few he had wouldn't dare interrupt a Redskins' game. Probably a Jehovah's Witness or Mormon missionary. If it was those damn missionaries again, he was going to rip them a new one…

His expression must have matched his thoughts when he yanked open the door, for the woman that stood there awaiting his arrival stepped back in wide-eyed alarm.

Sure enough, it wasn't anyone he knew. But one look made him wish he did. She wasn't all that young, probably early 40's, with brownish-blondish hair and green eyes, but she had the kind of pouty lips and high cheekbones that he absolutely loved. Curvy in all the right places, too.

"I'm sorry!' she squealed. "Is this a bad time?"

He felt the anger drain out of his cheeks, replaced by the fiery red of embarrassment.

"Uh, no, no, not particularly. Is there something I can do for you?" He was hoping there was.

The woman glanced nervously over her shoulders at the street below. Brady recognized the look. He'd seen plenty of sources make the same turn. She was worried that someone might see her there. Interesting.

"Are you Brady James?"

So, at least it wasn't a mistake.

"I am. And you are?"

The woman lowered her voice to little more than a whisper. "May I come in? I'd like to…discuss something with you."

Brady's intrinsic skepticism made him wonder if this was some new God Squad approach, but even if it were, he decided he would hear her out. *'Only being polite,'* he justified.

"Yeh, sure. Come on in."

He stepped aside to let her enter. As he did, he looked into his apartment and saw it just as she did at that moment. Dishes and pans from breakfast sitting on the stove and the counters. A Bud 12-ouncer, sides crushed, lying next to his chair. Sunday Post spread all over the worn gray couch. He hurried past her.

"Wasn't expecting company," he groused as he collected the various Post sections and cleared a spot on the couch. "Have a seat."

A look of doubt, or was it distaste, crossed the woman's face for just an instant. And then it was gone.

"Thank you," she said, sitting primly on the sofa.

"Can I get you something? Soda? Juice? A beer?"

As soon as he said it he wished he hadn't.

"Juice would be great. Thanks."

"I'll be right back. You like the Redskins?" he asked as he started for the kitchen, nodding idiotically toward the TV.

"The Redskins? Oh, I don't really follow football all that much."

He winced. *What is this, the high school prom?'* he chastised himself as he slipped the plates and pots into the sink as quickly as he could without making too much noise. *'I'm acting like a goddamn 17 year old.'* He opened the orange juice and sniffed it to make sure it hadn't gone bad. He grabbed a glass from a cabinet, held it up to the window to see if it were clean enough for guests, and then gave it a quick once-over with a paper towel just to be sure.

As he was walking back to the living room carrying the orange juice, he glanced at himself in an old wall mirror whose silvering was flaking badly. Through the blotches of disintegration he could just make out a 63 year old couch potato, some 6'1" of steely resolve and rubbery constitution, hair thinning precariously, his jaw a bit too prominent, his gut hanging over a battered belt tethered on its last way station to the next larger size.

He reflexively sucked in the gut. *'Not bad,'* he mused. *'Could be worse.'*

The woman was seated exactly where he had left her. *'Doesn't look like she moved a muscle,'* he thought distractedly. *'Could be a statue.'*

"So, what brings you to lovely northeast DC?" he asked as he handed her the juice.

She bit her lower lip and took a sip of juice. Brady knew she had something important – at least to her – on her mind.

"I...I'm not even sure if you're the right person," she began, her gaze riveted on an indefinite space a few feet in front of her. She hesitated.

He nearly jumped in to give her a push, but he held his tongue. He was in no rush, chancing a quick glance at her shapely legs.

"Hard to say," he finally tossed out to fill the silence.

"Yes. Yes, it is," she agreed. "You see, I'm not used to this kind of thing…"

"Look. I don't know what it is you want to talk about, but just relax, take a deep breath, and lay it out there. I don't bite – despite appearances."

He felt unexpected satisfaction when the woman smiled slightly.

"I'm sure you don't."

"Let's start with your name. How about that?" he coaxed. For the first time in over a month he wished he had a cigarette.

"Oh, I'm sorry. Anne. Anne Waznewski."

"Ok then, Miss Waznewski…" He tried not to emphasize the 'Miss' too blatantly, but he couldn't help himself. He paused for just a heartbeat, just long enough for her to correct him if he'd been wrong. She didn't.

"Anne. Please, call me Anne," she said instead.

He couldn't restrain a smile of his own. "Ok then, Anne, let's start at the beginning. What is it you think I can do for you?"

She closed her eyes, as if summoning the fortitude to launch into her story. When she opened them again, he learned why.

"You see, I'm Senator Blayton Wainwright's personal secretary. Was, that is." She looked for a second like she might cry.

"Yeh, I read about his drowning. Terrible tragedy."

"It wasn't!" she said with surprising forcefulness.

"A tragedy?"

"No! A d..r..o..w..n..i..n..g," she said as if whispering a common truth to a moron.

'Another conspiracy nut,' Brady thought with a shake of his head. "What exactly do you mean, it wasn't a drowning? I saw the pictures when they fished him out of the river."

"Oh, he drowned all right," she said, a bit of fire flashing in her eyes. "But it wasn't an accident."

"And you know this because…"

"As I said, I was the Senator's secretary. I screened all his calls, opened all his mail. I even had access to his emails."

"And…"

"And, I know that the Senator *never* took walks by the river, and I know that he was involved in something – something important. I'm not certain exactly what it was…"

"I thought you had access to all his messaging," Brady groused. He'd heard too many similar tales to take this one at face value.

"In the office, yes. But he had his Blackberry and his home phone. He might have even had other emails accounts."

Brady still wasn't convinced, but those legs were looking better by the minute. He sat down on a dilapidated leather hassock and pulled it close to the sofa so he could face her.

"Okay, so you saw some emails or heard some phone messages. What makes you think they had something to do with his death?

"Because of the way he was acting during those last few weeks."

"The Senator?"

"Yes, the Senator!" Anne answered, her irritation visible as well as audible. "He was…different."

"How do you mean?"

"I don't know…The Senator was always a very forceful, determined man. But in those last weeks it seemed that he'd lost his way. He seemed…lost."

Brady stared hard at the woman. She didn't seem like your average crackpot.

"But there was more to it than that. Right?"

She nodded. "I think he was frightened. He instructed me to not let anyone into the office who didn't have an appointment, and he seemed uncharacteristically jumpy. As if he expected something bad to happen. He was always so calm and in control…"

She sniffled and fished in her small black pocketbook for a handkerchief.

"And you think someone…killed him?" Brady asked, thinking that she was making quite a leap between a jumpy boss and murder.

Anne just nodded, the tears flowing freely now.

"I know it sounds crazy," she managed between sniffles.

"No, no, of course not," Brady interrupted, thinking all the while that it was absolutely bananas. "Have you talked to the police?"

"They are convinced it was just a drowning," she answered, her voice gaining strength once again. "They don't want to hear about my 'theories'."

He could imagine one of the DC detectives using just those words.

"I see. How about the FBI? He was an elected official, after all."

"I didn't have the heart, after the reception I received from the police."

Brady nodded. She wouldn't be the first person put off by the famous DC police charm. "Do other people in your office share your opinion?"

Anne hesitated just a moment. "I haven't really discussed it with them. I didn't want to…reopen fresh wounds." The way she said it suggested she wasn't too sure they would agree with her.

Brady took a deep breath. He knew what was coming next, and the smartest part of him said to show the woman the door before it came. But the journalist part said to dig.

"And so you came here."

"Yes. I didn't know where else to go."

He could have suggested a half dozen places. But he didn't.

"So, what is it you want me to do? I'm not a private investigator…"

"I know, but I've read your stories for many years, and I know that you have a reputation for getting to the bottom of difficult stories."

"Had a reputation. I retired a few months back."

"That's why I thought you might have the time."

He wanted to disagree, to tell her about all the important work he was involved in. Only problem was, he couldn't think of anything just then. Truth was, he was getting a little bored with this retirement thing.

She looked up at him with the wide-eyed stare usually seen on black velvet paintings. He knew right then he was about to break one of his most fervently held rules. He was about to take on an assignment with no clear direction and little hope of remuneration.

"I couldn't promise you anything," he said, hoping against hope that she'd back out if given a chance. She didn't.

"I wouldn't expect you to," she said, a hopeful light shining in her eyes. "And if there's anything I can do…"

He was about to reply with a scatological quip when he caught himself.

"Don't worry. I'll let you know. But first things first. I'll need to get acquainted with all the background info. How about family, friends? Was he married?"

"He was, but three years ago his wife and son were killed in a car accident. Drunk driver."

Brady nodded sympathetically out of habit.

"How about friends? People he saw frequently?"

"Quite a few, until three years ago."

"And more recently?"

She shook her head sadly. "The Senator often ate alone. As far as I know, he had no real regular communication with anyone, other than me, and that was all about the job."

Brady sighed. When things went bad, they really went bad. "Can you get me a list of all the Senator's calls and e-mails over the past month or so?"

Anne cocked her head appraisingly. "That's a lot of calls and e-mails."

"I'm sure. But somewhere in there there might be a lead. Can you do it?"

"I think so. Yes, I will."

"And anything else you can think of. A list of all his visitors during the same time period. The names of his friends, family, and close political associates. Places he frequented. Basically, anything that might help me understand what was bothering him these past few weeks."

"Of course. I'll start compiling the information tomorrow morning."

She seemed like a new person, confident, on top of it. He liked this person.

"Good," he said with a pleased smile. "As soon as you can get me that stuff, I'll start looking for leads. Of course, I'll need to be able to get ahold of you if I have questions or... get some new ideas." Brady tried to sound as neutral as possible, but the shy grin that greeted him suggested that Anne hadn't missed the overtones. And hadn't objected.

"Of course. I'd very much appreciate regular updates."

"Yeh, okay. No problem."

She gave him her office and home numbers as well as her cell, since she didn't know how long the Senator's office staff would be kept on now that he was gone. They had to close-up the office and transfer files, but there hadn't been any word yet from Tom Jeffries, the Senator's Chief of Staff, whether they were on a three week or six month schedule. She didn't think he knew either. They were all waiting to hear from the Governor's office who he would name as the interim successor.

"I really can't thank you enough, Mr. James," Anne said, rising from the sofa and offering her hand. "We all loved the Senator, and want to see justice done."

"Apparently not everyone," he said.

To her quizzical expression he quickly added, "Loved him. If you're right, someone didn't care for him at all."

"That's the person we've got to find," she said, with such finality that Brady almost believed it was possible.

"We'll give it our best shot."

He showed her to the door.

"I'll expect to hear from you soon."

"You will. I'm certain…"

She was interrupted in mid-sentence by a loud knock on the door.

"Excuse me," he said, stepping past Anne. "It's Holy Roller season." He grimaced and would've kicked himself if he could get his foot back there. He was so angry that he almost barked as he opened the door.

"What?!"

Both he and Anne stared out into open space, until a voice from roughly waist-high spoke up with undisguised irritation.

"You don't have to bite my goddamn head off! If any of your dwindling brain cells are still working, you might remember you asked me Wednesday if I wanted to watch the game."

Brady knew the source of that all too familiar voice before he even looked down, but Anne's mouth dropped open as she faced a short – no, very short – little man, perhaps a tad over 3 feet tall, with long black hair, bulging brown eyes, and a handsome, rugged face that belied his miniscule stature. She thought he was in his late 40's, but he could have been anything from 40 to 60.

When he spied her half hidden behind Brady, his eyes bulged even further.

"Oh. I didn't know you had company," he said smoothly, a smile replacing the scowl that had greeted them.

"Yeh, right," James muttered. He ignored the new arrival and turned back to Anne. "We'll be in touch. Let me know if you run into any…problems."

"I will," she said, looking from him to the little man just outside the door, and then back to Brady again. "And thank you again. I can't tell you how much this means to me."

"No problem. My pleasure."

Brady took Anne's elbow and was showing her out, with no recognition of his new visitor whatsoever, when the visitor took the initiative.

"I don't believe we've met," he said, lifting his hand so that Anne could shake it if she chose. "I'm Derek. Derek DiLaurain. And you are…?"

"You don't have to answer that," Brady cut in, the irritation showing on his face. "The lady was just leaving," he explained to the newcomer.

"I can see that. A pity."

James rolled his eyes. "Don't worry, he's harmless enough," he said to Anne. "But a real pain in the ass sometimes, albeit a *small* pain."

"HA, HA, HA!" Derek forced a sarcastic laugh. "Small jokes. Real classy, James."

"I'm Anne, Anne Waznewski," the embarrassed secretary said, stepping past James and taking Derek's hand. "Pleased to meet you."

"Likewise, I'm sure," the midget said as he stretched his neck to kiss her hand.

Anne looked stricken, but forced a wan smile through her bright red cheeks.

"Well, I really should be going…"

"Not on my account, beautiful," the little man said with a grin that approached leer-dom.

"As I said, we'll be in touch," Brady said, ignoring the comment completely. "I'm sure we can get to the bottom of this."

"Thank you," Anne said, looking intently into his eyes. "I will pray for it."

She stepped down onto the landing outside the door and forced a smile. "Very nice meeting you, Mr. DiLaurain." The smile disappeared before she'd even turned to go.

"Yeh, you too," Derek called after her. He turned to Brady with wide eyes and an appraising look. "What's that all about?" he whispered too loudly.

"Get in here!" James spit, grabbing him by the shoulder and dragging him through the doorway. "What is the matter with you?!" he raged as soon as the door was closed. "Do you have to hit-on everything in a skirt?"

"*That* was not just your common everyday variety thing in a skirt," Derek explained. "That was something else."

"*That* was someone who wants me to help find a murderer, so hands off."

"What?! I thought you were retired."

James shrugged. "I am. But this could be interesting. She thinks her former boss, Senator Blayton Wainwright, was killed. Wants me to see if I can find out how."

Brady could see his little friend's interest piqued. "Wainwright? The papers said he drowned."

"The papers are sometimes wrong. Or have you forgotten already?"

Derek worked from time to time as a private investigator and had helped Brady with a number of difficult crime story investigations. He knew full well how wrong the papers, even the good ones, could occasionally be.

"I haven't forgotten. But a Senator? The FBI looks into those cases. You think they'd miss something as big as the murder of a Senator?"

"I don't know. Seems unlikely, but unlikelier things have happened. Besides, even if there's no story, at least I'll have an excuse for seeing Miss Waznewski from time to time."

At that the little guy's face lit up. "Ah ha! I knew there was more to it. She is a real nice piece, ain't she?"

"She is, and a classy one at that. So just keep your distance."

"Alright, alright. I just said hello. Don't turn it into a rape case, for cryin' out loud."

James liked the little man. He didn't know too many midgets – little people – but Derek was all right. No chip on his shoulder. No hyper-sensitivity. He could laugh at himself, and perhaps that was why

Brady rarely thought of him as vertically challenged. And he was a good PI. Brady didn't know if his diminutive size made people overlook him, or whether they just underestimated him, but whatever the reason Derek had come up with details for a number of stories that no one else had even touched. Not even the cops. Maybe he could use him on this story, case, whatever. But not until he knew whether there was any story to be covered.

"Rape? With that little pickle of yours?" Brady jibed.

"Pickle? More like kielbasa," Derek came right back. "Speaking of which, I'm starving, what do you have in the fridge?"

"Look for yourself. This isn't a goddamn diner."

Brady went back into the living room to watch the game.

"And bring me a beer when you come."

As he settled into his easy chair, Brady's thoughts were only partly on football.

'Blayton Wainwright, huh?' he thought as the Cowboys tried a quarterback sneak to pick up a first down. *'This might be interesting.'*

CHAPTER 2

It had been four days since the unexpected visit of Anne Waznewski, and Brady was getting antsy waiting for the materials she'd promised. He'd done some homework on his own, of course, Googling the Senator and trying to find as many news reports as possible from the past year. But the real info, the real dirt, would be found in those phone call lists and emails – or so he hoped.

It was midafternoon when the phone finally rang.

"Mr. James?" came the familiar voice. "Brady?" He wanted to smile, but the tension in her voice made him hesitate.

"Anne? Is everything ok?"

"No, no it's not. Can you come down here…now?"

"Where's here?" he asked, his mind racing.

"I'm at the Senator's office, in the Hart Building. Do you know where it is?"

Brady had been there many a time. "Yeh, I know it."

"Please. There's something here you need to see. I'll leave your name with security."

His instincts told him to question her further to see if he could save himself a trip, but the anxiety he heard made him agree. *'Must be getting soft,'* he thought.

"Okay, sure. I'll be there in a half-hour."

Brady hurried to his bedroom and pulled out his best interview clothes: a fairly new brown permanent press shirt, brown khaki trousers (a tad wrinkled, but just a tad), and a brown plaid sports jacket. It wasn't particularly new, but since he rarely wore the thing except for high level interviews, it still had a lot of wear left in it. He started to look for brown dress shoes, when he remembered that he'd tossed them in the trashcan on his last day at the paper. "Damn!" He'd just have to wear the black loafers he had on.

He stuffed his wallet into his left inside coat pocket and a wad of ones and fives into his trousers. Grabbing the car keys off the bureau, he hurried out of the apartment, locking both the deadbolt and the handle lock before he rushed downstairs. His 2002 red Honda Civic sat in its usual street-side parking place. He jumped in and headed downtown, trying to keep his speed under the limit despite the worry that welled-up inside him.

'What the hell is this all about?' he wondered as he tried to imagine what could have prompted her call. *'I hope she's not some kind of nut case who's going to call me for every little bump in the road.'* Investigations like this one often had lots of little bumps.

James turned off Rhode Island Ave onto 6th Street, and then left onto Pennsylvania Ave. A left on Constitution and he was there in less than 25 minutes. The Hart Building, otherwise known as the 'new' Senate office building, was a million square feet of 1970's era glass and concrete. He entered the building on the 2nd Street side and went straight to the security desk.

"Brady James, to see Anne Waznewski," he announced to the guard on duty.

The guard picked up the phone on his desk and dialed an extension.

"Miss Waznewski? There's a Brady James here to see you. Yeh, sure." He hung up and turned to Brady. "She'll be right down."

Brady nodded, all too familiar with the security procedures in federal office buildings. He eyed with some disdain the huge black metal 'clouds' that served as artwork in the atrium, before wandering over to the window to look out at the people and cars hurrying here and there throughout the city. Until a few months ago, that had been him as well. Did he miss it? Not in the least. But, here he was, dipping his toe back into the same swift flowing stream of crap. *'I must be crazy.'*

As if on cue, an elevator opened and Anne click-clacked loudly across the polished marble floor to the security desk. Brady tried to assume the cool, calm, detached persona he had perfected after 30 years as a reporter, but those legs…

"Mr. James," Anne said with a nod of her head. Her voice was controlled, but the thin press of her lips told Brady the truth about her mental state.

"If you'll just put any metal in this tray and walk through the screener," the guard directed amicably.

Brady was already complying and was through the checkpoint and following Anne into the elevator in a matter of seconds.

"I'm so sorry to call you down here," she began as soon as the doors had closed. "But I think you'll see why in just a moment."

"What's happened? Are you all right?"

"I'm fine, thank you for asking," she said, and her smile made him glad he had asked. "It's the office…"

The floor indicator beeped and showed a large red LED '3' as the door slid quietly open. "Right this way," she continued. Her high heels echoed in the long corridor.

He was about to ask more about the problem in the office, when she stopped at an unmarked door and used her key to let them in.

"Staff entrance," she explained.

As soon as they stepped through the door it was perfectly clear why she had called. File drawers hung at crazy angles from a number of gray metal file cabinets. Manila files and a thick carpet of papers nearly completely covered the floor. A flower pot had been smashed, the poor withered greenery tossed aside. All in all, the place was a mess.

"Remind me not to use your moving company," he said softly.

But Anne didn't laugh. In fact, tears welled up in her eyes.

"Why would anyone do this?" she asked, her voice quivering. "Why?"

Brady absently patted her on the shoulder. "I don't know. But I'm starting to think your theory about the Senator's death may not be so far-fetched after all."

"Far-fetched?"

James could have kicked himself. "I'm a skeptic," he scurried to explain. "Everything is far-fetched to me until I see some hard evidence. This is pretty hard."

"So you think this might have something to do with the Senator's murder?"

Instinctively Brady looked at the partly open door out to the hallway and quickly pushed it shut.

"Are you sure you didn't share your thoughts about his death with any of your colleagues? Not anyone?" he asked once he was confident no one could overhear them.

"No, not really. Most of them have been on furlough since…that day. The only time I've seen them was at the funeral, and we didn't really talk much there."

"Good. For the time being, keep your thoughts to yourself."

"But why?"

"Whoever did this is worried – big time. To rifle through a Senator's office in a federal building takes guts and panic. Not a good combination. Have you called the cops?"

"Not yet. I wanted you to take a look before anyone else comes in."

"Okay, fine. Let me snoop around a little bit, and then you can call your security people. Have you noticed anything in particular that's missing?"

Anne surveyed the scene of destruction. "I really don't know. It seems like they went through everything. I didn't want to move anything, but I looked through my desk a bit while I was waiting for you to get here. I didn't notice anything in particular."

"Did you check your computer?"

"My computer? No, but even if they could have accessed my files, everything is backed-up on the central server."

"Good. We may need to see that back-up. Take a look anyway."

While Anne went to her desk to check her computer files, Brady systematically checked the rest. He wasn't exactly sure what he was looking for, but he was tantalized that it might have something to do with the Senator's death. There had to be something there that would point them in the right direction.

He took out his cellphone and began to snap photos: an overview of the entire office, close-ups of individual files, specific documents, Anne's desk, even the overturned plants. Just about everything, in fact. He didn't know what he might find, but he knew that once the police got there he probably wouldn't have access to the crime scene for quite some time. At least not until they'd mucked the place up, anyway. At one point he glanced over at Anne, wondering if she might object to his taking photos of the Senator's private files. But she was so involved in her computer scan that she apparently didn't give it a second thought.

He had pretty much finished his photo inventory when Anne gave a small gasp from behind her monitor.

"What? What did you find?" he asked, moving quickly to her side.

"I can't believe it," she said, shaking her head in bewilderment.

"Can't believe what?" he asked, looking over her shoulder.

"This!" she said, her voice rising as she pointed to the screen. "This was our phone log."

James scanned the screen looking for anything that resembled phone numbers. All he saw were garbage symbols. Gibberish.

"Did anyone else have your password?"

"No one. Not even the administrator. The Senator had a thing about individual responsibility."

"And did anyone else have access to this file?"

"Not this one. This one is my personal file. But there should be another copy accessible to the entire office…" she said, snapping her mouse around to dig into another drive. Neither of them said a word as she plowed into the shared drive. Brady found himself holding his breath as she clicked on the actual file.

Nothing. Just the same gibberish.

"I don't believe it! How is this possible?" Anne cried out, her voice on the verge of panic.

"Take it easy now," he said, resting his hand reassuringly on her shoulder. "Let's check a few other files. How about the visit log? You did keep track of everyone who came to this office, right?"

"Of course. As did the security people downstairs."

"Okay. Show me."

She quickly jumped to the visitor file and double clicked.

Gibberish.

"How about the Senator's personal phonebook? Do you have access to that?"

"I did," she said, clicking expertly. It was only seconds later when the same telltale nonsense symbols appeared on the screen.

"This is a nightmare!" She sounded ready to cry.

"Check one other thing for me, will you?" Brady interrupted. "Access any other file. Office supplies, or something equally mundane."

"But why…?"

"Just check – please."

She did as he asked, and moments later a list of supplies ordered and used appeared on the screen.

"Interesting…" he mused.

"What does it mean?"

"Well, I don't know for sure, of course, but it looks like someone went to great pains to erase only those files dealing with the Senator's contacts, by phone and in person. Someone good enough to break into this office and access your computer could easily have just erased the entire drive. But he – or she - didn't. Why?"

"I don't know…"

"Neither do I. But maybe the back-up has the information we need. Who do you need to contact to get access to the files?"

"The network Administrator. He has an office downstairs. I can call him."

"Ask him to come up here. Tell him…tell him it's important."

As Anne made the call Brady stalked the office, hoping to find anything that would shine a light on their predicament.

"The Administrator is on leave," Anne announced as she hung up the phone, breaking his train of thought.

"Too bad. When is he coming back?"

"Actually, it might be a good thing. His assistant is a young guy, really knowledgeable about computers. He's on his way up."

"Can he keep a secret?"

Anne bobbed her head appraisingly. "I think so. At least I've never heard a complaint."

"Good. But just to be sure, let's keep your murder theory just between us for now – okay?"

"Okay." She was still a bit shaky. James could feel it.

He was about to launch into his best buck-up speech when a knock sounded on the door behind them.

"Jesus, what did he do, run up here?" Brady asked as he went to answer.

"I said he was young."

Brady swung open the door and found himself staring at a tall, skinny 20-something with shaggy brown hair and intense dark eyes, wearing wrinkled jeans and a t-shirt that read 'What Part of $E=mc^2$ Don't You UNDERSTAND!'

"Uh, is Ms. Waznewski here?" he said after a momentary hesitation.

"Yeh, sure. Come on in."

Anne stood up from her desk and immediately walked toward the new arrival.

"Danny, thanks a lot for coming up."

"No problem, Ms. W. We all know how heavy it's been up here since…the Senator died."

'Classic geek,' Brady thought. *'All the finesse of a bulldozer.'*

"Yes, well thank you for that," Anne continued undeterred. "This is a friend of mine, Mr…"

"Just call me Brady," James said.

Danny blinked twice before shaking the outstretched hand.

"So Anne tells me you're something of a computer whiz," he said, hoping that flattery was the way to a geek's heart, or at least his head.

"I'm pretty good. What's the problem?"

He turned back to Anne.

"I think there's something wrong with my computer," she explained. "Some of my files are all messed up."

'Good girl,' Brady thought. 'Better to keep the truth to ourselves at this point.'

For the first time the young assistant administrator seemed to notice the chaos in the office.

"Not just your computer files," he said as he surveyed the scene. "What happened? Pissed-off employee?"

"We're not sure," James jumped in. "Maybe her computer files will give us a lead."

"Okay. Show me what's up."

Brady let Anne lead the way, but followed close on her heels. As soon as she brought up the phone file on her monitor, and the nonsense characters that had usurped the actual numbers, Danny clicked into high speed.

"Possibly a virus," he said, and indicating the keyboard added, "May I?"

"Of course," she said, getting up and turning her chair over to the suddenly energized computer whiz.

Tapping madly at the keyboard, his fingers moving faster than Brady could follow, Danny brought up a new screen in seconds.

"Can you recover the data?" James asked, his usual skepticism neutralized by this kid's obvious affinity for bits and bytes.

"Don't know yet. If anything can bring it back, this should do it." He turned back and smiled at Brady and Anne with a conspiratorial grin. "Same program the FBI uses," he explained. "Analyzes the free space on the hard disk and tries to reconstruct the files that were once there."

He punched in some data and waited while the computer did its thing. Or tried. After less than a minute a message in large letters composed of an assortment of letters, numbers and symbols filled the center of the screen. 'TOO LATE ASSHOLE!' it read.

"Damn it!" the assistant administrator mumbled. He looked up at Anne. "Sorry about that, but it looks like your files have been compromised."

"Meaning?"

"Meaning that some hotshot moron has hacked the file and obliterated your data."

"Why the message?" Brady asked, all the while having a pretty good idea himself.

"A calling card," Danny said. "Whoever did this thinks he's hot enough to get away with it. He's taunting us."

"Or she," Brady corrected.

"Huh?"

"Could be a lady asshole, couldn't it?"

"Oh, yeh, I suppose it could. But most hackers are men. Teenagers, usually. They think it's cool."

"So you think this is just some random hacker?"

"I don't know. Don't you?"

Brady met his eyes without flinching. "Could be. But I think there are a couple of other files that were also 'compromised.' Maybe you can learn something from them."

"Oh yeh? Show me."

Anne reached over the keyboard and brought up the visitors' log. Danny ran the same program and got much the same results. Only this time the message read, 'STRIKE TWO!' The young man was mumbling to himself as he typed in a long list of characters. Brady thought he might break his forefinger as he pounded ENTER.

As Danny studied the even longer list of characters that popped up on the screen, Brady could see the kid's lips move.

"Anything?" he asked.

"No. Nothing. Whoever did this knew what they were doing."

"How do you mean?"

"Well, they not only erased the headers, which any amateur could do, they overwrote the deleted files multiple times with multiple characters. And then they hid all signs of their handiwork. Or so they thought."

"Do you mean you can find out who did this?" Anne asked eagerly.

Danny smiled. "You have no reasonable expectation of privacy on this network," he said, quoting the standard Fed disclaimer on all their networks. "I should be able to find out when and where, if not who once I get back to my office. Can you give me a list of all the files that were hacked?"

"The ones I know of."

"That should be enough. We'll see how hot this dude really is." The young administrator's eyes virtually shone with anticipation. He had been challenged on his own turf, and he didn't like being made to look like a fool.

Anne jotted down the files and folders that she had found damaged and handed them to Danny.

"Cool. I'll let you know as soon as I have something," he said. With a nod to Brady, he headed downstairs.

"Well, what do you think?" Anne asked as soon as he had left.

Brady frowned. "He's certainly got the hutzpah, but I don't think we're dealing with some second-rate teenie hacker here. I think our guy is a pro. In fact, I'd bet on it. We'll have to see if Danny boy is up to the challenge."

CHAPTER 3

In a small but unobtrusively upscale house in suburban Billings, Montana, a flashing icon on a huge computer monitor went unnoticed for over an hour. When the young man living in the house finally noticed the signal, his smile was broad and instantaneous but cold as the winter nights in the nearby Beartooth Mountains.

"About time," he muttered as he sat down at the computer desk and began to tap away at the keyboard. After about five minutes he'd seen all he needed to see and shut down the program while dialing his cellphone.

"Grandpa, it's me," he said into his brand new IPhone. "Everything's going as we planned. They've finally discovered the missing computer files, but from what I can see they don't have a clue how they got hacked or what to do about it."

He smiled as he leaned back in the chair. "Yeh, I told you they wouldn't be all that sharp. Hell, they're government employees!"

He laughed as the voice on the other end ran through a well-worn litany of complaints about the 'lazy asses' who worked for the federal government. 'Sucking on the government tit,' as his grandfather put it. But the jocular good humor only lasted a few seconds. Before the younger man could fully savor his small victory, the older man was already barking orders.

"I told you I'd stay on him," the young geek complained as he reacted to being told the same directive for the third or fourth time. "Yeh, yeh, I remember... I'm on it!" he finally snapped. He knew as soon as he said it that he'd have to suffer through a tongue-lashing from the old man. He held the phone at arm's length and let his grandfather finish his rant.

"I didn't mean it that way," he said as soon as he could fire a word in edge-wise. Of course, he did mean it that way, but no need to get the old man any more worked up than he already was.

He listened attentively as the orders were repeated a second time, only grunting or responding with a noncommittal "uh huh" as needed. Finally, the lecture was finished. He hung up with a frown having replaced the icy grin.

"Can't even give me my props when I earn them," he muttered as he pushed himself away from the desk. "Eh, screw it."

He knew he should follow his grandpa's directions to the letter, but he wasn't feeling it. Besides, his girlfriend lived just a short distance away. She wouldn't give him grief for nothing. Not if she knew what was good for her.

CHAPTER 4

Brady made a perfunctory search of the paper files in the Senator's office, but he was pretty certain that the missing computer files contained the key to the break-in, and maybe more. He stayed with Anne for another hour, talking about the Senator, his private life and the legislation he was involved with, campaign financing, his staff, other Senators he worked with, and a host of other topics that boiled down to who liked him, and who didn't.

"Senators have an impact on just about everyone in their state, if not the whole country," Anne explained apologetically when he asked for a list of possible enemies. "Your list could contain half the people in Ohio."

"I thought he was pretty popular."

"He was," Anne said with a small smile. "Otherwise the list might be longer."

James nodded.

"Okay, then until Danny boy gets back to us, make me a list of everyone you can think of who might have held a grudge against the Senator. Not fender-bender stuff, but the kinds of things that could make someone take drastic action."

"Murder? I really don't know if anyone was that angry with the Senator."

"Okay, then anyone who might've wanted to punch him in the nose. And anybody who was calling him, or visiting him more than usual in the last month or so before his death."

"I don't know that I can remember every repeat visitor or caller."

"I don't expect you to. But at least we'll have something to get started with. Derek is getting antsy."

Anne couldn't disguise a startled twist to her lips. "The … small guy?"

"The little person. Yeh, that's him. He's between cases and wants to get a jump on this story before he needs to take on a paying customer."

"I'll do the best I can," she promised.

"That's all we can ask for. E-mail me the list as soon as you're done. Okay?'

Anne nodded pensively.

"Hey," he continued, resting his hands on her shoulders and staring directly into her eyes. "Don't worry. We're going to get to the bottom of this story, one way or the other. You can quote me on that."

She smiled. "I'll do that."

He returned the smile. "Call me if you have any questions, or get any ideas."

"I will. And Mr. James…"

"Brady."

"Brady. Thank you."

"Thank me once we have this thing figured out. Until then, keep your doors locked, and keep an eye peeled for anything or anyone unusual. I don't imagine that this little break-in is a one-of thing."

"You mean they might…come after me?" Her voice nearly broke.

"Unlikely, but they might keep an eye on you to try to find out what you know, or what you think you know. I might be overly cautious, but better that than the alternative. Right?"

"Right." She forced a smile.

"I'll call you tomorrow, if not before."

When he left the office he stood outside in the hallway until he heard the bolt catch. *'I might be wrong, but I don't think so,'* he thought as he headed for the elevator. *'This smells bad.'*

*****

It was nearly dinnertime when Brady received the e-mail from Anne. He called Derek, who promised to come right over when he heard that hot dogs and beer were on the supper menu. As he waited, Brady scanned the list of regular visitors and callers that Anne had assembled. Most of the names meant nothing to him. But a few names jumped out. James Westerly, Wainwright's fellow Senator from Ohio, had called or visited his cohort repeatedly in those last two weeks. Were the two of them always so close? He knew that Westerly was a Republican, and that Wainwright had been as Democratic as Democratic could be. Seemed unlikely. He'd have to ask Anne about that.

And then there was Simon Beddecker. He'd called the Senator a half-dozen times in the two days before he died. Why? Since when does a TV news personality make such calls himself? It should have been some little-known producer. Again, maybe Anne had some idea why.

Lastly, he saw the name Adam Hoch. Everyone who followed the national political game knew Hoch. A maverick oil billionaire, he was the man behind half the ultra-conservative political movements that had appeared on the U.S. scene over the past decade. He was secretive, smart, and ruthless in pursuit of his goals. Political as well as business?

None of it made any sense. Two right-wingers and a TV news host. Why would they be among the Senator's most persistent callers during his last few days? Of course, they were just the big names that jumped out at him with a quick perusal of the list. How many others would they find when they looked closer? Or if Danny Boy could find the actual logs?

His mind was whirling when a familiar knock sounded on the front door.

"Come in Derek!" he called out.

The door swung open and the diminutive private investigator strolled in.

"Hot dogs, eh? I brought some relish. You never have relish," the little man said as he dropped a small grocery bag on the kitchen table.

"You're a prince," Brady replied, not even taking his eyes from Anne's list.

"Hope I'm not interrupting anything important," Derek said as he walked to where Brady continued to study the names. "What do you have there: the Redskins' pass defense statistics against left-handed QBs?"

"A partial list of the people who visited Senator Wainwright in the last couple of weeks before he drowned."

Derek opened his hands as if to say, 'So?'

"Anything interesting?"

"Simon Beddecker and Adam Hoch were bugging the staff trying to talk to the big guy."

"You mean in person? Not staffers?"

"In person."

"That's something."

"And Senator Westerly, Ohio's Republican darling, actually paid several visits to his office."

"If Wainwright had been poisoned, we'd have a suspect. But drowning...? Doesn't seem like the kind of thing a big-time politician would get involved in."

"Yeh... But nothing about this story seems to make much sense. Like why was Wainwright nervous, or upset just before he died?"

"If he really was. Might just be the secretary trying to make sense of things as she looks back."

"Might be. But people don't break into a Senator's office and wipe very specific computer files for nothing. No, there's something here."

"The hotshot reporter has a feeling?" Derek jibed.

"Yeh, an emptiness in my stomach that only a few hotdogs can fill," James answered as he pushed the list away. "Let's get cooking."

Derek had visited the apartment enough times to know the routine: Brady always cooked the dogs himself, first boiling them in the same old battered black cast iron pot, and then dropping them on a hot grill just long enough to char them a bit on the outside – at the same time the buns were being toasted, of course. Derek's job was to dice some onions, locate the relish and mustard (no Dijon or any of that other fancy stuff; just good old French's would do), and insure that the buns didn't burn. Even the vaguest hint of carbonized bun would throw Brady into a tizzy.

It wasn't long before they had settled down in their designated spots – Brady in his easy chair, Derek at the dinner table (where he had been permanently banished after once dropping a dog slathered in mustard and relish on the couch). Brady pushed the play button on his VHS recorder, and the fuzzy videotape of a 2005 Redskins game against the Cowboys popped up on the TV. His mouth was poised to devour a good half of his first dog, when the phone rang.

"Damn!" he howled, staring at the bun for a long second before dropping it tenderly on his plate.

"Ignore it," Derek advised through a mouthful of pork and bread.

"Can't. I'm working on a story, in case you've forgotten."

He paused the tape and snatched the phone in one smooth motion. "Yeh?" he snapped.

"Brady?" the familiar voice on the other end asked tentatively.

"Anne! Yeh, it's me. What's up?"

"I hope I'm not bothering you…"

Brady blushed. He knew how he came across on the phone when either a game or a meal was being interrupted. Anne had managed the Daily Double.

"No, no, of course not. We were just sitting around watching an old ballgame. What's up?"

"I just heard from Danny."

Brady looked at his watch. It was nearly 7:30. Didn't that kid ever go home?

"And? What did he find?"

"It looks like whoever wiped my files tried the same thing with the back-ups."

"Tried?"

"Well, I'm not sure I understood it all, but what I think Danny said was that this hacker tried to erase a whole bunch of back-up tapes, going back over a month. But Danny had the last back-up in his desk and the hacker missed it."

Tapes. Who but the Federal Government still used tapes for back-ups?

"So he's got a good history of the Senator's calls and visitors?" Brady asked. He needed information, not tapes. If the kid didn't have the information, the tape was meaningless.

"I think so. We won't know for sure until tomorrow, when I can review the files. But from what Danny was saying, I think we've got it all."

"Well hallelujah. What time will you be able to look at the tape?"

"I'm usually in the office by 8. But the police said they'll have more investigators there in the morning. So, as soon as I can get to it, I guess."

"Okay. You'll give me a call as soon as you know if it's what we're looking for?"

"Of course. Would you like me to e-mail you the files too?"

"Yeh, that'd be great."

"It's a lot of material."

"Break it into a bunch of smaller files if need be."

"Will do. Is there anything else we need to discuss?"

Brady thought for a second. "Nah, that should do it for now."

"Okay then. Enjoy your game. I think I'll go fix some dinner."

He would've liked to invite her over for dogs and a beer, but he didn't think it would be her cup of tea, or Budweiser, as the case might be. When he hung up he saw Derek eying him.

"So?" the little man asked. "Did the geek save the files?"

"By sheer luck, but yes – it looks like we've got the files. She'll e-mail them over here as soon as she breaks them up into digestible chunks."

"Sounds vaguely like peristalsis."

Brady shook his head but smiled in spite of himself.

"You've got a real talent for analogies, you know that?"

"Uh oh. Once you start with the compliments, I know I'm screwed."

"I don't know about that, but I could use a little help sifting through the calls and visits."

"Looking for what, exactly?"

"Don't know. Anything that looks odd."

Derek got up from the table and carried his plate into the kitchen.

"I'd better grab another dog, then," he called back over his shoulder. "Sounds like I'm going to need the strength."

*****

The next day, while Derek pored over endless names and phone numbers, Brady contacted Simon Beddecker, the longtime host of a cable news political show and an even longer-time acquaintance of Brady's. The two had worked together at the Post nearly thirty years earlier. Beddecker had gone on to fame and fortune. James had received a nice watch when he retired.

To Brady's surprise, the great man was available and willing to meet with him that very afternoon. He pulled on the brown plaid jacket and hopped in his red Civic for the short drive down to First Street. The day was gray and overcast but hot and humid as ever. Brady made a note to have the car's a/c checked out.

Security at the Cable News offices was nearly as imposing as at the Hart Building. Searches, clip-on IDs – the whole works. James wasn't upset in the least, however. He knew how many crazies were out there just looking for a reason to take out their frustrations on a famous TV personality. And that was just in the general public. The criminal types were even worse.

Eventually a cute young blonde with nice tits and a round ass sashayed down to the security desk to show him upstairs. *'Good ol' Simon,'* Brady thought as he followed closely behind the assistant, his eyes riveted on her flexing backside. *'Always knew how to pick office help.'*

Beddecker's office was located on the fourth floor, a floor higher than the last time Brady had visited. If, as he supposed, the higher the floor the bigger the paycheck, he figured ol' Simon must be doing quite well.

"Please have a seat," directed the blonde – Alex, or Jamie, or something equally androgynous – smiling with a mouthful of perfect white teeth.

'Hate to have her bleaching bill,' Brady mused as he watched her butt bounce briskly out of the waiting room.

With nothing better to look at, he glanced around the room to see what it said about the network. A typical outer office for a TV entity: the walls were covered with huge blow-up photos of the famous personalities that graced the daily lineup. The one thing that caught his eye was the age of the photos. Or rather, the age of the people in the photos. Every one of them was a good ten years younger than the teleprompter kings and queens he saw on the tube every day. *'The crew is showing its age, and management doesn't like it,'* he surmised. *'Be looking for some turnover if I were them.'*

He was wondering if even the legendary Simon Beddecker would be immune to a youth purge if it swept through the network, when the great man himself opened the door into the inner sanctums.

"Well, well, well, Brady James. To what do I owe this great honor?" Beddecker asked with just enough smile to demonstrate clearly he was only being polite.

Brady smiled back with equal sincerity.

Simon Beddecker was the archetypical modern TV newscaster: square jaw, piercing blue eyes, perfect coif, probably six foot two, trim yet buff. Brady almost felt ill looking at him stride purposefully across the room.

"I'm working on a story, and your name popped up," James explained as he shook hands with his old cohort. He took some pride in the realization that his handshake was firmer than Simon's.

"Really?" the TV newscaster said, tilting his head ingénue-like while narrowing his eyes in surprise. "About what?"

Brady lowered his voice. "Can we talk someplace a little less…public?"

"Sure. Of course," Beddecker answered without hesitation. "Come on in. We can use my office."

Simon led the way through the swipe-card protected door, down a long corridor lined by shoebox offices, conference rooms the size of walk-in closets, and darkened edit bays, to what Brady immediately recognized as the high rent district. There was a central shared meeting area, or 'socializing space' as modern designers tended to call it, off of which led four solid wood doors. One was for the News Director, one for the Sales Manager, one for Simon's female equivalent, and one for good ol' Simon.

"Make yourself comfortable," Simon said as he made his way to a small all-glass portable bar that was parked next to a massive mahogany desk. "Can I get you something to drink? A scotch, perhaps?"

Brady wondered if Simon really didn't remember that he only drank beer, or if he were rubbing it in that he could afford the good stuff.

"You got water? Faucet's okay."

"I think we can do better than that," Simon said, bending down to access a small refrigerator built into the desk. He came up with a bottle of mineral water.

"I hope it's okay that it's imported."

"Sure, unless it's from China." Two could play this game.

"Still the bon vivant, eh Brady?" He handed him the bottle and plunked himself down in the high-backed leather chair that faced the sofa where Brady had landed.

"Nothing but the best."

Simon sipped single malt scotch from a lead crystal tumbler. "I heard you retired. Got sick of the daily grind?"

"Yeh. Didn't see myself banging out stories about scumbags until I was 70. You? Still love the cameras?'

Simon shrugged ever so slightly. "More than they love me, I'm afraid. Makeup only covers so many sins."

"Come on," Brady said with sincerity he didn't feel. "You're still the king. They'll keep you on the network until you drop dead. Larry King redux."

Beddecker stared out the window at the city below. "I don't think so. Truth is, they're already grooming some young studs to take my place. Off the record, of course."

"I'm not here to do a profile."

"No, I didn't think so. But now that you mention it, why exactly are you here? I haven't seen you in, what, 5-6 years? What's up?"

Brady had already decided he wasn't going to share too much with his old colleague. Just enough.

"I'm working on a story about Senator Wainwright. Freelance thing."

Simon nodded thoughtfully. "A shame about the Senator. He was a good man."

"Yeh, that's what everyone says. So, I'm interviewing people who knew him, personally or professionally, and when I asked his secretary for a list of people who he'd seen or talked to in those last few weeks, your name came up. Were you working on a story?"

Simon hesitated, for just a second, but long enough for Brady to notice.

"I was. Ohio is shaping up as quite the battleground for the Presidential election, and I wanted his take on how the Buckeye state might tip the balance one way or the other."

"Anything you can share? I mean, was he looking forward to the election? Was he optimistic?"

"Is that your angle? How his death might influence the election?"

"Something like that. I mean, he apparently had a lot of clout back home. His death may give the Republicans a real shot at winning the state." Brady was winging it. He hadn't really thought too much about the election.

"He did, and they do," Simon said, sipping freely from the scotch. "Wainwright was pumped up. He couldn't wait to get home and bang the Democratic drum. He was very confident that they would carry the state."

"And now?"

"Now?...well, I hear the Governor may name Congressman Jessup to the vacant seat. He's a good politician, but he's no Wainwright."

"So you think the Republicans can pull it off?"

Simon tilted his head. "I think so."

Brady processed the information. He didn't see how it fit Anne's theory about the death, but if there was one thing he'd learned from 30 years of reporting, it was never to shitcan any information until the story was completed.

"So did you ever record any video with him? I don't remember seeing a story by you after his death..."

"No, no we didn't. Played phone tag for a couple of days, and then he was gone. We barely even scratched the surface."

"Pity. I would've liked to have seen it. For a bit of context. Maybe pull a quote or two."

"Sorry."

"Yeh, well, do you by any chance remember anything specific he said that I could use? About the election..."

"No, not really. I only talked to him on the phone that one time. And it was pretty brief. We were going to try to get together that next week."

Brady shook his head. "Murphy's Law of interviews."

"It'll get you every time."

It sure would. This one hadn't worked out too much better for Brady. But maybe it could still be saved.

"Hey, you wouldn't know any politicos who might be willing to talk about Wainwright and how his death could influence the election, do you?"

Beddecker smiled. "Do I get paid for doing your legwork for you?"

"Could be. At least a mention in the story."

"You're too generous. But it doesn't really matter, because I really don't. Sorry."

Brady sighed. "Doesn't hurt to ask. Well, I won't take up any more of your time…" He moved as though to stand.

"Really was a shame, wasn't it?" Simon suddenly asked, staring out the window at nothing in particular.

"The Senator? Yeh. Like you said, everyone said he was a good guy."

"I've been wondering myself how his death might influence things. You never know…" Brady wondered if it was the scotch that was making Simon so reflective. It seemed out of character for the hard-ass reporter he knew.

"Anyway," Simon said, turning back to James as if he'd heard his thoughts, "I guess there's nothing we can do about it now. Except maybe that story you're writing."

"Yeh. We'll see if I can come up with enough to make it interesting."

Simon stood. "You do that. I think the Senator would've liked it."

He put his arm on Brady's shoulder and walked him out through the hallway to the waiting room. They didn't say much, just a word here or there about the offices.

"If there's anything I can do to help with your story, like maybe put you in touch with some politicos, just let me know – okay?" Simon said as they stood by the door that led out to the elevators.

"Great. Thanks," Brady answered, a bit taken aback by Simon's sudden cooperativeness. "Keep up the good work."

"Yeh, you too."

The last thing Brady saw as he pushed the down button in the elevator was Simon looking after him, his eyes narrowed and his lips a thin line of thoughtful contemplation, or was it confusion?

What the hell was all that about?' Brady wondered as the elevator brought him down to the ground floor. *Wonder if he's been hitting the booze too hard.'*

He nodded at the security guard as he traded his ID for the driver's license he'd left behind. As he walked out of the building he noticed one last big promotional poster above the exit doors. It showed a smiling Simon surrounded by a small host of fellow reporters. *Looks like Grandpa surrounded by his grandkids,'* Brady thought to himself as pushed open the glass door and collided with the warm humid air outside. Maybe he had retired at the right time, after all.

*****

He'd called Derek on his cell during the drive home, and the little guy was already waiting in his big old Cadillac when Brady pulled up. James watched in the rearview mirror as his friend got out of the black tank and waddled over to where he'd parked the Civic. *What a pain,'* he thought, not for the first time, as he watched Derek struggle to get down from the Caddy and then make his way to where he was getting his things together.

"So, you got this story all tied up yet?" the little man asked as soon as the car door swung open.

"I was going to ask you the same thing."

"Fair enough. What do ya say we have a beer and talk about it."

A quick jolt of adrenaline shot through the veteran reporter. "Did you find anything?"

Derek smiled evasively. "A nice cold beer would taste pretty damn good just about now."

"Jesus," Brady swore, slamming his car door. "Now I gotta bribe the little asswipe to get any info out of him."

"Couldn't hurt," Derek said, the smile growing wider.

"All right. You're just lucky I'm a bit thirsty myself. Let's go see what you've got."

After uncapping a couple of cold ones, Brady sat down with his PI friend to go over the caller and visitor logs.

"Most of it is just the usual day to day stuff you'd expect from a Senator's office," Derek explained, kneeling on a chair in order to be able to lean far enough over the print-outs he'd spread out on the kitchen table to point out the data he was indicating. "Complaining constituents, staffers, family…the usual."

"But…?" Brady prompted, certain that there was more to it.

"But, notice these calls in yellow, and these visits in blue. These are definitely NOT just the usual daily routine. All of these here," he said, identifying a host of closely bunched calls, "were from your old buddy Simon Beddecker. Seems like he was talking to the Senator every couple of hours the week before he died."

"Or trying to. Simon told me that they'd played phone tag for a while and then he died. I got the impression that they really didn't have much time for conversation."

Brady saw the quizzical look on Derek's face before he even opened his mouth.

"What?" he asked.

"Well, maybe I'm misreading these records, but according to what it says here, they talked at least seven different times during that last week. Nearly two hours in one call."

"What? That doesn't jive with what Simon was telling me."

"Here it is, in black and white."

What was going on? Why would Simon give him the impression that they'd barely talked if they'd spent so much time on the phone together?

"And that's just the calls," Derek interrupted his thoughts. "See this notation here? The great Mr. Beddecker came to the Senator's office at 5:15 pm and stayed until 7."

Brady stared at the paper. "Hmmm."

"I take it he didn't mention his little visit?"

"No he didn't. And I can't think of any good reason why not."

"Maybe you'll have to ask him."

"Maybe. But not right now. What else did you find?"

"These calls," he said, indicating another dense grouping of calls. "All from Senator Westerly."

"Well, they were both Senators from the same state."

"And that would make perfect sense. Except I asked Anne for her records going back two months, and guess what? In that period Westerly only called four times. In the last ten days before Wainwright croaked? Seventeen times."

"Maybe they were planning a cruise together," Brady quipped.

"Maybe Wainwright should've been wearing his life preserver."

Brady didn't smile. Yeh, it was funny, but not in these circumstances. What had begun as a secretary's paranoid musings was starting to stink to high heavens. "Anything else?" he asked, half-hoping that there wasn't.

"See these three calls?" the little man said, his pudgy forefinger stabbing at the repeated numbers just hours apart. "Guess who?"

Brady was in no mood for guessing games. "Brad Pitt."

"Close. The numbers were all blocked, but thanks to my old buddy at the phone company, I tracked them down." Derek seemed to have buddies just about everywhere. Another reason he was such a good PI.

"And? Do I have to keep guessing?"

"Ever hear of Hoch Industries?"

"I was a newspaperman, not a TV talking head," Brady sneered. "You mean old man Hoch called?"

"That's the guy – Adam Hoch. Rich as God. Nearly as hard to talk to. And yet, here he was, calling your man Wainwright three times in less than 48 hours."

"How do you know it was actually him? I mean, couldn't it have been someone else at his company, or just using his phone?"

"Could have been. Except I checked with Anne, and she remembers the last call. It was Hoch himself, or so the guy at the other end said. And he was apparently pretty ticked off."

"About?"

"She didn't know. And Hoch wasn't sharing."

Brady stared at the numbers as if hoping they'd speak to him. Westerly, Simon and now this guy Hoch – what could they possibly have in common? Other than Wainwright, apparently.

"Strange."

"To say the least," Derek said, swigging his beer expansively. "I'd call it downright spooky, especially with Wainwright ending up in the bottom of that river just a few days later."

"Coincidence?"

"Could be. But you and I have both been around long enough to know that coincidences aren't usually coincidental. Especially when a Senator winds up dead."

The little guy didn't pull his punches. And in this instance, Brady didn't disagree with him.

"I don't suppose there's much chance we're going to be able to talk with this Hoch guy…"

"Unlikely. He makes Howard Hughes look like a socialite. Unless…"

"Yeh?"

"Like you said, he's big with the right-wingers. Do we know anyone who knows anyone who hangs with those schmucks?"

Brady thought about all the hundreds of journalists and politicos he'd run into during his thirty years in DC.

"Let me think about it," he finally said. "I'm sure there's someone we could talk to. But for now, I think I need to talk to Senator Westerly. How'd you like to go visit this Hoch Industries?"

"What do you want me to do – apply for a job?"

"No, nothing quite so dramatic. But I'd like you to talk to some people who work there, maybe have a drink or two with someone who's been there a while, or even knows Hoch."

"You know they're headquartered out in Montana, don't you?" Derek didn't sound enthusiastic.

"I didn't, but I do now. What's the problem, don't like Big Sky country?"

"Don't like rednecks. It's something about how they use little people for bowling balls. Strikes me the wrong way, sort of speak."

"So stay out of the bowling alleys."

Derek frowned. "I take it you're paying?"

Now it was Brady's turn to frown. "Yeh, I guess so. Unless you've got frequent flyer miles you want to donate."

The frown turned to a mocking smile. "Man, I don't know whether you've had too many beers, or too few. But in either case, there's no friggin' way."

"Probably too few. Let's see if we can remedy that," James said, popping another Bud. "And then maybe we can check the flight schedules."

The little guy groaned.

CHAPTER 5

Senator James Westerly didn't have offices in the Hart Building. As the junior Senator from Ohio, he'd landed in the older Russell Office Building, a classy turn of the century grey marble and limestone monument to former Georgia Senator Richard Russell. Within view of the Capitol dome, the building offered proximity in place of modernity.

Brady waited patiently for the security process to unfold. He'd developed a sort of zen approach to all the searching and pocket emptying. *'They're just doing their jobs,'* he repeated to himself, admittedly more often when the process stretched out inexplicably, like a mantra. Finally, it was determined he posed no real threat to the Senators and their staffs, and with his temporary ID clipped ever so visibly to his collar, he followed one of the Senator's people into the elevator and up to the second floor.

"A pity about Senator Wainwright," the middle-aged secretary said as the doors slid shut. "He was a good man."

So she knew why Brady was there, or at least what he'd told Westerly.

"So I understand. I guess it was pretty tough on all of you, huh?"

"Horrible. I thought the Senator was going to have a breakdown for a while there." She paused for just a second before catching herself. "Not really. I mean, he was quite upset."

"Understandably. Were they close?"

"Not really," the woman said. "Professionally yes, but they didn't spend much time together outside the office, if that's what you mean."

Brady nodded. Like most low level insiders, she was eager to share the little info she possessed. He was about to ask a few more seemingly innocuous questions when the floor bell rang.

"Here we are," she said, holding the door for him.

He followed her into the waiting room, a plain, barebones space that no doubt would have pleased the Senator's Midwestern constituency. She plopped down behind a well-used dark wood desk and punched a button on the telephone. "Mr. James is here to see you," she said into the mouthpiece. She nodded at the response. "He'll be right out," she said to Brady as she hung up the phone. "Can I get you anything? Coffee?"

James politely refused as he settled into a moderately uncomfortable wooden chair and grabbed a magazine. Normally, 'right out' meant anything from five to ten minutes, depending on how important the person thought himself to be. For a Senator, ten seemed about right.

Surprisingly, he had barely finished the first paragraph of the editorial he was perusing when the door opened and Senator James Westerly bustled out to greet him. Westerly was young, at least compared to most Senators. Forty-four according to his bio. He had the kind of Bobby Kennedy hair that looked sculpted instead of cut, and a toothy smile that screamed 'politician'. At least to Brady.

"Why Mr. James, what a pleasant surprise!" Westerly said, hand extended. "Haven't seen much of you lately."

In fact, the Senator had only met Brady once, or was it twice. In either case, they were hardly best buddies.

"I retired a few months back," Brady said, perfectly willing to play the game. "Needed to make some time to watch the Redskins lose."

"It is a sin, isn't it? All those fans, so excited about having a new coach, and this is what we get."

"It'll take time," Brady said, trying to convince himself as much as Westerly.

"I hope so. I really do. Come – let's go into my office." He turned back to his secretary just before passing through the doorway out of the reception room. "Hold all my calls, will you Janet?"

Brady hid a smile. It was so Washington. Anything to make a visitor feel important. Anything that didn't cost votes or money.

Westerly's office was just a few doors down a narrow corridor, but provided a stark contrast to his public waiting room. Larger than Wainwright's office at Hart, it was filled with brown leather, polished hardwoods and gleaming brass. More like what Brady would expect from a senior senator, or the CEO of a multinational corporation.

"Can I get you anything?" Westerly asked, at the same time motioning to an elegant chair placed directly in front of his paper-strewn desk.

"No, thanks. Your secretary was already kind enough to ask," James said, knowing from his many years in DC the benefits of praising the power behind the throne to the king.

"I can offer something a bit…stronger," the Senator pressed with a mischievous smile, indicating a good-sized wet bar just behind the desk.

"Nah. It'd only put me to sleep this early in the day. But don't let me stop you."

"Don't mind if I do," Westerly said, pouring himself a stiff whiskey straight up. "So, you're writing a story about how Blayton's death might affect the upcoming Presidential Election, huh? Interesting idea." He lowered himself into the deep cushioning of his high-backed leather chair. Brady noticed immediately that the desk chair was a good six inches higher than the visitor's chair he sat in. *'Better to set the pecking order right-off,'* he thought.

"I'm thinking about it. Just doing some research at this point."

"Freelance? I mean, since you're retired…"

"Yeh, it's a bit of a gamble. But I still crank one out every once in a while if a topic catches my interest."

"And this one does? I thought crime is your forte'."

"Was. Now I'm free to write about anything that strikes my fancy." Brady was tired of answering questions. It was time to ask a few. "Okay if I turn this on?" he asked, hauling out his ancient Olympus recorder.

"Fine."

Brady placed it on the desk directly in front of the Senator. "I imagine it was quite a shock – hearing about Senator Wainwright's death and all."

"Terrible. We were quite close, you know."

Brady didn't blink. "No, I didn't know. Had you been friends for a long time?"

"Over ten years. From before I first ran for Congress."

"Then I guess you were as familiar as anyone with his clout back home in Ohio."

"Oh my, yes. Blayton was a pillar of the Democratic Party back home. Make that 'the' pillar."

"He was probably a big thorn in your side – politically I mean."

Westerly's smooth smile wavered. "We...respected each other as professionals. After all, we both wanted what's best for the people of Ohio – and the country." His smile was back.

"What now? Who's going to lead the Party into the next election?"

"That's really not for me to say. The Dems have several good, competent people to choose from. I have no doubt that they'll find someone to give us a good fight for our money."

"But now you're the top dog in Ohio politics, right? You and the Governor."

The Senator's face fell into the 'aw shucks' mask that James had seen many times before. He knew that the next thing out of Westerly's mouth would probably be bull-pucky.

"I don't know that I would characterize my position quite that way," he said smoothly. "But I have some influence in Ohio politics, yes."

"Well, using the insight that comes with your 'influence', how would you describe Senator Wainwright's clout on the home political scene? Is his death a major blow to Democrats' chances in Ohio?"

Westerly shook his head. "I wouldn't say that, exactly. It might make it a little harder for them, without Blayton's leadership and savvy, but I'm sure they will bounce back."

"But his death will make it harder." It was a statement, not a question.

"I think so. Yes."

Brady nodded appraisingly. "That's what I've been hearing. Some Democrats are downright despondent about his death. Politically as well as personally."

"I think they may be over-reacting just a bit."

"Was that what you were talking to Wainwright about – the upcoming elections – in the weeks before he died?" Brady loved to change the pacing in an interview. Shake it up a bit.

"Excuse me?"

"Oh, sorry. I'd heard that you called and visited the Senator a number of times in those last few weeks. I was wondering if you were discussing the elections."

Brady saw the smile waver. Westerly weighed his words carefully. "Blayton and I kept up quite regular communication."

"Oh sure. But from what I've learned, you two were talking more than usual. Several times a day on occasion."

"And your point is?"

"No point. Just wondering what the two big dogs in Ohio politics were discussing so feverishly."

"I don't know that I would characterize our communications as feverish."

"Feverish, unusually frequent – call it whatever you will. I would imagine you must've gotten a good sense of how Wainwright was viewing the elections."

"It wasn't all about politics." Westerly didn't look, or sound happy.

"Oh? So just shooting the breeze then?"

"We talked about a number of things," the Senator said crossly. "Did you have any other questions about Blayton's influence on Ohio politics?"

The unspoken suggestion was clear: Get back to Ohio politics, or the interview was over. Brady was relatively certain he wouldn't be getting anything more of interest at that point, but he couldn't resist one last stab.

"No, not really. Oh, one other thing: Congressman Jessup. Do you think he'll be named to finish Wainwright's term?"

Westerly paused. "That's up to the Governor, of course. But he's a good man."

"So you know him then? As friendly with him as you were with Wainwright?"

"We were in Congress together." A longer pause as the two men stared at each other. "Is that about it then?" Westerly couldn't have been clearer.

"Yeh. I think that gives me a bit of context for my article. Thanks for your time." Brady packed up the Olympus and stood. The Senator was already headed for the door.

"No problem. By the way, where exactly will this story appear?"

Brady smiled. "That's the beauty of freelancing. It'll go to the highest bidder. Maybe the Post, maybe not. We'll just have to see."

"Let me know when it's running," Westerly said, but his tone suggested he didn't give a damn if it ever appeared.

"Will do. Thanks again." The handshake redefined perfunctory.

"No problem. You can find the waiting room, I expect?"

"No problem." Brady couldn't resist. The door behind him shut solidly before he could take two steps.

"Did the interview go well?" the secretary asked as he passed in front of her desk.

"Yes, yes it did. Thanks for your help."

"My pleasure. Just give us a call if there's anything else we can do for you."

Brady showed his brightest journalist smile. "I will." And he meant it. Not much chance he'd be talking to her boss anytime soon, but if he needed to chase down anything in that office, she might be just the source he'd need.

He gave one last wave as he left. The elevator was empty as he traveled down to ground level. *What was he so antsy about?'* he wondered as he walked out into the lobby and then outside. *'There's something there that's making him nervous.'*

If Brady hadn't been so preoccupied he might have noticed an unremarkable older model Ford Taurus parked just three spaces behind his Civic. And he would've surely noticed it pull out and follow him as he headed back to his apartment. As it was, he didn't notice a thing.

CHAPTER 6

The airport in Billings was about what Derek had expected. It was relatively new, and certainly large enough to handle the 35 or so flights that departed at least once a week. He marveled at the rugged mountains that provided a backdrop to the runway. Not so much the horse statue in the center of the baggage claim carrousel.

'Friggin' rednecks,' he thought as he endured the blatant stares of several locals as he collected his bag. *'Haven't they ever seen a city boy before?'*

He rolled his suitcase over to the rental car booths, where he signed the paperwork for his modified Ford Fusion. He quickly checked out the hand controls to ensure that they'd compensate for stunted legs that didn't reach the pedals, particularly when he used a special seat cushion to see over the steering wheel. In just a few minutes he was on his way into town. He had booked a couple of nights at the Old West Lodge, since it was centrally located and just a couple of blocks off of 27th St, a main drag that ran straight into downtown Billings. It was a classic old style western motel, complete with exposed beams and fireplace in the lobby, and knotty pine trim and mock kerosene lanterns in the rooms. Besides, it was cheap.

When he'd unfinished unpacking, he put his laptop and a few paper files on the small table next to the window. He reviewed everything he'd already dug up about this Hoch fellow. Seems he had come out of the Korean War a smalltime military hero, and had parlayed that fame into a job with a local oil company, Amkota Oil. He didn't know much about oil, but his wartime honors made him the perfect front man to raise money for drilling. People had speculated there was oil near the Montana/North Dakota border ever since the turn of the century, but precious little evidence had been brought up to back their suspicions. Then, in the early 50's, real, commercial oil deposits were identified near the town of Williston, ND. Hoch was nothing but a PR man at that point, and a junior one at that. But from what Derek had been able to uncover, sometime in 1953 Hoch had befriended a wealthy businessman from New York who had come out to Montana to take a look at the new rigs. Hoch had been assigned to wine and dine the potential investor. How it came to be, no one seemed quite certain, but somehow Hoch persuaded the older man, one Edgar L. Holliford, to name the young war hero as his personal contact person with the drillers.

There came a period, about 1958, when Amkota fell upon hard times. Too many dry wells, not enough fiscal smarts. In any case, Hoch persuaded Holliford to loan the company enough money to carry them through another 6 months of exploration. As collateral, he received the deed to a huge expanse of oil rights that Amkota had purchased from the government for peanuts just a few decades earlier. As luck would have it, Amkota drilled through that money with nothing but broken bits to show for it. The company collapsed, and Holliford took ownership of the rights. For more than 30 years he refused all offers to sell, despite a singular lack of production in the area. Holliford died in 1998 with his Williston rights judged to be, if not worthless, not worth much. In his will, he left them to his longtime associate, Adam Hoch, who by this time had made something of a name for himself in the Big Sky oil business.

Then, in 2000, geologists determined that new drilling methods and new cracking procedures had raised the amount of recoverable oil by nearly ten times the original estimates. Suddenly, Adam Hoch's worthless rights were worth millions! And then, as if Hoch's fortunes had not improved sufficiently, a federal government report upped the estimates to nearly 2 *trillion* barrels of oil in the region! Hoch was suddenly a billionaire.

Derek reviewed the news reports on Hoch and his Big Sky Oil. Until 2000 he couldn't find a single reference to the oil man anywhere in the state. However, beginning in that year Hoch's name began to pop up in business and civic groups. In 2004 the first photo appeared of Hoch with a local candidate for public office. For a few years he was a local superstar. There wasn't an election of note anywhere in the state, and sometimes even across the border in North Dakota, in which Hoch didn't play a major role. Suddenly in 2008, all that changed. Fewer photos of the great man appeared in the media, but more articles about Hoch's influence in the radical right political scene.

'This guy sees himself as a kingmaker,' Derek thought as he read an article cataloging Hoch's efforts on behalf of candidates who espoused limits on gun control, tax relief, and railed against abortion rights.

At the same time his political machinations were increasing in size and scope, he himself had become somewhat of a recluse. Derek hadn't been able to find a single image of Hoch since 2009. It was clear from the public record that he had married in 1963, but whether he was still married, and what had become of the two children of that marriage, was anyone's guess.

'Howard Hughes the Second,' Derek reflected.

He closed his laptop and tidied up the files. He had enough to get started, and since he knew darn well that Brady wouldn't be paying his usual rate, he wanted to wrap this up as quickly as possible and get back home to DC.

One of Derek's favorite sources was always the local press. Journalists were usually among the best informed people in any town, and given the right motivation – often liquid and alcoholic – they were willing to share their information. He left the Lodge from a side exit, avoiding the lobby entirely. No need to advertise his comings and goings.

His first stop would be at the Parmly Library. He wanted to review their archives on the local newspaper, the Gazette. See what the local press had to say about Hoch and his businesses over the years. He parked on a nearby street and walked up the long right-angled stairway that led to the front entrance. He had to admit, the building was striking. Looked like a hundred year old stone Hansel and Gretel castle, with two unmatched turrets on either side of arched doorways. He was lucky enough to find a helpful research librarian, and in just a few minutes he was engrossed in the Gazette microfilm. There was plenty to review, but nothing too controversial. Like in most small towns, it looked like the locals avoided biting the hand that fed them. A little over an hour later, Derek had seen enough.

With the basic background firmly in hand, it was time to go to the source: The Billings Gazette. The local paper of choice for 125 years, the Gazette mixed just enough national and international news with complete coverage of everything Montana to keep its loyal following. And who couldn't love a paper that listed two AA meetings as part of its top news of the day?

The Gazette offices were just a few blocks from the Lodge – one of the reasons he chose the classic motel in the first place. As he pulled up in his silver Fusion he surveyed the layout. The two-story concrete and stone building was relatively modern, resembling a library or post office with a big American flag flying out front. Just a half block away was the Yellowstone Art Museum. Derek had always liked landscapes and this area had nicer settings than most. He decided he'd try to stop by before he left.

He locked the Fusion and strolled confidently to the Gazette's double glass doors, ignoring the honking of a battered red pickup truck that cruised by on 28th Street. He was so used to causing a stir in public that he really didn't notice it anymore. At least, not much. By the time he sauntered up to the service desk, he'd almost completely forgotten the pencil-necked, pimply-faced hick driving the truck.

The receptionist was glued to her computer monitor.

'Probably reading her Facebook wall,' Derek decided. He cleared his throat.

The young woman looked up from the monitor, flipped her long brown hair off her face, and for just a second saw nothing.

"Good morning," Derek spoke up, stepping back from the counter so she could see him a bit better.

"Oh!" the girl said, with the wide eyed look he had become accustomed to. Almost. "I'm so sorry. May I help you?"

"I was wondering if I might have a short meeting with your Financial Editor, Mr..." He took a notepad out of his pocket. "...Worthington. Is he available?"

"Do you have an appointment?"

"I don't," Derek said apologetically. "I'm only in town for a couple of days, and I was hoping I might catch him in."

"May I tell him what you would like to talk with him about?"

"Adam Hoch. Tell him I'm doing some research for the Washington Post, and hoped to add his perspective to the article." A little name-dropping and a stiff dose of flattery never hurt.

The receptionist's head popped up from the note she was jotting. "The Post?" He could see the name had worked its usual charms. "That's really a great paper. I've seen 'All the President's Men' three times."

"Woodward isn't that good-looking," Derek joked.

"That's okay," she said with a broad smile. "He's still a great man. And your name is...?"

"DiLaurain. Derek DiLaurain."

"Like the car?"

He was surprised. He might have underestimated this lovely young thing. "Yeh, kind of. Spelled a little differently, but close."

"Have a seat. I'll see if Mr. Worthington is in."

He didn't actually sit. Scrambling up to chair-level tended to diminish the professional aura he worked so hard to create. So, as usual, he stood, looking at the photos and clippings on the walls. It couldn't have been more than 30 seconds later when the receptionist interrupted him.

"Mr. Worthington will be right out. Can I get you anything?"

He bit his tongue. He wasn't sure how his DC flippancy would go over in Billings. "No, thank you. I'm fine."

She nodded and smiled. *'Too bad I'm only in town for a couple of days,'* he thought.

His imagination was just coming to full fruition when a tall (or maybe he just seemed tall) man in his mid-fifties, graying black hair, skinny in a tough, cowboyish kind of way, came out from a side door.

"Mr. DeeLurean?" he asked.

Derek was once again tempted, but just reached out a welcoming hand. "Mr. Worthington?"

"Name's Carl. Only my kids call me Mister. Come on back."

He held the door for his diminutive visitor and then stepped past him to lead the way.

"So you're working on a story about Mr. Hoch?" he said as they walked past the usual glass-encased cubby holes.

"I am. With the election coming, we thought we'd profile some of the bigger contributors on both sides of the aisle."

"Oh?" Worthington looked ill at ease. "Then this isn't another of those left-wing attack articles..."

Derek realized he had stepped in it. *'Should have said it was for the business section,'* he groused to himself. "No, no – nothing like that," he said aloud. "Just a straightforward story about how Mr. Hoch has been a mainstay of the New Conservative movement in this part of the country."

"Not just in these parts," Carl said, showing the PI into his small office. "He's been a mainstay of the national movement. *The* mainstay, some might say."

"I can see you're pretty well-versed in the politics of big business as well as the financial side," Derek praised the editor. Maybe Carl would try to show him how much he knew about Hoch and his political dealings.

"A bit. In small towns like Billings, we all have to know a bit about everything."

"Well, what I'm most interested in is Mr. Hoch's financial support for various conservative candidates and groups. Are you familiar with any of that?"

"A bit. Not as much as our political guys, I'd guess, but I do know that Mr. Hoch has been extremely generous with his donations."

Derek pulled out his cellphone. "Do you mind if I record our little conversation?"

"Not as long as it's all off the record. You can ask if you want specific quotes."

"Deal. So, how generous has Mr. Hoch been? I mean, do you know how much he gives to his various groups?"

Carl pursed his lips as if considering the number. "Can't say, exactly. But if you said 'millions' I don't think anyone could argue."

"And that's nothing for someone like Mr. Hoch, I assume."

"His company is worth about 12 billion. And he's sole owner."

"That's a lot of oil," Derek said, trying to ease around the political questions without raising Worthington's skepticism.

"Not just oil. Not anymore. Sure, he started with the Williston wells, but these days he's pretty well diversified: manufacturing, transportation, communications – you name it, Hoch Industries does some of it."

"I assume he doesn't do all the political giving himself. Who's his exec in charge?"

"Of political contributions? They say he handles a lot of that himself, but his public face is Earl Henson. VP of Communications, I think his title is."

"Do you know him?"

"I've met him a couple of times. That's about it."

"What's the story on him? Good guy?"

"I think so. Haven't heard much of anything to the contrary."

"Much of anything?" Derek knew that little words often meant bigger things when people were being interviewed. "So there has been some criticism?"

Worthington shrugged. "Oh, there was a story a few years back about a DUI that never made it to court. And you sure don't want to cross the guy, but nothing serious."

"Don't want to cross him? Why's that?"

"Well, aside from having Mr. Hoch on his side, he's an ex-Marine. Looks like one of those UFC fighters."

'Great. All I need,' Derek thought. "Think I could get an interview with him?"

"Might do. You have the number over there at Headquarters?"

"Probably, somewhere. You have it readily available?"

Carl started flipping through an old style Rolodex. "I think I have it in here, somewhere…Yeh, here it is. 423-3141. His secretary's name is Jillian."

"So you must've called over there a few times then, huh?"

"Anytime we want to talk to Mr. Hoch, it all goes through Earl."

"Okay. Thanks. Can I keep you a couple of more minutes?"

Carl looked at his desk clock. "Sure. I need to get crackin' on today's column, but I think I can spare another little bit."

"Great. So, how would you describe public sentiment regarding Mr. Hoch?" Derek realized he needed to appear a bit more journalistic if he wasn't going to arouse suspicion. "Is he a popular guy?"

"Well, Mr. Hoch isn't just a businessman. He gives a great deal to charities each year."

"You don't say."

He did, and he kept on saying for another ten minutes. Long enough to seem like a real interview, according to Derek's inner clock. Worthington didn't seem political enough to know any deep dark secrets on that end, and was too circumspect to reveal any financial hanky-panky, even if he knew about it. It was time to go.

"Well, I want to thank you for all your help," the little man said as soon as he found an opportune moment to interrupt Worthington's monologue. "Is there a decent restaurant where a guy can get lunch and a beer nearby?"

"Just down the block – Hannah's. Great sandwiches, decent chicken, and cold beer."

"Just what the doctor ordered. Hey, thanks again for seeing me on such short notice."

"No problem. Good luck with your piece."

Derek felt pretty good about himself as he bid Carl goodbye and headed for Hannah's. He hadn't found any smoking guns, but he'd uncovered a few new leads and had a better understanding of Hoch's place in the community. He might not have been so self-satisfied, however, if he'd seen Worthington pick up the phone and call a familiar number just moments after Derek left his office.

*****

Hannah's was a quaint little place, complete with antlers on the walls and photos of hunting trips dating back 30 years. *What a hicky dump,'* Derek thought as he moseyed up to the bar and hopped up onto a towering stool. *'Did I remember to bring the Pepto?'*

"What can I get you, pardner?" the cute young barmaid asked with no sense of irony as she plopped down a cardboard coaster. She couldn't have been more than 23, with light brown hair streaked with blond, pulled back into a short ponytail. She wore a tight knit shirt cut to reveal significant cleavage. A tattoo of barbed wire encircled her sculpted bicep. *'Maybe this place isn't so bad after all,'* Derek decided.

"How about a beer," he answered. "What's the best local brew?"

"That's a matter of opinion. A lot of people'd say Red Lodge, but I like Blackfoot or Big Sky, myself."

'Wow. I'm not in Kansas anymore,' he thought as he looked into her soft brown eyes. Glancing down, he noticed the coaster was from Big Sky. "Let me try one of these," he said, pointing to the logo.

"You got it."

He watched her move behind the bar. No wasted movement, no fumbling. She was a pro.

"You just visiting Billings?" she asked as she poured his beer.

Good. A talkative wench. "I am. Here on business. You from Billings?"

"Lived here all my life."

As the only patron at the bar that early in the day, Derek didn't have to compete with anyone to keep the conversation going. He learned more than he cared to about her life story, invented some enticing facts about his own, and then steered the chat toward the real reason for his visit. Turned out, as he'd suspected, that a number of the Gazette folks lunched at Hannah's nearly every day. Tina, the barmaid, knew most of them by name.

Derek pulled out his notepad and flipped through the pages until he found the name of a Gazette reporter he'd unearthed at the library.

"Does, uh, Greg Eddler ever eat here?" he asked, naming a political writer who had penned a recent series of less than complimentary features about Hoch and his political dealings.

"Greg? Sometimes. Maybe two or three times a week. Why?" He couldn't say for sure, but she seemed a bit skeptical, protective.

"I, ah, I'm working on a story myself, and read his series on Hoch Industries a few weeks back." Might as well keep his cover story consistent.

"You're a writer?" She seemed genuinely interested.

"I am. Mainly freelance, but I publish articles in the Washington Post from time to time."

"DC or state?"

Derek almost smiled, until he realized she was serious. "DC."

"Cool. So, did you like Greg's articles?" Her tone was non-committal.

He knew his answer might well determine whether he got to speak with Eddler or not. In his mind he flipped a coin. "Thought they were very well done," he said, hoping to split the difference.

He knew he'd succeeded when he saw her shoulders relax. "Yeh, me too. Not everyone saw it that way, you know. Some folks got downright angry that he had *dared* to criticize the patron saint of Billings. Took it personal."

"Not me. Just thought it was well done and hoped to talk to him a bit. Think he might come in today?"

She thought for a second. "Hard to say. Might. If he does, it'll probably be right around 12. All of the reporters come in early if they're not covering a story, so they can finish their articles before the 5 pm deadline."

"Seems like you really know your customers."

Tina smiled. "You know the definition of a bartender: half shrink, half confessor."

He returned the smile. "Hadn't heard that one." Derek looked at his watch. 11:40. Not a long wait. Just enough time for one more beer. "Guess I'll wait and see if he comes in. Can I try one of those Blackfoots?"

"Comin' right up."

Their small-talk continued for most of those 20 minutes, interrupted a couple of times by locals apparently just as thirsty, just as early, as Derek. He tried to start up a conversation with a good ol' boy sitting one bench away, but when his request to pass the peanuts was met with a stony stare and not one word in reply, he rethought the prospect. Finally, at 12:09, a small group of young men and women came in. They looked like journalist types, or at least what he imagined Billings journalists would look like. A couple of them waved to Tina the bargirl.

She waved back and then stepped out from behind the bar and went over to where they'd filled two booths. He tried to watch inconspicuously as she whispered something to a young guy with close-cropped brown hair, glasses, and the kind of All-American look that Madison Avenue would've paid big bucks for. They both looked his way, and Derek tried to act as if he hadn't noticed. A few seconds later he looked up to see the same young guy standing beside his stool.

"Howdy. Tina there says you were asking about me," he said matter-of-factly. That close, Derek could see he wasn't quite as young as he'd first thought. Probably around 28. Maybe 30.

"You're Greg Eddler, the Gazette reporter?"

"I am. What can I do for you?"

"Derek DiLaurain," the PI said, holding out his hand. "I'm here in Billings working on a story about the upcoming elections, and was hoping to pick your brain a bit about Adam Hoch and his influence on the local political scene."

"Did you see my series on Hoch and his company?"

"I did. Very well written. You got a couple of minutes?"

Eddler considered the possibility. "Yeh, why not."

"How about over in one of those?" Derek directed, indicating three empty booths on the other side of the bar. It would be quieter there, with less chance of someone overhearing their talk.

He grabbed his remaining sip of beer and hopped down off the barstool. When he noticed the good ol' boy watching him with an ill-disguised grin, he couldn't resist. "Nice talkin' to you," he said, and without waiting for a reply waddled over to the booth where Eddler was already seated.

"So, did Tina get it right that you're writing for the Post?" the young journalist asked before Derek had even settled into his place.

"Almost. I'm a freelancer. Sold them a few things before, and thought I'd give it another try."

"And what exactly is this one about?"

'Damn reporters,' Derek thought. *'Almost as snoopy as PIs.'*

"It's a feature about the upcoming elections and the powers behind the throne. The big-money power brokers who stay out of the public eye but have tremendous influence on what happens within our political system."

"That's Hoch alright," Eddler said without missing a beat. "But he isn't just local. He's gone national – big-time."

Something about the way he said it made Derek think he wasn't a big fan of the Big Man.

"So I've learned. They say he's the money behind some of the big conservative political groups out there."

"I didn't say that."

Suddenly the young reporter seemed nervous, or was it scared?

"No, no you didn't. Actually, I wondered about that. Your series was pretty exhaustive about Hoch and his company. But nothing about the national conservative groups. Any reason?"

Eddler swallowed hard. "Anything I tell you will be completely off the record – right?"

"Absolutely." He didn't know how far off the record it'd be.

The reporter glanced around – to see if anyone was watching? He leaned in toward the midget.

"I got some phone calls, and e-mails," he whispered. "Telling me to stick to the local political scene."

"And? A couple of crank calls and emails stopped you from following up?"

Eddler took another glance at the dozen or so people in the joint. "They were…not very pleasant."

"Oh, come on. You're a journalist, for Christ's sake. You must get nasty reactions fairly often – if you're doing your job."

"Nasty is one thing. These were threatening."

Derek felt his pupils dilate. "How so?"

"'Stay away from the American Rights party or it'll be your last story – ever.'"

"Did you tell anyone?"

"My editor."

"Not the cops?"

"We decided not to make a stink over some rightwing hotheads."

"But you didn't print anything about American Rights."

"No."

Derek had heard this song before. "I bet Hoch Industries is one of your biggest advertisers."

A resigned smile. "The biggest."

Of course.

"Did you have anything?"

The young reporter nodded and lowered his voice even further. "I found an accountant who had worked with them. Got fired when he complained that a good bit of the PAC money Hoch doled out couldn't be documented. Told me that Hoch has channeled millions under the table to get AR situated in all 50 states."

"Credible?"

"I thought so."

"Can you tell me his name?"

Eddler's eyes narrowed. "I don't want to seem… disrespectful, but I don't know you from Adam. And I don't reveal sources."

"What if he wanted to talk to me? Maybe he'd like to see Hoch get his comeuppance in the Post."

"Maybe. That'd be up to him."

"Can you ask?"

Eddler took a deep breath. "Yeh, I can ask. But it may take a while. I haven't kept in touch."

"I'm only supposed to be here through tomorrow, but I could extend if there's a real chance I can talk to this guy."

The reporter stared at Derek. "This isn't just some profile of Hoch, is it?"

"Not exactly," the PI admitted. "More of a preliminary fact-finding to see what the real story might be."

"Okay. I can live with that. I'll try to track him down. Where can I get a hold of you?"

"I'm at the Old West Lodge."

Eddler smiled. "I thought the Post would have bigger per diems than that."

"I like rustic."

"Fair enough. I'll let you know if I can locate him." He started to slide out of the booth, and then stopped. "One other thing: I'd watch my back, if I were you. A lot of people think pretty highly of Hoch in this town, and it's not as though you're going to pass unnoticed."

Derek winced ever so slightly. "Suppose not. Thanks for the tip."

The kid nodded and then went back to his friends.

Derek paid the bill and slipped out of Hannah's without even saying goodbye to his new friend Tina. Eddler's words echoed in his mind. He hadn't thought of this assignment as particularly dangerous, but Hoch was the 800 pound gorilla in these parts of the woods. He'd keep his eyes open.

It was barely 3 minutes later, as he was opening the door to his parked Fusion, that a large, black SUV cruised to a slow stop just within his peripheral vision. *'Probably wants my parking space,'* he told himself, even though there were several others available close by.

"Mr. DiLaurain," an unfamiliar voice suddenly called out.

Derek turned slowly, trying not to show the surprise he felt. The passenger window of a Lincoln Navigator slid open, and a man with a long narrow face, razor-cut graying hair and icy blue eyes peered out at him.

The PI walked toward the Lincoln. "I don't believe we've met," he said in lieu of an answer.

"No, we haven't," the man said. "My name is Henson, Earl Henson. I work for Hoch Industries."

"And?"

The smile that slowly emerged on Henson's face reminded Derek of ice cracking in the spring thaw.

"And my employer would like to have a word with you, if you have a moment."

"Your employer?" Derek had no intention of making this easy.

The smile faded almost imperceptibly. "I believe you know who I work for, Mr. DiLaurain."

"Do I?"

The smile disappeared completely. "I am Mr. Adam Hoch's Public Relations Chief."

"Ah. I thought the name seemed familiar."

"With all the conversations you've been having about Mr. Hoch, I'm not surprised," Henson said coolly. "So, can you spare a moment?"

The chance to talk with Hoch himself was more than Derek could have hoped for. But this was not the introduction he would have expected – or wanted. Still...

"I suppose I could make some time. What would work for Mr. Hoch?"

"How about right now?" The casual way Henson said it sent a chill down Derek's short but sensitive spine.

"Now? Well, I was going to do some research..."

"Mr. Hoch is a very busy man. I don't know if he will be able to see you before you leave our little town, unless you can make it now." It was more an order than an explanation. Derek got the distinct impression this man wasn't used to people saying no to him.

"Okay. I suppose I can reschedule my research. So, where do I meet your boss?" He pulled out his notepad to jot the address.

"Hop in," Henson said. "We'll give you a lift."

Derek could barely see through the heavily tinted windows; he couldn't tell for sure if there was anyone else in the car with Henson and the driver. In any case, it didn't feel right.

"That's okay. I don't want to put you out," he stalled. "Besides, I have GPS – I can find my way."

"It's no trouble at all. Is it, Tommy?"

At that moment, the driver's door swung open and a massive black man – the only black man Derek had seen thus far in his short stay in Billings – stepped out and walked around to tower over the PI.

"None at all, Mr. Henson," the man agreed.

Derek craned his neck to look up at the man.

"Hop in," the PR man repeated. This time it was definitely not an invitation.

"Yeh, yeh sure. Let me just lock up the Ford," Derek said, feeling inside his jacket to reassure himself he carried the 9 millimeter he always took with him on investigations.

The huge black man followed close behind as Derek locked his rental, and then walked with him to the far rear passenger door of the Lincoln. He opened the door and stood aside to let the tiny PI climb in.

"Thanks," DiLaurain said as he clambered up into the SUV. *'Hate these damn high-clearance fashion trucks,'* he fumed, knowing how ridiculous it must look to the giant behind him.

"I'm sure Mr. Hoch will be pleased to meet you," Henson said with no sincerity whatsoever as Derek slid into the seat next to him. It was the last word he would say to his guest during the entire 20 minute drive.

Nestled down into the luxurious black leather, Derek could not see much more than building tops and sky. After the first few minutes the man-made features disappeared entirely, replaced by towering pines and firs, and the occasional aspen. Beyond, in the distance, jagged mountain peaks slashed his horizon.

'Where the hell are we headed?' he wondered as it became clear that they had left the city far behind. He absent-mindedly nudged his gun with an elbow. He'd heard too many stories of one-way trips to the boonies to feel entirely comfortable.

About 15 minutes into the trip, the car turned off the smooth asphalt of the highway and onto a dirt road. Although the Lincoln ate up the small bumps effortlessly, even its silky suspension could not absorb some of the larger gullies, as they slowed to little more than a crawl. After another few minutes the car stopped and the big black dude got out. Derek heard a gate screech open, and a few seconds later – after the gate was closed (and locked?) – they were on their way again.

The last leg of the trip was brief. Only a few hundred yards from the gate, the big SUV slid to a stop.

"This is it," Henson announced as he opened his own door.

Derek lifted himself up as best he could in the seat and peered out the side window. They had parked next to a small but expensive-looking cabin hidden in the midst of deep forest. A man stood in the doorway. The PI couldn't be sure, but it looked a lot like the photos he'd seen of Hoch.

His door suddenly opened. "Mr. DiLaurain," Tommy the gate-opener intoned.

Derek took a deep breath and slid carefully out. He began his turn to circumnavigate the car, when the black hulk stepped into his path.

"What?" he asked, staring up into an expressionless face.

"My apologies, Mr. DiLaurain," the man standing in the doorway explained, his voice relaxed and, if not friendly, at least not angry. "Standard procedure. You understand, I'm sure."

It took just an instant for Derek to realize what he was talking about. "Oh, yeh, no problem," he said, even as felt his heart rate skyrocket.

Tommy crouched to pat him down. It didn't take more than five seconds to find the 9mm. He turned the little man roughly and finished the task.

"Just this," the large dark man said, holding the 9mm up between thumb and forefinger like some toy for his boss to inspect.

"Not the usual equipment for a journalist," the man at the door said cheerily. "More like what I would expect from, say, a private investigator." Derek could hear his heart pound in his ears. "Bring him here, Tommy."

The bigger man grabbed Derek by the lapel and half-dragged him to the bottom of the four steps leading up to the cabin door.

"Hey, take it easy, bro – your steps are a lot bigger than mine!" he protested, but Tommy didn't seem to hear.

His mind was racing as he waited to see what came next. *'So he knows who I am. Not surprising. He's got the resources, and as the kid said, it's not as if I was going to pass as one of the locals. Maybe it's better this way. At least I don't have to bs him... Breathe, damnit, BREATHE!'*

"Welcome to my little getaway," the man in the doorway said, breaking his increasingly panicky thoughts.

"Mr. Hoch, I presume," Derek said as he climbed the steps, his lips barely moist enough to get the words out.

"Indeed. My pleasure." He shook Derek's hand with surprising vigor for a man of his age. Adam Hoch was 74 years old, 6'1", 185 pounds, with pale gray eyes and the square Montana jaw that Derek was beginning to detest. His hair, at least, had grayed and was none too thick. "Come in, come in."

His tone was reasonably warm and affable, but Derek did not consider lowering his guard for even a moment. Hoch was from the end of the political spectrum that the PI mistrusted instinctively, and was filthy rich besides.

"Have a seat. Can I get you something to drink?" the billionaire asked.

"A glass of water?" At least it would help him lubricate his suddenly dusty tongue.

"I think we can handle that. Janine?" A plump, middle-aged woman appeared from the far end of the room. "A glass of water for our guest."

Derek scanned the room. It was simply but elegantly furnished and bigger than it looked from outside, probably a good 35 feet long and 20 wide, with a huge exposed beam – more of a tree trunk, actually – spanning the entire length at a height of some 18-20 feet. Derek could never understand why people liked to have their ceilings so damn high, but he understood that his distaste was probably based on his own situation.

"So, I understand that you're writing a story about me," Hoch said as he settled into a huge chair directly opposite from where Derek had been directed. The PI felt like a serf come to beg for food from the Czar. *That's probably the exact sentiment he wants to convey,'* he thought drily.

"To do some research, actually," he said. "With the elections coming up, there's a lot of interest about political movers and shakers, especially about those less visible to the public."

"And you think I am one of those 'movers and shakers'?" Hoch said with a disarming smile.

"Not just me. Just about everyone I talk to."

"Really. And who would that be?"

It was Derek's turn to smile. "Journalists don't reveal their sources," he said with just enough pompous self-righteousness to sell his reticence. Or so he hoped.

"Yes, so I've heard. And does that hold true for private investigators as well?"

Derek didn't flinch. "When they're working for a newspaper, yes."

"Ah, yes. The Post, if my sources are correct."

"That will be our first pitch, yes."

"Our?" Hoch said, leaning forward ever so slightly. "So you're working with someone else?"

This time the PI did flinch. He'd have to be more careful. This old guy still had a lot on the ball.

"I don't write, just research."

"Am I familiar with your partner? I read the Post most every day. Perhaps I've read some of his pieces."

"I'm sure you have. But, we PIs don't talk about our clients," he said, hoping to sound more confident than he felt.

"Yes. Very admirable." Just then the housekeeper came in with Derek's water. "Janine! Come in, come in," the older man said with poorly feigned enthusiasm. "I'm sure Mr. DiLaurain would welcome something to drink right about now."

At that, the conversation ended abruptly until she delivered his glass and slowly padded back to her room. For several long seconds the two men stared at each other, with Tommy standing behind and to the side of Hoch, and Henson sitting just to his left. *Looks like a scene from the Godfather,'* Derek mused in the eerie silence of the rustic cabin. He took a big sip of the cool mountain water and tried to relax.

"So, since you're obviously interested in my political dealings, I thought it might be helpful for you to talk with me directly," Hoch continued as soon as the kitchen door closed.

"Actually, I was going to request an interview once I had enough background to know what to ask," Derek countered, trying to keep his head above water.

"And? Do you have enough now?"

"I think so. Are you…amenable to answering a few questions?"

"That's why we're here. Right?"

There was something about his tone that didn't sit well with Derek, but there wasn't much he could do about it at that point.

"Right. So, I understand that you've been quite active with your contributions to various political groups and parties. Could you tell me a little about who you're backing, and why?" He reached into a pocket to grab his cellphone recorder. As he did, Tommy took a step forward and reached inside his jacket. Hoch held up a hand to stop him.

"Mind if I record this session?" Derek asked quickly, holding up the phone to make clear it wasn't loaded.

"Not at all, do we, Earl?"

The publicist looked less than thrilled. "I suppose not. Of course, we'll do the same." He deposited a compact digital recorder on the coffee table in front of them.

"Cool. Stereo," Derek quipped. No one else smiled. "Yeh, cool... So, about your contributions?"

"What would you like to know, exactly?" Hoch asked, stressing the last word noticeably.

"According to government records, you've donated over $30 million to various conservative political groups over the past three years. That would make you one of, if not the biggest donor in the country. My question is, why? Why give so much money?"

"Have a theory?" Hoch teased. "Perhaps a conspiracy theory?"

"I thought I was going to ask the questions."

Hoch's eyebrows shot up. "Touché. Okay, let's take it one step at a time. First of all, I take some exception to your use of the term 'conservative.'"

'Here we go,' Derek thought. *'He's going to nickel and dime me to death.'*

"I give money to organizations that I believe can do something important for this country. I don't choose them for their political slant or following, but for their capability."

"Admirable," the PI said, purposely echoing Hoch. "So then, can you give me the names of a few non-conservative organizations you've given money to?"

"That information is publicly available," Henson interrupted, "as you no doubt are aware."

"Is it? I must have missed it in my research. The only organizations I've seen supported are either conservative Republican PACs, or new fringe groups like American Rights."

Derek knew he'd hit a sensitive spot when Hoch's eyebrows knitted.

"I'd hardly call AR a fringe group," he said more calmly than he apparently felt. "They have candidates registered in all 50 states."

"But they only have 3 Congressman and one Senator," Derek countered. "Hardly mainstream."

"They're a new party, but with a little help I'm confident that they can help turn this country around."

"Turn it around? Is it heading in the wrong direction?"

Hoch's eyes narrowed. "Isn't it obvious? We are about to be overtaken by the Chinese – the Communist Chinese, for Chrissakes – as the number one economy in the world. Our military, the largest and best-equipped on earth, can't defeat a few thousand nomads in Afghanistan. The federal government wants to restrict our use of firearms – in direct violation of the 2nd Amendment, may I point out, and now this idiotic health care bill will bankrupt small businesses just to give a few thousand illegals and some inner city blacks the kind of medical care they haven't earned and don't deserve! And that's just the tip of the iceberg," Hoch continued, his voice rising and his face glowing red. Seemingly in spite of himself he winced, shifted in his chair, suddenly uncomfortable. Derek glanced up at Tommy, who showed no emotion at all.

"It's a national tragedy," Henson interrupted, using the exact wording DiLaurain had seen on the AR website. Hoch used the interruption to catch his breath and lower his blood pressure.

"And what – you think AR can change all that?" Derek didn't even try to keep the skepticism out of his voice.

"I don't know. We will see," the billionaire said softly, making a concerted effort to control his temper. "What I do know is that the Democrats, and even the Republicans haven't been able to handle the job. In my business, if someone can't do the job, you fire them and hire someone else."

Derek waited a beat. "Is that how you see yourself – as the CEO of AR?" he finally asked, hoping it would push the old man's buttons. It did.

"CEO?! Hell, I'm just a good ol', God-fearing, red-blooded American who wants to see this country get back to where it used to be. I would think even you journalist types would be able to understand that."

"Is that why you were trying to meet with Senator Wainwright, just before he died?" Derek asked, hoping Hoch's temper would get the best of him. "To try to convince him to back the AR?"

The silence was complete.

"Wainwright? What does he have to do with anything?" Henson finally asked.

"Yes, what?" Hoch echoed.

"I was hoping you'd tell me," Derek said with more sangfroid than he felt. "We were talking with the Senator just before he died, and he mentioned that you had been trying to get a hold of him."

"Did he?"

"Are you saying you didn't?"

Derek saw the PR man glance over at his boss. Hoch did not return the gaze. He stared at some indeterminate point in space as if debating his reply.

"I called the Senator's office a couple of times, yes," he finally said, meeting the PI's stare. "I wanted to discuss Ohio politics with him."

"Just state politics? You didn't chat about the national scene?" Derek was fishing, but he felt on fairly solid ground.

"I really don't remember. Probably. I mean, Layton was one of those 'movers and shakers' that you referred to. He knew just about everyone worth knowing."

"And yet the polls were saying he might have a tough re-election fight. Did you offer your support?"

"Me?" Hoch laughed. "Layton wasn't exactly the conservative type. Quite the contrary, as you no doubt know."

"Which is why we were kind of surprised when we heard that you two had been talking. It's hard to imagine that you shared a whole lot of philosophy or outlook."

"Even Liberals can be patriots," Hoch said with more animation than he probably intended. "Senator Wainwright always had this country's best interests at heart, even if he was mistaken in the direction it was headed."

"But he stopped taking your calls after a while. Why?"

Hoch's eyes clouded over with anger. "That's none of your business."

It grew uncomfortably quiet in the cabin. *'Hmm. A definite sore spot.'*

"Okay, let's put that aside for now. Shift gears a bit. What are your predictions for the upcoming election?"

"Still some time before November 4th," Hoch said, clearly back in control again. "A lot can happen between now and then."

Derek glanced down at some notes he had scribbled in his pocket notepad. As he looked back up he thought he caught the tail-end of a meaningful look between Henson and his boss. They both seemed to be suppressing smiles. *'What's so funny about that?'* the PI wondered.

"What if you had your druthers?" he asked. "Who would you like to see win?"

"Ah. That's a different question all together. There are a number of good candidates out there. Both Jacob Elias and Ned Blackburn would make a better President than either the incumbent or any of the Republican front runners," Hoch answered, naming the two most prominent AR candidates.

"Do you think either of them has a chance?" Derek couldn't keep the incredulity from his voice.

"Stranger things have happened."

Again the knowing glance from Hoch to his PR guy. What was that all about?

"And what about you? Could you see any situation in which you'd run for office?"

A big smile. "I have a company to run. I'd be happy just to help a real professional get to the top."

"An AR professional?"

"Preferably. But if not, the man..."

"Or woman," Hanson added.

"...or woman who best represents the principals I hold dear. Me and a great many other Americans, may I add."

Derek asked a few more questions to make it seem more like a real interview and after ten minutes or so reached for his recorder. "Anything else you'd like to add?"

"Just that this election might be the most important in the recent history of this great country. We've lost our way. We're losing our place on the world stage. Unless we act soon, and act aggressively, the U.S. will cease being the agent for good that it has been for over 200 years. Not only we Americans, but the whole world will be worse off if that happens."

Derek could almost feel the intensity Hoch threw off. The words of Barry Goldwater reverberated in his mind: "Extremism in the defense of liberty is no vice." The PI wasn't so sure.

"Okay then. Thanks for the interview," he said, packing up the recorder and his notepad.

"My pleasure. So, when will we see this masterwork of yours?" Hoch asked as he stood at his chair.

"Hard to say. We're still doing the research. I'd guess two or three weeks, if the Post buys it, of course."

"Of course," the billionaire echoed, but his tone was pure skepticism. "Tommy here will get you back to your car." He started toward the door. "Are you planning on staying on in our little town for a while longer?"

"Not sure," Derek lied. "Maybe a day or two. Depends."

"On?"

"On how my research goes. You never can predict."

"No, you certainly can't." The oil man stopped at the doorway. "Well, safe journey. We'll be looking for your article."

"Thanks again." The two men shook hands as Henson looked on from inside the cabin. "You're not coming?" Derek asked when the PR man made no effort to follow.

"No, I'm afraid Mr. Henson and I have some things to discuss," Hoch answered for his employee. "Business – you know."

"Yeh, of course."

A chill swept through his tiny body as he turned to head down the stairs. He was almost at the bottom of the staircase when a thought jumped into his head.

"Can I ask one more question?" he said, turning to look up at the billionaire.

"Of course. How can I refuse the Post?"

"I was so focused on Senator Wainwright, I forgot to ask: now that he's gone, will you be discussing your plans with Senator Westerly?"

Hoch's superior smile faded and almost disappeared, like a plate sliding off a table. "I discuss politics with a good many people," Hoch equivocated. "I would think a good Republican like James might be one of them."

"Okay. Thanks again."

Hoch merely nodded as Tommy opened the rear passenger door and held it for Derek. The last thing he saw before the car pulled away was Hoch and Henson, filling the front doorframe, watching him closely. They did not wave goodbye.

*****

"Must be interesting, working for a man like Mr. Hoch," Derek said after several minutes of silence on the drive back to Billings.

"It is," the driver answered simply.

"You been working for him long?"

"Long enough."

"He spend a lot of time out at that cabin? Seems kind of rustic for such a wealthy guy."

"Sometimes yes, sometimes no."

'Good thing I wasn't coming out here to interview this guy,' Derek thought. *'Like trying to wring water out of a dry mop.'*

"The boss travel a lot?" he tried one last time.

"A bit."

For the rest of the ride the only sounds to be heard were the hum of the tires and the wind rushing past the dark tinted windows. It was only when he finally caught a glimpse of the upper floors of a building he thought he recognized that Derek relaxed. He hadn't thought Hoch was angry enough to try anything stupid, but one thing he'd learned over the years was, you never knew.

Twenty minutes after they'd left the cabin the Lincoln pulled up next to his rented Fusion.

"Uh oh," Tommy grunted nearly imperceptibly.

"What?"

"Looks like someone isn't too happy with you."

Derek tilted his head unthinkingly. *'What the hell is he talking about?'* he wondered.

The large black man climbed out of the SUV and opened the PI's door.

"Want me to call someone?"

Derek was just about to ask why, when he looked out at the left rear tire of his car. It was as flat as his ex-wife.

"Goddamn it!" he spit before he could stop himself. "Hick assholes!"

"You got a cellphone?" Tommy asked.

"I can change a goddamn tire," Derek grumbled. "But thanks for asking."

"No problem. Here." He handed Derek his 9mm. "Take care of yourself, little man."

"Yeh, you too," Derek answered as Tommy returned to his side of the SUV, "big black man."

The driver stopped in his tracks. *'Uh oh, this could get nasty,'* Derek fretted.

Instead, Tommy turned to him with a big smile. In the twilight all the PI could see was teeth.

"Big black man. Good one," was all he said as, shaking his head in amusement, he climbed into the Navigator and gunned it down the street.

Derek exhaled. *'That was dumb,'* he chastised himself as he opened the trunk and started pulling out the spare and jack. *'Pretty damn dumb.'*

CHAPTER 7

By the time Derek pulled the Fusion back into the Lodge parking lot, it was pitch dark outside. He was tired, sweaty and his hands looked like he'd been greasing a pig. He slammed the car door shut and tramped wearily into the motel. He was nearly to his room when he first noticed the shadow at the end of the corridor, not 15 feet from his door. The person was nearly invisible in the dim hallway light, but Derek was just paranoid enough to check every nook when he was on foreign turf. He was just about to turn and feign having forgotten a bag, when a familiar voice called out to him.

"Mr. DiLaurain. May I talk to you for a minute?"

Greg Eddler stepped out into the small circle of light thrown by the feeble bulb overhead.

"A bit dramatic, don't you think?" the midget groused. "You're lucky I didn't pull a gun on you."

"Sorry about that. Didn't mean to scare you. But there's something I need to tell you," the young reporter said, his voice dropping to little more than a whisper, "in private."

DiLaurain hesitated. He'd already pushed his luck by going along with Henson out to Hoch's cabin in the middle of nowhere. What if this kid wasn't as country simple as he seemed to be? *'Only one way to find out,'* he decided.

"All right. Come on in," he said, turning the key and throwing open the door to his room.

As Eddler went inside Derek scanned the hallway to make sure no one else was loitering out there. When he was confident that they were alone, he went in and closed the door behind him.

"So, what's with all the mumbo-jumbo?" he said, tossing his notepad on the bed.

"I...I didn't feel comfortable discussing everything I uncovered about Mr. Hoch in Hannah's. Too many people around," he said anxiously.

"Okay. Not too many here. Have a seat and tell me about it."

The young reporter did as he was told.

"Want something to drink? I have water, and water."

Greg smiled. "Some water'd be great."

Derek grabbed a plastic glass from the kitchenette counter and knelt on a chair he kept stationed by the sink in order to reach the faucet.

"Oh! I can do that," the reporter offered, jumping to his feet.

"Don't wet yourself," the PI growled. "I'm short, not helpless." He filled the glass and waddled over to where Eddler had sat back down.

"So, what's so hush-hush?"

Eddler took a big gulp of water. "I talked to that accountant I was telling you about. The one who told me about Hoch's under the table contributions..."

"Yeh, I remember. I thought you didn't keep in touch."

"I just said that in case anyone was listening. Anyway, he'll talk with you."

"When?"

"Tonight, if that works for you."

Derek was bone tired, more from the adrenaline rush of visiting Hoch's little getaway than from any real work he'd accomplished. But this was too good to pass up.

"Yeh, okay, we can do it tonight. How do I reach this guy?"

"Here," the reporter said, slipping Derek a slip of paper with an address on it. "You can meet him here at 8 o'clock."

"There's no name," the PI said. "Who do I ask for?"

"He'll know you. I...described you to him." The kid seemed genuinely embarrassed.

"Okay, fine. Anything else I need to know about this guy?"

"Just that he's been laying low ever since he was let go by Hoch. He's even thinking of moving to another state. So if he seems a bit nervous, he has his reasons."

"Such as?"

"I'll let him talk about that."

"Okay, thanks – I appreciate it."

The kid nodded. "One more thing."

"Yeh?"

"When I was doing my interviews I had two separate sources tell me that Hoch has something big in the works. Something to do with American Rights."

"And? I mean, that's his baby, right?"

"It is, but this is something big enough that two separate operatives knew about it, but secret enough that neither of them knows what it's all about. Or so they said. Seemed pretty odd to me."

"Yeh, I see what you mean. Did they mention anything else? Names, places?"

"No, not really…Oh, wait. One of them said something about Ohio. He said Hoch was focused on Ohio."

Derek sucked in a quick gasp of air. Ohio. Coincidence?

"Interesting. Nothing else? No names?"

"Not that I remember. But I can tell you that if those guys think it's something big, it is BIG."

"And yet you didn't use it in your series."

"Didn't have enough details. 'Something big' isn't what I'd call news. And I couldn't find anyone else who knew anything about it. Or at least they wouldn't tell me."

Derek nodded. "Yeh. Makes sense. So, anything else?"

"Just remember what I said – watch your back. There are people here in Billings who wouldn't take kindly to an outsider asking too many questions about Mr. Hoch."

"Thanks. I'll do that." He debated whether or not to tell Eddler about his meeting with Hoch, but finally decided he'd earned the trust. "One thing you might find interesting – I met your Mr. Hoch today."

The kid looked surprised. "You did? How'd that go down? It took me over a month to just get an appointment."

"They found me: his PR guy, Henson, and a big dark fellow named Tommy."

Greg nodded. "His inner circle. Everything goes through Henson, and Tommy is always somewhere nearby. Jeff wasn't there too?"

"Jeff who?"

"Hoch's grandson, Jeffrey Simpson Hoch II. About 23, geeky little s.o.b. with a bad attitude. But they say he's smart as the dickens."

"What's he do for grandpa?"

"Computers. Supposedly a whiz-kid. Dropped out of MIT."

"What's his Dad do? I didn't hear his name mentioned."

"He died a few years back in a car crash. People say that's when Hoch turned to politics."

"Why?"

"Jeff Sr. was the real political one. In fact, he was running for mayor of Billings when he died. People say the old man took it hard and decided he was going to carry on for his son – but on a bigger stage."

"And that's when American Rights burst on the scene?"

"More or less. They were a tiny right-wing fringe group until Hoch decided to finance them."

"And now they have representatives in Congress. Big change."

"Just the beginning, if you listen to the AR flaks. They expect to become a real Third Party on the national scene. And soon."

"Great. Just what we need. Lunatic conservatives with money."

"Patriots who love their country, is how they put it."

"Right. I feel much better."

Eddler smiled. "You're not the only one with misgivings. Not all of us out here are gun-toting wackos just looking for a Commie to burn."

"Or an East Coast midget?"

"Like I said, watch your back."

"Don't worry, I will," Derek said, climbing down off his chair. "So, if I have any other questions, can I get in touch with you?"

"Sure. But, call me at home. Here's my number," Greg said, scribbling it on a scrap of paper. "Too many 'interested parties' at the paper."

"Will do. Thanks again."

"I'll be looking forward to your story. I think I just scraped the surface with my series. I really feel there's something much bigger here."

"We'll see."

The two men shook hands and Derek looked both ways down the hall before letting Greg leave. When he closed the door he let out a big sigh. There *was* something much bigger going on; he felt it too. Maybe the accountant could help him find out what it was.

*****

After a quick bite to eat and a shower to revive his flagging spirits, Derek Googled the address Eddler had given him. It was located over on the south side of town, the closest thing to a 'rough' section Billings could offer, according to a blog he scanned. The PI printed off a map with directions and headed out to meet his man.

It didn't take him long to see why the blogger had characterized the area as he did. He passed a large trailer park with dozens of quasi-permanent doublewides parked cheek by jowl in a sad looking tract, and then turned left into an older neighborhood with small, seedy houses on threadbare lots. He saw a sign for 'Massages' in the window of one house in the middle of a block.

'Tempting,' he thought as he continued on his route.

When he finally turned onto the street Eddler had indicated, he double checked the address. It appeared to be nothing more than a peeling, two-bedroom shack with no lights on inside and no car outside. He cruised past the house slowly and parked just down the block to surveil the area. *This is where the former accountant for Hoch Industries hangs out?'* he wondered suspiciously.

He was a few minutes early, as was his habit. He hated people who came late to meetings. Thought they were irresponsible at best and self-centered asses at worst. He watched the street with feigned nonchalance, glancing regularly into the rear and side mirrors to make sure no one or nothing was coming up behind him. At 8 o'clock on the dot a single light popped on at the house in question.

'What the hell?' he thought. *'How'd he get in there without me seeing him?'*

Whatever the answer to his question might be, he knew it was showtime. He checked his 9mm in the shoulder holster one last time and climbed down out of the Fusion. Looking left and right for more than just traffic, he crossed the road and made his way slowly to the crumbling shack.

He rang the doorbell and waited. After just a few seconds the door opened a crack.

"Yeh?" a male voice asked tentatively.

"Greg Eddler sent me," Derek said, feeling a bit like a thug at a speakeasy in Chicago in the 20's.

"All right. Come on in."

The door opened slowly to reveal the archetypical accountant. He was probably in his mid-fifties, balding, and wore brass-rimmed glasses. He was barely 5 foot ten, if that, and slightly overweight, maybe 180. His chin was a bit weak and his nose a bit sharp.

"I'm Derek DiLaurain," the midget introduced himself.

The accountant closed the door securely and made sure the deadbolt was thrown before turning to face his guest.

"Anthony. Anthony…" He stopped in the middle of his introduction. "Just Anthony. Okay?"

"Fine with me. Hey, thanks for agreeing to this meeting."

"Greg said it was important. That you might be able to help me."

Derek wondered why Eddler had used that entre´. He decided to play along.

"Yeh, maybe. You wanna sit down someplace?"

The idea seemed to hit Anthony unexpectedly.

"Oh, yeh, sure. Let's go into the kitchen. More private there."

As he followed the accountant past worn furniture and flaking wallpaper, he considered whether the meeting might have been a mistake. *'Only one way to find out,'* he decided.

"Can I get you something to drink?" Anthony asked as they stepped into the dimly lit kitchen. "I don't know what they have in the fridge, if anything."

The PI glanced at the dirty counters and greasy linoleum floor. "No, thanks anyway. I'm good."

The accountant motioned for DiLaurain to sit at a Formica dinette table with one leg propped up on a wooden block.

"So," he began as he sat opposite the PI, "I understand you're writing something about Hoch."

"Doing some research, actually."

"For the Post?"

"That's who we hope will take the story, yes."

"You understand, if I tell you what I know, you can't use my name." His voice trembled.

"Understood. The Post never reveals its sources. You remember Deep Throat?"

The quizzical look on the man's face told Derek he didn't.

"He was the source for most of Woodward and Bernstein's articles on Nixon. They *never* revealed his name."

"Yeh, good. Okay then, what do you want to know?"

"May I?" the PI asked, putting his cell recorder on the table.

"I…I suppose so."

"Thanks. So, Eddler tells me that you worked for Hoch Industries. Is that right?"

"At first. But then I was 'transferred' to a subsidiary. Montana Oil, he called it."

"Hoch?"

The accountant nodded. "It was just a shell, really. No assets, didn't do anything. Just a place for Mr. Hoch to launder his PAC money – *before* the Supreme Court's Citizens United ruling."

"I'm not sure I understand," Derek prompted, hoping to get Anthony to explain in his own words.

"It was quite elegant, actually," the man began, warming to his subject. "Hoch created this company, which – on paper – was a hard-luck drilling concern. Terrible luck. Never hit one single wet well."

"Is that unusual?" Derek didn't know squat about drilling.

Anthony smiled. "Not if you don't drill. You see, Hoch had this rig that he sent around here and there as if they were prospecting. They'd set it up, drill for a day or two, and then report problems – broken bits, machine failure, injuries, you name it. Thing is, they never got down anywhere near where the oil would be, if there was any in the first place. But they kept records that indicated that they had spent weeks, even months at each site, and so racked up imaginary costs. And the tax right-offs that came with them."

"Wasn't that pretty dangerous? I mean, if anyone had found out..."

"It was just one crew, and they were all Hoch lifers – been working for the old man for 30 years or more. They got hefty bonuses under the table and knew that if they talked, well, it wouldn't go good for them."

"The theory didn't seem to work with you."

"I wasn't supposed to know. I think they thought I was just some dumb numbers guy that they could keep in the dark. Problem was, I did find out. They were good with rigs and all, but they didn't know much about bookkeeping. I kept seeing discrepancies and couldn't figure out why. And whenever I mentioned anything to my boss, he'd tell me to just shut up and work the numbers."

"So why'd you leave?"

"It got out of control. At first Hoch was just hiding a few hundred thousand dollars in phony wells. But then, starting a few years ago, suddenly he ramped the whole process up a notch and started hiding millions, tens of millions of dollars a year. That was too much for me. I didn't mind small time fudging. They all do it. But tens of million – well, I'm not going to prison for anyone. Certainly not Hoch."

"How'd you get out without them getting suspicious?"

The accountant grinned proudly. "Faked an ulcer. Complained for a couple of weeks about stomach pains, then went to my doctor and got a prescription. I took days off nearly every week for a month, so they didn't complain when I finally told them I had to leave – for my health. I thought it was pretty clever – a fake ulcer to get away from fake wells."

"So why all this cloak and dagger? If they don't know you know about their little game, what are you so nervous about?"

The accountant sighed. "One of Hoch's people saw me talking to Greg. We had been pretty discrete, meeting in a little out of the way bar in mid-afternoon. But, just my luck, one of his people saw us. I begged Greg not to use anything about the phony wells in his series, and, thank God, he didn't. But I got a voicemail a day or two later – I didn't recognize the voice – that said my health would get a whole lot worse if I didn't stop talking to reporters. Since then, I don't do anything out in the open. I'm even thinking of moving out of Billings. Maybe out of the state. Only, all my friends and family live around here. It'd be hard."

Derek felt real sympathy for the guy. He was caught in a bad place, no doubt about it. But there were a few things the PI didn't understand about the scheme.

"Why would a man like Hoch risk so much for so little return? I mean, he's already got billions, for Christsakes."

"Ah. That's the interesting part. You see, even someone as wealthy as Hoch couldn't channel the kind of money he wants to the politicians he's backing. It would leave a trail that even the Feds could follow. We're talking more than $27 million over the past three years alone. It's illegal. But, the money that he invested in drilling all those dry wells was invisible. Lost. On paper at least. In reality, he still had all that cash. All he had to do was set up a string of front companies, and have them donate to individual candidates and national PACs on behalf of themselves and phantom or unknowing employees, and abracadabra: the money disappears. I can't prove it, but I'm pretty sure he gives millions to those wackos out of his own pocket as well."

Derek shook his head unconsciously. "Wow. Do you have anything on paper? Anything that can prove what he's doing?"

The grin faded. "Most everything was done electronically. And Hoch's grandkid had the system locked up tight. I couldn't risk downloading a thing."

"So it's just your word."

"Sorry. That's all I have. But maybe you can find a way to get to it."

"Maybe," Derek said. "But it sounds doubtful. Let's get back to those contributions – why's Hoch so generous to those right-wingnuts? I mean, $27 million is nothing to sneeze at."

"And it's probably more. Why? Who knows. I mean, if you look at the timing, I'm sure it's no coincidence that his son died just a few months before he started the real big donations."

"The politician?"

"Yeh. Jeff Senior. Actually, not a bad guy. But when he died, something snapped in the old man. Not just the big illegal contributions. He made a lot less public appearances, didn't even attend most board meetings. Became a bit of a recluse."

"Howard Hughes Two?"

"Something like that. Rumors around the water cooler say he even let a lot of the decision-making devolve down to his managers. Never used to happen. He made every major decision about that company, right down to the color of the paint on the headquarters building. Now, not so much."

"Sounds almost like some kind of breakdown."

"There are those who say that's exactly what it was. And I don't know anyone who says he's recovered since then. A few who say he's gotten worse."

"Interesting. Any idea why this has never come out in the media?"

"He's rich, he keeps his friends close to him, and…"

"And?"

"Rumors say that his enemies have…accidents. That's one of the reasons I've been keeping a low profile. I don't think I'm on their radar, but I don't want to take any chances."

Derek immediately thought about the flat tire. A warning?

"I certainly understand that," he said to the accountant. "So, anything else you want to tell me?"

Anthony fidgeted in his seat. "Well, it might be kind of tacky, but if this story sells, I wouldn't mind if you sent me a small…honoraria, you know, for my information. It's been a bit…thin since I left Hoch."

Derek looked more closely at the accountant and saw the tired eyes and worn shirt collar. Thin indeed.

"Yeh, sure. If this gets into print and we get some money, you'll get a piece. You earned it."

His smile showed more relief than the promise deserved. "I'd appreciate it. Especially if I decide to move on, I'll need a nest-egg."

"I understand." Derek turned off the recorder and slipped it into his pocket. "Well, thanks again. If we can find a way to document any of this info, I'm pretty sure we'll be able to sell the story. It'll be big news." He stood.

"I'll keep my fingers crossed."

The accountant walked Derek back to the front door in silence. There really wasn't much more to say.

"Drive safely," Anthony said as he unlocked the door and swung it open.

"Thanks. And good luck with that move," the PI answered, shaking the offered hand. "I'll let Greg know if the story gets picked up."

"Great. Good night."

"Night."

Before he'd even taken a step, the door behind him snapped shut and he heard the deadbolt slide into place.

'That's one nervous guy,' the little man thought as he walked back to his parked car. *'Seems there's more to this Hoch than meets the eye.'*

As he climbed into his Fusion and pulled away from the curb, he was too lost in thought to scan the street in either direction. If he had, he might have seen a rusty brown pickup sitting a few houses down from where he'd parked. The moment the Fusion's tail lights disappeared around the corner, a man got out of the pickup and walked carefully, stealthily, toward the house where Anthony was getting set to leave. He did not go to the front door, and he did not ring the doorbell.

*****

By the time Derek got back to the Lodge, he was tired, confused and famished. He didn't have the strength to go out, so he broke his own rule and ate in the onsite restaurant. As he sat in the red leather booth waiting for his meal, he glanced around at his surroundings: men wearing white cowboy hats and tooled leather boots, women with teased 60's-era hair and more makeup than anyone not working Times Square should ever consider, and the heads of deer, elk and even a bear gracing the walls. *'What am I doing here?'* he thought, not for the first time. *'I feel like I stumbled into the Wild West version of a Fellini movie.'*

As he sipped a beer he tried to wade through all the leads he'd uncovered. It was clear that Hoch was up to something, but it still made no sense to him why the guy would risk serious jail time to support a bunch of drooling idiots in races they could not hope to win. Or at least not so many as to make a real difference in the status quo. Or could it? He was no political expert, but it didn't seem likely that American Rights could get enough Congressmen or Senators elected to even hold the balance of power in the legislative branch. *'Maybe he just wants to influence a few states.'* Or maybe it was something else. Whatever it was, after talking to Anthony he felt it in his bones that Wainwright's drowning might not have been as innocent as first suspected.

He finished his venison steak smothered in wild mushrooms and sipped the last of his Bitter Root beer, trying to ignore the blatant stares of a good many of his fellow patrons. He was pretty much used to it, after all those years, but he still didn't appreciate it. As soon as he had finished the last bite of rhubarb pie, but not one minute before, he paid his tab and made his way back to his room. He double-checked the locks on the door, pulled off his clothes, brushed his teeth and washed his face, and then virtually collapsed into bed. He was asleep in moments.

He awoke at 6:30 the next morning, feeling no worse for wear. He showered, dressed and had just stepped out into the hallway on his way to breakfast when the front page headlines on the complimentary Gazette laying at his feet caught his eye. There was the usual stuff about state politics and warnings about lingering unemployment, but what made him look twice was a small photo just above the fold. It couldn't be...

He picked up the paper and read: "Local Accountant Killed in Hit and Run". It was Anthony all right. The story said he'd been hit by a passing car after stopping to fix a flat just a few blocks from where they had met. A flat? Derek didn't believe in coincidence, and this was more than just coincidence – this smelled of murder.

As soon as he could choke down a breakfast of scrambled eggs and toast, he hurried back to his room and called Eddler, hoping to catch him at home. When he got the answering machine instead, he hung up and called the Gazette.

"Greg Eddler," the familiar voice answered, sounding more somber than Derek remembered.

"We need to talk," he said. And waited.

"I told you not to call me here," the reporter whispered nervously. "Especially not now."

"You saw what happened to our friend?"

"I saw." Defeated. Or was it angry?

"We need to meet. Can you get away?"

A long pause. "10:30. The Library. Fiction section. Hemingway." Dial tone.

The PI hung up the receiver. This was getting interesting.

*****

He had no problem finding his way back to the library. He went upstairs to the Fiction section and feigned looking for a good read, all the while scanning the stacks out of the corner of his eye. He could keep the 'H' section easily in view while ensuring that no one came or went by the stairs or elevator. 10:30 came and went and no Eddler.

Did he chicken out, or did he have an accident too?' Derek wondered as he flipped through the latest, well-read issue of GUNS & AMMO.

He didn't have to wait long. At 10:43 the reporter emerged from the elevator wearing a wrinkled blue and white short-sleeve shirt and dark sunglasses. He looked around with forced casualness until, finally, he spied Derek sitting not 30 feet in front of him. He nodded conspiratorially and motioned with his head to indicate that the PI should move from his exposed seat into the more private space of the fiction stacks.

Derek was about to mutter under his breath when he remembered Anthony. He got up and did as the kid suggested.

"This had better be something important," Greg began before he'd even said hello.

"You can take off your sunglasses now," Derek replied. The reporter sheepishly obeyed.

"Sometimes I forget I've got them on."

"It's not a good look indoors if you're trying to be inconspicuous."

"I guess I'm not used to all this sneaking around."

"Well get used to it. If the accountant's death wasn't an accident, and I have my doubts, you'd better keep your head on a swivel."

He could see the kid's eyes widen. "So you think it was suspicious too?"

"A former employee of Hoch meets with an out-of-town PI and dies in a hit and run accident fifteen minutes later? You tell me."

"It was the first thing that crossed my mind."

"Good. You may live to be an old reporter. Now, let me ask you a few questions and you can be on your way."

"Okay."

"Anthony told me that Hoch had channeled millions to conservative PACS illegally. Did you know about that?"

Eddler fidgeted. "I, I knew that something funny was going on."

"And yet you didn't use it in your series."

Greg's smile was more grimace than grin. "How long have you been here in Billings?" he asked.

"Two days."

"Unless you're the least observant researcher in the history of journalism you must've noticed that Adam Hoch pretty much runs this city."

"Including the media?"

"Including everything."

"So what happened? Did he pick up the phone and call your Managing Editor?"

"Didn't have to."

"What do you mean?"

"Let's just say that if Hoch Industries decided to withhold its regular advertising budget for more than a week or two, I'm not sure how long we could stay in business."

"Right. And while I'm at it, how about these American Rights people? Do they have an office here in Billings?"

"Just a small one. Despite all their bravado about protecting the little guy and states' rights, the principal advisers and money raisers are in DC – northern Virginia, actually."

"Yeh, makes sense." Derek flipped through his notes. "Hey, this may seem a bit out in left field, but did the name Blayton Wainwright ever come up in your interviews for the series?"

"The Senator who died?"

Derek nodded.

"No, no I don't think so. Why?"

"Probably no reason. How about anybody else from DC? Any politicians, or… I don't know, whatever."

Greg was shaking his head when suddenly he stopped. "Just that Cable News guys – Beddecker, isn't it?"

"Simon Beddecker? How's he fit into all this?"

"Not sure, but once I was sitting in Hoch's lobby waiting to meet with his PR guy, Earl Henson…"

"Mr. Personality?"

This time the smile was genuine. "I see you've met him. Anyway, I was waiting for my appointment when I heard one of the secretaries say 'Sorry Mr. Beddecker. He's not in just now. Of course, I'll give him the message.' The name caught my attention. Then she turned to the other girl working the phones and said, 'Mr. Beddecker again. Do you think CN is doing a story on Mr. Hoch?' When I brought the subject up with Henson you'd think I accused him of child pornography. He basically told me to mind my own business if I wanted any cooperation from H.I."

"Hmm. Interesting. Anything else I might want to follow-up on?" the midget asked Eddler.

"If you mean about Hoch's contributions, no. Anthony never really opened up to me, like I take it he did to you?" He was definitely fishing.

"He told me a few things. But he was scared. He even talked about possibly getting out of Billings. Not now, though."

Eddler grimaced. "No, not now. So, is that all?"

Derek thought for a moment. "Yeh, I think that'll do it for now. But if I have any other questions, can I give you a call?"

"At *home*," the reporter stressed.

"Yeh, yeh, of course. So, thanks again. You take care of yourself, you hear? And I don't mean just wearing sunglasses indoors, either."

"Don't worry. I can take care of myself," Eddler said. "I just hope you get the whole story. It'd be a doozy."

"You'll be the first to know. Maybe we'll even add you as a contributor. Would you like that?"

"In the Post?"

"Wherever."

"Sure. Thanks."

"My pleasure. Now go write stories to make Billings safe for women and little children."

"I'll do that."

They shook hands and then the reporter was gone. Derek put his pad away and flipped through the last few pages of G&A. *'May as well give him plausible deniability in case anyone is watching either of us,'* he thought as he stared at a scantily-clad bimbo stretched across the hood of a pickup while a smiling redneck held his 30.06 as if in a trophy photo. *'Man, these hicks know how to live,'* he thought sarcastically.

Ten minutes later Derek pushed open a rear glass door and left the library as inconspicuously as someone of his stature was able.

As he walked to his car he made a decision: with all that had happened, caution had definitely become the better part of valor - it was time to leave Billings. He called the airline on his cellphone and changed his reservation to the next available flight. He drove to the Lodge and quickly packed his few belongings and went to the front desk to check out. But before the clerk could even prepare his bill, she handed Derek a sealed envelope.

"What's this?" he asked the young woman behind the desk.

"A message, I assume."

"From whom?"

"Got me," she answered with a shrug. "It was sitting here on the counter when I came out from the office."

Derek nodded absent-mindedly and turned away from the counter to open the envelope. Inside he found a piece of white paper with five words scrawled in red crayon: "Good riddance. Don't come back."

"Hospitable folks you got around these parts," he muttered aloud.

"You'll never meet friendlier people," the girl replied without even looking up from her computer screen.

"I can try," he whispered.

He paid the bill and drove straight to the airport. On his way out of town he could see the expansive grey headquarters building of Hoch Industries sitting in the foothills to the north.

'Wonder what that old bastard is up to,' he thought as he turned into the rental return lot. *'No good, I'll bet on that.'*

CHAPTER 8

Brady was trying to pry a burnt piece of toast from his toaster when the doorbell rang.

"Come in, it's open!" he yelled over the blare of the TV.

DiLaurain strolled into his kitchen looking much the worse for wear.

"Breaking another small appliance?" the midget quipped as he pulled out a chair and hopped up into it.

"Screw you too," Brady answered as sparks flew from the toaster.

"You don't have that thing plugged in, do you?"

"You get toast out of your toaster your way, and I'll do it mine."

"I'll notify Emergency Services."

Brady grimaced as he yanked the plug out of the wall and turned to face his small friend.

"Great to have you back, kind of."

As he took a closer look at Derek his eyes narrowed. "Jesus! What did they do to you out there in Bull Moose country, or whatever they call it?"

"Friendliest people you'll ever meet," he said in a squeaky falsetto.

"Do I detect a hint of sarcasm?"

"Never could fool you."

Brady smiled and pulled up a chair. "Okay, give it to me."

"On an empty stomach?" the PI whined.

"What, you don't have food at your place?"

"Perhaps you've forgotten: I was gone for a couple of days, on a mission of mercy for a dipstick I thought was my friend."

James shook his head. "If they ever give graduate degrees in guilt-laying, you'll get the first PhD," he said as he pushed the chair away from the table and stood up. "All right – what'll be?"

"How about two eggs over easy, with a couple of pieces of toast." He paused for effect. "Oh, I almost forgot, your toaster is 'indisposed'. How about a Bloody Mary instead?"

"Just one," Brady answered gruffly. "We still have work to do today."

"More than you realize."

Over breakfast the PI told the entire story of his brief stay in Billings. Brady interrupted from time to time to ask questions, but for the most part he listened silently.

"Jesus H. Christmas," he said when Derek finally stopped. "This is looking like a real pile of dog crap."

"Or pig vomit. Depends on your point of view."

"Whatever, it's looking nasty."

"I don't know, you might say it's looking up. At least we've got some leads."

"I don't think that accountant would say so, or Wainwright."

"Yeh, well their points of view are somewhat limited right about now," Derek said without a smile. "I hope they're the only ones connected with this story that turn up with that particular malady."

"That makes two of us. Speaking of which, I'd better give Anne a call and let her know to keep her eyes open."

"How is the Senator's foxy secretary?" Derek asked with a sly smile. "You get into her pants yet?"

Brady glared at the PI. "You are one nasty little dude," he finally muttered.

"And damn proud of it."

"Even worse. You know…" James was about to add a good deal more, when the phone rang.

"Damn!" Derek jibed, "I was hanging on your every word."

"You will be hanging from a coat hook if you don't clean up your act," Brady said back over his shoulder as he went to answer the incessant ringing.

"Hello," he said with the impatient, almost angry tone that was his habit. That tone changed almost immediately as he heard who was on the other end of the line. "Anne! I was just about to call you. Uh huh…uh huh…"

As he talked he caught a glimpse of Derek leaning around the corner, lips puckered and eyes aflutter.

"Jerkoff," Brady muttered as he turned away from his friend. "No…no. I was just talking to Derek, his usual charming self," he explained into the phone. "Anne says hi," he informed the chortling midget, who waved. "Derek says hi back. So tell me about this paper you found."

After listening carefully to what she had to say, he filled her in about Derek's trip out west and cautioned her to keep alert. A few minutes of back and forth, and he closed the conversation by suggesting they should get together sometime soon.

"Anne found something that might be relevant to our little investigation," he said as he flopped into a seat opposite Derek at the kitchen table.

"Condom?"

Brady smiled as he shook his head. "It's really been that long since you had any, huh?"

"I've started flipping through old National Geographics."

"You are truly pathetic. But that's obvious. What isn't so obvious is why Senator Wainwright was apparently doing some research of his own just before he died. Ever hear of the Vulnerability Assessment Team of the Argonne National Laboratory?"

"Semi-pro ball?"

"Enough with the jokes," Brady snapped. "Anne found a file in Wainwright's desk that contained a white paper by this Vulnerability group about the possible ways hackers could sabotage electronic voting machines. Kind of an odd thing for a Senator to be looking into, don't you think? Especially without sharing the task with his secretary, or at least someone on his staff."

"Are we sure he didn't? I mean, maybe he tasked someone without telling Anne."

"She asked around. Nobody's even heard about the group."

"And they're legit?"

"She Googled them. Big-time hush-hush government agency located just southwest of Chi-town. They look extremely legit."

"So – what now?"

"Well, I think we need to follow-up on these VAT folks, and we need to talk with the American Rights leaders too. I haven't been out to Chicago in a while, and you're buddy-buddy with all those right wing politicos, so…"

"So I get the kooks and you get a good steak. Ok. I've had enough traveling for a few days anyhow."

"Good. I'll try to book a flight tomorrow, and you see what kind of connections you can dig up to get to the leadership of AR."

"Sounds good," Derek said draining the last of his Bloody Mary. "But for now, can I guy get another one of these?"

*****

Brady had booked a flight to O'Hare first thing the following morning, but he decided – for personal as well as professional reasons – to see Anne before he left. She seemed warmly receptive to the idea, so he was in good spirits as he drove over to her place to pick her up.

She lived in a high-rise apartment complex within spitting distance of Capitol Hill. It was one of those typically DC arrangements with four thin splinters of brick all linked together by a central plaza, complete with occasionally-functioning fountain. The view of the majestic Capitol building was possibly worth the exorbitant monthly rent, Brady mused, but not to him.

Anne buzzed him in and was waiting in the doorway when he stepped off the elevator. She was wearing a slinky blue-green designer dress, a string of sizable black pearls, and the kind of high fashion heels that Brady thought were reserved for models. 'Not *bad,*' he thought with a dazed smile.

"My god, I think I'm underdressed," he said as he approached the door.

"Not at all," she said forgivingly, leaning over to kiss him gently on the cheek. "Oops, let me get that," she added as she wiped a small lipstick smudge off his reddening skin.

"You look...incredible."

"Thank you. Shall we have a drink before we head out?"

"I could be persuaded. What do you have?"

"You name it. A good Congressional secretary always keeps a well-stocked bar."

He wanted to ask for a beer, but decided it would seem too mundane. "How about a scotch?" he finally decided.

She opened a mirrored cabinet to reveal bottles of every shape and size.

"Blended or single malt?"

"Wow. I've been to bars that didn't have that kind of selection."

She smiled. "Actually, most of it was from the Senator's office. He kept a little of everything on hand for visits from his fellow representatives."

"A skunked Senator is a friendly Senator, is that about right?"

"Something like that. What can I get you?"

"You don't happen to have a Tomintoul, do you? I had a taste once when I was over in Scotland, and I've never forgotten it."

Anne looked through the various bottles. "I don't think so, but how about a Longmorn? I know the Senator had a soft spot for it."

"Hey, what the heck. You can't grow if you don't try anything new," he said, cringing as he realized how his words might be misinterpreted. Or interpreted, anyway.

"Coming right up," she continued as she brought out the cut glass tumblers. "Neat?"

"I wouldn't add DC water to oatmeal, let alone single malt whiskey."

"Fair enough. I might even join you."

Brady strolled to the windows to look out at the Capitol dome. "Beautiful place you have here. Great view."

"They charge for it, believe me. But, I don't have that many other vices, so may as well spend it on the view."

"Not that many other vices? So there are a few?"

Her smile was broad and genuine as she brought his drink to him. "We can talk about that over dinner. Cheers."

They touched glasses and sipped the scotch.

"Mmmm. Kind of sweet," Brady said, holding his glass up to the light to marvel at its golden color.

"Told you. The Senator was something of a connoisseur."

"Speaking of which, I hate to mix business with pleasure…"

"Don't be silly. I would if you didn't."

"Okay. Then, I just wanted to double-check a few things on this report you found from the Argonne Lab. Where, exactly, did you find it? I mean, you'd gone through the files pretty thoroughly, I thought."

Her face turned serious. "That's the odd part of all this," she began. "I went through that office with a fine tooth comb looking to see what files might have been taken or destroyed in the break-in. Then yesterday, after the police finally gave us the okay, I was cleaning out the Senator's desk, putting everything in boxes to send to his family. I was looking through the middle side drawer when suddenly I saw a tiny flash of white paper. I thought at first it was just a scrap of something sticking up out of the drawer below. But when I opened that drawer, there wasn't anything there. So I got down on my knees to see what was what – and I found a file in an envelope velcroed to the bottom of the middle drawer!"

"Was it just the report? Anything else in there?"

"A few notes the Senator wrote himself. Nothing that seemed too extraordinary. But here," she said, walking over to a plain white oversized envelope that sat on her dining room table, "take a look for yourself." She handed him the envelope.

"Have you told the cops about this?" he asked as he flipped perfunctorily through the dozen or so pages.

"Not yet." She smiled. "Thought you might want to have a chance to go through it; maybe even make copies."

Brady nodded as he reviewed the first page of the report. "You're starting to think like an investigative reporter."

Her smile grew broader. "I try."

"Very interesting..." James muttered to himself as he read the executive summary.

Anne was watching him closely. "So, do you think this might have something to do with the Senator's death?"

"I don't know yet. Perhaps."

"But how? I don't think Senator Wainwright had any connection to Argonne Laboratory."

"It seems there may be a few things no one knew about the Senator. And besides, maybe it didn't have anything to do with the Lab. Did your boss, by any chance, have anything to do with electronic voting machines in Ohio?"

"Well, he certainly wasn't involved in the nuts and bolts, if that's what you mean," she said dismissively. "But if you mean, was he involved in the overall process – of course! He was the former state party chairman and had his hand in everything that happened in Ohio politics."

"Maybe there's a link there," Brady said, his face a thoughtful mask. "But we can think more about that tomorrow," he added, closing the envelope and tucking it under his arm. "I'm getting hungry. You?"

"Very."

"Then let's get going before they give away our reservation." Brady gulped down the last few sips of his scotch and felt the warming burn surge down his throat and into his brain.

*****

The alarm clock sounded at 5:30. It was still dark as he reached to turn it off and found – nothing.

What the…?' he thought wearily. Suddenly, the alarm stopped.

"Rise and shine," a pleasant, familiar voice coaxed.

Brady rolled onto his other side and found himself nose to nose with Anne. In an instant he remembered the scotch the night before, followed by wine with dinner, the laughter and easy conversation, the hand touching, the nightcap back here at her apartment, and then…

"How'd you sleep?" she asked.

"Fabulously!" he said with more energy than he felt.

She snuggled closer and slipped her hand between his legs. "I'm not surprised," she cooed. "You expended a lot of energy."

"Whoa, tiger," Brady said, gently taking her hand in his. "If we get started in that direction I may miss my plane."

"And we wouldn't want that, would we?" she asked in mock horror. But before he could answer she kissed him on the forehead and sat up. "Okay, so what'll it be for breakfast: eggs, toast, cereal?"

"Smart, beautiful, and you cook? I could get used to this."

"Don't get ahead of yourself, buddy," Anne said with just enough humor to let him know she was only partly kidding. "First date is always an aberration."

"But a nice one," he countered with a knowing grin.

"Get yourself up and showered," she said as she pulled on a fluffy white robe and slippers. "I'll meet you in the kitchen in 20 minutes."

"Yes, sir!" he said, watching her pad off.

'I bet she's one hell of an office manager,' he thought as he stretched and pulled his battered body out from under the sheets.

*****

The hassle at Reagan National was as bad as usual, but Brady was so engrossed in thought about the Argonne Lab report he barely even noticed the endless, crawling security lines, the smiling but unfriendly TSA agents, and the dazed travelers who dragged themselves through the terminal like extras from 'Night of the Living Dead'. He reread the report as he sat waiting for his flight, trying to divine why Wainwright would have kept, let alone hidden, such an arcane document. *'This is really deep in the weeds,'* he thought as he perused paragraphs that Wainwright had apparently highlighted, for the most part dealing with security weaknesses in the electronic voting machines that were already being used in most parts of the country. *'Including Ohio?'* he wondered. He decided he'd have to check on that.

The flight was uneventful, except for the hyperactive 10 year old sitting behind him who kept kicking the back of his seat until he peered around the edge of the row and nailed him with a stare so evil that he thought the kid was going to start crying. He got the message. Less than an hour after landing, Brady had already collected his luggage and rental car and was on his way southwest down I-55 toward Argonne.

He had booked a room at the Argonne Inn, located just south of the Labs. From the name, he'd assumed that it was a quaint mid-west B&B type of establishment. *'Something out of American Gothic,'* he remembered thinking when his agent had suggested it. So he was more than a bit surprised when the GPS instructed him to turn into the driveway of a modern, glass box hotel straight out of 'Clockwork Orange', or was it 'Blade Runner'? Whatever, it wasn't quaint. It was, however, clean, scientifically efficient (what did he expect five minutes from the Labs?), and the bed seemed relatively comfortable. Besides, at $70 it fit his budget. He checked in, unpacked his single carry-on suitcase, and called the contact he had identified at Argonne. They reconfirmed a one o'clock meeting with Dr. Theodore Davis, one of the co-authors of the report and the Deputy Director of the Vulnerability Assessment Team.

With a little over an hour to kill, Brady made his way down to the Inn's coffee shop and ordered a burger and fries. As he waited for the food to come, he eyed his fellow patrons. He would have expected a scene from 'Geek Squad,' complete with horned-rim glasses and pocket protectors. What he saw instead was a scene from 'Wall Street': trim, leggy young women who looked like they could handle themselves in the UFC Cage, and slightly older, slightly more conservative, professorial men dressed in $500 suits. *Probably sales people pitching the Labs,'* he decided. *'From the looks of them, there must be money to be made here.'*

Service was good and the burger edible, so he arrived at the Lab gate a few minutes earlier than he had planned. He cleared security and received his clip-on badge and parking pass, which he dutifully hung from the rearview mirror. As he drove along the narrow, two-lane access road that encircled the Lab buildings, he was struck by how much like a college campus it all appeared. Admittedly, more like a good community college than Harvard, but impressive nonetheless. Several clusters of two-story 1950s' era brick buildings were highlighted by the occasional modern white concrete and glass structure, all separated by strapping oaks and rolling green landscaping extending along a half-mile stretch of good prairie countryside. *'Must be 1500 acres here,'* he thought as he made a complete loop around the 'campus' to check it all out. He was just turning back by the main gate to make his way to the building where Dr. Davis waited, when an unmarked black sedan pulled up next to him. The uniformed guard inside motioned for him to roll down his window.

"Lost?" the guard asked cheerfully.

"Just looking around," James admitted. "I think I can find my way. Thanks."

"Okay. Have a good day."

The guard rolled up his window and then waited as Brady pulled ahead and slowly made his way to the building where the interview was scheduled. He glanced in his rearview mirror and noticed the black sedan following at a polite distance.

'Trusting souls, aren't they?' he thought with a smile.

He found the building without problem and gave the security guard a casual wave when he cruised by. Inside, there was another security desk and another magnetometer, but within just minutes he was following a tall thin redhead through the somewhat sterile corridors to his scheduled interview.

She led him to a large office with floor to ceiling windows that looked out on the rolling greenery and woods in the distance. 'Dr. Theodore Davis' the nameplate on his desk read, and the man who rose to greet him fulfilled his every preconception: balding, maybe six feet tall, thin with a bit of a paunch, Davis met his gaze directly with piercing dark eyes half-hidden behind rimless glasses.

"Mr. James," he said in a voice a full octave deeper than Brady might have expected, "glad you found us here."

The men shook hands. "Thanks for seeing me on such short notice."

"I must admit, we haven't had too many journalists calling about that old report for over a year now. I was a bit taken aback to hear you'd just stumbled upon it."

"I don't usually work the tech beat," Brady explained, "but with the elections coming up in the fall, we thought it'd have broader interest."

"Makes sense. What can I do for you?"

"Well, although your report makes it pretty clear that your Team had theoretical concerns about the security of electronic voting machines, I was wondering what probability you put on someone actually being able to tamper with a machine in the real world, and also whether your opinions had changed since you wrote the report – either because of a new generation of machines, or for whatever other reason."

Davis leaned back in his black high-back leather chair and let out a long slow sigh.

"Good questions. Let me take the first one first. At the time we originally wrote that report – and that was the summer of 2008 – the first generation of machines was just being widely deployed and used in actual elections. They were a novelty, and our report was more meant to open people's eyes to the possibilities than to cast doubt on the feasibility of using them in general elections. To be honest, we were a bit surprised by the panicked response we got from the media and a number of election boards across the country."

"You said that someone with a screwdriver and five minutes time could pop open a machine's back panel and cross a few wires to create fraudulent results. And that they could remotely manipulate the machines from a distance of a half-mile away so that they could pass pre-election scrutiny and still give the required results. You didn't think that would raise concern among election officials?"

Dr. Evans smiled. "Let me reword that. It was the panic we didn't anticipate. We assumed that election officials would have had the machines tested for every kind of tampering long before initial deployment. We thought we were merely confirming what they already knew, and were taking steps to correct."

"And?"

"And, it turns out we were wrong. The manufacturers had put the onus for keeping the boxes safe entirely on the elections people. The elections people were under the gun to come up with an alternative to the 'hanging chads' that had been such a scandal in the 2004 Presidential election. They both knew about the shortcomings but basically disregarded them."

"Not exactly the kind of public stewardship we expect from our officials, eh?"

"You said it, not me," the Deputy Director said. "We simply said that there were problems that someone needed to address."

"And, have they? I mean, are electronic voting machines safer now than in 2008?"

Davis tilted his head from side to side as if trying to decide. "That depends on your point of view. Newer designs have made it more difficult, but not impossible, to access the innards of the boxes and make the initial alterations, but software has progressed to the point that a really good programmer, with the help of a decent mechanic, can install self-replicating viral instructions on just a handful of machines a few months beforehand that can infect an entire system."

"Can it be detected?"

"It would be very difficult. Unless you know what you're looking for, it's not so easy to find. And worse of all, there are still thousands, maybe tens of thousands of the old machines still in use. They've come up with new protocols for storing and installing the machines, but if I were a betting man – and I am – I'd bet everything I own that a really determined hacker could get access somehow and wreak havoc on election day."

"Without being detected?"

"Possibly."

"Wow."

"Exactly. We're so concerned, we're thinking of putting out an update to the original report. But, with budgets the way they are…"

"It's looking unlikely."

Davis nodded resignedly. "We'll just have to keep our fingers crossed that the elections people are on top of the situation."

"You didn't tell me you were a longshot player."

Brady couldn't tell if Davis was smiling or scowling.

"It's a sad situation, that's for sure."

"And dangerous. Hey, is there any chance I could see a demo of how someone would jerry-rig one of those machines? Do you happen to have any here at the Labs?"

"In fact, we just dragged a couple of them out again a few weeks back when we thought we might get the money to produce another report. Come on. I'll show you myself."

Dr. Davis led Brady through the pathologically clean glass and steel hallways of the Labs to a large well-lit room with spotless white walls. In one corner stood two upright devices that could have been mistaken for video poker machines at a distance.

"Here we are. How familiar are you with these gadgets?" Davis asked as he rolled one of the machines into a position where he could plug it into a wall socket.

"Not very. Never used one myself." As he watched, Brady realized that the actual voting machine was only the very top section of the cabinet. "I thought it would be bigger," he said.

"Like most things electronic, it could be even smaller. The only reason it's this big is to give us humans enough room on the touchscreen to easily read and access the candidates' names." He pushed a switch on the back of the device and the screen leapt to life. "There we go."

James glanced down. '2008 Presidential Ballot' was lettered at the very top of the high def screen, with the names of the various Presidential and VP candidates listed just below. A large square was positioned next to each team. 'Barack Obama/Joseph Biden. John McCain/Sarah Palin. Mickey Mouse/Donald Duck.' "Quite the impressive list of candidates you have here," he joked.

"What? Oh – the guys had a little fun there," he explained following Brady's gaze. "But the results of their findings are dead serious. You see, with just a basic screwdriver," he continued, producing one from the cabinet below the screen, "a person who knows what he's doing can sabotage one of these in minutes." He went behind the machine with Brady close on his heels. "You just remove these screws," which he did in less than a minute, "open this back cover, and…voila´ -- you have access to the electronic guts. From here all it takes is a few cables and adapters, a laptop and the right software, and you're in business. Less than five minutes from start to finish."

"And no one could tell by a visual examination that anything was amiss?"

"You tell me." Davis turned the other voting machine around and undid the rear screws. He put both machines side by side. "Which one has been tampered with?"

Brady studied the electronic innards closely. They looked identical. "I have no idea."

"And neither would anyone else. To the naked eye, they are exactly the same. But even worse, watch this." He turned the first machine so that the touchscreen faced them and took a small netbook computer from the cabinet below the screen. He led Brady all the way across the room, a good thirty feet from the machine.

"Imagine I'm parked in a car outside a voting center, as far as a half-mile away. The elections officials have just completed their pre-vote screening, and the real voters are just starting to stream into the center. I push a few buttons," he said, demonstrating by punching some instructions into the netbook, "and I now control the voting machine – and any others I've managed to infect through the network that ties them all together. How many votes would you like Obama to have?"

"27,234," James said, pulling a number out of thin air.

"And McCain?"

"Six," James deadpanned.

Davis smiled. "Do I detect a bias here?"

"Just wanted to make the demonstration more striking," Brady lied – badly.

"If there were at least 27,240 voters at that center, we could make it happen, no problem. In fact, here's the printout the folks at Election Central would see." He showed Brady the netbook screen. It showed columns of numbers, but at the bottom the totals read, 'Obama/Biden – 27,234, McCain/Palin – 6.'"

Even as prepared as he was, Brady shook his head in disbelief. "Is it really that easy?"

"It really is. Of course, if someone was actually trying to rig an election, as opposed to just showing off their hacking abilities, they wouldn't make the differences so 'striking', as you put it. But they wouldn't have to. Just a shift of a few percentage points at some key polling stations, and the results could be quite different."

"But couldn't the election officials do a post-mortem on the machines and see that they've been tampered with?"

"If the hackers were sloppy, maybe. But if they're any good – very unlikely. The same way they'd program their instructions to spread virally, they'd instruct them to self-erase completely – throughout the network. A minute after the polls close, the system would look as good as new."

"This is scary stuff," Brady finally managed to mumble.

"Very scary. A handful of guys could break into some of the warehouses where these machines are stored between elections, access the electronics and plant their viral instructions, and no one would be the wiser."

"This undercuts the very foundation of democracy."

Davis nodded thoughtfully. "With every technological advance comes new challenges. Electronic voting is faster, easier, and usually more accurate. But those very traits also make it more susceptible on a much larger scale. You see now why we wrote that report?"

"In spades. One more question: is there any way to make the machines foolproof? I mean, is electronic voting doomed?"

"Anything a human being can design, another human being can figure out how to hack. The machines are getting more secure, but foolproof? Not as long as people are involved in the process."

"So electronic voting is…what? Just a flash in the pan?"

"Not likely. You've got to remember that states have spent millions, maybe billions by now in buying and installing the framework for these machines. They can't back out now, even if they wanted to. And, to be fair, no system of voting has ever been 'foolproof'. The difference here is, if they let their guard down just a micron, someone could steal a whole election – maybe even at the national level."

James whistled. "Why haven't we heard more about this?"

"We tried. But it fell into the media pool and sank with barely a ripple. I think people just don't want to believe it's true. They want to believe that their vote is sacrosanct."

"Well, maybe we can help get the word out," Brady said, thinking that he might just have to write a real article for publication once this whole Wainwright thing was settled.

"You'd be doing a real service to your country."

"I don't know about that, but a journalist's job is to let people know the truth about the world around them. Or, at least that's what I've always thought."

"Keep on thinking that way."

The two men chatted a bit longer about the electronic voting machines, and about the Labs more generally, until Dr. Davis had to excuse himself for another meeting. They shook hands, and Davis called an assistant to show Brady to the exit.

It was just a bit after two when he drove out of the gates of Argonne Laboratories and headed back to Chicago for the flight to DC.

'There's something of Alice in Wonderland to all this,' he thought as he drove on the Interstate. *'It just gets curiouser and curiouser.*

*****

At about the very same time, Derek was just arriving at a concrete grey two-story office building in Fredericksburg, Virginia, about a half hour south of Washington. Located in a slightly rundown strip mall, no signs or banners announced that this modest structure housed the headquarters for the American Rights Party. He parked in their ten-space lot and made his way to what appeared to be the main entrance.

The PI had always prided himself on his sensitivity to his surroundings – his 'gut' feeling – and at that moment his gut was telling him something was not quite right. *'A bit too easy,'* he judged as he pushed open the glass door and faced a sign directing visitors to everything from 'Tan's Nails' and 'Burton Optical', to the AR offices, which were located upstairs. He'd been able to make the appointment to meet with AR officials with just one phone call. In fact, the press person had seemed almost as if he were…expecting the call. But easy or not, he and Brady needed to get a feel for these people, and he intended to do just that.

He found another glass door at the top of the stairs, and was surprised when it swung open from his push. He did notice a camera mounted in the hallway, but otherwise it appeared that AR was a good deal more relaxed about their security than most such organizations. A young woman with teased blonde hair and pink lipstick sat at the reception desk.

"May I help you?" she asked with a pleasant smile, looking down at him with no sign of surprise or unease.

"Derek DiLaurain, to meet Roger Goodman," he announced boldly.

"Ah yes, Mr. DiLaurain. Mr. Goodman is expecting you. Please have a seat and I'll let him know you're here."

Derek remained standing, looking around the office at the various photos and framed documents that dotted the walls. He saw a number of faces he recognized, mainly from the far right wing of the Republican Party. But most of the people were unknown to him. *'Probably former governors of hick states that only their staffs could identify,'* he decided.

He was inspecting one particular photo that featured a young, dark-haired man shaking hands with Ronald Reagan, when a decidedly older version of that same man appeared in the reception area.

"Mr. DiLaurain!" the man said with the wide smile and welcoming expression Derek had learned to expect from top-level political operatives. "I hope you found us without any problems."

"None at all. Mr. Goodman, I take it?"

"I am. I see you were admiring that photo – it's one of my favorites."

"Understandably. President Reagan was a great man." Two could play this game.

"Indeed. We could use more like him today."

"That's a pretty tall order."

"Yes, I'm afraid it is. But we can always hope. So, why don't we go into my office and I'll try to answer your questions."

"Sounds good."

Derek followed Goodman through a door located directly behind the receptionist's desk and into a narrow hallway with tiny offices lining both sides. The PI noticed that the entire wall shook when the door closed behind them.

"How long have you been here in Fredericksburg?" DiLaurain asked as they made their way to Goodman's office.

"Just a few months. But then again, we've only been legally constituted for a little over two years," he said, stopping at a slightly larger office on their right. "Here we are. Make yourself comfortable." He punched a button on the desk intercom. "Roberta? Ask Jeff to come down to my office please."

He sat behind the very used looking desk and leaned back in his chair. "Can we get you anything – tea, coffee?"

"No, nothing thanks. I'm fine. Mind if I record our interview?" Derek asked as he pulled out his cell recorder.

"No problem. We'll do the same, I imagine." Just as he finished, a perfunctory knock sounded on his office door, which swung open immediately. A thin, wiry young man in his late twenties strode in. Having seen the expression many times before, the PI was not surprised to see the newcomer's eyes open wide when he saw Derek.

"Jeff, this is Mr. Derek DiLaurain," Goodman introduced. "He's here to interview me for an article he's helping put together about the upcoming elections. You remember, I mentioned him to you."

"Oh yes, pleased to meet you," the young man said with a plastic smile and dead fish handshake.

"Jeff is our Public Relations person," the AR Chairman explained to his visitor before turning to the PR man. "I was just telling Derek that we usually record all interviews."

"That's right," Jeff agreed cheerfully as he pulled out a digital recorder that bore a striking resemblance to Derek's cellphone.

"Just be sure they don't get mixed up," Derek said.

Jeff looked at the two recorders and laughed with the pro-forma, unamused laughter that public relations people everywhere seem to master from birth. "That could be embarrassing," he said with mock joviality.

"Yes, it could," Derek agreed coolly. "But I think we'll work it out. Are we ready to get started?"

"Any time," Goodman said. "Fire away."

"Okay. Well, the main thing that I think people want to know is how AR came into existence, and how you've become such a major national player so quickly."

"I wouldn't call us a major player – yet," Goodman said with a smile that didn't hide his pride, "but we're getting there. As to how we got started, I'm sure you've visited our website…"

"I have," Derek interrupted, "but it was a bit…general. What I'm looking for is the backstory. Who did what, when? You know."

"Ah, yes. Well, I suppose it all goes back about four years ago when a number of disaffected political activists met in Houston to discuss ways we could move the political dialogue in the direction we thought it needed to go."

"They were mainly Republicans, I take it?"

"Mainly. But a number of the participants would likely call themselves Independents, or Libertarians. You see, it wasn't a political party that brought us together, but our belief in critical core values: individual freedoms, a strong military, sound economic policies – things like that. And what came out of those meetings was a decision to form a new political party that would owe nothing to the existing political structures and would, eventually, move this country toward the original vision of the Founding Fathers."

"And are those people who met in Houston still the backbone of the party?"

"For the most part, yes. Of course we've added some new faces, and lost a few…"

"But not many," Jeff chimed in.

"No, not many," his boss agreed with a nod. "We've been blessed to have some very determined members on our National Committee."

"And are there other supporters, people who are not on the Committee, who carry a lot of weight inside the Party?" Derek asked, trying to sound as innocent as possible. He watched Goodman's eyes closely, but detected only the smallest of reactions.

"We do have some important supporters who are not formal members of the National Committee," he said without hesitation.

"Can you identify a few?"

The Chairman's unflappable smile wilted just a bit. "Not everyone is interested in becoming a media sideshow, Mr. DiLaurain. I'm sure you can understand that. And we certainly support their right to maintain their privacy."

"So does that mean you can't, or won't reveal the names of any key supporters who aren't members of the Committee?"

"Those supporters who wish to publicize their support have already done so. The others, well, they've made their choice as well."

"But even those supporters must be acknowledged in the campaign finance reports, right?"

"Of course," Goodman agreed. "But there are hundreds, if not thousands of people on those lists. Not all of them could be called 'key' supporters, by any stretch of the imagination."

Derek reached into a jacket pocket and pulled out a printed list of names. "So, would you say any of the following were 'key' supporters?" He read about seven names of the AR's largest contributors, when the PR guy interrupted.

"I think Mr. Goodman already explained that some supporters do not wish their participation to be publicized."

"I understand," Derek countered. "But surely you, Mr. Goodman, in the position you occupy, appreciate that the citizens of this country have an interest – and the right – to know who is backing which candidates. How else can they really know what those candidates stand for and who they really represent?"

"Our candidates state quite clearly what they stand for, and we submit every document required by law," Goodman answered solemnly. "I'm quite sure the major parties are no more forthcoming."

"But the major parties have been around for a hundred years or more, while AR has seemingly just popped up on the scene. Can't you understand how that might make some people wonder who's behind such a fast-rising group?"

"Excuse me," the PR guy interrupted, color rising to his cheeks, "but is this so-called article about the upcoming elections, or is it about AR's backers?"

Goodman held up a hand to calm his associate, before turning back to Derek. "I understand what you're saying, Mr. DiLaurain, but you must understand that we have an obligation to our supporters to maintain their privacy, if that's what they prefer. So, I'm sorry, but this is an area we just cannot expand upon. Do you have any questions that are about our party, its policies or candidates?"

"I can get most of that from your website," Derek answered sullenly. "How about your future plans – can you discuss those?"

"Of course. What would you like to know?"

"You've got, what – one Senator, a couple of Congressmen and three or four governors right now?"

"Four governors," Jeff interjected.

"Okay. So how long do you think it will take before you become a major national player? I mean, before you have, let's say a dozen Congresspeople, five Senators, or someone in the White House?"

The Chairman's eyes sparkled. "Perhaps not as long as you think," he answered with renewed charm. "But it's not always just numbers that equate to influence. I think we're already well on our way to influencing the direction of the political debate in this country. Definitely on the conservative side."

"So you aren't aiming for bigger and better returns? You have no aspirations for the White House?"

Goodman laughed, and for the first time since they'd met, Derek judged his reaction to be genuine. "No politician worth his or her salt would ever say they had no aspirations for the top office in the land. That one person has a greater impact on what this country does, and more importantly what it represents, than all the others put together."

"Okay, so when do you see this as a real possibility? When would you hope to see an ARer in the White House?" Derek pressed.

Goodman pursed his lips thoughtfully. "Well, it's all just pie in the sky at this point, but the way things are going I would be surprised if we didn't have a strong candidate competing for a place on a Presidential ticket within 10 years. How's that? Good enough quote?"

It was Derek's turn to smile. "Yeh, that's a good one. Thanks. Anything else you'd like to get out there to the electorate?"

"Just to remind them that neither the Democrats or Republicans were around at the founding of this great nation, and that we actually have a pretty strong history of third parties contributing to the national good – a history that goes back almost to the very beginning of the Republic."

Derek recognized the zeal of a true believer. The hairs on the back of his neck stood up.

"That's another good one," Derek complimented, trying to hide the unease from his voice. "All of a sudden you're a virtual quote machine."

"Worth the ride down here?" the PR assistant asked.

"Absolutely. I can almost see the headlines now."

"Can you?" Goodman asked, and something in his tone put Derek even further on his guard. "That's good to hear. We'll certainly be on the lookout for the article."

"In the Post, is that right?" Jeff asked.

"That's our hope. I'm sure you know how tough the freelance market is these days."

"So we've heard. Keep us informed, in any case. Anything else we can answer for you?"

The PI feigned deep reflection. "No, not really. Oh, one thing: is there anyone else you would recommend I should talk to, to get further perspective?"

"Senator Graceworthy has always been very willing to spare some time for the media," the Chairman said. Derek suppressed a smile. Graceworthy was one of the biggest media hogs in the entire Senate.

"Can I tell him you sent me in his direction?"

"Oh, by all means. In fact, we'll give him a call to let him know you may be in touch. Okay, Jeff?"

The PR guy nodded resolutely.

"Great. Thanks." Derek was confident he would either find the Senator unavailable, or the interview would be one step below pabulum. But he smiled as he stood and collected his recorder.

"Got the right one?" Jeff taunted.

"I think so. If you push play and hear me reciting my grocery list, you'll know I was wrong."

All three men faked a chuckle.

"Well, thanks again. And good luck with the Party. It'll be interesting to see how it evolves."

"Yes, it will," Goodman said as he shook Derek's hand. The PR guy, on the other hand, just nodded, tight-lipped.

"A definite pleasure," Derek quipped as he turned to leave. "We'll be in touch."

"I'm sure we will," the Party Chairman said, and Derek felt those hairs on the back of his neck tingle once again.

As he pulled out of the headquarters parking lot to head back up I-95 to Washington, a very used grey sedan pulled out of a lot on the other side of the street and followed him at a discrete distance.

CHAPTER 9

Brady reshuffled the layer of papers that covered his kitchen table as he tried to make heads or tails of the Wainwright story. He'd returned late at night to Reagan, and after a short ride home had slept like a rock. But even a good night's sleep hadn't brought order to the jumbled mosaic that included the Senator, Hoch, American Rights, and all the others. What was going on?

If Anne was correct, and he was giving her intuition more and more credit with each passing day, then Wainwright's death was not an accident and the cause of his death might very possibly be found in the jumbled mess that confronted him. He ticked off the facts: it wasn't a robbery. The Senator didn't seem to have had any enemies – even within his family. His finances were in good order. He didn't drink to excess, he never used drugs, and if he had a secret life it was a secret from everyone who knew him. No, it didn't seem likely that he was killed for any of the 'usual' reasons. The only logical reason Brady could come up with, and he admitted to himself that it was a reach, was that Wainwright might have known something, or stumbled upon something, that someone didn't want him to know. A week ago he would have pooh-poohed that reasoning as the typical leap of illogic that so many families or close friends came up with when a death was particularly inexplicable. But with bizarre leads taking them out to Billings, Argonne and now Fredericksburg, it no longer seemed quite so far-fetched. He was still mulling the possibilities when the annoying front door buzzer clattered in the familiar, 'shave and a haircut, two-bits' pattern.

"Come on in, Derek!" he yelled back over his shoulder.

The screen door slammed shut and the diminutive PI waddled into the kitchen.

"You're a little late to be filing your taxes," he said, eying the pile of paperwork.

"And you're a little short to be playing center for the Lakers," Brady shot back with perhaps a bit more annoyance than he intended.

"Whoa – that time of the month?"

"This whole damn Wainwright thing is giving me a headache," he admitted wearily. "I know that there's something here staring us in the face, but what is it?"

"I always think better when I'm sucking on a cold one. Can I get you one too?" Derek headed straight for the refrigerator.

"Did you actually bring a six-pack?" James asked in amazement, looking up from the paperwork.

"No, of course not. Why would I bring a sixer when I know you've always got some chilling in the frig. Tell you what – next time you're over my house, the beer's on me."

"Right. By that time we'll have men living on Mars."

"Then they can supply the beer. I really don't care who, as long as it's cold." He pulled two longnecks out of the frig and snapped the tops off by snapping his fingers to send them sailing in the general direction of the sink. One found its mark, while the other bounced around on the linoleum floor.

"Are you the stupid s.o.b. who's been clogging my garbage disposal with caps? I should send you the plumber's bill!"

"As long as your plumber doesn't mind waiting a while, maybe a long while, be my guest. It's not like I'm hauling in the big bucks just now, you understand," he explained drily.

"Yeh, right. Who knows, maybe there's actually a story in this mess after all."

"So you think Wainwright really did take that dip against his will?"

Brady took a big gulp from his beer. "Don't you? I mean, he had no obvious problems, he was intensely involved in planning for the next election, everybody loved the guy, and he was a U.S. Senator, for

Chrissakes! That's the next best thing to the Playboy mansion for attracting good-looking nookie."

"I thought he was still bummed from his wife's death."

"True, but he was a man. Even if he wasn't looking for a long-term thing, I'm guessing he wouldn't have said no to some prime groupie T&A if it fell into his lap. Just doesn't make sense. So where does that leave us?"

The midget swigged his beer. "Well, we've got all that back and forth with Hoch."

"Yeh, we do have that. But I just can't bring myself to believe that one of the richest men on this planet would kill Wainwright over some political dispute. Doesn't ring true."

"So, how about the Argonne crew? Did they shed any light on the subject?"

Brady spread his palms skyward. "Yes, and no. I mean, they definitely have an axe to grind over the security concerns they've identified with these new electronic voting machines. It's absolutely a disaster just waiting to happen. But, again, what's it have to do with Wainwright?"

Derek played with his long hair, curling and uncurling several strands as he pondered the question. "Well," he finally offered after another sip of beer, "he was closely connected with the election process in Ohio, right?"

"He was. Definitely."

"And does Ohio use electronic voting machines?"

"Just about every state uses them to one extent or another."

"So, maybe Wainwright found out that someone was going to sabotage the machines in Ohio, and they decided to get rid of him. People have been killed for a lot less."

"I thought about that. But who would benefit? I mean, Ohio's a pretty big state. To rig a statewide election wouldn't be easy. And then, even if you could pull it off, what would be the value to you? A Senator is only one of a hundred, a Congressman one of more than

400. Trying to get a Governor elected might make sense, but Ohio isn't electing a Governor in this next election. So why bother?"

"Maybe those American Rights bastards just wanted to get another Congressman or two to help cement their position as up and comers."

"Maybe, but enough to kill a Senator?" The incredulity in his voice brought a nod of agreement from Derek.

"Yeh, a stretch. So, where to from here?"

"I need to get some insight from someone who really knows this political biz. It's not exactly my forte´."

"You got somebody in mind?"

"Actually, I do. I've been talking to a few old buddies at the Post, and they say I need to talk to a Professor James Beardsley over at George Mason. They say he knows the right-wing politicos better than just about anyone."

"George Mason?" Derek asked, his tone suggesting that he wasn't fully convinced of the University's credentials. "Doesn't Georgetown have someone who knows the skinny?"

"They probably do," Brady explained, "but apparently George Mason is the hotbed of libertarian ideology in the DC area these days. And if you want to know about bears…"

"You gotta go to a cave. Yeh, I know. So who's it gonna be – you or me?"

"I'll take this one. I want you to see what you can dig up about the Ohio political scene. Who's the big cheese now that Wainwright is out of the picture? Who makes the decisions about where and which voting machines are used? Basically anything and everything about the upcoming elections out there. Can you do that?"

"For you, and a couple of cold ones, I can do just about anything," Derek answered with a blurry grin.

"Your loyalty is touching. And get me another one too while you're at the frig."

"You read my mind," the PI said as he drained his first beer.

"Not that hard. I mean, it's not exactly 'War & Peace'."

The midget's grin grew even wider as he flipped his empty bottle in the general direction of the yellow plastic trashcan in the corner on his way to the refrigerator.

"Sticks and stones may break my bones, but beers will never hurt me."

Brady shook his head. He only hoped that the beers wouldn't run out before his patience. Derek handed Brady his beer before making himself comfortable. The two men proceeded to discuss their separate trips to Illinois and Fredericksburg at some length while nursing several more cold ones, before turning on the Redskins-Eagles game. It would be a long afternoon.

*****

George Mason is a state university with its main campus located in suburban Fairfax, Virginia, a bedroom community for the tens of thousands of government, think-tank, and related employees who work in and around Washington, DC. Just thirty years ago the school would have been categorized as average at best, the kind of place 'C' students went to get a piece of paper that said they had graduated from college. Then, starting in the late 80's, the University expanded its campus, increased its student body, and went on a recruitment drive to land 'star' professors in economics, computer and neurosciences, and public policy, among others. Government grants began to pour in, and gradually the University began to evolve. The university is still well back in the pack as far as overall national prominence, but in a few specific areas they have achieved hard-won distinction.

Foremost among those areas is public policy. Championing a hybrid philosophy of conservative and libertarian values, GMU has become a focal point for policy planners and political conservatives throughout the country. It was just the kind of place that American Right-ers would feel right at home, Brady mused.

As Brady drove through the densely populated Northern Virginia neighborhoods of townhouses and garish MacMansions situated on postage-size lots, he marveled at what a difference a few miles could make. His area of NW D.C. was just a short drive to the north, but in stark contrast to the soulless landscape he stared out at, his neighborhood was comprised of smaller, 1930's and 40's-era single and two-family houses with their own sizeable patches of lawn, interspersed with classic old row houses. Northern Virginia seemed to him a classic example of development run amok. Too many people. Too many cars. Not enough roads and diversity. Oh, there were plenty of Asians and not a few Middle-Easterners, but they were all middle class types with the same middle class values. It felt claustrophobic, and, well, junky to him. True, there were some very nice places, like Spook-Central around Langley, but by and large it was not his cup of tea.

GMU was, to some degree, an oasis in the sea of sameness. Its numerous low-rise red brick buildings could hardly be called radical, or even architecturally stimulating, but the large open green spaces and innumerable flowering bushes gave it a sense of spaciousness and calm in the confined, congested world of northern Virginia. As he turned off of Braddock Road and into the campus, he literally sighed with relief.

He parked in one of the visitors lots and made his way to Prof. Beardsley's office. As he walked through the campus he felt the late fall heat rise up off the cement walkways, and before he could even reach the Professor's building he was sweating profusely.

'Nice,' he growled. *'Nothing like looking like an overworked stevedore to give a favorable first impression.'*

He found Beardsley's building without any trouble, but was taken aback to find that the entrance to the Professor's office was just another unremarkable wooden door in a long corridor of similar doors, without secretary or waiting room. *'I guess fame doesn't necessarily bring perks at ol' GMU,'* he thought as he knocked loudly.

"Come in!" a strong but aging voice called from inside.

Brady opened the door and was once again struck, this time by the very basic nature of the eminent educator's digs. The room was small, by any standard. Probably not more than 12 x 15. With Beardsley's large wooden desk taking up half that space, most of the rest was covered by a snowstorm of paper, books and...well, just junk. Beardsley himself seemed strangely incongruous in the midst of all that chaos. Not a tall man, the balding professor sported a perfectly manicured moustache and gray goatee streaked with black. He wore an expensive brown houndstooth sport jacket over tailored brown trousers, with a conservative silk tie that spoke of elegance and wealth, not absent-minded disorganization.

"Looks like it's a tad warm out there," the professor commented as he glanced at James' matted hair and the rivulets of sweat streaming down his forehead.

"It's fall in DC."

Beardsley smiled. "That it is. Have a seat, if you can find one under all this trash."

"Thanks. And thanks for seeing me on such short notice."

"Not a problem. So, you're researching for an article on the upcoming elections, eh?"

"I am. There are a number of interesting facets I'm hoping to explore."

"They must be quite interesting to pull you off your crime beat. That is what you won your Pulitzer for, isn't it?"

Brady's eyebrows shot up involuntarily. "I'm impressed. Been doing your research as well, I see."

"Google is a wonderful thing. Not much you can't find on the Internet these days."

"Oh, I don't know," Brady challenged Beardsley. "I really haven't been able to find all that much about American Rights, for example. Oh, I've looked at the press releases on their website, but it's all boilerplate. On the other hand, I've been hearing through the grapevine that they're hoping to make a big move this election season."

"Don't all politicians hope to make a big move in every election?"

"I suppose, but not all of them have such significant financial backing." If Brady thought he might get a reaction from the professor, he was mistaken.

"And where did you hear that?" he answered without blinking an eye.

"From a number of sources," Brady lied. "How about you – have you heard anything of the sort?"

"Well, I have to admit that I have heard some rumblings about a swelling war chest," Beardsley said, leaning back in his chair. "But when you take a look at their Federal filings – and I have – their successes have been...incremental. Hardly noteworthy."

"And do all contributions show up on those filings?" Brady knew he was walking a fine line, but he was growing frustrated with their inability to find a connecting thread linking AR, or Hoch, or anything for that matter, to Wainwright's death.

This time he thought he glimpsed a bit of a reaction.

"How do you mean?" the professor asked, shifting forward to lean on his desk.

"Well, there's a lot of money floating around out there. Individual contributions, corporate, and a whole lot more from PACs and SuperPACs. Surely not all of that is picked up by the filings."

Beardsley's eyes narrowed. "It should be." He stared directly into Brady's eyes for an uncomfortably long moment. Then he exhaled deeply and fell back into his chair. "But, of course, especially now that the Supreme Court has ruled that corporations should have First Amendment rights when it comes to financing campaign advertising, as long as it's not given directly to the candidates themselves, well, it's a whole new world out there."

"And is AR benefitting from the new rules?"

"They all are. But as a smaller party, trying to get themselves recognized as a national player, sure, they will probably benefit more than most. Now, I'm not saying that I have any evidence of wrongdoing on their part..."

"No, of course not," Brady quickly reassured. "But, what have you heard?"

"Off the record?"

"If you'd prefer."

"I would."

"Then sure, off the record it is."

Beardsley nodded acceptingly. "Okay. Well, the rumor among some of the more conservative operatives is that AR has found a Sugar Daddy – a wealthy donor, or two, or three, who knows? – who is channeling them enough money to make a much bigger splash this time around. And there's enough optimism in the AR brain trust to reinforce those rumors. Is it a fact? Who can say? But I know that there's a feeling among the movers and shakers that they're going to surprise a few people in the next elections."

"And these Sugar Daddies are keeping their identities hidden? Is that legal?"

The professor tipped his hand to and fro. "So-so. If they're giving the money through a PAC, they really don't need to make their personal identity known. Of course, company ownership is a matter of public record."

"But, in theory, the corporation could be just a front to give donations?"

Beardsley raised one eyebrow. "You really are onto something, aren't you? That's exactly what a lot of us warned when the Supreme Court issued its decision. But the boys – and girls – in black don't care about such piddling details. They interpret the Constitution. Keeping our election system honest is somebody else's job."

"So, is it possible? I mean, not theoretically, but in the real world? Could someone hide their ownership in a corporation sufficiently well that their support for a candidate – or party – could be unknown to the general public?"

"They could certainly make it hard enough to unravel the ownership that an election could come and go before their support was widely known, yes. And if it was convoluted enough – you know, off-shore holding companies and dummy shells – it's possible that no one would ever take the trouble of tracking it down unless they had a very specific reason to do so."

"And then the candidate or party could use the money any way they wanted?"

"Not exactly. They could use it for all the advertising in the world that supported their 'core values', a sort of stealth support in which everyone in the world would know that the ads were for that candidate, or party, but they'd never actually name them. And then the candidate or party could use the money that they'd normally put into advertising – the largest portion of campaign spending, may I add – on other expenses. Peter paying Paul, as the old saying goes."

"Slick."

"Very. And threatening to the very core of our democratic system."

"How do you mean?"

"Well, if the super wealthy can channel huge sums of money through real, or dummy corporations or PACS, they can – in theory – influence elections to ensure that candidates beholding to them win critical posts. And then the whole concept of democracy is turned on its head."

"You don't seem to have tremendous confidence in the common man's common sense."

Beardsley shrugged. "I think most people have pretty good common sense. But when they're told over and over again on TV, radio, and now more than anything, the Internet, that such and such economic, or foreign, or social policy is either God's gift to man or the Devil's own handiwork, a sizeable proportion of people are going to believe it enough to cast their vote to the person – or party – that mouths the same policies. We're all only human. We want to believe that we know better than our neighbor. That we hold ourselves to a higher standard than our co-workers. But just look at Bernie Madoff – even the most sophisticated among us can fall victim to a slick presentation repeated convincingly with great frequency."

For a moment Brady didn't know what to say. It was even more horrible than he had feared. But despite that realization, he still wasn't convinced that he'd found the motive for Wainwright's death. Could the Senator have found out that Hoch, or someone else, was going to give large sums of money through dummy corporations to AR? But even if he did, would they kill him for that knowledge?

"Not a pretty picture, is it?" the professor asked. Brady realized he'd been staring into space for quite some time.

"No, not at all. In fact, worse than I'd thought. This Sugar Daddy you've heard rumors about, any ideas who he – or they – might be?"

"Not really," Beardsley said with a shake of his head. "There are a lot of wealthy people out there who want to get the federal government off their backs, and some of them are definitely ethically challenged."

"Yeh, I saw a lot of that in my former incarnation."

"I bet you did."

The two men chatted for more than a half-hour about AR and its founding fathers, and more specifically about known or rumored wealthy benefactors. Hoch was definitely among the latter, but he was just one of several. At the end of their meeting, after all the give and take, Brady was no more confident of why Wainwright was killed than when he arrived, but was approaching 100 percent certainty that it was not an accident.

*****

Brady drove home slowly, trying to synthesize all the data that was floating around in his overstuffed brain. He had a hunch that he'd reached critical mass with the myriad pieces of this puzzle, but still couldn't identify the boundaries that would allow him to begin filling in the empty spaces. He'd had the same sensation many times before when covering crimes for the Post. He knew the only solution to the frustration he was feeling was more research, more reflection, and – most importantly – a little luck.

He passed the National Cathedral as he cruised up Wisconsin, but it wasn't until he'd actually turned onto Lowell Street that he first noticed the smoke in the distance. At first it was just an oddity, one of those 'what the heck is that?' moments. But as he came closer to his building he saw the red trucks and white police cars, and suddenly he had a bad feeling.

He parked as close as he could, given that the cops had the street blocked off a good hundred yards from his place. He tried to keep his calm, walking at a normal pace, trying not to hyperventilate. The rancid smell of smoke filled the air. Radios squawked unintelligible gibberish. A few dozen neighbors braved the smoke and chaos to congregate on corners, watching the whole drama unfold. *'Probably the only time most of them have ever talked to each other,'* Brady thought as he continued toward his building.

Suddenly a hand grabbed him hard by the elbow and pulled him to an abrupt halt.

"Sorry, buddy. No one gets closer except the firefighters," a young black cop explained. "Too dangerous."

Brady realized he'd been so involved in his own thoughts that he hadn't even noticed the sawhorse barriers and yellow tape, both in the street and on the sidewalks.

"I think that might be my apartment," he said numbly.

The cop's expression softened. "Sorry to hear that. But I'm afraid you still can't go in there until they get the fire under control."

Brady nodded. "Any way I can find out for sure if it's my place?"

The cop scanned the mass of public safety workers. "Try that guy over there," he said, indicating an older firefighter in a blue dress uniform. "I think he's calling the shots."

"Thanks."

The cop let him slip under one of the yellow tapes and he made his way directly to the officer.

"Excuse me," he said, "that might be my apartment that's burning."

The firefighter turned toward him. "8I?" he asked.

Brady let out an involuntary sigh. "That's me. Brady James is my name," he added, offering his hand.

"Captain Jeffries," the firefighter introduced. "Sorry about your apartment."

"Thanks. When did this all happen?"

"We got the call around 40 minutes ago. By the time we got here, it was burning pretty hot."

"Anybody hurt?"

"Not that we know of. So far, it's just the one apartment."

"Have any idea what caused it?" Brady thought of over-taxed outlets and worn power cords.

"Not yet. We'll get the inspectors in there as soon as it's safe."

No sooner had those words escaped his lips, however, than an ash-smudged fireman came stomping over to the Captain in his heavy rubber boots. In his gloved right hand he carried a large blackened gasoline can.

"Found this inside," he said, his voice rough from the smoke. "From the burn patterns on the walls and floors, looks like it might have been torched."

"That belong to you?" the Captain asked Brady.

"No. Never seen it before," he answered, but he couldn't help hypothesizing where it might've come from.

"You'll need to make yourself available to our inspectors, and maybe the police too if it turns out this was arson."

"As soon as I know where I'll be staying, I'll let you know."

"You do that."

From the way the Captain said it, Brady knew he was a suspect.

When the two firefighters resumed talking about the fire, he turned away and flipped open his cellphone. He pushed the Contacts button and hit #2. The phone rang almost instantly.

"DD PI," a familiar voice answered.

"I'm standing on the sidewalk outside my building watching a dozen firefighters trying to put out a fire that completely destroyed my apartment. Better yet, it was arson and they think I might have done it."

"Did you?"

"Your sense of humor is appalling."

"You think it was because of our Wainwright project?"

"It crossed my mind."

"Yeh. Well, it's obvious these bastards aren't kidding around. Maybe we should go to the cops."

"And what, tell them we think a Senator was murdered but we have no evidence and don't even have a reasonable theory? Yeh, that'll impress them."

"How about Chesley? He was always a good contact. He'll listen."

Brady stopped for a moment. He hadn't thought about Chesley. "Maybe. I'll have to ponder it."

"You do that. But while you're pondering, could you use a place to stay for a while? I could shovel some of the crap off the spare bed."

"Is it a full size? I don't sleep too well with my legs hanging off the end of the bed."

"Funny. So funny I'm thinking you must be lookin' to spend the next couple of weeks in a motel."

"Just trying to keep things in perspective. Sure, I'll take you up on that offer. I'll even bring a six pack or two."

"That'd be good for an overnighter, but if you intend to hang around for a while, a couple of cases might be more appropriate."

Brady shook his head. "I'll see what I can do. You there now?"

"Actually, I'm on my way to the DMV to get my license renewed."

"You know you can do that online?"

"You can, but only if your current license is still active."

"You're driving on an expired license?"

"I've been busy."

"So when will you be back? I don't really have any place to hang out just now."

"It's the DMV. Could be anything from an hour to all eternity. You know where I keep the spare key – let yourself in. Of course, you'll have to shovel the crap off the bed yourself."

"I'm a big boy. I think I can handle it. And Derek…"

"Yeh?"

"Thanks. I appreciate it."

"Don't go getting all mushy on me. I figure I'll break even on free beers alone. See you when I get back."

The phone went dead.

Brady smiled. It was a good thing to have a real friend in a situation like this. Even if it was Derek.

CHAPTER 10

DiLaurain lived in a brick and glass apartment building located off New Hampshire Ave just south of Dupont Circle. The brick was supposed to make it fit in with the older homes that dominated the area, but there was no way to hide a seven-story building among all the single and two-story residences. Still, it was a pretty nice place to live. Nicer than his own, even pre-fire, Brady had to agree.

He carried the CVS bag with toothbrush, toothpaste, deodorant, and shampoo into the building and took the elevator up to the fifth floor. He'd have to make a stop at Wal-Mart or some other big box store to get enough clothes to make it through the week. And the beers, of course. But that could wait. For now he just wanted to get to a landline and call his insurance guy, so that he might collect at least a couple of bucks on the fire before he died of old age. Then, as soon as Derek returned he'd get on a computer and try to recreate his notes as best he could from memory. And maybe he'd call Chesley. He didn't like to get the cops involved in a story investigation, but he really didn't much care for the direction this whole thing was taking.

He casually glanced up and down the hallway in front of Derek's apartment before he bent down and flipped over the Welcome mat. He tugged at a small black tag in the top left-hand corner that blended almost perfectly with the black surround of the mat. With the familiar sound of Velcro separating, a small rectangular section of the mat pulled away, revealing the spare key. He quickly opened the door and replaced the key, reorienting the mat. He wasn't going anywhere until the little guy got back.

It had been a while since he'd visited his friend's apartment, and he was once again impressed by the size and décor. *'Overcompensation?'* he wondered as he walked through the massive living room with its nine-foot ceilings, Corinthian columns, and museum quality oil paintings. He might argue with the taste of the decorator, but not the impact of his work. A big guy lived here, in spirit if not stature.

As he walked down the corridor that led to the three bedrooms in back, he glanced at the photos that lined the walls: Derek with celebrities, Derek with good-looking babes, even Derek with Bill Clinton. Had to hand it to the little schmuck, he got around. Brady stuck his head into the master bedroom and couldn't help but smile: over the king-size bed was a full-length, gilded mirror that no doubt had seen its share of action over the years. *'Casanova DiLaurain,'* he mused.

'His' room was the last one on the right, just past the smallest bedroom, which had been converted into a home office since the last time he'd been there. As promised, he found a pile of clothing, bed sheets and assorted odds and ends piled waist-high on the full size bed. *'Must be The Dumping Ground,'* he decided, thinking back to a room of the same description he maintained in his apartment. Or used to maintain. He was guessing it was a bit less cluttered right about then. It briefly crossed his mind that this room could use the same treatment, but decided to play nice and so began to shift all the clothes to the closet and the sheets and assorted junk to an oversized bureau. As he worked he caught sight of himself in a mirror. He stopped momentarily and focused on the old guy with the ever-growing paunch that stared back at him. He thought he looked spooked. *'Not too surprising,'* he decided. *'I guess I am.'*

He was just about to call his insurance agent when he caught a whiff of smoke a la sweat on his clothes and hair. He decided a shower was job number one.

A half hour later he eased into a velvet cushioned easy chair in the living room and dialed the agent. He explained what had happened and answered the agent's sympathetic, yet businesslike questions.

"Oh, and one other thing," he added before his brain could edit his tongue, "the cops might think I started it."

There was a long pause at the other end.

"Is that going to be a problem?" Brady finally asked.

"Not unless you did it," the agent said, and then laughed. "No, I think we're good, Mr. James. I'll try to get over there tomorrow morning to get some photos, and then I'll contact the fire investigators to see what they've come up with. Barring unforeseen circumstances, we should be able to get things moving pretty quickly. Do you need us to get you a motel room?"

"Nah, not just now anyway. I'm staying with a friend for a while."

"You know, we probably can't reimburse you for that."

Brady smiled. "Yah, I know. Don't worry about it. Just get me some money to get some clothes, and a computer, and a TV. All that stuff."

"We'll do our best, Mr. James."

By the time he hung up, Brady had a pretty good feeling about his immediate future. He had a place to stay, his insurance company wasn't jerking him around, and he'd remembered in the shower that he e-mailed Derek a fairly long document with key facts and possible conclusions about the Wainwright story just the night before. At least they'd have something to start with.

He was just jotting some notes, trying to reorganize the basic facts of the story, when the apartment door flew open. He knew at a glance that Derek was not in a good mood.

"Sons of bitches!" the PI muttered loudly before he'd even closed the door. "Goddamn sons of bitches."

"Not a good day?" Brady said without getting up.

Derek threw some papers on top of the dining room table and marched straight to the kitchen. Brady heard the refrigerator door open.

"I don't know what they think we're getting close to, but it must be something."

Brady sat up in his chair and removed his glasses. "What do you mean?"

"Where are the beers?!" the PI bellowed, appearing red-faced in the doorway back into the living room. "I almost get killed and I can't even suck up some suds to ease the pain?"

"I've been a bit preoccupied trying to get my life back in order. I'll get your freakin' beers when I go out. What's all this about almost getting killed?"

Derek flopped down on the seven-foot sofa. He looked like a kindergartner trying out his father's oversized chair. "I was on my way back from DMV – and that was a story all its own, believe me – when I decided to cut through Archibald Park on Mass Ave. Get a break from all the asphalt and noise. So I'm just cruisin' along, listening to the radio, when suddenly this big black pickup truck starts to pass me. Well, I don't think anything about it, other than maybe wondering where he was going in such a hurry, when the bastard jerks the truck back into my lane not three feet in front of me!"

"Did you hit him?"

"Almost. I slammed on the brakes and steered to the right, trying to stay off his rear end. I was doing okay until I hit a rough section of pavement and the tires lost traction. Shot off the pavement right into a small stand of trees. Ended up with a nice little four-inch diameter maple as a hood ornament."

"Did the truck stop to see if you were okay?"

Derek stared at him as if he were nuts. "What do you think? The bastard stomped on the gas and took off. Luckily, a good Samaritan came along about two minutes later and helped me out."

"Were you hurt?"

"Nah. A bit dazed, maybe. I got a tow truck to haul me out of there and drag the Caddy over to my repair guy. Radiator's shot and the sheet metal will need some work, but I got lucky."

"Was it just some drunk redneck, or…something else?" Brady asked. He had his own suspicions, but wanted to hear Derek's thoughts.

The sarcasm in the PI's voice was unmistakable. "Let's see: your apartment decides to burn up, probably from arson, and I get run off the road, all within a couple of hours of each other. Does that sound like an accident to you?"

"No, it doesn't. It sounds like someone doesn't like the story we're working on. I think I'll give Chesley a call, after all."

"Yah, sounds like it's about time to get the cops involved. I don't know if these were just warnings, or if they were trying to screw us up and didn't get it done. In either case, I'm not happy."

"You know, if this is getting too heavy for you, I'd understand if you…"

"Get out of here," Derek interrupted. "Do you really think that I'm going to let some assholes run me off a good investigation? Not a chance. All they've done is piss me off."

'Their mistake,' Brady thought, looking at his stony-faced friend. *'You really don't want Derek mad at you.'*

Not long afterwards Brady tried to reach his friend Chesley, but the detective was out on a case and wouldn't be back until the next day. He decided not to leave a message. *'Must be getting paranoid in my old age,'* he thought.

He and Derek spent the next couple of hours running through scenarios and reconstructing the interviews and research they'd compiled before the fire. This time they emailed everything to themselves, creating a permanent online file. By the time they finished, they'd pretty much decided that Anne's intuition about her boss had been right on. They also decided to be even more careful about their comings and goings.

For that very reason, among others, Brady called Anne to fill her in on the day's activities and to warn her to stay vigilant. As he listened to her phone ring, he decided that perhaps it would be better to explain to her in person all that had occurred. Even though it was nearly six, he invited her for "a quick bite" and was inordinately pleased when she accepted.

He didn't have anything to wear that didn't reek of smoke, so he made a quick jaunt to a nearby Suit Warehouse and spent more time than was necessary picking out just the right clothes for their little dinner – casual yet classy.

'This is ridiculous!' he chastised himself after twice choosing, and returning, a shirt. Yet he continued his sorting until he was satisfied that he looked as good as he possibly could, given what he'd started with. *'All I need now is the corsage,'* he jibed, but he smiled as he did.

Anne buzzed him up to her apartment and met him at her door looking like something out of a fashion magazine. Oh, she was casual, all right, but with every hair in place, her makeup a work of art, and her outfit perfectly integrated from head to toe. Impossibly, she also looked like she'd somehow managed to shower in the hour or so since he'd called. And the plunging neckline of her blouse did not escape his notice.

"Wow!" he muttered. "I guess Mickey D's is out of the question with an outfit like that."

She smiled broadly. "Wherever you want to take me, I'd be happy to go."

Brady felt inappropriate stirrings south of his beltline and blushed.

"I think we can find someplace a little more appropriate. You ready?"

"If you are." Her smile and twinkling eyes complemented the seductive coo of her voice. Or was it just wishful thinking on his part?

"Let's hit it, then," he said, trying his best to ignore the impulse to scoop her up in his arms and throw her down on a bed.

"So what's all this news you wanted to share?" she asked as they made their way down the hall to the elevator, her arm firmly interlocked with his.

Brady glanced behind them without thinking. Anne noticed and frowned.

"What? Did something bad happen?" she asked anxiously.

"Well, yeh, I guess you'd have to say that." He'd considered downplaying the whole affair, but decided it was better for her to know the truth. "I think we've stirred up a hornet's nest. My apartment caught fire earlier today and the cops think it may be arson."

Anne turned to face him and grabbed him by the shoulders. "No! Was anyone hurt?"

"Thankfully, no. But it was pretty much a total loss."

"My God. You think the fire had something to do with the Senator's death?" Suddenly her smile was gone and her eyes shone with fear.

"More likely it was our snooping around," Brady explained as the elevator started down. "Someone is sending us a message."

"But it could be just a nut, or maybe some criminal you wrote about in the past?" She was obviously searching for any answer other than the obvious one.

"Possible, but not likely given our other little treat today."

"Something else? You've got to be kidding!" Her voice sounded a little panicky.

"Somebody forced Derek off the road in Archibald Park."

"Oh my God! Was he hurt?"

"Nah. Take more than a fender bender to hurt that little s.o.b."

"But his car was damaged?"

"A few dents here and there. He'll have that big old pig back on the highway in no time."

"Did he call the police?"

"Not yet."

"Brady, we've got to! This is serious."

"We will, we will. I have an old buddy downtown I'll call tomorrow morning. See if he can give us a hand."

Anne was silent for several seconds.

"Hey, don't worry too much about it. We're both insured."

"That's not the point, and you know it. You both could've been hurt – even killed! I just knew something wasn't right with the Senator's death."

"Looks like your intuition was right on," Brady agreed. "But the main thing we can all do at this point is to be a bit more careful than normal. I mean, if you see any strange people hanging around, or a car following you, for instance, give me a call."

Anne stopped in her tracks. "Following me? You think they might follow me?" Her nervousness was unmistakable. He frowned. This wasn't going well at all.

"I mean, it's a possibility," he said evasively. "Not very likely, but it's better to be prepared, right?"

He saw her take a deep breath. "Yes, of course it is. It's just, well, I'm not accustomed to this sort of thing. The most dangerous situation I usually face is an upset constituent, or another Senator who didn't get his way."

Brady grabbed her arm lightly and turned her to face him. "Look, Anne, Derek and I aren't going to let anything happen to you. If you want, we'll get someone to keep an eye on you 24/7."

She smiled. "I don't think that will be necessary. But thank you."

"You're welcome."

Afterwards, he couldn't remember how it happened, whether he kissed her or she kissed him. But kiss they did. All he really remembered was the softness of her lips and the intoxicating scent of her perfume. The rest of the night was a blur to him, although he was pretty sure that she had as good a time as he did. All too soon, however, they arrived back at her apartment.

"Can I interest you in a nightcap?" she asked at the door.

Part of him wanted to scream "Yes!' before she even finished asking. But another part, an annoying voice in the back of his head, made him hesitate. "Are you sure? I mean, I know we had our one night, but I don't want to take advantage of the situation."

To his amazement, she laughed out loud. "My God, Brady! Perhaps you can't tell in this dim lighting, but I'm not 22 years old. I wouldn't invite you in unless I wanted to. And yes, I realize there might be…complications. I'm looking forward to them."

"Well, if you put it that way…"

She grabbed him by the arm and pulled him into the apartment. "I do," she said with mock severity. "And I won't take no for an answer."

He made sure to lock the door behind them.

*****

By the time he awoke, Anne was already up and gone. He stretched languidly and realized he ached in places he hadn't ached in a long time. After a long hot shower he made his way to the kitchen to see what was available to silence the increasingly formidable growls emanating from his gut. On the small dinette table in the breakfast nook he found a note addressed to him. 'Brady: Last night was wonderful! We'll have to do it again sometime – soon, I hope. Help yourself to whatever you can find in the frig – sorry, I wasn't expecting guests. BTW, I was thinking – if it doesn't work out with you staying with Derek, let me know. As you can see, I have a spare room too. All your current problems stem from me anyway, so it'd be only fair. And fun, too. Anyway, think about it. Have a great day! Anne."

Brady smiled and winced simultaneously. On the one hand, it pleased him no end that this lovely, classy, sexy woman would even think of inviting him to stay in her place. On the other, things were moving a lot faster than he had planned, or probably even wanted. No, he decided on the spot, Derek's place would have to do for now. Even if it cost him a king's ransom in beer.

He found eggs and bread and made himself an omelet while only slightly burning the toast. When he'd finished and cleaned up his mess, he nursed a second cup of coffee while he called Chesley once more. This time he was in his office. Brady was afraid to go into any detail over the phone, so he persuaded his old contact to meet him for lunch. They decided on a little Chinese joint in Arlington at 1:15. "Most of the office workers should be done by then," he'd suggested. Besides, he had errands to run.

He jotted a short note to Anne – friendly but absolutely noncommittal – and headed back to Derek's apartment. He was late enough to have missed most of the commute and so made good time. DC was the kind of place that five minutes one way or another could make a huge difference with the traffic. He'd called Derek before leaving, both to see what the PI was up to, and, given the day they'd both had yesterday, to let him know he was okay. Derek asked him if he could run him over to the collision repair place so he could negotiate with the owner in person, and he'd agreed. James also wanted to go back over to his apartment and see what he could see, but the cops had told him the place was off limits until the fire investigators had completed their job. He asked when that might be, and was told "I have no bleep-ing idea." Always helpful, the DC police force.

By the time he found a parking place and made his way into the building, the temperature had warmed and he was sweating. The icy a/c felt particularly gratifying. As he rode up to the apartment he ran through a mental list of all the places he needed to visit, starting with Wal-Mart and concluding with a couple of real estate agents he knew who might be able to help him land a good temporary apartment. It was fine staying with Derek for a short while, but he expected it might take a few months before this was all sorted out. Too long to be freeloading. Besides, he liked his place, and if the insurance people gave him enough money to refurnish the apartment – and the owner still wanted him there after rebuilding, he intended to move back in.

Derek answered the door after a single buzz.

"Got lucky, eh?" the little man said with a huge cat-ate-the-canary grin.

"You know how it is: Yin and Yang and all that crap. I was due."

"I'm happy for you. Now you just need to find me a nice young lass."

"If you wait for me to find you a girl, you'll be filing for social security before you get laid again," Brady said, flopping down on the oversized sofa. "Besides, I'll be a little busy getting my life back in order for a day or two. And then there's the Wainwright thing."

"Okay, I'll let you off the hook for now. But speaking of Wainwright, I spoke with some people I know over at Democratic National Headquarters, and they put me in touch with a guy out in Ohio…" He flipped through some notes. "David Hockney is the guy's name. He's the Elections Supervisor for the state. Which means, he's the guy who knows what's what with the electronic voting machines."

"He's in charge of voting for both state and national elections?"

"Not exactly. Turns out that the Secretary of State of each state is the person who has the overall responsibility, but all of them devolve it down to an Elections Supervisor of one kind or another, and they pass it down to county boards of election."

"And? Was he helpful?"

"I wouldn't use that particular adjective. As soon as he found out I was asking about electronic voting machines, he snapped shut like a clam near a BP rig. I got the distinct feeling he was expecting my call."

"Why? You didn't use your real name, did you?"

"I'm short, not stupid," Derek snapped. "I told him I was calling from USA Today, but as soon as I started asking about electronic voting, he asked me who my editor was and said he'd get back to me. I don't expect any return calls."

"No, I wouldn't think so. Can your DNC friends get you an appointment with the Secretary of State?"

"He's a Republican. Doubtful."

"Know anyone over at the RNC?"

Derek scrunched up his face as though the thought process hurt. "Maybe one. But we didn't exactly part on the best of terms. I'm not sure she'd want to hear from me."

"Love 'em and leave 'em," Brady said with a shake of his head. "All right, let me see what I can do. I'm meeting Chesley for lunch. I'll jump on the phones after that. Let's see how many errands we can knock off between now and then."

"Just get me over to the repair joint. I've already arranged for a loaner until they can straighten out the Caddy."

"Give me five minutes to cool down. Then, we're off."

"You got it."

It was more like fifteen minutes later when the two men finally left the apartment. After the PI locked his door, he bent down and attached a small piece of clear scotch tape extending from the corner of his door to the jam.

"What's that all about?" Brady asked.

"I'm not taking any chances. Anyone tries to get in while we're gone, I'll know."

Brady nodded. He wasn't going to argue against taking precautions.

The temperature had gone up another couple of degrees in just the short time he'd been inside, and the heat and humidity hit them like a wet fist as they stepped outside. Brady double-timed it to his car, leaving Derek to waddle along as best he could in his wake.

"Hey, what's the rush?" the PI called after him. "A sale ending at Wal-Mart?"

"It's too goddamn hot out here," Brady called back over his shoulder. "Feels like September instead of October."

By the time he got to Brady's Honda, the a/c was blasting but the temperature inside still approached the surface of the sun.

Brady dropped his friend at Cesar's Auto Repair and headed straight to Wal-Mart. He had always found the big box stores fascinating. God knows how many square feet of cheap Chinese junk produced by people earning $3/day. He'd bet half the people that went in there, especially in the DC area, considered themselves good Christians, or Jews, or Muslims. Yet they supported a company built on the exploitation of workers. Workers in other countries, yet. With that thought firmly in mind, he parked the Civic and went in to buy his share of the Asian Dream.

He wasn't a fussy shopper, so it was less than an hour later when he emerged into the sauna that is DC in the Fall. His shopping cart was filled to overflowing with permanent press casual shirts and pants, a sports jacket, underwear, even two pairs of shoes. He didn't expect any of it to last much more than a year or two, but then again, who cared? By then he hoped he'd have the insurance money from the apartment and could visit real stores with real clothing – also made in Asia, but at twice the price. Somehow it would make him feel better.

He hid his new wardrobe under an old blanket in the trunk. As soon as the steering wheel was cool enough to touch, he headed off to Arlington for his lunch meeting with Chesley. Arlington was an interesting case study. A sleepy little upper middle class bedroom community for DC until the mid-70's, the character of the place changed dramatically when thousands of Vietnam refugees showed up after the fall of Saigon expecting their slice of the American pie. Then 10-15 years later, an influx of Salvadorans and other Latinos changed the complexion of the town once again. It hadn't bothered Brady, who thought of himself as a liberal, and rarely crossed into Virginia unless it was absolutely necessary anyway. Besides, the restaurants were fabulous and relatively inexpensive. But some of the locals had gotten positively steamed at the temerity of the newcomers to dare intrude on their good thing. Some had moved. Others had tried to change zoning and other regulations to make it harder for 'them' to get established. Only problem was, 'them' were harder working and more determined than the locals, by far. *'Another thirty years and they'll own this town outright,'* he thought as he slipped into a parking place in the mini-mall where the Golden Dragon restaurant was located. Personally, he wouldn't lament the change.

As soon as he stepped into the tiny hole-in-the-wall restaurant, he spied Chesley sitting in a booth at the back of the room. *'Smart man, always keeping his back covered,'* Brady thought, and then wondered if his current circumstances had prompted the observation.

Chesley noted his entrance immediately with a nod and a tight smile. The longtime detective was 50 years old, give or take a few years, and had the craggy look of an African-American version of Harrison Ford in the Indiana Jones movies. Grey, close-cropped hair, dark eyes, still in good shape for a guy who spent too much time at a desk or eating doughnuts and pizza.

"Long time no see," he said, getting up to shake hands.

"You don't look any the worse for wear."

"You should see it from my angle," he joked.

Brady patted his expansive gut. "At least you haven't picked up one of these yet."

"Can't afford that much beer."

"Lucky for you."

The cop smiled understandingly. "So, how's the retired life treating you? Staying busy?"

"Spent the first few months just trying to unwind and catch up on sleep. But it's been busy lately."

"What, cashing social security checks and watching the Redskins get their asses handed to them?"

Brady chuckled. "Wait till RG3 gets back in the groove."

"*I'll* be collecting Social Security before those bums get their act together."

"We can always hope."

"Right. So if the Redskins aren't keeping you busy, what is?"

Brady glanced around casually. It did not escape Chesley's notice.

"Uh oh, don't like that move. What nasty crap have you got yourself into this time?"

"Like I told you when I called," Brady said, leaning forward and dropping his voice to little more than a whisper, "I'm working on a story that has gotten…strange."

"Gee, you working on a weird story, how unusual."

"This one's weirder than most. Maybe weird enough that I might need a bit of help from you and your buddies."

Chesley's eyebrows shot up. As opposed to many other local reporters, Brady had made a long career out of writing solid crime stories without relying on the police force to do all his work for him.

In fact, Chesley had probably gotten more tips from James over the years than he'd given him.

"Shall we order first?" he asked as a young Chinese waitress sidled up to their table.

"Might be a good idea. This may take a while."

While they waited to be served, Brady ran through the basics of the Wainwright story. He stripped away some of the details to keep the full extent of the scheme to himself, but revealed just enough to whet his friend's appetite for depraved criminality. Chesley listened intently, showing little reaction. *'Must be a damn good poker player,'* Brady thought as he finished his presentation.

"So, let me get this straight," the cop said when he'd finished. "You think someone killed Senator Wainwright, despite the fact that the coroner says he drowned."

"Oh, I don't doubt he drowned, but I'm thinking someone helped him do it."

"Okay. And on top of that, you think that one of the country's richest men is somehow involved."

"I can't prove it, yet, but I'm almost positive he had something to do with it."

"And all of this is somehow tied-in with the upcoming elections and maybe American Rights?"

"You got it. Told you it was kind of weird."

Chesley smiled and shook his head. *"Kind of_weird?* James, your life makes the Twilight Zone look like Main Street. But I'm pretty sure you didn't invite me here just to outline a story. What do you want me to do about it?"

Brady had been pondering just that question ever since he'd decided to call his old friend.

"Well, I was hoping you might be able to check into a couple of people for me. Some folks Derek ran into out in Montana."

"Let me guess: these people have something to do with Adam Hoch."

"They work for him."

"Do you realize what kind of shit will hit the fan if Hoch finds out the cops are investigating him? I don't even want to think about all the legal bullshit we'll have to wade through."

"I know, I know. But I'm telling you Chez, there's something very wrong with this story. And just think, *if* Wainwright was killed, and we break the case, you'll be a big hero and probably get promoted."

The cop stared at him with a blank look. "And if you're wrong? I'll be lucky to be pounding the New York Ave beat. More likely I'll be working as a security guard at K-mart."

"You'll probably get 20% off."

Chesley smiled. "I must be nuts. Okay, who do you want me to check on?"

Brady told him all they knew about Hoch's driver, Tommy, and his PR guy, Henson.

"And one other person: Hoch's grandson, Jeffrey."

"You never make it easy, do you?"

"Don't want you to get bored."

"Bored's okay. Fired, not so much." Chesley sighed. "Okay, I'll see what I can dig up. Just remember to make me a hero if this wild goose chase turns out to have any basis whatsoever."

"I'll do my best."

The two men continued their banter throughout lunch, with Chesley probing ever deeper into the strange story of Wainwright and the upcoming elections. By the time Brady paid the bill, the police detective had to admit even to himself that it didn't sound as far-fetched as he'd initially thought. In fact, it was clear that something wasn't right. The question was, what?

*****

Brady had been glued to the telephone for over an hour by the time Derek returned to his apartment.

"So, how'd it go?" he asked when the PI came in.

"Not bad, I suppose."

"Not exactly a ringing endorsement. What's the problem, didn't they have a loaner for you?"

"Oh they had one, all right. Come here – take a look." He directed Brady to the windows that overlooked the parking lot. "Take a guess which one's mine."

Brady separated the venetian blinds and looked down at more than 50 cars parked below. He scanned the assorted makes and models wondering how the heck he was going to pick out Derek's loaner from that distance, when suddenly his eyes settled on one car in particular.

"The pink one," he said, staring with a smile at the massive convertible parked like a flamingo amid several dozen sparrows.

"Bingo. Apparently it belonged to one of those make-up salesladies, and it was the only Caddy they had available."

"So why didn't you ask for some other make? It's not like you need a car as big as the Superdome."

"I'll ignore the crack. As you know all too well, I'm a Caddy man. I've never owned a car that wasn't a Caddy, and I don't intend to start now, unless I have to. Besides, it had to have the special gear for me to be able to drive it. Kind of limiting."

"Then drive it with pride," Brady said, walking back to the dining room where his notes spread out over half the table. "Pink is just a frame of mind."

"I don't know what the hell that means, but I can tell you that if anyone gives me crap about driving it, they're going to get a face full of one pissed-off midget."

"I'd pay good money to see that confrontation."

"I need a beer," Derek said, walking into the kitchen. "Want one?"

"A little too early, even for me. I'm still making calls, but I think I may have found us an entrée to the Ohio Sec State."

"Nice. Who'd you track down?"

"A former political reporter for the Post. I remembered that he'd done a cream-puff piece on the RNC a year or two ago that had them eating out of his hand. He got me through to one of their money people, who gave me the number of the Secretary's Chief of Staff. I was just about to call her."

"Don't let me stop you," Derek said, tossing himself into a throne chair and chugging his beer.

As Derek chugged, Brady dialed.

"Belinda Carlisle," an authoritative voice on the other end of the line answered.

"Ms. Carlisle, my name is Brady James, and I'm doing some research for a feature article I'm writing about the upcoming elections."

"*Feature* article," Derek mouthed, just loud enough for Brady to hear and wave him off with irritation.

"I was hoping that I might be able to interview Secretary Owens about his role is overseeing the vote in Ohio, and in particular about the increased use of electronic voting machines in the election," Brady continued.

"Who are you writing for?" the chief of staff asked.

"Well, it's freelance, but I was a staff reporter for the Washington Post for many years and I'm hoping to tailor it for them."

"'Tailor it'," the PI said aloud, raising his eyebrows in mock admiration. "Lah-di-dah."

Brady flipped him off and turned so that he couldn't see the little s.o.b.

"Who's the editor you worked with there?" she asked.

'No nonsense in this one,' James thought. "Jimmy Ogden," he said, naming the crime beat editor he'd worked with for the last five years before retiring.

"Okay. If you don't mind I'll give Mr. Ogden a call, and if he vouches for you, I'll see if we can squeeze it into the Secretary's schedule. Did you want to do this in person or over the phone?"

"I'm old school," he said, "I like to see the eyes of people when I'm interviewing them.'

Behind him, Brady heard Derek hum a few bars of the theme from 'The Good, The Bad, and The Ugly.'

"Fine. And what was your timeframe?"

"Well, I'd like to get this written and out there before every reporter in the country comes up with their take. The sooner the better. Later this week, if possible."

"I'll see what I can do," Carlisle said in the officious tone that Brady recognized from all his years talking with government types. "But the Secretary is extremely busy. I can't promise anything."

"Your best is good enough for me," Brady said, and immediately heard Derek echo him in a high falsetto.

"Fine. Give me your phone number and I'll get back to you as soon as I know something."

Brady did as asked. "Can I give you a call if I haven't heard back by Wednesday?" he ventured after she'd read back the number, knowing full well there was a better than fifty per cent chance he'd never hear from the woman unless he pushed the issue.

"Sure. That'd be fine with me."

He thanked her for her help and hung up the phone.

"Jesus, another gatekeeper with a stick up her ass," he bemoaned to no one in particular.

"And we both know what stick you're dreaming it could be," Derek quipped between gulps.

Brady stared at him, shaking his head. "What in god's name are you drinking?"

"A PINK Cadillac," was all his friend could say. "PINK!"

"Not worth having a stroke over," Brady muttered, and quickly dug up the phone number of his former editor.

"Hey, Jimmy," he said as soon as the phone was answered. "It's Brady."

"Well, well, well, the man of leisure. How the hell are you?"

"I'm doing just fine Jimmy. You?"

"Same old same old," he said tiredly. "The more things change…"

"Yeh, yeh. But you can retire soon can't you?"

"Not soon enough."

"Tell me about it. Hey, Jimmy, I have a favor to ask of you."

"What's up?"

"The Chief of Staff of the Ohio Secretary of State may give you a call to check up on me, to see if I used to work for you. Belinda Carlisle."

"What, are you trying to get laid?"

"Just doing some research on a possible story idea."

"Did her boss pocket the budget?"

"No, no, nothing like that. It's a political story, actually. Setting the scene for the upcoming elections."

"Political? I thought you hated those bastards."

"It beats writing for the AARP monthly."

"Ah, I see. Okay. Sure. What do you want me to tell her?"

"Just the truth – I was one of your finest reporters and you're damned sorry I decided to retire."

"Wow. And you think she's gonna swallow that?" the editor joked.

"She's from Ohio."

"Good point. No sweat. Be my pleasure."

The two men reminisced a bit before ending the conversation.

"So, all set?" Derek queried as soon as he hung up the phone.

"All set. Now we wait for the Chief of Staff to contact him, and then it's off to Ohio to interview the SecState."

"A phone interview would be a lot easier."

"I want to see his reactions. And there's always something unexpected that pops up when you're on-site. Never happens on the phone."

"You mean like someone trying to force you off the road, or an unexpected hit and run?"

"I'll keep my eyes open."

"You'd better. So, what's next here?"

"I was thinking, I'd really like to take a look at Hoch's computer files. I bet they're enlightening."

"And you were thinking what, that he'd invite you over for a file reading party?"

"Not exactly. But if someone could hack a Senator's system, why not Hoch's?"

"Isn't that against the law?"

"Only if you're caught."

"And who's going to perform this electronic skullduggery? Certainly not you, who can barely send an e-mail."

"As a matter of fact, I think I know just the person." Brady smiled.

*****

O'Riley's is a small, dark, pub-ish bar located in the shadow of the Capitol building. You'd never see a Congressman or Senator in there, but their staffers kept the place alive. With plenty of booths and the dim lighting that encourages free and open exchanges, it was where they aired their petty grievances and made their off-the-grid rendezvous. It was just the place, Anne decided, to meet the tech whiz who could help them break into Hoch's computers.

"I feel like Methuselah in here," Brady griped as he settled down in a back booth beside her. "What's the average age of these kids, 28?"

"Working for a Senator or Congressman is not for the faint of heart," Anne explained. "You need a lot of energy and the ability to function with little or no sleep. Kids are the only ones who can hack it."

"Better them than me. Do you come here often?"

It was a good thing the lighting was so bad or she would've seen him blush when he realized what he'd said.

"Not so much anymore," she answered with no sign of amusement. "When I first started working here on the Hill, oh so many years ago, I did visit here once or twice."

Brady was just about to embarrass himself further with a corny line about it not being all that long ago, when he saw Anne's eyes elevate to meet a new arrival. Brady turned to face a familiar face. He struggled to his feet.

"Danny. Glad you could join us."

The young computer geek from the Senate Office Building was dressed in another notable tee-shirt ("Thou Shalt Not Reboot") and looked even more disheveled than the last time Brady had seen him.

"Mr. James. Ms. Waznewski. Hope I'm not interrupting anything."

His leering smile annoyed Brady, but he refused to let it show. He needed the young doofus.

"Not at all. Glad you could join us."

Brady stepped out from the booth and let Danny squeeze past him.

"So, I understand you might have a freelance job for me?" he asked before James had even sat back down.

"We might," Brady said. "Depends."

"On what?" There was a note of indignation in his tone.

"On a couple of things. First of all, we need someone who can keep his – or her – mouth shut. This is not something I want to see in the Federal Diary."

"No problem. Heck, there aren't that many people I talk to anyhow."

'I can believe that,' Brady thought. "Good," he said.

"And second?"

"It will require considerable computer savvy. Not just the usual virus protection and software updates."

"Look – I know computers. If it can be done, I can figure out how to do it."

"Very impressive," Brady said, turning to Anne. "Don't you agree?"

"Very," Anne said assuredly. "That's why I suggested him. He's good at what he does."

Brady noted the 'Aw shucks' look on the kid's face. It was time to lower the boom.

"Oh, there is one other thing."

"And that is?"

"Well," James said, lowering his voice for dramatic effect, "this job we have – we're not sure if it's exactly legal."

Brady didn't know what reaction he expected, but a big smile and excited eyes was probably not it.

"Cool! You want me to hack someone?"

Brady motioned with his hands for a little more self-control and a little less volume. "In a nutshell, yes."

The young computer whiz leaned back in his seat. "As they say," he said, "you've come to the right place. Before I decided to work for the Government, I was pretty well known in hackification circles, if I do say so myself."

"So, do you think you could, say, access the information in a private company's system, without their knowing you'd been there?"

"How well is it protectified?"

Brady tried not to react to the sudden grammatical slaughter. "We really don't know. But if I were a betting man, I'd say it's probably just this side of Fort Knox."

"A challenge! Cool. As we always used to say, if it has a front door, it has a back door too. You just have to figure out how to get in."

"I bet you don't say that much in your current job," Brady said.

Danny grinned. "Only when I'm campaigning for a raise and want to scare the be-Jesus out of them."

"There is one other thing," Anne prompted. Brady stared at her. Another 60's moment. *What is she talking about?'* he wondered.

"The person who more than likely controls that system..." she coaxed.

"Ah, yes, of course! How are you with revenge?" he asked the mystified geek.

"Okay, I guess."

"So you wouldn't mind getting back at the s.o.b. who hacked your system and erased Anne's documents?"

A small, tight smile crept across Danny's lips. "Would I ever. I owe him one, in spades."

"Then I think we may be able to do some business here," Brady said, putting out his hand to shake.

The three conspirators talked further over lunch. To Brady's great relief, the more Danny learned, the more excited he became. He wasn't intimidated in the least to learn that the company was a large one, or that the target of their raid would be one of the country's richest men. In fact, the more he learned, the greater his interest. By the time they finished, he probably would have hacked Hoch for free. But they offered him a modest stipend anyway. Better to keep it purely professional. In an off-the-grid, slightly illegal way, of course. Where's the fun otherwise?

They bid Danny goodbye at the end of his lunch hour and sent him on his way, back to the Senate office building. That left just the two of them.

"You have any plans for the rest of the afternoon?" Brady asked.

Her sly smile said it all.

"Not that I couldn't put off. Have anything in mind?"

"It's such a beautiful day, why don't we go back to your place and spend the rest of the afternoon in bed?"

Her smile widened. "You read my mind."

"I'm more interested in other parts of your anatomy just now."

Her blush was genuine.

*****

They didn't have to wait long to hear back from Jimmy. The next morning Brady got a call at 9:30.

"I just got off the phone with your Chief of Staff," the Post editor explained. "She doesn't seem so bad."

"And? Did you feed her the line about me being an ace reporter?"

"I did."

"Did she swallow it?"

"Hook, line and reel. The second I mentioned Pulitzer she just about melted. I think you could get them to pay for the air ticket at this point."

"You are a true scholar and con artist. I owe ya' one."

"And don't think I won't collect on it. Maybe not this week or next, but sooner or later I'll be calling with an offer you can't refuse."

"You got it, whatever it is. In fact, I just may have a story for you in a couple of weeks. A BIG story."

"Exclusive?"

"I wouldn't have it any other way."

"I'll be sitting by my telephone, awaiting your call."

"Try to get a paper out while you're at it. It won't do either of us any good if the Post folds before I can nail the story."

"You got it, James. Hey, we should take in a Redskins' game one of these days. My oldest is coming up with his two sons in two weeks. Think you could stand a family outing?"

"What kind of beer do they drink?"

"We'll have to see about that. But I'll let you know. I'm sure the boys would love to see their 'Uncle Brady'."

"No accounting for taste. But yeh, that sounds good. Would it diminish the Kumbaya factor if I brought along a lady friend?"

"A lady friend? You? Hell no, drag her along! Add a touch of refinement to the outing."

"Okay, I'll let you know. Take care, Jimmy."

"Yeh, you too, James."

As he hung up the phone Brady experienced a momentary stab of regret that he no longer worked at the newspaper. But it lasted less than a second. *'A story is a story, and this is a whopper,'* he thought as he began to decide what he would pack for the short jaunt to Columbus. He only hoped they could tie up all the loose ends before someone got hurt – especially if it was him.

CHAPTER 11

Columbus is a small but surprisingly sophisticated Midwestern city located in the large and not so sophisticated state of Ohio. In the 1970's and 80's a number of large corporations built distribution centers just outside the city, taking advantage of its location at the confluence of Interstates 70 and 71. It was an ideal spot to reach the population centers of both the Northeast and the Midwest. What had been a somewhat sleepy little state capital suddenly came to life with an explosion of new arrivals and a corresponding blossoming of the cultural and social scenes. It wasn't Paris, but it wasn't the old Columbus either.

The Port Columbus Airport reflects the evolution of the capital. Small but efficient, it reminded Brady of a scaled-down version of a big city airport with all the basic amenities you could hope for as you await your departure. There's a good sampling of decent local artwork, and even a Lichtenstein located outside the middle of three concourses. Brady was surprised at the number of flights listed on the arrival and departure boards.

He rented a Toyota Corolla and threw his carry-on into the back seat. Relying on the GPS, he drove down Interstate 670 to 71 South before exiting on East Broad Street. The traffic was mid-morning light and it was an easy drive. He could see the Statehouse off to his left as he continued on to Front St, and then left to Doubletree. According to his travel agent it was the closest major hotel to Capitol Square and the high-rise government building on Broad Street, and one of the easiest to find. Besides, there was a reassuring sameness to Doubletree, as with all the majors. No matter the location, you could be assured that the front desk and reception area would look pretty much the same, and you always knew where the bathroom would be if you woke up in the middle of the night and couldn't remember instantly where you had landed. For Brady that was an important consideration, since after a few beers he quite frequently woke up in the middle of the night.

He checked into his room, which was thankfully available even though it wasn't quite yet noon – let alone the 4 pm check-in time. He unpacked a few things, then sat down and dialed the State office building. Secretary Harris' assistant answered.

"Secretary of State's office."

He identified himself and reminded her of his 2 pm appointment with Harris.

"Oh yes, Mr. James. Secretary Harris is expecting you. Will you be able to find your way here to the State office building all right?"

"I'm not exactly a human GPS," Brady admitted, "but I'm only a few blocks away – at the Doubletree."

"Oh, no trouble then. See you at 2."

Brady hung up and took the elevator downstairs to the Caucus Room restaurant. The eatery was bright and unassuming, divided into small nooks and decorated in Early Businessman, topped off by a Muzak bar located up a short flight of stairs. A cafeteria-style buffet ran some twenty feet along one alcove, illuminated by mock antique dropped lighting. He was disappointed that he couldn't see the Scioto River from his table, but decided he'd make up for that shortcoming at dinner. For now, a quick lunch and a shower would suffice. He had awoken more than thirty minutes late that morning, having snoozed his way through the alarm on several occasions.

A somewhat attractive but undeniably chunky middle-aged waitress bustled over to his table with a sweet, caring grin.

"Would you care for a menu?" she asked.

"Sure, thanks."

'I might not be in Kansas,' he thought as she handed him the laminated tri-fold menu, *'but it's pretty damn close.'*

He chose the Buckeye burger with fries and a Coke. He would've preferred a beer, but thought that Bud breath might be a poor first impression for the Secretary. He continued to gaze nonchalantly at his fellow diners, until he became convinced that they were just what they appeared to be – plain old Columbus folks. After that, he concentrated on his upcoming interview. He always tried to come up with a few questions that would frame the discussion, steering it in the direction he wanted it to go without appearing to do so. The framework was inevitably fairly loose, since he'd learned long ago that every interview took on a life of its own; he wanted to be able to go with the flow. The added complication with this interview, and any others dealing with the Wainwright story, was Hoch. If they were right, if Hoch was somehow involved in the Senator's death, then he needed to tread very carefully. A good story was worth its weight in gold, but not worth dying for.

He tipped the smiling heifer and went up to his room for a short nap. At one-fifteen he showered, dressed, and headed out of the hotel. The State office building was close enough that he decided to walk. The bulge at his waistline hadn't gotten any smaller over the past few weeks. Anne hadn't mentioned it, but he thought he'd seen her eyes glance down in that direction the first time they bared all. He was pretty certain she hadn't been sneaking a peek at his male equipment. If she had, he only hoped she could see it past the gut.

With that on his mind he double-timed it up Broad Street to the glass and steel high-rise that housed a number of State offices, including the Secretary of State's. He went through the usual security rigmarole with his usual smoldering impatience, and was all ready to find a seat for a few minutes when an attractive 30-something blonde wearing a dark blue pants suit appeared from a hallway to his left.

"Mr. James?" she asked with an ingratiating smile. "Belinda Carlisle. Did you have any trouble finding us?"

"You're the second person to ask me that today," he answered with a smile of his own. "Do Ohioans have a hard time navigating the mean streets of Columbus?"

She laughed, an honest, open laugh. "No, not usually. But we're always concerned that out-of-towners might get confused and head for the Statehouse. It's happened more than a few times."

"No, no problem at all. The Secretary's assistant was quite clear in her directions."

"Good! So, shall we head upstairs?"

"By all means." As they walked, Brady took the lead on the required small talk. "So, have you worked for the Secretary long?"

"Three years. Before that I worked on the Governor's staff."

"A real politico, eh?"

She chuckled. "Yeh, I guess you'd say that. And you? I understand you worked for the Post for quite a while."

"Nearly thirty years. Just retired seven months ago."

"A real reportico, eh?" She glanced over with a smile.

"You can take the boy out of the pressroom…"

"Do I understand correctly that you're interviewing the Secretary for a story about the upcoming election?" Her tone was suddenly less jovial.

"I am. How Ohio fits into the big picture. That kind of thing."

"But you were primarily a crime reporter, weren't you?"

He admired her attempt to spring it on him. But she was dealing with an old pro, not some kid fresh out of grad school.

"I was. But when you're freelancing you've got to go where the editorial interest lies. Otherwise, you won't be selling many stories."

"I can imagine." Just then the elevator floor indicator pinged. "This is us."

She held the door open to let him pass, but he insisted she lead the way. Not only was it gallant, but he had a much better view of her backside.

The offices were typical of the various government workplaces Brady had visited: just nice enough to keep everyone happy, but not so nice that a disgruntled taxpayer could get any traction with a complaint. The smiling receptionist looked like a younger sister of his lunch waitress. Or were all women of a certain age beginning to look the same to him? That would be sad.

"Mr. James – I see that you found us!" the receptionist announced cheerfully.

He glanced at the nameplate on her desk. "That I did, Miss Winlock. Thank you for your concern."

"I really wasn't concerned, just trying to be helpful."

"That you were," he answered as he swept past her desk and followed Brenda down a corridor lined with offices. At the very end of the hallway, the name 'Edward R. Harris' was prominently displayed on a bronze plaque beside an expensive oak door. Brenda knocked twice lightly.

"Come in, come in!" a muffled voice responded.

The Chief of Staff showed Brady into a large office dominated by a bright blue rug with the state seal of Ohio woven into the fabric and a mahogany desk that was either an antique or just had seen better days. One entire wall consisted of floor-to-ceiling windows.

"Nice view," Brady said as the Secretary turned away from his computer and stood stiffly.

Secretary Harris glanced over his shoulder at the vista that stretched out before him. "Yes, it is. I get so tied up with that darn computer that sometimes I forget how lucky I am. Ed Harris," he continued, reaching out to shake hands.

"Brady James. Thank you for taking the time for this interview."

"No problem. Have a seat." Harris gestured to one of two leather chairs posed respectfully in front of the big man's desk. As he sat, Brady looked at his subject more closely: six-two or three, probably 210, graying black hair, the kind of face that was both strong and soft at the same time. Brady decided he liked the guy.

"So, can we get you anything? Coffee? Tea?"

"No, thanks. I just ate lunch before coming over here."

"Do I remember correctly that you're at the Doubletree? The lunch buffet is pretty decent. Or at least it was the last time I was over there."

Brady could picture him there for a political fund-raiser or community function. "Good memory. But I try to stay away from buffets. My waistline thanks me," he added, patting his expansive midsection.

"Ah. I know that one. With the years come the pounds. So, how do you like our little city? Have you been here before?"

Brady hid a grin. *'Typical politician,'* he thought. "Very nice," he said. "And no, this is my first time. I've been up to Cleveland, but never made it down here."

"Well we're happy you could visit with us. Columbus is a great little city. Although I'm biased – having been born here – I honestly think it's one of the nicest cities its size that I've ever seen."

"I was reading some of the tourist literature in my room. It is impressive, what with all the cultural and business opportunities."

"And we pride ourselves on being a bit of a political center as well. I take it that's why you've come out to interview me."

Straight to the point. Good. "It is. As you are no doubt aware, this next election is shaping up to be another close one, and unless I'm very much mistaken Ohio will once again be a key state in determining our next President."

"Perhaps the balance in the House as well." An unmistakable sense of pride colored his words.

"Perhaps," Brady answered agreeably. "But however it works out, your state is going to play an important role. And as one of the key players in the local political scene, I'd like to hear your ideas of how it's all going to shake down. Democrat or Republican, or could a third party have any chance here?" He watched for the Secretary's reaction. He didn't have to wait long.

Harris grinned broadly. "Whose press releases have you been listening to? If you listen to them all you'd think that every group of more than ten Ohioans is going to form their own party – and win! Fortunately, I think that possibility has been greatly exaggerated."

"So who do you think will win?"

The smile was replaced by a thoughtful grimace. "Well, as a good public servant I guess I should really say that it's not for me to predict a winner. We've still got a couple of weeks to the election, and I certainly don't want to bias anyone out there who hasn't made up his or her mind."

"Don't you think most people already know who they'll vote for?"

"The opinion polls say that 25-30% still haven't made up their minds, and as a public servant I'm not allowed to proselytize, or even predict – which is pretty much the same thing."

"Do you see any of the current crop of smaller parties having a real chance?"

"Unlikely, but remotely possible. If the Republicans had nominated someone else, perhaps a third party might have found more space to contend."

"More likelihood on the right than the left?"

"I don't know about more…"

The interview continued along the same lines for the better part of an hour. Brady got the impression that Harris was a solid, knowledgeable, close-to-the-vest public servant who knew a lot about the election but scarcely anything about the voting process itself. Just to be sure, he decided to drop the 'H' bomb.

"What do you think about some of the players behind the scenes, like Adam Hoch for instance?"

Harris didn't blink. "He certainly seems determined to put a conservative in the Oval Office, but I don't think this is his time. Maybe in four years." Either he was a magnificent liar, or he didn't know anything about a Hoch-run conspiracy. Brady asked a few more innocuous questions to disguise his interest in Hoch, before turning to his next lead.

"I understand you're in the process of phasing-out paper ballots. I'd like to take a look at Ohio's electronic voting procedures while I'm here. Is there someone I should talk to?"

"Ted Wyman's the man you want. Technically, I'm in charge of the vote, but these new machines are too complicated for an old bureaucrat like myself. Ted is our tech person; he oversees the entire network. Of course, our Boards of Election in each of the 88 counties have a local person who can do basic repairs on Election Day, but Ted has the best overview of the machines and the process."

Brady got the contact information for Wyman and thanked the Secretary for his time.

"It's my pleasure," Harris said graciously. "Besides, it's been good practice for all the other interviews that I expect will be coming my way as we get closer to election day."

"You're a pretty popular guy in November?" Brady asked as he packed up his recorder.

"Very. Especially since we've had such close elections in the recent past. I mean, back in 2000, a shift of some 80,000 votes out of nearly 5 million cast in the Buckeye state would have made Al Gore President, and if a few thousand Ohio votes had gone to John Kerry instead of Bush, he would have been President in 2004."

The hairs on the back of Brady's neck stood on end. "Really? But it won't be that close this time, will it?"

Harris smiled with a shrug. "Who knows? The country is still terribly divided, and I don't see anyone running away with the polls. No matter what the polls say today, it'll get close by election time. You know what they say, 'whoever wins Ohio wins the Presidency.'"

"Just a saying, right?"

"I'm not so sure. We've voted for the winning candidate 25 out of the last 27 elections. Not a bad record."

James swallowed. His mouth had suddenly become dry. "So what you're saying is that a shift of maybe 100,000 votes out of 5 million could not only decide the Ohio race but the national election as well?"

"Well, don't quote me on that," the Secretary said with a chuckle. "But off the record, yes. It could happen."

Suddenly, Brady began to see a scenario that he hadn't even dreamed about until that moment. If someone could control the electronic voting machines, could they shift 1 percent of the votes from one party to the other, resulting in a net shift of 100,000 votes?

"Jesus H. Christmas!" he mumbled under his breath.

"Excuse me?" Harris asked.

"No, nothing. Just had a thought. So, anyway, thanks again. You've been *very* helpful."

"I'm glad it was useful. If you have any other questions or follow-up, just get a hold of Belinda and we'll try to get you some answers."

"Appreciate it, sir. Good luck with the elections."

Brady was half in a daze as he made his way out of the building. He exchanged some idle chit-chat with Ms. Carlisle as she showed him downstairs, but all the while his mind was whirling. Could Wainwright have discovered all this just before he died? Was Hoch, or perhaps even someone else, planning on just such an attack on the Ohio voting machines? This wasn't just an attack on the Ohio election system, this was an attack on the entire American democracy!

'*Get a hold of yourself,*' he thought as he hurried back toward his hotel. '*You're getting ahead of the facts. Just because someone could be planning to sabotage the election, doesn't mean it's going to happen. I gotta talk to this Wyman character. But I better call Derek first. This might be a bigger hornet's nest than we'd thought.*'

As soon as he got back to his room he dialed the P.I.

"Hey, Bossman, qué pasta?" a familiar voice answered.

Brady was just about to launch into a detailed regurgitation of his suspicions when another thought stopped him in mid-sentence.

"I just finished interviewing Harris," he began, "and…"

"And what? Alzheimer's kicking in again?"

"Uh, do you have a…more secure way for us to communicate?" he asked, trying to keep his tone as neutral as possible.

"What, you afraid 'They' are bugging the phones?"

"Something like that. Yes."

The little man hesitated. Brady was hoping he'd gotten the message.

"You're serious?"

"Completely."

"Ok, sure. I think I can come up with something. Let me get back to you in say, 20 minutes?"

"That works. Thanks."

While Brady waited he called the contact number for the tech supervisor Harris had recommended. The phone rang four times and then was answered by voicemail. "This is Ted. Leave me a message after the beep and I'll get back to you as soon as I can," a pleasant, seemingly middle-aged voice announced. Brady told him that Harris had recommended he interview Wyman for the story he was working on and suggested they get together later that afternoon or the following morning. He hung up and paced the room while he waited for Derek's return call. What had begun as just a hunch by a secretary with great legs had evolved into a possible murder and national vote-rigging conspiracy. *'What have we gotten ourselves into?'* he wondered.

Not ten minutes later, his phone rang. "James," he answered.

"Mr. James, this is Ted Wyman," the voice from the voicemail began without formalities. "Do I understand correctly that you'd like to interview me about the upcoming elections?"

"You do, and I would. I'm only in town through tomorrow though, and was wondering if you could make some time to sit down with me. It won't take long – probably just a half-hour or so."

There was a short pause. "I suppose so, but I really don't know what you can learn from me that Secretary Harris hasn't already told you. I mean, he's the big fish. I'm just a minnow in the pond."

"Sometimes minnows have their own perspective," Brady improvised. "Besides, the Secretary said you're the man to talk to about the new electronic voting machines. We're looking for a fresh angle, and technology always creates interest, especially with the younger readers."

Another, longer pause. It was obvious that Wyman wasn't terribly enthusiastic about doing the interview. "We can keep it off the record, if you'd prefer," he added, hoping that anonymity might persuade the techie.

"Well, okay I guess," came the lukewarm reply. "I guess I can make some time this afternoon. Say, around 4?"

"Just tell me where you'd like to meet."

"Well, how about a little bar over on Parsons? The Golden Buckeye. It's quiet there, especially during mid-afternoon."

"I don't know the place, but since I'm not from here that's not a surprise. I'm sure I can find it. Four o'clock."

"Fine. See you then."

As he hung up, Brady analyzed the conversation. He wasn't really surprised that Wyman was hesitant to talk to the media – in his experience a lot of techies kept pretty much to themselves. But the fact that he had asked to meet in a bar did surprise him. Usually government officials, even relatively low level ones, wanted to meet in their offices. Starbucks at the worst. Only the criminals he'd talked to had insisted on dark, out-of-the-way bars. A feeling of disquiet rumbled through his ample stomach.

He was perusing a map of the downtown area, trying to identify the best route to The Golden Buckeye, when his phone rang.

"It's me," Derek announced without intro. "Go downstairs and find a payphone. Write down the number and then go to a different payphone and call me at 202-477-2137. Got it?"

Brady fumbled with a pen and jotted down the number. "2137?" he double-checked.

"That's it. I'll be waiting for your call."

The call disconnected.

What do you know, the little fellow is treating this like the real thing,' he mused as he dialed the front desk. Truth be told, he was glad the PI wasn't fooling around.

"Do you have any payphones in the hotel?" he asked the clerk.

"Downstairs, outside the Caucus Room."

"Great, thanks."

He grabbed his pen and a notepad and headed for the elevator. Three phones were banked together right across from the bathrooms. He picked up the receiver at the first phone and listened for a dial tone. When he was certain it was working, he jotted down the phone number. Then he went over to the next phone and dialed Derek. The phone rang only once before it was answered.

"What's the number of the other phone?" the PI asked brusquely.

Brady read him the number.

"Okay. Stand by. I'll call you in a few seconds."

As soon as the phone rang, James picked it up.

"Derek?"

"No, Santa Claus," came the sarcastic reply. "Wanted to find out if you're naughty or nice. Of course it's me." Brady smiled despite himself. "I'm calling you from a second payphone. Unless someone's very good, they'll never be able to trace this until we're long gone. So, what's the scoop?"

Brady explained about his interview with Harris and how the mention of the recent close elections had made him view their investigation in a different light.

"So you think Hoch, or someone, might be planning to steal the Presidential election by rigging the Ohio vote?" He whistled loudly. "Jesus, that's ballsy, even for a rich bastard like Hoch."

"I know it sounds far-fetched, but I have a feeling about this one. I'd like you to check with some of the political pollsters, and maybe that Poli-Sci professor over at Georgetown. What was his name...? Petigrew. Jeffrey Pettigrew. He's always blabbing about something political on the radio talk shows. See if you can find out how close they think the election is going to be. And ask what three or four states are going to likely have the closest votes."

"Why three or four?"

"If I were going to rig an election, I'd want to cover my bets. If I only had to shift the least number of votes in the closest states, I could still make a huge impact on the Electoral vote. Maybe even change the outcome."

"Wow. If Wainwright found out about this..."

"Yeh. That's just what I was thinking. If we're right, this might be the biggest story we've ever worked on."

"If you're right, this could the biggest story anyone has ever worked on. I'll get right on it. Are you still coming back tomorrow?"

"That's still the plan. But I'm meeting in a little over an hour with the techie in charge of the electronic voting machines out here, a guy named Ted Wyman. We'll see if that opens up other avenues."

"All right. Let me know. But as long as we've started down this James Bond route, let's assume they're wise to us, whoever 'they' are. If they're good enough to steal an election, they may already have our phones tapped. So, let's throw'em a curveball. If you're coming back on the 10 o'clock flight, just leave me a message saying 'The Skins sure looked good last night.' If you're changing flights, tell me 'Old number 'whatever the time of your arrival' looked like crap. Got it?"

"Skins looked good if I'm sticking to my schedule, and the hour of my arrival looked like crap if I'm coming back later. Got it. And Derek?"

"Yeh?"

"Be careful."

"Yeh. You too."

Brady hung up and took a deep breath.

CHAPTER 12

This time the flashing message on his computer wasn't received with a welcoming smile.

"Damn it all!" the young man said as he scrambled to see who had tried to hack the system. His fingers danced over the keys as he tried to pinpoint where the attack had come from, and what files, if any, had been compromised. With each successive attempt, his frustration grew.

"They're good, I'll give 'em that much," he said to himself as he struggled to get one step ahead of the invader.

Fifteen minutes later he did something he had promised himself that he would never do: he pulled the plug. Literally. He powered down the entire system. The fact that it was after business hours made it easier to justify, but his hands were still shaking ten minutes after the LEDs went dark. He'd already decided to broadcast some kind of 'Sorry for the disruption. Routine housekeeping' message, and he assumed the vast majority of the staffers at his grandpa's headquarters would accept the message at face value. Some of the folks in the IT Department might ask questions, but a combination of fancy footwork and in-your-face bravado would almost certainly silence even the geekiest of that crew.

No, it was his grandfather's reaction that worried him most. He had promised the old man that no one could penetrate his security systems. And now this. He could hear the irritation and disappointment in his grandpa's voice now.

Damn it! Someone was going to pay for this.

Pay big-time.

CHAPTER 13

Brady drove south under Interstate 70 and then east on Whittier before turning right on Parsons Ave. As he drove past check cashing services and boarded-up storefronts, it was clear that Wyman hadn't chosen the high rent district for their meeting. Still, compared to some of the areas he'd frequented while working the crime beat in DC, this was pretty tame. It took him only 15 minutes to find the Golden Buckeye; he was lucky enough to find a parking spot right out front. He double-checked that the car doors had auto-locked and went inside.

The bar was like a good many he'd visited before. Dark, slightly claustrophobic, with the unmistakable smell of stale beer, body odor and two-day-old puke.

'Nice,' he thought as he looked around, letting his eyes adjust. 'He obviously wants to make an impression.'

There were only three people in the place at that hour: a young, dread-locked bartender, an old man who seemed to grow out of the stool he occupied, and a tattooed construction-type who was coddling a beer at the far end of the bar. All three glanced up at him as he came in. Only the bartender showed any interest.

"Hey, how's it goin'?" he asked with the absolute minimum amount of energy required to exhale the words.

"Good, good," Brady lied.

"Can I get you something?"

"I'm waiting for a friend. Should be here momentarily."

"Cool. Just let me know when you're ready."

Brady nodded. He looked around the room as his vision adjusted to the dim light. An old classic jukebox stood in one corner, behind six tiny tables with two battered chairs at each. The walls were dotted with beer and booze signs and an occasional black and white photo. He glanced at one but couldn't identify anyone in the shot. The bar had the kind of bottle collection on the back wall that spoke of bare necessity. Where a yuppy joint might have 50 bottles in the display space, this place had about 15. Make that 17. It was like looking at the decimated shelves of a Blockbuster the day before it went out of business. He was beginning to feel depressed when the door opened and a forties-something white guy wearing a plaid short sleeve permanent press shirt and black-rimmed glasses strolled in. His very being screamed 'Geek!'

"Ted?" Brady ventured.

"You're the reporter?" came the response.

"Brady, Brady James," he said, offering his hand.

Wyman stared at the dangling hand for what seemed like 30 seconds, but was probably just five. Then he shook it, briefly, without commitment.

"Let's sit."

As Brady followed him to a table in the far corner, he wondered how Danny was doing with Hoch's computer system. He had the feeling that if they had to depend on this guy in front of him, they wouldn't be getting anywhere quickly.

"So, what do you want to know?" Wyman asked before Brady's ass had even hit the chair.

"Nice place. One of your favorites?" James asked, hoping to loosen the mood.

"No, not really. I just thought, well, maybe it'd be better if nobody saw us talking." The look on the techie's face was a cross between despair and terror.

'What is this?' Brady wondered. *'He looks like he's ready to jump out of his skin.'*

"Any reason? I mean, that you wouldn't want anyone to see us talking?"

Wyman looked down at his folded hands.

"This is all off the record, right? I mean, my name doesn't get mentioned."

Brady nodded. "However you want it. You're in charge."

Wyman leaned forward conspiratorially. "They know you're here," he said in a low voice. "They told me you might try to get in touch with me."

Brady tried to control his expression. "Who? Who told you I was here?"

He swallowed heavily. "I don't know. I don't know who they are, but they're powerful and they know everything that's going on. And I mean everything."

Pay dirt. Brady leaned back, trying not to look overly interested. "I don't know about you," he said casually, "but I could use something to wet my whistle. Draft okay?"

The change of subject caught the techie by surprise. "Huh? Yeh, sure, fine."

James caught the bartender's eye. "Two drafts!" he called out.

Wyman fidgeted as they waited for the beers. "Mind if I take some notes?" Brady asked, pulling out his pad even as he spoke.

"No...Yes, I mean, just don't use my name in anything."

"No problem." He opened the pad and clicked his pen. "I think you'd better start at the beginning." Wyman looked as if he were going to speak, but just then the bartender brought their drafts. He stopped abruptly and sat staring at his hands until the man had returned to his post behind the bar. "So, how did you come into contact with these people?" Brady prodded.

Wyman took a long gulp of his beer. "They contacted me, oh, probably five, six months ago. At first it was a phone call. Somebody I'd never talked with before called me at home – my number isn't even listed! He wanted to talk about a contract job. He was a little evasive, but nothing too strange. So, I said, sure. I mean, I like to pick up extra money just like the next guy."

"Of course. We all do. Go on..." Now that he was talking, Brady wanted to keep the story flowing.

"He said that the group he represented was fighting to keep America free and needed my help. I said 'okay, what do you need me to do for you?' I mean, I'm a good American and all – registered Republican for over 20 years. But I'm not an idiot. My antennas were already up by then, but I guess I was curious. So, he said it was nothing all that difficult, just tracking down someone who'd hacked into their system. He said I'd be well-compensated, but it was hush-hush. Okay, fine. So I agreed. They gave me the name of the site – it was one of these American Rights sites, and I tracked the hacker and gave them the info. Did the whole thing from my home computer. Two days later I get $5000 in my PayPal account!" He was getting agitated, spitting out words as if they burned his mouth.

"Did you ever meet the guy, or at least learn his name?"

Wyman shook his head miserably. "He said I could call him Mr. Black, but I was pretty sure that wasn't his name. It was weird, but five grand is a lot of money."

"Not bad work if you can get it, huh?"

"That's what I thought. But a few weeks later, I get an e-mail on my private account, with a URL attached. Now, I normally wouldn't get within a country mile of that kind of thing – phishing and all – but I thought I recognized the sender. I mean, it looked like a message from a guy I know. So anyway, I click on it, and there are some pictures of me...and a woman I know."

"*That* kind of picture?"

Wyman nodded silently. Brady almost felt sorry for the guy. "Worse thing is," he finally spoke, his voice shaking, "I'm married."

"And the woman in the pictures wasn't your wife, I take it."

He shook his head and then took off his glasses and rubbed his eyes intently. "It was just a couple of times..."

Brady had a hunch. "How did you meet the woman?" he asked. "Was it through your work?"

Wyman slowly put his glasses back on. His eyes were rimmed with red. "No. As a matter of fact, I met her at a bar I used to go to after my Wednesday bowling night. A few of us just stopped there for a beer before heading home. Reliving the game, you know? And one night, when I came out of the men's room I literally bumped into this woman. Tall, trim, not a stunner but pretty cute. Maybe 35 or so. I apologized, she was very nice about it, and that was that. Or so I thought. But later that night, as we were leaving, I found a note under my windshield wiper." He reached into his back pocket and pulled out his wallet. Reaching inside, he removed a folded piece of paper and handed it to Brady. 'Nice bumping into you. Maybe we should do it again,' the note read. And then there was a phone number.

'Classic setup,' Brady thought. *'Poor bastard. Never saw it coming.'*

"And one thing led to another," he prodded.

"Yeh. I guess that was pretty dumb, huh?"

"Everybody wants a little attention from time to time."

"This was more than a little." Brady thought the geek might actually cry. He suddenly felt overwhelmingly sorry for the guy.

"So what came next?" he asked to bridge the sniffling silence. He was pretty sure he already knew.

"They told me that a certain anti-American group had planted some dangerous code in the voting machines' programming, and that they would be able to control the outcome of the next election. They said they'd taken their information to the Secretary of State but that he wouldn't listen. They didn't know if he was just naïve, or if he was in on it too."

"Why didn't they just ask you to help? Why the girl?"

"I asked them the same thing. They said that if Ed Harris was in on it – he's our Secretary of State, then they couldn't trust anyone in the government. They said they were sorry to have to do it to me, but it was the only way they could ensure that I wouldn't tell Harris."

"I take it they threatened to make the photo public?"

"And send it to my wife," the techie answered somberly. "Look," he continued, leaning forward with pain brimming in his eyes. "I love my wife. Really, I do. But Amy was... exciting, and fun and..."

"And she didn't ask anything from you other than your attention when you were together."

"Yeh, exactly." The awe in his voice was unmistakable.

"You're not the only guy in history who's bought that pitch," Brady said, thinking back to the young reporter who proved to be the death knell for his own marriage. "We all have to be reminded from time to time that there's no free lunch."

"You'd think I would've learned that by now," Wyman said with a sigh as he leaned back in his seat.

"It's a difficult lesson to learn. But once you have, there's no forgetting it. I can tell you that from personal experience. But let's get back to the guys who wanted access to the voting machines. How did they communicate with you?"

"Online, at first. They somehow got a hold of my office e-mail address and sent me the photos. A couple of days later they called – on my cell."

"Office or personal?"

"My personal phone."

"Do many people in your office have that number?"

"That's the weird thing – hardly anyone. And the few that do only give it out to close friends and family. I really don't know how they got the private number."

'They have their sources,' Brady thought. "And so you agreed to give them access?"

"Not right away. I told them I needed time to think it over. They gave me 24 hours. I debated going to the police, but…"

"You kept imagining your wife's face when she saw that photo."

"Well, yeh. And then too, I couldn't completely rule out the possibility that they were right. I mean, maybe someone on the inside *had* tampered with the machines."

Brady hated to erase the earnest look from the techie's face. Could he have repeated the line to himself so many times he actually believed that crap?

"Is it possible?" he said, softening his initial reaction. "Could someone from inside get access, without anyone else finding out?"

"I did."

Brady nodded. Maybe the machines weren't as secure as the government officials who were touting them suggested. Wouldn't be the first time that politicians got it wrong. He decided to give Wyman the benefit of the doubt.

"What then?" he asked.

"Then, I did what they asked me to do."

"And that was?"

Wyman looked down at his hands. "I accessed an electronic voting machine in storage and installed a piece of software they provided," he said softly. He looked up at Brady as if expecting a tongue-lashing – or worse.

But Brady wasn't thinking about the techie by that point. He was wondering if this could be the mistake that led him to Wainwright's murderer. "So if we could get someone to examine that machine we could show that it had been tampered with?" he asked, trying to keep his tone as calm as possible.

"I don't know. I don't think so."

Brady felt the excitement drain out of him like a leaky radiator. "What do you mean, you 'don't think so'?"

Wyman shrugged. "From what I overheard one of them say, they can activate it or deactivate it remotely. That's what I'm guessing they did when the State Elections people inspected the machines after the primary."

"I thought *you* were the State Elections people."

"Just the head of one section. We've got probably 70 people working in three offices here in Columbus and another one up in Cleveland. And that's just at the state level. There's a lot more locally."

"I take it the machine passed the inspection?"

"With flying colors," the State employee said with a mixture of pride and embarrassment. "They didn't have a clue."

"And what could these people do with that piece of software in a real election?"

He shook his head. "I really don't know. I mean, they didn't exactly share their plans with me. Maybe they're just monitoring what those other guys are doing."

"But you don't think so."

A shrug. "If they're as good as they seem to be, they could pretty much do whatever they wanted. They might even be able to control the machines remotely. They could take votes from one candidate, give then to another, add write-ins – you name it." His eyes shone.

"So what you're telling me is they could steal the election."

"Absolutely. That's why I'm here."

"Have you told anyone else?"

"Of course not! I can't go to the police. I'm not exactly sure, but I imagine I've probably committed a crime of some kind. Besides, the people behind all this would release the pictures." He looked down at his hands again. "I was kind of hoping you could...handle this. Quietly, I mean."

Brady stared at him. Was this guy for real? Or was it some kind of set-up?

"What makes you think that?" he asked, watching for any sign of a con.

"If they're telling me to stay away from you, it means they're afraid, or at least concerned. That means you must have some clout. I Googled you – Pulitzer, Washington Post – all that. You must know a lot of big time politicos – right?"

"A few. But without proof, it'd be your word against theirs. And we both know how that would turn out."

"We've got to do something! They're already getting set for the election."

"How do you know that?"

"They told me. They said they'd need me to stand by to possibly provide access again. Only this time it'll be for real."

"Over the phone? They told you this over the phone?"

Wyman shook his head. "In person. Two of them met me at a motel off the Interstate. A big black guy and a skinny white guy."

"Would you recognize them if you saw them again?"

He shook his head no. "They wore masks. The big guy looked like Obama, and the white guy like Jimmy Carter. Pretty weird, huh?"

"Yeh. Pretty weird." Brady was thinking he had a pretty good idea who those two might be. But how to prove it?

"Can you remember anything else about them? What they wore, how they spoke…?"

"I might be able to recognize their voices if I heard them again."

He didn't sound very certain.

"Okay, that's good," Brady said, trying to keep the guy feeling positive. "So, when is this all supposed to go down?"

"They said they'd get back to me. But if it's like the test run, probably a few days before the election."

Brady thought for a few seconds. He could feel Wyman watching him. "Can you do it?" he finally asked.

The techie stared at him in open disbelief. "I thought you wanted to stop the bastards!"

"I want to *catch* them. But from what you're telling me, they already have the software loaded. Why do they need you?"

"I don't know. Maybe they're thinking they might need more machines, or more districts."

"Okay, but if they do call you, could you do it? Get them inside again?"

"Of course. There's really nothing to stop me. The guys in charge are too busy to pay much attention until the day of the election, and the public doesn't have a clue."

"So then it comes down to whether there's a way to bust them while they're changing votes. Is there?"

Wyman nodded thoughtfully as he ran scenarios in his head. "Maybe."

"Is that the best you can do?" Brady said more forcefully than he'd intended.

"Hey, look. I'm a computer guy, not James Bond. I'd have to ponder it a bit and run some simulations. I don't even know how many people have access to the machines."

"How soon will you know – if you can detect them or not?"

"I don't know...Maybe a week or two."

"Okay, good." He scribbled a number on a business card and slid it over to Wyman. "This is my private cell. Disposable, unlisted, and as far as I know, untraceable. Call me when you know. Call from a pay phone and just say, 'It's me. I'll call you tomorrow at...whatever time you can call.' Then make sure no one follows you and call me from a different pay phone the next day. Got it?"

"These guys are big fish, aren't they?" Wyman said, his voice cracking ever so slightly.

"Yeh, they're big fish. Sharks, who'll gobble up our whole system if we let 'em. But, we won't let 'em, right?"

"And the photo?"

Brady was tempted to harangue the guy for his selfishness, but thought better of it. He really wasn't James Bond.

"Maybe we can hack into their computer system and erase it. And if not, maybe the feds can cut a deal with one of them to trade it for a reduced sentence. We'll think of something." He wished he were as sure as he sounded, but he couldn't let Wyman get cold feet, no matter what. "Don't worry. Our fish are even bigger than theirs."

"Yeh. FBI, and all that. Right?"

"You got it."

He sipped his beer, giving the frightened man sitting across from him time to compose himself. Wyman took the cue and finished his glass in one long glug.

"Anything else?" he asked Brady after wiping his mouth with the back of his hand. "I need to be getting home."

"Don't know. You tell me: anything more you can add about who these people are or why they picked you?"

"I think we know why they picked me. I have the access, the know-how, and…" he paused and shook his head, "I handed them the weapon to force me to do it. As to who they are, your guess is as good as mine. Maybe better."

"Okay. I guess that's all for now." He started to shut his notepad as Wyman pushed his chair away from the table and stood.

A thought suddenly jumped into his mind. "Did these guys mention anyone else being involved? I mean, did they say anything about any other state?"

Wyman squeezed his eyes shut as he tried to remember.

"Not about another state," he began, "but they did have me send the software to four other email addresses."

"Do you still have those addresses?"

"I think so."

"Send them to me at this email address," Brady said, jotting down an address he seldom used any more.

"You *will* stop them, won't you?" the techie asked softly.

"*We* will stop them. And thanks. I know this wasn't easy."

A weak smile crossed the techie's face, the first time Brady had seen it since the state official had come in. "Just because I was stupid doesn't mean these guys get to steal the election," Wyman said. "There really wasn't any other choice."

They shook hands. "Call me when you know," Brady reminded.

"Don't worry. I will."

Wyman walked quickly to the door and, with a nod, stepped outside. Brady watched through the dirty front window as the tan Chevy pulled away. As the taillights faded in the distance, he called Danny back in DC and told him to expect a forwarded email with some addresses he needed traced. Then he paid the bartender, left a bigger tip than the service deserved, and slipped out into the cool blackness of the night.

'*I sure as hell hope I wasn't feeding that poor guy a line,*' he mused as he climbed into his rental car. True, he felt more confident than he had before their meeting, but if it came down to Election Week and they hadn't figured some foolproof method for catching these bastards, he'd have to call the FBI – photos or no photos. But with no physical evidence, no way to link Hoch to the plot, and no good reason why someone like the eccentric billionaire would risk everything to rig an election in which he had nothing much to gain and everything to lose, he knew how far he'd get with the Feds. All he really had was Wyman's story and a hunch. But as a U.S. Senator and a former Hoch Industries accountant might have pointed out, if they were still able, it was very dangerous to have a story to tell if Mr. Hoch was involved.

CHAPTER 14

The trip back to DC had been uneventful, although he'd felt like an idiot telling Derek that the Redskins looked good the night before; they'd lost 31-6 with 4 turnovers. *'If anyone is bothering to listen-in they must think I'm out of my mind. Maybe I am.'*

The PI was even then on his way over to Georgetown to talk to the Poli-Sci prof he'd recommended. He was pretty certain what Pettigrew would tell Derek, but he wanted to be sure. This story was growing by the minute, and he needed to get his arms around it.

As soon as he got home he tossed his suitcase on the bed and threw his dirty clothes into the pile in the closet before calling Anne at work. The phone rang four times before she answered.

"Senator Wain...Senate offices," she corrected herself.

"Still can't get used to it, huh?" Brady asked sympathetically.

"You're back!" Anne said with just enough enthusiasm to stir feelings he hadn't experienced for years. He'd have to watch himself. He was getting a little too fond of this woman...

"Yeh, just got in. Thought I'd see how things were going over there."

"Fine," she said without conviction. "Or at least as good as can be expected."

"No problems?"

"With our 'friends'? Nope. No sign."

"Glad to hear it. And with everything else? Have you heard anything from Danny?"

She lowered her voice. "I had a voicemail from him that was sufficiently cryptic to suggest he might have something to share. But he can't get free until lunchtime."

Brady looked at his watch. It was already 11:30. "I could probably get down there in an hour or so if you think it'd be worthwhile."

"I can't speak for Danny, but it'd be fine with me," she said provocatively.

"I'll give you a call when I'm five minutes out. Maybe we can get out of that building to someplace a little more…intimate?"

"I'm sure Danny would be thrilled."

"Tell him in person, okay?" He knew it was ridiculous to think that anyone who could tap their phones would be put off by their rudimentary code, but it was worth a try. "And have him meet us there." It wouldn't be smart for the three of them to march arm in arm through the streets.

"Will do." She paused for just a heartbeat. "By the way, do you have plans for tonight?"

"None that I couldn't change – given the right motivation."

She giggled. He found himself smiling as well. The sound of her laugh was becoming inordinately pleasing to his ear.

"We'll see what we can come up with."

"Then I'll see what I can get up as well." The juvenile humor was pathetic, he knew, but somehow it seemed right.

"Anyone ever tell you you were a dirty old man?"

"Not lately. Maybe you can tell me tonight."

"We can discuss it at lunch."

"Now I'm certain Danny will be thrilled."

"See you around 12:30."

As he hung up, Brady had a nearly overpowering urge to whistle. *'Jesus H. Christmas. What the hell is happening to me?'* And then he began to whistle.

*****

Georgetown is a city university. Its campus lies just a stone's throw from the Potomac River, just a couple of Metro stops from the

Mall and the beating heart of DC. At first glance the architecture is reminiscent of jolly old England, with imposing gray stone facades and towers that conjure images of princesses in distress. However, as the oldest Catholic university in the country, founded by Jesuits at that, you might instead imagine the tortured cries of heretics (or learned astronomers) emanating from those same imposing towers. But you would very probably be wrong. For although Georgetown is titularly a religious school, its greatest renown arises from its international studies program and its close connection to politicos past, present and to come. Cabinet members and assistant Secretaries of State have been known to cool their heels teaching a course or two at old GU while awaiting the cyclical return of their party to power. And what better locale than a 100 acre educational preserve in the midst of the decaying capital, complete with thousands of eager and impossibly earnest young men and women who yearn to study the realities of politics at the feet of former A-list party hacks whose theories of world dominance are, momentarily, out of fashion.

Derek thought about none of this as he made his way to his meeting with Professor Jeffrey Pettigrew, former Assistant Secretary of State for... something or other. Derek had forgotten. Not that it mattered. Brady thought the guy had a decent grasp of the current political scene, and that was good enough for Derek. He stopped to watch two lithe young women running and jumping as they chased a thrown Frisbee, both wearing the ever so trendy short shorts that barely covered the bottom curve of their respective butts. '*Ah, to be young again*,' he thought as his gaze shifted to include literally hundreds more of the lovely young things, all similarly attired, all competing to catch the eye of one of the buff young dudes who lazed, or tossed a ball, or surreptitiously swigged a beer on the grassy quad between several red brick dormitory buildings.

Somewhere a clock chimed the hour, snapping him out of his deepening reverie. '*Damn, better get a move on*,' he thought as he pulled himself away from the enticing scene and hurried on short little legs to get to his appointment before the self-important Prof closed up shop and went home for a martini or three.

Luckily, Pettigrew was still in his office when Derek finally tapped on the stained oak door.

"Come in," a middle-aged voice called out in reply.

Derek opened the door and stepped into a comfortable office, its walls lined with bookshelves positively stuffed full with biographies of Winston Churchill, John Adams, and hundreds of other equally deceased former political big-wigs. On closer inspection it became clear that some weren't bios at all but mea no-culpas written by the politicos themselves to justify their screw-ups. Derek preferred sci-fi.

"Come in!" Pettigrew called out once more, this time with noticeable petulance.

"I am in," Derek answered calmly, despite his inclinations.

The professor shifted in his chair and leaned forward over the paper-strewn dark wood desk. Only then did he see the PI standing just a few feet in front of him.

"Oh, so you are," he said without apology or, apparently, embarrassment. "You must be the investigator. Have a seat."

He motioned to one of the two green and gold upholstered chairs that fronted the desk. Derek ignored him for the moment and approached close enough to toss his business card to the nonplussed academic. Out of necessity he'd developed a flick of the wrist delivery that had proven pretty effective at skimming cards across imposing office desks, dinner tables...and bars, when necessary.

"Derek DiLaurain," he said, using his best Sam Spade delivery. "I work with Brady James."

"Right, right, the Post guy. So, what can I do for you?"

"Well," Derek said, scooting up into the visitor's chair with as little evident effort as possible, "Mr. James is currently researching a story about the upcoming elections. He wanted to pick your brains about the lay of the land."

"And he couldn't come here himself?" Pettigrew asked, staring intently at the PI.

Derek knew the type. Too important to speak to underlings. "He's out of town just now. But he wanted to be sure that your contribution to the story was included. Specifically, he was wondering which states – in your expert opinion – would be too close to call in the coming Presidential balloting." He knew just how to stroke this kind of guy, and when he saw the professor ease back in his chair and assume the 'political guru' pose, he knew he'd succeeded.

"Well, of course it's always dangerous predicting elections, even this close to V-Day," he began, and Derek knew he was about to do exactly that. "But, I'd say that Pennsylvania, Ohio, Missouri, Colorado, Washington, and, of course, Florida are the most important. There are a number of others as well, but those six are bellwethers. They will set the stage for the northeast, midwest, southeast, mountain states and far west."

"And just how close do you think they will be? I mean, are we talking tens of thousands of votes, or something less?"

Pettigrew stared out into the indefinite distance as if deep in thought. "I'd say each of them could, and I stress *could*, be decided by less than 1% of the total vote. And one or more of them could come down to a Florida in 2000. Of course, that's all dependent on a number of factors, most notably the economy. There's an old saying, 'incumbents don't win when the Dow is down.' And I'd add, when unemployment lines are long. As of this minute, both those factors favor the challenger. But the incumbent is still reasonably popular, so...who knows."

"You'd say it's pretty wide-open at this point?"

"Impossible to predict. Too many variables."

Derek glanced down at his notepad. "What do you know about the smaller parties, like American Rights? Are they real players?"

"Players? Yeh, sure. I mean, there's no way that they can elect a President on their own, but they might be able to swing enough votes in key states to make the difference in a tight election."

"And what would they ask in return?"

Pettigrew looked at the PI with increased interest.

"What did you say this article was about, again?"

"The upcoming elections. In particular, how smaller parties could influence a close election."

The professor nodded to himself. "Yeh, yeh I can see that. If AR, or one of the other splinter groups, could scare-up a few thousand votes for one side or the other, they could definitely influence the outcome." He paused for a second. "Don't use that comment about 'splinter groups'. They probably wouldn't like that."

Derek pounced on the correction. "And that would bother you – that they didn't like it?"

He nodded absently. "We academics walk a fine line. We try to maintain some semblance of impartiality, but we can only function if we get access. And you don't get access from people who don't like you, or think you don't like them."

"Off the record, then, what do you think of AR?"

Derek could see the glassy veil of distrust slide across the professor's eyes. "You seem pretty interested in such a small party…"

"Like you said, small in size, but potentially big in influence. Our readers should know what they're all about."

"Off the record?" Pettigrew repeated after a moment's consideration.

"Completely."

"Real died-in-the-wool conservatives, with overtones of religious and even social fanaticism."

"Racists?"

Pettigrew hesitated. "Certainly anti-immigration. And maybe worse."

"Abortion?"

"The majority won't even accept it in cases of rape."

"Big government?"

The professor smiled. "They don't want any interference in their daily lives by Washington bureaucrats. Except when there's a flood, or tornado, or they're thrown out of work. Then they're first in line with their hands out, and first to criticize slow response."

"Are they dangerous?"

Pettigrew's eyes narrowed. "This isn't about an election article, is it?"

Derek hesitated. If he told the whole truth, he risked that word of their investigation might reach Hoch and his people, either by design or a slip of the tongue. If he was too evasive the professor might clam up. "I think Brady intends to write something, eventually," he finally said noncommittally.

"But there's something else, another reason why you're looking into AR." It was a statement, not a question.

"There is another reason, but I'm afraid I'm not at liberty to reveal it." The PI sat up as tall as he could in his oversized chair, trying to appear authoritative.

Pettigrew stared at Derek for several long seconds. And then he sighed.

"Not really any of my business, I suppose." Derek let out an audible sigh of relief and slumped back down into a more comfortable position. "But as to your question, I don't think the vast majority of ARers are any more dangerous than a cross-section of the population as a whole. Oh sure, some of them are angry, and quite a few of them say things that are ill-considered. But dangerous? Not 99% of them."

"And the rest?"

"There are *some* people who identify themselves with AR who could be categorized as…radical. Not many, maybe not more percentage-wise than any other party."

"But there are some?"

"I don't know any of the more radical members, if that's what you want to know. But I've talked to enough people in the movement to know that there is a small subgroup that is growing impatient with the glacial pace of politics in this country. They want to take things into their own hands and make the changes they believe are important."

"Revolutionaries?"

"They'd call themselves 'patriots', I'm sure."

"And what would you call them?"

Pettigrew stared out the window behind his desk. For a moment, Derek thought he hadn't heard the question or wasn't going to answer. But after a painfully long wait, he turned back to face the PI.

He shook his head thoughtfully.

"Crazy," he said softly. "Absolutely nuts."

*****

The Capitol Hill Grille is located just six blocks from the Russell Senate Office Building. Close enough that you could walk there without too much effort, far enough that the vast majority of lazy secretaries and office geeks, as well as most self-important policy wonks, wouldn't be bothered to make the journey. There's no eatery within a mile of the Capitol that isn't frequented by at least a couple of staffers every now and then (and certainly no bar that doesn't suffer their often loud and acronym-infected debates), but the Grille is one of the few decent restaurants within walking distance where you can usually find a dark corner at lunchtime and hear yourself – and whoever you're with – talk.

Brady had decided to meet Anne and Danny there, figuring that the two of them would be less noticeable leaving the Russell Building than he and either or both of them together. As had become his custom in recent days, he took a circuitous route to the Grille, turning down streets that ran opposite to his ultimate direction and even racing the wrong way on a one-way street for just a block to keep things interesting. Whether it was his Steve McQueen driving or something else, he didn't spot anyone tailing him. He parked around the corner from the Grille and cut through an alley that bisected the block. Still no one. He checked his watch. He was early, but instead of killing time, he went straight to the restaurant and got himself seated at the most remote, poorly-lit table in the place. And then he waited.

12:30 came and went, with no Anne and Danny. 12:45. 12:50. He found himself staring at his watch compulsively. This wasn't like

Anne. As a tiny ripple of concern raced through his stomach, he realized just how much she had come to mean to him. Where the hell were they?!

He pulled out his phone to check on the two of them, only to find himself facing a blank screen. It took him a second to process the fact that it was turned off. Sheepishly, he turned it on and saw at once that there were two voicemails from Anne. Before he could access them, however, the door opened and he saw her come into the Grille, followed less than a minute later by Danny. He felt an embarrassed grin of relief spread across his face as he stood to greet them, but he didn't care.

"Sorry about that," she began as she approached the table. "Senator-designate Jessup's staff 'absolutely needed' to discuss some administrative details with me just as I was headed out the door."

Without thinking, he reached out and hugged her close.

"Woa! What's that all about?" she asked as he loosened his bear hug.

"Just happy to see you," he dissembled.

"And what about me?" the young computer tech teased as he arrived at the table. "Are you happy to see me too? You should be..."

"Why? You pickin' up the tab?" Brady said straight-faced.

"Better," Danny said, dropping his voice and glancing around appraisingly as he sat at the table. "I got something on the asshole who hacked the Senator's account."

James didn't even try to disguise the excitement in his voice. "Do you know who it was?"

"Not quite, but close. I know where he is."

"Where?"

"This guy's good, very good. But I think he's a little full of himself. I mean, he was just a little sloppy, and it cost him."

"Ok, so the guy thinks he's hot stuff and you kicked his butt. Got it. But where is he?"

"You know that system you wanted me to hack?" he said softly.

Brady nodded.

"I found some files from the Senator's computer on it."

Brady suppressed a whoop. "Good work. Now where is he?"

The tech wasn't through explaining. "He tried to strip-off all identifiers by running the hack through secondary scrubber servers and using some kind of proprietary anonymizer…"

"Look, Danny, I'm not really much of a computer whiz, okay? So your explanation is just pearls before swine. All I want to know is where the guy is located."

The disappointment on the younger man's face passed quickly, replaced by glowing pride. He leaned in toward Brady with a self-satisfied smile. "Montana," he whispered.

"I knew it!" Brady hissed. "I knew it was that bastard Hoch, or one of his flunkies."

"Adam Hoch?" the techie asked in awe.

"So you think his calls to the Senator in the days before he died were all part of this?" Anne chimed in.

"It's certainly beginning to look that way."

"But why? Hoch's already got all the money in the world. Why would he want to hurt the Senator?"

"You think Adam Hoch had something to do with the Senator's death?" Danny asked a little too loudly, his eyes wide with disbelief.

"Keep your voice down!" Brady barked, a little louder than he had intended.

Danny looked around in uneasy embarrassment. "Sorry. But, Adam Hoch…"

"May or may not be involved in this whole thing," Brady interrupted calmingly. "We don't really know for sure. But obviously, all this needs to be kept very close-hold." Brady had learned long before that a few well-placed buzzwords could work wonders with federal bureaucrats.

"Oh, yeh, yeh. I got it."

"Good. So, did you get anything else?"

"I'm zeroing in on the specific area of the state, and I might be able to track the IP address, but I'm not really sure that'll help much."

"Get all you can. But I'm pretty sure I know exactly where the hacker was located, right down to the building."

"Brady, if Hoch is involved, we should call in the big guns: the FBI, or at least the Capitol police," Anne warned.

"Too early. That guy's got his tentacles into everything. I don't want to tip him off that we know so much about him and his little game."

"What game?" Danny asked eagerly.

"You don't mean you think he could influence the FBI?" Anne asked, surprise tinged with indignation.

"Security types aren't exactly known for their liberal tendencies," James explained. "I wouldn't be shocked to learn that his outfit has sympathizers in just about every Washington agency."

"What outfit?" the techie asked.

"It's better if you don't know," Brady said. "Nothing personal, just standard security ops."

"Oh, yeh, right," Danny replied, his disappointment poorly hidden. "Loose lips and all that."

"*I* don't even know all the details," Anne added, hoping to blunt the blow.

"But you'll both be among the first to know once we can pin it all down. Fair enough?"

"Fair enough," Danny said with a small smile.

"Works for me," Anne agreed.

"Good, then let's order. Some of you need to get back to work."

Brady tried to project relaxed confidence, but despite his best efforts he couldn't get Hoch and the AR election scammers out of his mind. He picked at his food and lost the thread of the conversation on several occasions. His tablemates couldn't help but notice, but they kept their observations to themselves. Brady, for his part, played with all the pieces of the story like a jigsaw puzzle, trying to complete the picture before it was too late.

There had to be a way to get Hoch to show himself. But how?

CHAPTER 15

Adam Hoch didn't like surprises.

"What do you mean we had 'an intruder'?" he asked, his voice a sharpened dagger.

Jeff had been around his grandfather often enough to know *that* tone when he heard it. "I mean I think someone has accessed our computer system," he said calmly, trying to diffuse his grandfather's fury. "Probably from a federal government server."

"You 'think', or you know?"

The younger Hoch hated when his grandfather pulled this crap. He was a smart guy. He already knew what had happened. All the rest, that was just to make a point. Well he was a smart guy too, and two could play his game.

"I'll know for sure when I finish my analysis," he continued as though nothing were wrong. "But it looks like a tripwire was activated, and that usually means unauthorized access."

"How the hell could this happen?!" the elder Hoch began to ramp up his anger. "I thought you were one of the best."

"I am one of the best," Jeff answered definitively. "But there's no such thing as a network that can't be hacked. I've told you that a thousand times."

"And you also told me that the idiots in the government couldn't get past your security in a million years!" Adam bellowed. "It doesn't look like a million years to me!"

Jeff bit back an ill-considered retort. He *had* told his grandfather exactly that. He quickly evaluated his options and decided that evasiveness would only lead to a bitter ending. Checkmate in four or five moves. Better to own up to it.

"I underestimated them," he said softly. "It won't happen again."

"You're damn right it won't happen again! I'm going to find a computer expert who deserves the title and turn it all over to him – or her!"

Jeff refused to let his grandfather see the effect his words were having on him. He knew the old man had only suggested the possibility of a woman network manager to piss him off. Adam would never consider putting a woman in that position. Public Relations? Sales? Sure. But something that really mattered? No way.

He concentrated on relaxing the muscles around his eyes, the way top-level poker players did. No stress, no worries. No nothing, just a blank page staring back at the old man. He kept all emotion from his voice, and placed his hands where his grandfather could see just how unperturbed he was. Of course, it was all Zen bullpucky, but he knew for a fact that it worked.

"That would be a mistake," he answered, his tone permitting no contradiction.

"And why would that be, Mr. Computer Hotshot?" The sarcasm was still there, but Jeff could already hear some of the steam draining out of the old guy.

"For two reasons: because no one will do a better job than I will," he began, blending just a touch of sincerity with the arrogant certainty, "and because you'd have to let at least one more person into your inner circle, and that's one more chance that your little plan to take over the country will leak. And that, Dear Grandfather, would be catastrophic."

The younger Hoch took just a slightly deeper breath, knowing that this would be the tipping point. Either the old man would buy his pitch and back down, albeit without admitting that he'd been wrong, or... Or his ass would be in a sling and he'd have to start maneuvering behind the scenes ASAP to regain his position at the grownups' table and ensure that his inheritance wouldn't be touched. He renewed his focus on his eye muscles and reminded himself to blink.

Like a sheet of ice on the windshield of a wintry car with the defroster blowing full tilt, the angry scowl of Adam Hoch slowly melted, transformed into a begrudging smile.

"Maybe you are my blood after all," he said calmly, leaning back into his plush leather chair. "Any way to know how much he learned?"

"I'm on it. But probably not very much. I don't think he penetrated the encrypted drives."

"Some good news, at least. But we need to be sure." His voice hardened. "Do you know who did this to us?"

"Not yet. But I will."

"Good. And when you do, I think we're going to have to teach the bureaucratic bastard a little lesson. Do you agree?"

"Oh, absolutely," Jeff cooed. Nobody made him look like a fool. Particularly not to his grandfather.

CHAPTER 16

Brady felt as if he were being pulled in a hundred different directions at once. There was the murder, and the election scam, and AR, and Hoch, and now Anne was a factor to be considered in whatever he did. Even Orakpo and Cooley were having a dry spell, and they had been the Skins heart and soul over the last three games.

'*Jesus. You'd think they could at least make it to the playoffs one of these decades,*' he thought as he drove towards Anne's place just before 7 pm on a Tuesday night. Traffic was light, which was a good thing. As usual, he was running late.

After his lunch downtown, Derek had briefed him on the Pettigrew visit, stressing the possibility of violent action from the AR fringe. Not that Brady was surprised.

"Those bastards think they have an exclusive on the truth," he'd told the diminutive PI. "When you get right down to it, they're really not much different than the fanatics in the Mid-east: they're right, everyone else is wrong, and they're gonna make damn sure we all do it their way."

"At least we have our guard up for the suicide bombers. I'm not sure anyone is really taking the nut cases in our own country very seriously," Derek had agreed.

"We are."

But even now, with the near-certainty that Hoch was part of whatever happened to Wainwright and was involved up to his neck in some kind of plot to rig the upcoming election, Brady wasn't sure what to do about it. He knew Hoch had friends in high places, and he was equally convinced that AR had a good many sympathizers in government, law enforcement and the military, so who to trust? He and Derek had discussed the possibilities, but they couldn't agree on a course of action.

"FBI?"

"Only if we could be sure that the investigation would stay compartmentalized. If it were widely known we were after Hoch, I can virtually guarantee one of his buds would shut it down, or at least tip him off."

"Do we have a good enough friend in the Bureau?"

"I don't."

"Then how about the Attorney General's Office? They certainly are no friends to Hoch."

"All government agencies leak like sieves. You should know that by now, after all the stories we've done. If you want to know a secret, just ask a bureaucrat...or two."

"State authorities?"

"What state? Ohio? I sure as hell don't know anyone out there. It'd be like Russian Roulette. Pick the right contact, we win. Pick the wrong one...we might not be around to see the results of the next election."

When it came right down to it, the only person they knew and trusted in law enforcement was the same Don Chesley who was already investigating Hoch's flunkies. They decided to stick with him, for the meantime, and made plans to get together the following afternoon to sketch-out their next steps.

'Reminds me. I need to get back to him and see what he's found out,' Brady mused as he turned into Anne's apartment building lot a few hours later.

He parked in a visitor's space and nodded to the concierge as he entered the building. By this time they all knew him by sight. To his surprise, it didn't bother him in the least. He rode the elevator to her floor and knocked lightly on a familiar door. He saw a shadow pass over the peek-hole from inside the apartment and heard the soft click of the deadbolt.

"Why Mr. James, what a pleasant surprise," Anne said leaning forward to kiss him hello. She wore a low-cut sheer blouse and had clearly spent some time on her makeup and hair. He had to admit, she looked great. Better than he deserved.

"I brought you a little something," he said, handing her the brown paper bag that contained a bottle of Napa Merlot. One of her favorites.

"If I didn't know better I'd think you were trying to get me drunk," she teased.

"To take advantage of you?" he leered.

"One can only hope…"

Inside, over a glass or two of wine, he caught her up on their latest bits of information. Her smile turned somber.

"Brady, I really don't like the way all this is heading. Adam Hoch is a very powerful man. He's not going to take kindly to anyone exposing his little shenanigans. You need to find someone to help keep you guys safe."

"Just what Derek and I were discussing this afternoon," he reassured her. "We're working on a plan." He didn't want to lie to her, but didn't feel she'd appreciate the unvarnished truth.

"Well, I hope so. I wouldn't want anything to happen to the two of you."

Her concerned look touched him.

"Getting sweet on the little fellow?"

Her smile returned. "Something like that."

The warm glow of the wine spread throughout his body. "Should I be jealous?" He slid closer to her, looking into her hypnotic green eyes. A small flush to her cheeks told him that she was feeling the wine as well.

"I wouldn't think so," she said softly, stroking the side of his jaw with her hand.

He fumbled to place his wine glass on the coffee table and leaned in closer. He could feel her breath on his lips.

"I'm happy to hear that."

He kissed her deeply and she slipped her hand behind his neck.

"We're going to be late for dinner," she whispered.

"We can eat cake," he said. Food was the furthest thing from his mind just then.

*****

At nine o'clock sharp, Brady pulled himself out of bed and poured himself a cup of coffee. Derek was already up and about. "On a real, paying case," as he'd put it.

Anne had wanted him to stay the night, but he had things to do. Important things. Not that he wouldn't have liked to wake up next to her. But first things first.

When he was confident that his head was clear enough to risk a serious conversation, he dialed his old buddy Chesley. The phone rang twice before the detective picked up.

"Chesley."

"Chez – it's Brady."

"Brady. How they hangin'?"

"I'm okay. Hey, have you had any luck with the people I asked you about?"

"What, no foreplay?" the cop joked.

"Sorry. Guess I'm losing my touch."

"You're gonna make me think you only want me for my sources."

"A big strong police detective like you? No way."

"Jeez. Now you got me all squishy and breathin' hard. What were we talkin' about?"

Brady smiled to himself. "The guys you were going to take a look at…"

"Oh yeh. Interesting group." His voice dropped as if he were covering the mouthpiece with his cupped hand. "Maybe we should have a cup of coffee and discuss it?"

Brady took the hint. "Absolutely. I'll even buy."

"You're a prince. How about 10:30. The usual place?"

"You got it. See you then."

Brady showered and shaved before straightening up his room a bit. It wasn't likely Derek would care, or even notice, but he didn't want his friend to start thinking of him as the unwanted slob of a guest who'd outstayed his welcome. At least not so quickly. He'd talked to an agent about seeing a couple of new apartments to rent while they were rehabbing his. But most of the good places were beyond his limited means. It might take a while to locate a place that was both livable and affordable. Until then, it required precious little effort to keep his space – and some of Derek's too – looking at least a notch above a college dorm room.

Café Red was just that: a small red brick building that had the curb appeal of a squatter's shack but served some of the best 'jo' in town. And it was out of the way. Brady had met Chesley there a few dozen times over the years. This time he felt a bit more nervous than most of the others. The detective was already there waiting for him when he arrived.

They shook hands and sat without a word. Chesley looked on edge, and that worried Brady.

"So, you got something for me?" he asked, trying to act more relaxed than he felt.

"Yeh, a few tidbits. But before I pass them on to you, I gotta warn ya, these are some heavy hitters you're playing around with."

Brady felt a chill run up his spine. "Meaning?"

"Meaning I hope you got one tough bodyguard keeping an eye on you, or at least a ton of life insurance."

"Do I need it?"

"You might. You know that driver you asked me to check out…?"

"Tommy?"

"His name's Thomas Jefferson Clark. Rap sheet as long as your dick. Make that as long as mine. Assault, B&E, attempted rape. Just about the only thing that guy hasn't done is fix an election. That we know of."

"And the PR guy – Henson?"

"Earl Wayne Henson, aka Earl Hayes, aka Wayne Hayes, aka a half-dozen other aliases. That guy would try to sell the Brooklyn Bridge to the mayor of New York. He served 3 years in the late 90's for stock fraud, but the Feds think he might have been involved in bunko, extortion, blackmail – a real prince. Just couldn't make anything else stick. The guy's slick – and good."

"And now they both work for Hoch. Great."

"I don't get it, Brady. Okay, so they want to steal an election. Why all the high tech shenanigans and heavy-duty thugs? Can't this Hoch guy just buy an election in a nice hicky place like Ohio?"

"I don't think it's Ohio they're thinking about," Brady said, dropping his voice to little more than a whisper. "I think it's the White House."

Chesley blinked. "The White House? Are these guys completely nuts?"

Brady scanned the tiny coffee shop before he answered. "I think they might be able to pull it off," he finally said.

"By tinkering with electronic voting machines?" The note of incredulity in his voice did not escape James.

"Listen: the difference of a few thousand votes in key states could have changed the outcome of at least three presidential elections since 1960. With Bush-Gore it was less than a thousand."

"That's all well and good," the detective argued, "but how are they going to get one of their guys on the ticket? I don't care how much money Hoch has, the Republicans aren't going to run an AR candidate for President. And even if they did, changing a few thousand votes in a few states wouldn't do it. This makes no sense."

"I don't know. I only know that they're planning on rigging the election, and I think Wainwright found out. And that's why he's dead."

"You have proof?"

"Some."

"So let's take this to the Feds, then. The FBI loves this kind of case."

"How long do you think this story would stay secret once the FBI got a hold of it? An hour? I'm betting there are more AR sympathizers in the Bureau than Democrats."

Chesley smiled. "You may be right. So what do we do then? We're a bit outmanned here."

"Out-moneyed, yes. Outmanned? I don't think so. If we can catch these bastards in the act, and maybe wheal a confession out of them regarding Wainwright, then we can go to the Feds."

"You're not asking for much, are you? You got a couple of divisions of Marines stashed away somewhere to come to your rescue when these very nasty guys decide they don't like you snooping around their business?"

"I've got you. And Derek. And me."

"Jesus, I feel better already," Chesley said, taking a big sip of his coffee.

"Plus, we have "Wainwright's former secretary and a computer whiz at the State Dept."

"Great. Maybe we can get by with just one division of Marines." The detective shook is head in concerned bemusement. "Who's the geek? Is he any good?"

"Very. He's already been able to track the person who hacked the Senator's computer back to Montana. With any luck, he'll take it right to Hoch's door."

"Yeh, well if my sources are right, it might be his grandson's door."

"Jeffrey?"

"They say he's a real piece of work. In college his grandfather supposedly bought off at least two girls who wanted to bring assault charges against him. His freshman roommate requested a new room after less than a month, as did the person they brought in after him. He lived in a double all by himself for the entire second half of the year."

"A chip off the old block."

"Oh, and one other thing. If you don't already know, he's a bit of a computer genius. Sky-high IQ, but not much with the social graces."

"So we won't invite him to dinner."

Chesley's smile barely moved his lips. "All kidding aside, this is going to be tough sledding. He's got all the resources in the world and a solid core of criminal minds surrounding him. And that doesn't even take into account the AR nut cases who'll help him out for political reasons. You sure you don't want to call the Bureau, or somebody?"

"Not yet. If he knows we're closing in on him, he'll just lay low for a while. Nobody's going to keep surveillance on a well-connected billionaire for very long. We need to get enough proof to make the story air-tight."

"Okay," the detective said, shrugging. "It's your story. But you'd better be on your toes. This could get messy."

"It already *is* messy. Just ask the Wainwrights."

Chesley nodded sadly.

"So, are you willing to risk your badge a couple of more times?" Brady pressed.

The DC cop shook his head in disbelief. "What do you need?"

*****

Brady drove around the city for quite a while after his meeting with Chesley. He often did that, drove aimlessly, when he was trying to think through a particularly complicated story. The flow of the traffic somehow stimulated the flow of ideas. Unfortunately, the traffic was bumper to bumper on many of the main roads, and his thinking wasn't much better. There had to be a way to force Hoch out into the open. He knew Hoch was keeping an eye on him, and probably Derek as well. But he was pretty sure the Montana oilman didn't know what they were really researching. If they did, he and the tiny PI would probably be studying the root structure of ditch grass from the prone position. And he didn't like confining spaces.

There had to be a way…

CHAPTER 17

Jeffrey had been staring at his computer screen for hours. He found it hypnotic, even when the monitor showed nothing more than the automatic sorting or crack sequencing of long strings of numbers. He had a big office, bigger than anyone else in the building, except his grandfather, of course. But it was empty, except for his desk and his computer. He didn't need anything else. Extra chairs would only make people think he wanted visitors. And he didn't. He enjoyed working with machines. They were predictable, for the most part. They didn't go off on emotional tirades or sulk over infinitesimal nothings. Oh sure, he liked to get laid every now and then. But he'd learned long ago that a good hooker satisfied his lust as well as any girlfriend. No need for constant explanations and excuses. No long heart to hearts over nothing. No expectations. Besides, as the heir apparent to a huge fortune, he knew damned well that any girl who made a play for him was only thinking about the money anyway. Or almost only.

Suddenly the endless stream of letters and numbers on his screen came to a screeching halt. He leaned forward and examined the single line of information that remained.

"Got ya' you little son of a bitch," he muttered. And he smiled.

*****

Danny usually didn't bring work home with him. At five o'clock he left the office, and whatever was on his desk stayed there. But this Wainwright job had wormed its way inside his head, not just because he liked and admired the Senator, but because the hacker who had accessed his files was so damn...arrogant! And, he had to admit, because the guy was good. Very good. Using all his skills, and 'borrowed' software developed for use by the FBI, Danny was still barely able to follow his tracks. But ultimately, it was that arrogance that was going to be his Achilles' heel. He had left just a little too much info on the net, and Danny was finally closing in on the guy.

He parked his 2002 BMW 325i in the apartment garage and took the elevator up to the 9th floor. He was running through the steps that he would take to nail the scumbag and wasn't really focusing much on what he was doing. If he had, he might have noticed a shadow appear behind him when he left the elevator and turned toward his apartment door. He might have heard footsteps, soft but insistent, trailing just behind him. He certainly wouldn't have fumbled with his keys after opening the door, hesitating just enough so that the footsteps could quickly close the gap between them.

When Danny woke up, he found himself lying on the floor. At first he couldn't understand what he was doing there or why everything seemed so... different. He tried to sit up, only then realizing he had a splitting headache. He reached for the spot that throbbed so violently and his hand came away wet with blood. As if in a dream he glanced up and saw... chaos. He stared blankly, not quite able to understand what had happened. It was all like looking through fog. But then he saw the scattered foam from sofa cushions torn to shreds, food from his refrigerator dumped unceremoniously in the sink and on the floor, CDs and DVDs, thumbdrives, cables – nothing had gone untouched. And then it finally dawned on his battered consciousness: someone had trashed his place and slugged him from behind! Was the person still in the apartment?!

A stabbing shard of fear cut through the fog. Danny turned his head to look into the bedroom – too quickly. The pain rushed back; he nearly blacked out. His breathing was ragged now, whether from fear or the pain he didn't know.

'*Gotta call 911,*' he thought woozily. '*Gotta call...*'

He managed to drag his cellphone from his pocket. He had trouble focusing his eyes on the tiny numbers, but finally managed to thumb the emergency call.

"911. What is your emergency?" an efficient female voice answered.

"Need an ambulance," Danny managed to mumble, his tongue fat and flailing. "Need…"

The phone dropped from his hand as his head slid slowly to the floor. Darkness flowed over him.

*****

When he opened his eyes he saw Anne's worried face staring down at him.

"Danny! Danny, you're in the hospital. Don't try to sit up. You've been injured," she explained, her voice soft but clearly upset.

"You took a good one to the back of the head," Brady James said just a second before his face leaned into view. "Hope they didn't break their sap."

Danny tried to smile but his mouth barely moved. *'Must have me drugged up,'* he thought. "Hope he broke his hand," he muttered.

"How are you doing?" Anne asked.

"I've felt better."

"I bet," Brady said. "Did you happen to get a look at them?"

Danny tried to shake his head but the pain throbbed intensely. "No. Didn't know anyone was there until I woke up and saw the mess."

"Yeh, according to the police report they pretty much tore the place apart."

"They were looking for info on the Wainwright hack, weren't they?"

Anne and Brady exchanged glances. "Most likely," James answered. "Unless there was some other project you were working on…"

"Nah. I usually don't take work home. But they didn't get much. I keep most of my data in the cloud, and it's all encrypted."

"Danny, I hate to ask you this while you're just coming around, but did you have any info lying around about Anne, or Derek, or me?" He tried to keep his tone level, but even he could hear a tinge of concern in his voice.

"No, no I don't think so. And even if I did, you were all coded."

"So they wouldn't be able to identify us?" Anne asked, the concern in her voice undisguised.

"Well, not from anything they found in my apartment. At least not without a lot of effort."

'But combined with what they already know about us, they'll almost certainly put two and two together,' Brady thought, but he kept his thoughts to himself.

"That's a relief, anyway."

"Worse thing was, I almost had them," Danny added, his voice a bit stronger. "I was zeroing in on the origin of the hack. Had pinned it down to Billings, and was on the verge of pinpointing the IP address. As soon as I get out of here…"

"You just worry about recuperating," Brady said, patting the young techie on his leg. "We can handle the hack for now."

"That's right!" Anne added. "Your job is just to get better. Don't even think about the jerks who hacked the Senator's computer."

"I think that's about enough for today," the voice of a nurse called out from the open doorway. "He needs to get some rest."

"We were just leaving," Brady answered. "You take care of yourself, Danny. No heroics. For the next few days you listen to what the doctors tell you, and you'll be back in the office in no time."

"Not the best motivation in the world," Danny deadpanned.

"That's right!" Anne agreed. "He'll be up and around and walking outside in this beautiful weather we've been having the last few days. Not slaving away in his office!"

"Whatever spins your hard-drive," Brady quipped, resulting in a well-deserved groan from the young computer manager.

"Let's go. You're only making him worse," Anne chided with a smile. "I'll try to be back to see you tomorrow," she added, leaning down and kissing the young man on the forehead.

"Thanks for coming by, guys," Danny said, and then he fell back into his pillows and closed his eyes.

Brady took Anne's arm and together they walked out past the waiting nurse.

"How's he doing?" Brady asked as soon as she shut the door behind them.

"He took a nasty blow," the nurse explained. "Lucky they didn't fracture his skull. As it is, he's got a severe concussion. We're keeping a close watch for any swelling of the brain."

"So far, so good?"

"Barring unforeseen circumstances, it looks like he should be well enough to go home in 2-3 days."

"Great. Thank you, nurse. And please keep an eye on him. He's a good kid.

"My pleasure."

Neither Anne nor Brady said much as they left the hospital, Brady because he didn't want to risk being overheard, and Anne because she was worried sick about her young friend. When they got in the car, however, Brady was all business.

"I'm going to ask Derek to find you a bodyguard for the next little bit," he said as soon as her car door slammed shut.

"What for?! I already have you."

Brady almost answered with one of his usual self-deprecating quips, but decided put-downs were better suited for beer-soaked outings with Derek or old newspaper buds.

"And you've definitely got the body I want to guard," he said instead with a lecherous grin he hoped would lighten the mood. "But these folks play hardball. My pen may be mightier than a sword, but I don't feel confident putting it up against a nine millimeter. Ok?"

"Do you really think they might come after us?"

'*Us.*' Despite living alone for years and liking it, he had to admit that right then he liked the sound of '*us*' even better, thank you very much. "They might. We still don't know for sure what happened to the Senator, but it definitely looks like Hoch and his friends might have been involved. I don't want to take any chances."

"Well, I suppose so. But how am I going to explain some big hulking guy hanging around me wherever I go?"

"I don't know – how do you do it now?"

She smiled in spite of herself.

"They all think you're writing a story about the Senator."

"And I might, when all this is done and finished."

"That will be soon, won't it?" she asked, and for the first time she sounded truly worried.

He didn't know what to tell her. So he did what he always did in that kind of situation. He lied.

"We're closing in on the bastards. That's why they went after Danny, I'm sure," he explained without much conviction. "With any luck, we may be able to take them down in just a few weeks." Without luck, it might be months or perhaps never, he thought, but he kept his mouth shut. Anne put her hand on his leg and smiled. The warmth he felt from reassuring her more than compensated for the chill he felt for lying to her. He only hoped it wasn't too much of a lie…

*****

Adam Hoch's face was a deep, dangerous purple.

"You stupid, STUPID kid!" he screamed at his grandson, who had just reported the messy confrontation that had occurred at the apartment of the State Department flunky. He thought his grandfather would be pleased at his initiative. He was wrong.

"Do you have any idea what you've done?!!" When no explanation was forthcoming, he plowed on, ignoring the shocked and slightly fearful look plastered on his grandson's face. "You've given them all the reason they need to keep on with their little investigation, and maybe even take it to the police! You've jeopardized the future of this country!"

Jeffrey had heard and seen his grandfather in this state of frenzy enough times that he knew to keep quiet. It would pass in a few hours or days. It always did. Hell, maybe the old buzzard would work himself into a heart attack or stroke, and he could start enjoying the money even sooner than he'd hoped. Then again, he was such a tough old s.o.b. that he'd probably live to be a hundred.

"Don't you EVER think before acting?!"

He looked up to see the white-haired billionaire staring at him with bloodshot, bulging eyes. He fought back an urge to slug the old man.

"I'm sorry, grandfather," he said with as much sincerity as he could muster. "It won't happen again."

"It better not," the elder Hoch said, his voice dropping to a cool rumble. "If you screw this up, I'll turn you over to our AR friends and they'll have your balls for dinner."

'Don't push it old man, or I'll have your head on a platter,' Jeffrey countered in his ongoing internal dialogue. A slight sneer worked its way unconsciously to his lips. He wiped it away as soon as he became aware it was there.

"What should we do now?" he asked instead, knowing that the fastest way to get his grandfather to drop his diatribe was to get him talking.

"'We' aren't going to do anything," Hoch snapped. "I am going to call some friends back in DC and have them watch James and his little friends. If it looks like they're getting too close, well, then we'll have to take some action."

Action. That's what Jeffrey was looking for. Enough of this tip-toeing around. It was clear to him that the old man was losing it. But he'd be gone soon enough. And then Jeffrey would be in charge, and things would be different.

*****

Derek knew that Brady was upset before he even said a word. Normally his friend was calm to the point of somnambulance. Today he was jumpy, distracted.

"Okay, so what's going on?" he asked as he sat down at the dining room table where James was already seated, drinking a cup of coffee and working on his third jelly doughnut. "A bad habit I picked up hanging out with cops," he'd explained once.

"This attack on Danny has me worried," he said, staring at the PI with that 'I'm really serious with this one' look he'd come to know so well over the years. "As long as they were just blowing smoke about us doing a story, I didn't really care. But this takes it to a whole new level. I think they're getting nervous, and nervous people do stupid things."

Derek agreed completely. In fact, he had planned to raise the subject if Brady had not. "So, what're you thinking? 24 hour guards?"

"For Anne, yes. For us, I think maybe you'd better start carrying that new gun you always talk about but never take out of the safe."

Derek had bought a Smith and Wesson .357 magnum a few months back, but other than taking it down to the range a few times to keep in practice, he'd never taken it out of the gun safe he kept hidden in the apartment. For one thing, even though it was a snubby, it still looked oversized in his small hands, and its weight was annoying after a few hours packing. But when he did snap off a few rounds, he appreciated the minimal recoil and substantial stopping power. A couple of .357s and even the biggest perp was going down.

"Are you sure that's necessary?" he asked. "The 9 millimeter usually gets the point across."

"You don't use a peashooter against an elephant, unless you want to find yourself floating in a river somewhere without your water wings."

"We don't know if that was Hoch, or even if it was murder."

"Since when do you believe in coincidences?"

Derek sighed. Of course, he didn't believe in coincidences, and he didn't believe Hoch was completely innocent, either. But carrying the .357?

"Yeh, all right," he finally conceded when he saw Brady's set jaw. "So that takes care of Anne and me. What are you going to do to stay safe? Or do you see yourself as some kind of invincible newspaper hero, like Clark Kent?"

Brady smiled. "I was thinking more like Iron Man."

"I don't think you'd fit in the suit," the PI said, patting his stomach. "All kidding aside, what's your plan? If they'd go after anyone, it'd be you."

"I've never fired a gun in my life, and I'm not going to start now. We can't afford a 24 hour guard following both Anne and me, so that's out. I'm just going to keep my eyes open and my fingers crossed."

"Yeh, and always look both ways before crossing the street and wear clean underwear. Sounds a bit…understated."

Brady shrugged. "Best I can do for now. Chesley knows what's going on, so at least we have that."

"Great. So he'll have a head start investigating your death. Pretty reassuring."

"Hey, I've always got you. Don't ever underestimate a pistol-packing pint-size PI."

"Your confidence is touching. At least program your cell for a one touch 911."

"Already there, my apprehensive friend. Don't worry, I've stayed alive this long, I'm not going to stop now."

"You better not. Hard to find somebody else stupid enough to watch all the Redskins games and provide free beer."

"Glad to be of service."

"Yeh. I bet. So what now? How do we get the evidence we need to lock those s.o.b's up?"

"As a matter of fact, I've got a plan," Brady said nonchalantly.

"Oh really? Going to share it?"

"Is there any more coffee?"

Muttering, the little man shuffled into the kitchen to fetch the pot.

*****

Simon Beddecker hadn't sounded happy when Brady spoke with him on the phone. More like nervous. Very nervous.

Now, as Brady rode up the elevator to the newsman's office, he debated how to approach the conversation. Should he finesse the subject, waiting for Simon to come clean? Or should he confront it head on? As the floor bell rang and the elevator doors slid open, he decided to play it by ear.

Beddecker didn't come out to greet him as he did the last time. The receptionist called to announce Brady's arrival, and a few minutes later a young, attractive secretary, or intern, appeared to show him back to the big man's office. Simon was seated behind his impressive desk, feigning real work just as they did for all the cut-aways on his news network profiles, and looked up as if caught unawares when the young woman accompanying Brady tapped on his office door.

"Brady, come in, come in!" he said with more volume and less sincerity than the occasion called for. "Have a seat. Hadn't expected to see you again so soon."

"Hadn't expected to be back so soon," James said, stalling while the intern closed the door behind her as she left.

"So, what can I do for you?"

"Remember when I was here last time, I asked about some calls you made to Senator Wainwright's office just before he died?"

"Yeh. And I told you we just played phone tag."

"Well now it appears that Wainwright's death might not be an accident."

"What's that have to do with me?"

Brady tried not to display any reaction. He'd expected at least a show of mock surprise when Simon learned that Wainwright might have been murdered. But he didn't even blink. '*He must be more uptight than I'd thought*,' Brady decided. '*Maybe a little push will put him over the edge.*'

"That's what I've come here to find out," he said distractedly, glancing through a notepad he'd pulled from his pocket. "Do you know Adam Hoch, by any chance?"

He looked up in time to catch the flash of fear reflected in the newscaster's eyes. "Hoch, the billionaire? Everybody knows him."

"Have you ever spoken with him?"

Beddecker looked like he might answer, but then caught himself. "Hey, what is this? What's Hoch have to do with anything?"

"I don't know. Was hoping you might tell me. He apparently made several calls to the Senator's office just before he died as well. Just a coincidence that both of you decided to call Wainwright repeatedly in the days before he died?"

"What else could it be? I mean, I'm certain that Hoch didn't know about my story, and I certainly have no idea what he might have wanted to talk to the Senator about."

"None? Not, say, the 2012 elections? And electronic voting machines?"

Beddecker gulped for air like a fish out of water.

"Voting machines? What about voting machines?"

Brady eyed him closely. He seemed genuinely confused.

"Are you telling me Hoch didn't tell you about the Ohio voting machines?"

"I don't know what you're talking about."

"This is no game, Simon. I don't know how you got yourself into this mess, but people will be going to prison over it."

"Prison?!" He held up his hands as if fending off an attack. "Hey, all he asked me to do was hook him up with Wainwright. I don't know anything about voting machines." Brady saw drips of sweat running down Simon's temples.

"And what were you going to get out of it?" Brady asked coolly.

The newscaster seemed to debate for a second before he sighed and shook his head dejectedly. "My own show," he said in a half-whisper. "And then the News Director's slot." He stared at his shoes for a long moment before looking up. "They were going to let me go!" he added, the anger in his voice raw and volatile. "After all these years, they said I was too old! Then Hoch called me out of the blue, and he knew all about it. He knew they were planning on bringing in those two bimbos to take my place. I don't know how he knew; maybe he was behind it. I didn't know and didn't care." The words flowed freely now. Brady had seen many a thug go through the same cathartic release. "All I knew was that Hoch could help me, and all I had to do was convince Wainwright to sit down and talk to him."

"Wouldn't the Senator be willing to do that anyway? I mean, Hoch *is* a billionaire."

"That's what I thought. I even told Hoch that. But he told me that the Senator wasn't returning his calls. He knew that I'd done a profile on Wainwright just a few months earlier and thought I could get through to him."

"What was so important that he needed to talk to Wainwright so urgently?"

"I have no idea."

"You didn't ask?" Brady had been a journalist long enough to know that the good ones, and Beddecker had been pretty good once upon a time, always asked.

"No, I didn't ask. I didn't want to know."

"So you knew something was fishy?"

Simon fidgeted. "I... Billionaires don't call me to make introductions. I knew something was...strange."

"So, did you make the introduction?"

"Yeh, I made it. I set up a meeting between the two of them."

"And when was that?"

"The meeting? April 11."

"Three days before he turned up dead."

"Yeh. Three days." His voice was low, wavering.

"Did you tell the cops about the meeting?"

"They said it was an accident. Why would I tell them about it?"

"Because you knew something wasn't right. Because you thought Hoch might have had something to do with it."

"I didn't say that!" the newscaster said with less vehemence than it deserved.

"You didn't have to. I've been interviewing crime witnesses for 30 years, Simon. I can tell when they're holding back. And you are."

"So you say." Peevish. Uncomfortable.

"So I say. You knew damn well that Hoch wouldn't be offering you your own show and the ND spot unless he wanted to keep you quiet. But you went along with it."

"And you wouldn't? How the hell did I know Wainwright would turn up dead?! I thought Hoch just wanted to buy his vote. Happens every day."

"And after his death?"

Simon stared blankly. "I was scared, James. I mean, Jesus, if they could get to a U.S. Senator, what would an old, beat-up newscaster mean to them? Nothing."

Brady was ready to jump all over him, to let him have it for letting Hoch and his flunkies get away with murder. But he saw Beddecker's fingers quiver, and he remembered how he felt when he'd heard that Danny'd been mugged. No, he couldn't pretend that he'd have done any different. They were both journalists, after all, not friggin' Marines.

"Yeh. Maybe I would be too," he said softly. "Have you heard any more from Hoch?"

"Not from him directly. But from some s.o.b. who works for him."

"Henson?"

Simon looked up, surprised. "You know him?"

"I know of him. Haven't had the privilege myself."

"Consider yourself lucky. Cold as my ex-wife's love taco. He called me a few days after Wainwright died. Told me, 'This is just between Mr. Hoch and yourself, right?' What was I going to say?"

What could he say? Not much if he wanted to keep his fancy new show and big corner office. Hell, if he wanted to stay alive.

"Did he threaten you?"

"Not in so many words. But it was pretty damn clear: 'keep your mouth shut or else.' So, I kept my mouth shut."

Brady couldn't argue the logic. "Anything else you can think of about that time? Anything Hoch might have said, or done?"

"Not that I can think of right off the top of my head. Hey, nobody needs to know about this, do they? About me, I mean."

His smile was crooked and tight-lipped.

"Not from me," Brady said. "And I'd appreciate the same consideration."

"You were never here," Beddecker said. Brady could hear the relief.

The two men exchanged pleasantries for a few minutes, but both knew it was pure gesture. Brady wanted to get moving, and Simon wanted him gone. In the minimum time it took to seem civilized, that's exactly what happened.

CHAPTER 18

"It's this weekend?" Derek asked when Brady raised the subject of a big Republican/AR pow-wow at lunch that afternoon.

"Monday, the 25th. I think we need to be there."

"October in Florida? Do I get bonus pay for braving hurricane season?"

"Sure. Make it double your daily rate."

The PI smiled. "Cool. Double nothing is...not so much, now that I think about it."

"And you're worth every penny."

Derek ignored the slam. "So what will we be doing down there – other than trying to keep from getting blown all to hell?"

"*We* won't be doing anything. I'll go down there myself. You stay up here and see that someone keeps an eye on Anne."

"I thought *we* needed to be there."

"The royal *we*. In other words, me. I'm going to see what Hoch and his people are up to, and how AR is represented. Maybe I'll find someone who knows what's going on and is willing to talk about it."

"More likely you'll find a .38 caliber slug between your shoulder blades. You aren't exactly Dick Tracy, you know."

"Thanks for the positive vibes. The way I look at it, I'm a known quantity so they are less likely to try to make me disappear."

"Wainwright was a known quantity too. For all the good it did him."

Brady notched an imaginary digit in the air. "Chalk one up for the little guy," he said. Then, turning more serious, he added, "I didn't say it was foolproof, but we need to get in Hoch's face if we want to break this open. Otherwise, it's just Wyman's word against the world, and I wouldn't be too confident that Wyman would still be around if Hoch found out he was talking to us."

"So you're the bait to get Hoch out in the open?"

"Something like that. Worried people make mistakes. We need to get Hoch worried."

"Well, you've succeeded in getting *me* worried. You're halfway there."

"I appreciate your concern, but unless you can think of another way of getting his attention, I'm going after Hoch."

"And me? What do you want me to do while you're chasing around Disneyland?"

"Disneyland is in California. Disneyworld is in Florida – Orlando."

"You know what I mean…"

"Yeh. Well, I think we need someone in Billings to keep an eye on Hoch's grandson. If we can't get the old man to play our game, maybe we can interest the kid."

"Any ideas how to go about that?"

Brady smiled. "That's why you make the big bucks."

"Great. Thanks for the insight. I'll arrange for someone to watch Anne and see if I can catch a plane out there tomorrow."

"Great. Call the agency if you can't find anything online."

"Will do. And Brady – be careful. I'm not fond of funerals."

"Better as guest than host."

"Better not at all."

*****

Derek felt only slightly more at home in Billings this time than last. The people still looked like something out of *Gunsmoke*, but at least he recognized some landmarks and knew his way around a bit. He rented another hand-control Fusion from Enterprise, but this time got the GPS and the XM radio. *'As long as I'm only getting expenses, I may as live it up,'* he decided as he clambered up into the seat and cruised over to the Old West Lodge.

Once ensconced in the rustic simplicity of the Lodge, he decided to contact Greg Eddler over at the Gazette to see if he could provide any leads on the Hoch kid. He dug out the reporter's home phone number from the scribbled note he'd stashed in his wallet, and stretched out on the queen size bed as he called. His feet didn't even reach the middle of the mattress, but he didn't notice, and wouldn't have cared if he had.

The phone rang four times before the voicemail picked up.

"This is Greg. Leave a message after the tone and I'll get back to you."

"Hey Greg, it's your ol' buddy Derek from DC," the PI said glibly. "Out here looking for a good time, and thought you were just the guy to show me around. I'm at the Old West Lodge again – glutton for punishment. Room 222. Give me a call." He thought it wiser to keep the details of his visit for a face to face discussion. No telling if Eddler's phone was tapped and no need to take the chance.

He considered taking a ride over by Hoch's headquarters, but he knew he wouldn't get closer than the guarded entry gate, so kicked off his shoes and flipped on the TV. As he grazed the 186 channels he was struck by how many fishing, hunting and even farming shows populated the local cable. Back in DC, he'd be lucky, if that's what you'd call it, to bump into a couple such programs in a full day of scanning. Here, it seemed like you could watch some high school dropout wielding a $500 fly rod or a thousand dollar shotgun land a trout or blast a deer every 15 minutes or so. He wondered how many times someone could watch such drivel before they headed for the local bar to rub elbows with other NRA pervs who reveled in secondhand images of dead and dying animals. *Maybe I'll start my own cable station,'* he thought as he popped a cool one and guzzled half the bottle. *'Nothing but the moment of the kill. The blast of the gun, the splatter of blood – maybe the NRA would even sponsor it. Call the show, 'Dead and Deader', or something equally attractive. Maybe have a spinoff for kids, 'Blast Bambi'.'* He smiled to himself and finished the rest of the bottle in one swig. He found a rerun of James Garner in 'Rockford Files' and settled back to await the reporter's call.

It was a little more than two hours later when a soft knock sounded at his door. "About time," he muttered as he rolled off the bed, avoiding the small pile of beer bottles that had accumulated on the floor below him.

"Coming, coming," he growled when the knock repeated. "Gave the butler the afternoon off."

He was still smiling when he pulled open the door and a black gloved fist crashed into his face, knocking him backwards like a bowling pin. Before he could even think to react, a pointy-toed leather boot implanted itself in his ribs, followed by a half-dozen equally vicious stomps and kicks. He could hear the grunts of effort his attacker made as he threw his full weight behind each swing of his leg. Derek struggled to suck in a breath as the blows suddenly stopped. A boot rested on the side of his head, pinning him to the floor.

"Welcome to Billings," a young, snide voice announced. "Now get the hell out of town or the next time we'll do some serious damage. Understand?"

Derek tried to move his mouth, but all that emerged was a feeble groan.

"I asked if you understand!" the voice shouted, and the pressure from the boot sent pain searing through his skull.

"Yeh, yeh, I undahstahn.." the PI managed to mumble.

"Too bad. I always wanted to do some bowling with a little half-pint like you. But...I guess kickball will have to do."

Almost before the words came out of his mouth the same pointy toe imbedded itself in Derek's groin. The rest was blackness.

*****

When the midget finally opened his eyes, the room was pitch dark except for the ghostly light of the TV. An overweight good ol' boy was getting ready to blast an elk, or was it a caribou? Looking up at the TV with one side of his face pasted to the carpeting, Derek wasn't sure.

He quickly took stock of his injuries, wiggling his feet and moving his arms to ensure they were still in one piece. A deep breath demonstrated that the kicks to his ribs had left him bruised but without anything obviously broken. He winced as he rolled gently onto his back. He reached up to his swollen lip and found coagulated blood running from his nose down his chin.

'*Some bastard's gonna pay for this,*' he pledged as he pushed himself up to his elbows.

As he did, a sheet of paper slid off his stomach where it had been tucked into his pants. He picked it up and, squinting, read the crudely lettered note:

'There's a United flight leaving for DC tomorrow morning at 8:25. Be on it.'

His immediate reaction was to wad the paper into a tight ball and toss it across the room. Then he realized he might be able to get some prints off the paper, or even identify the writing sample.

"Goddamn it," he muttered as he struggled to stand. It felt like he'd been run over by a truck – probably a pickup with a gun rack in that neck of the woods. As he tried to walk, the two bowling balls between his legs screamed bloody murder.

"When I get ahold of those assholes…" Derek threatened through clenched teeth. But at the moment it was all he could manage to put one foot in front of the other. He considered falling back down on all fours and crawling, but refused to give his attackers the satisfaction – even though they weren't there and would never know. By the time he got over to where the crumpled note lay on the kitchenette linoleum, he was sweating. He took a deep breath, bent down, and grabbed the paper as if snatching hot chestnuts from a campfire. His head spun slightly as he stood back up. He closed his eyes, took a deep breath, and stumbled the three feet to where he could collapse on his bed.

"They're gonna wish they were never born…"

*****

As Derek struggled to drag his carry-on to the boarding gate of United flight 6115, he glanced surreptitiously from side to side trying to identify anyone who might be watching him. He assumed that his *friends* would want to make sure he followed the advice they'd given him the night before. He saw the usual Western types with their $200 cowboy hats and $300 boots, their women bedecked with enough turquoise to sink a Spanish galleon. But no one stood out as a Hoch operative. Maybe they were good. Maybe they were so sure he'd leave with his tail tucked between his legs that they didn't even bother to send anyone. But he doubted it. Hoch's people had already made a few mistakes. He didn't think the old man would allow many more.

He saw most every eye in the waiting area slide his way, some furtively, some with brazen disregard for human decency. On the other hand, the tiny PI realized he must cut quite a figure – disheveled, with a swollen lip, one black eye, and limping like a lame pony that needed to be put down. Or that's what he hoped they were thinking. The more convinced they were of his decrepitude, the less likely they were to think him capable of deceiving them. But he was utterly capable, as he would soon demonstrate.

The smile on the gate attendant fizzled to a look of sincere professional concern as he presented his boarding pass.

"Car accident?" she asked with about as much real interest as if he'd had a hangnail.

"Woman trouble," he lied. "Mixed up my date nights."

"You must be one heck of a loverboy to get two women that ticked off at you."

"Why don't you have dinner with me next time I'm in town, and maybe you'll find out."

People behind Derek in line tittered. The gate attendant blushed a bright red.

"Not sure my husband would appreciate it much," she said with a forced smile.

"Would he have to know?"

The woman shook her head. "Now I can see why those women were upset."

"You know what they say about good things in small packages…"

"Hey, if you two'd like to be alone, do you think you could do it somewhere else so we can get on the damn plane!" someone shouted from the back of the line.

"Just hold your horses," the attendant called back, her expression a mix of embarrassment and irritation. "The plane won't be leaving without you." Turning to Derek she added, "I think you'd best be getting on board, sir."

"As you say, darling. But you don't know what you'll be missing…"

"I guess I'll just have to always wonder," she said with a pleased grin as she tore the end off his boarding pass. "Have a good flight."

"Thank you," the PI replied, his smile seemingly bigger than his bruised face.

Derek waddled his way down the jetway until he reached the last turn in the passageway, just a few feet from the service door at the entrance to the plane. There he opened his small carry-on suitcase and started sifting through its meager contents, as if trying to find something before boarding the jet. He took his time with the sorting, allowing the other passengers to pass him by. He smiled at their occasional snide remarks, keeping his razor-tongued responses to himself. When he saw that no one else was coming down the jetway, he waited until the flight attendant was distracted and then slipped quickly out the service door to the metal stairway below. With all the baggage loaders busy closing up the bins on the other side of the plane, the diminutive PI scampered down the stairs, walked nonchalantly to the next jetway, climbed up the companion stairway, and slipped into the empty walkway. With his head on a swivel to make sure no one had noticed, he made his way back to the terminal and tucked himself behind an unused boarding gate departures sign. He pulled out his I-phone and spent the next 15 minutes blissfully surfing the Net. When he finally heard the airline people pack-up and leave his original gate just next door, he made his way to a side exit, keeping to the edges of the terminal and away from prying eyes. Once outside, he grabbed a cab and had them take him to the Hampton Inn off of I-90, where he registered as Tulu S. LaTrec. The 20-something desk clerk didn't get it.

As soon as he got to his room and closed the door he called the Gazette. Eddler wasn't in. Hadn't been 'for a few days', according to the indignant young lady who answered the phone on the 27th ring. She had no idea where he was or when he'd be back. Derek assumed the worst. He called several no-name car rental companies until he found one that would rent him a hand-control junker for cash. He didn't really think Hoch's minions would be scanning his credit card purchases, but decided to err on the side of survival.

After a short rest and a half-dozen Advils to dull the pain, he took an elevator down to the ground floor. He didn't exit through the lobby, but made his way down a seemingly endless hallway to the parking lot where he'd left the wreck. He scanned the tastefully landscaped patch of asphalt just to be sure no one was surveiling him. When he was confident no one was watching, he sidled up to the vintage Olds, stacked two phone books behind the wheel of the massive black beauty, and climbed up into position to start 'er up. With a cloud of smoke and the growl of an asthmatic dragon, the engine roared to life.

'Nothing like the hum of a V8,' he thought as he dropped the tranny into Drive.

Derek headed northwest up Laurel to 27th from the Hampton towards an address he'd identified back in DC. He was still aching from head to toe, but somehow the thought of screwing with Hoch's grandson made the whole day seem just a little brighter. He headed out Rimrock Rd and found himself in the kind of yuppie-class townhouse village he was accustomed to seeing in northern Virginia. Too many coffee shops; too many dry cleaners. He had expected to find Jeffrey living in one of the newer brick and granite developments, and had been somewhat surprised when he'd gone on Google Earth and found himself virtually surveying a relatively modest one story home just beyond the townhouses. Now he parked his classic Olds across the street and a few hundred yards past the kid's house, close enough to watch who came in and out, but hopefully far enough to not be 'made'.

He plugged his ear buds into the IPod and sat back to listen to some classical music while he waited - Rachmaninov's Second Piano Concerto was first up on his play list. He liked listening to classical music when he was staking out a 'person of interest', particularly something with energy and complexity. He found that it kept him focused (or "awake" as Brady would put it), while not involving him so deeply that he missed anything going on. He still remembered an incident when he was younger and had been rocking out to "Magic Bus" by the Who, singing along at the top of his lungs, when the perp snuck out the back door. He'd attacked Derek's client that night, his ex-girlfriend, putting her in the hospital. Derek switched to classical that very day and had never looked back.

Most PIs, and just about every cop he'd ever met, hated stakeouts. Surveillance was usually handed out to cops as punishment. It was time-consuming, tedious, and just plain boring. Worst of all, you could rarely break a case through a stakeout, but you could sure as hell blow one. No upside and loads of down. Derek, on the other hand, saw this as an opportunity to get back at Hoch and his people for the beating he'd received, and for Danny, and Wainwright, for that matter. Even the smallest contribution to stopping Hoch, and perhaps even putting him – or at least some of his flunkies – in jail made the long hours of waiting all worthwhile. He shouldn't have screwed with the little guy. He'd have to be taught a lesson.

It was just a shade before noon when a big, black SUV backed into the driveway of the kid's place and the garage door flipped up.

Derek stopped the music and sat up attentively. Just a couple of minutes later Hoch's grandson came out of the house and jumped casually into the back seat of the car. The SUV pulled out into the street, and started off in Derek's direction. The PI ducked down behind the steering wheel as the car approached and sped past. *'I'd like to see Shaq get down like this,'* he gloated as the SUV disappeared from his side mirror. He waited for five minutes before driving up to the house next to the kid's place and parking at the curb. He reached into the glove box and pulled out a pad of paper and some restaurant takeout menus he'd picked up at the hotel. Always paid to look like you were doing something worthwhile when you're casing a place, he thought. Especially when you're three feet tall and stick out like a sore Thumbelina.

The PI strolled up the driveway as if he hadn't a care in the world, except, of course, the aches, pains and bruises from the beating he'd received the day before. He rang the doorbell, just to be sure there wasn't anyone still in the house. After a few seconds he knocked. When no one answered, he slipped a menu under the door and walked around the side of the house as if he knew what he was doing. He did, but it wasn't what any of the neighbors might think.

He'd already checked the place out online, and so knew that a wall of tall shrubbery surrounded the yard, giving him all the privacy he could want. He glanced in through the open blinds in several of the back windows, checking once again that no one was home. When he was convinced as he could be that he was alone, he made straight for the back door. He reached into an inside jacket pocket and pulled out a small, zippered leather case. He examined his picks and chose the pick and tension wrench he thought would do the trick on the typical Yale throw-bolt that secured the back door. Back in DC he'd use his electric pick for a straightforward job like this one, but he hadn't wanted to raise any questions passing through security at the airport, so had brought just the hand picks.

Manipulating the pick and wrench like the old B&E guy he was, he had the door open inside of a minute.

'Getting old,' he thought as he put the tools away in their case. *'Time was, I could crack a sucker lock like this in 15 seconds.'*

He opened the door slowly, listening not only for any housemates who might have been in the shower or listening to headphones when he rang and knocked, but any dogs whose bite might be worse than their bark. All was quiet. He closed the door behind him and moved silently through the kitchen and into the living room. He scanned the top corners of the walls for motion sensors, but saw none. In fact, the house was not much more lavish inside than out. Except for a 50 inch TV, a realtor would call it underfurnished. Until the PI opened the door to what was undoubtedly the computer room, that is. The place was packed with computer equipment, including scanners, faxes, copy machines, even four stacked 32" LCD monitors. And a bunch of stuff Derek couldn't even identify.

'This guy is a classic geek,' he thought. *'No concern for anything other than his computer.'*

Derek looked through papers scattered on the massive glass and chrome workspace, but saw nothing that would help with his investigation. He unzipped his jacket and pulled out a tiny netbook that Danny had modified just for this visit. He put it on the desk and went around to the back of Jeffrey's desktop, where he quickly unscrewed the side panel and pulled out the two hard drives. He connected them to one of the adapters Danny had provided and booted the netbook. He wasn't enough of a geek himself to open the kid's files, or probably even access them. But Danny had a neat little program on the netbook that his friends in Langley had provided. Within less than five minutes he had copied the drives onto a 2-Terabyte thumb-drive.

'The kid would have a goddamn bird,' Derek thought with a smile as he disconnected the patch cable and remounted the drives in the desktop. Back home in DC, Danny could take his time analyzing the info. And if he couldn't access it, he damn well knew someone who could. They could only hope that the arrogance the grandson had

shown when he accessed Wainwright's files carried over to his home computer.

While the drives were copying, Derek swept the rest of the house looking for wall or floor safes, fireboxes, anything that might hold additional info. He didn't find a thing of interest. Either the kid was much better at hiding his stuff than the PI figured, or he was stupid enough to keep everything on his computer. If that were the case, this whole damn trip might actually turn out to be worth the effort.

Derek was just finishing straightening up the kid's computer room so that no one would ever know he'd been there, when he heard a car pull up in the driveway.

"Damn!" the little guy spit when he peeked out the window and saw the black SUV in the driveway.

Tucking all his equipment back into his jacket, he scampered through the house and back out the back door just as he heard the lock open in front. He closed the door as softly as he could, and tip-toed back around the side of the house to where the SUV was parked.

'Manna from heaven,' he thought as he realized that no one was waiting inside the car. If there had been someone there, he would've had to wait for them to leave before he could make his getaway. And better yet, this gave him an opportunity he'd been wondering how to create. He pulled a tiny, quarter-sized device from his pocket, and crawling low below the house windows made his way to the parked SUV. He tucked the device up under the bumper, where its self-adhesive bonded the GPS tracker to the body of the vehicle. He had just crawled back to a hiding place behind some shrubs a few feet from the house when the front door opened and a familiar large black man came hurrying out. Tommy jumped into the car without so much as a glance at his surroundings and gunned it out of the driveway. Derek waited for several minutes to be sure the SUV wasn't coming back. Then he walked down the center of the driveway, 'reviewing' non-existent notes on his pad and whistling a merry tune.

'*They don't know who they're dealing with,*' he thought, '*but they will soon.*' And his smile broadened.

*****

As soon as Derek got into the Olds he opened the glove compartment and pulled out a small LCD screen. Connecting it to the lighter socket by the attached black plastic adapter, he slid a rocker switch and turned on the GPS tracker. The reassuring beep of the tracking device was soon matched by an overlay of greater Billings, with a blinking dot to identify the location of the SUV.

"Got 'em," he said to himself, and with a mighty roar and a cloud of swirling gray exhaust he set off in pursuit.

Within minutes it was clear that Tommy was headed to Hoch's headquarters. Knowing he'd find it difficult if not impossible to get inside the compound, the PI instead drove straight to the nearest FedEx location and overnighted the thumb drive with the two ghosted hard drives to Brady. They had discussed downloading the info and sending it electronically, but had decided that FedEx was safer. If he had somehow screwed up the data during transmission, he'd have to break into the house again. Getting in and out the first time was a testament to his skill and preparation, and still he'd almost been caught; the second time would require more luck than he was willing to risk.

As soon as the drive was on its way, Derek cruised over to the last known address for the newspaper reporter, Eddler. It was a twenty-something year old apartment building, brick and concrete, five floors, probably dating from the 70's. He knocked on Eddler's door but no one answered. Checking the mailboxes, he found the manager's apartment number. An elderly man in his late 70's answered the door.

"May I help you?" he asked.

"Perhaps. I was looking for an old friend, Greg Eddler?"

Derek noticed a narrowing of the manager's eyes. "Haven't seen him for several weeks," the manager said tight-lipped.

"Don't suppose you have a forwarding address or phone number."

"Don't think so. But hang on a second." He disappeared into his apartment. A minute or two later he reappeared holding an envelope.

"What was your name again?" he asked Derek.

"Don't think I gave it. But it's DiLaurain, Derek DiLaurain."

The manager looked at the envelope in his hand and then turned it over to the PI.

"Think this is for you. Greg asked me to give it to you if you showed up looking for him."

"Thanks. Appreciate it."

"No problem. Have a good one."

"Yeh, you too."

Derek felt the old man watching him as he walked away. He resisted opening the envelope until he was safely in his locked car. Inside were two pieces of paper.

'Derek,' a handwritten note read, 'If you're reading this it means you've come back to Billings looking for me but can't find me. That's a good thing. In the week after you left I received three threatening calls and the note I've included for you to take a look at. I decided that I needed a vacation and have left town – for parts unknown, as they'd say around here. Please don't try to find me. When I think the coast is clear I'll get in touch with you. Good luck, and stay safe!'

The exclamation point drove home the warning.

'Couldn't have gotten this to me yesterday,' the PI complained as he opened the second piece of paper.

'We don't like traitors in Billings!' screamed familiar block letters. 'Your time is up!' The last line was underlined three times and a stick figure of a man hanging from a noose accompanied it. There was no doubt in Derek's mind that Hoch's people were responsible. He felt a twinge of guilt for endangering the reporter, but was relieved that the kid had chosen the smart route – out of town.

He put both notes back in the envelope and slipped it inside his jacket. If they needed proof, they could analyze the writing and try to pull some DNA from the licked envelope. But he was pretty much positive he knew who'd written the note, as well as who'd planted his boot firmly in Derek's balls. *'I'm gonna get that little s.o.b. Jeffrey,'* he thought as he pulled away from the apartment building. *'One way or the other.'*

*****

With the GPS tracker showing the way, Derek spent the next two days following the Hoch SUV all over Billings. It was a typical tail: the PI spent the vast majority of his time listening to music and reading e-books while the grandson did whatever techies did, and then scrambled to follow the SUV at a safe, non-detectable distance during the few times a day when it moved from the Hoch building. It wasn't a total waste, however. He learned that Jeffrey had a fondness for pizza, draft beer, and a long-legged blond pro named Nina. He also learned that the nerd spent 90 per cent of his time locked-up in the Hoch headquarters. Tommy ran errands during the day, but with the dark tinted windows Derek couldn't be sure that Jeffrey wasn't inside and so he had to follow him – to the dry cleaners, to the gas station, to the grocery store… pretty much the full spectrum of tedious modern day drudge activity.

He had just about decided that his continued stay in Billings was shaping up to be something of a boondoggle, when a call came through on his cellphone just after noon on the second day. As he had agreed with Brady before leaving DC, Derek went straight to a payphone and called his friend, who answered on his new pay-as-you-go cell.

"How's our little cowboy doing out there in the wild, wild west?" Brady teased when he recognized the familiar voice.

"If I never see another cowboy hat or hear the word 'pardner' again as long as I live, it'll be too soon. What's up?"

"Danny's friends in Langley accessed the ghosted hard drives. They couldn't see everything, but enough to indicate that Ohio wasn't the only place that Hoch was up to no good. Florida and Missouri were the proving ground for his plans. He rigged the vote in a half-dozen key districts in those two primaries. Both use the same type of electronic voting machines as Ohio."

"What's the point?" Derek asked. "A half-dozen districts out of what, a couple of thousand nationwide? AR will never get enough votes to win the Presidency, with or without those states. You know that."

"They never intended to run a Presidential candidate, not in the end game. Thanks to the primaries that Hoch fixed, Ned Blackburn had enough conservative support to make him a king-maker at the convention in Tampa. He supported Andrews under the radar. That was their goal all along. He's not going to run for President, he's going to accept the Republican VP nomination. At least, that's what I surmise from what they've been able to dig out of those drives."

"And what about Van der Meer? Is he just going to go along with all this?"

"Don't know the arrangement, but I'm betting he was always just window dressing. Probably going to get a Cabinet position, maybe just cash."

"Jesus Christ. And I thought this business was dirty. Won't the AR faithful scream bloody murder?"

"Not if the Republicans promise them key points from their platform."

"But even so," the PI added, "why would Blackburn accept the slot? I mean, being VP is like being first runner-up in the Miss America pageant. It's a great honor better left to someone else."

Brady chuckled. "Good point. There isn't anything in Jeffrey's data that tells us the answer to that one. But it's clear from Hoch's actions up til now that he thinks it's important enough to risk his entire empire, even to kill for. He's got something up his sleeve."

"So don't we have enough now to go to the FBI, or somewhere?"

"Unfortunately, Jeffrey was either too smart, or too lucky to put it all in black and white. There's still a large amount of data that's encrypted. The Langley crowd is working on it, but they aren't going to invest a great deal of time in something that might prove to be a wild goose chase."

"And you think you're going to find enough hard facts in Tampa to change their minds?"

"I think I'd better."

CHAPTER 19

Tampa in October. About as comfortable as Siberia in April.

Brady stepped out of the Tampa Airport terminal and was welcomed by a wall of humidity that hit him flush in the face like a steaming sponge.

'Always great to be back in Florida,' James lamented as he wiped his face with a handkerchief and waved for a cab to move up to where he was already sweating profusely.

The cab drove east on US 275 before exiting on S. Florida Ave. In minutes he was unpacking his carry-on at the Embassy Suites just a couple of blocks from the Convention Center. Thanks to his old buddy Jimmy Ogden at the Post he'd managed to secure press credentials for the convention. He just hoped no one would ask what a retired crime reporter was doing at a political lovefest.

"More of a fit than you might think," he was tempted to answer.

He walked over to the convention center to get his bearings and, with any luck, talk to a few reporters already on the scene. He got in line with a half-dozen other early arrivers and waited to receive his credentials. He made small talk with a reporter from the LA Times who stood just in front of him in the line, but learned nothing that he couldn't have read in the Times itself. The Times guy didn't even mention AR until Brady raised the subject.

"So do you think AR will drain off enough votes from the conservative side of the GOP that they'll guarantee a Democratic victory?" he'd asked innocently.

"Could happen," the Times guy said convincingly. Brady loved the way reporters at the big papers, the networks, and now even at internet blogs, assumed the role of all-knowing authority even if they barely knew which way was up. "From what we've learned, however, the vote counters for Van der Meer are convinced that he can bring enough of the right wingers back into his camp that they'll give up on the idea of putting forward a candidate with AR and will back the Grand Ol' Party instead."

"Do you really think that's a possibility? I mean, AR has gone to a lot of trouble to establish itself as a legitimate third party…"

The Times guy smiled. "If they can win a few Congressional seats and maybe even one on the Senate side, they'll breathe a sigh of relief and declare victory. Most of the AR honchos are already looking ahead to 2016. This is just to lay the groundwork."

"I don't remember hearing that from any of their front men."

The Times guy barely resisted rolling his eyes. *'Must think I'm a complete idiot,'* Brady thought with a suppressed smile.

"Not publicly. That'd undercut their bargaining power. They still want to get some of their key planks into the GOP platform. But you watch, as soon as the Republicans promise AR that they'll include some of their key demands, they'll fall into line behind the GOP ticket."

"Pretty slick. Anybody on the AR side that would confirm that strategy, even if not for attribution?"

"I doubt it. But you could talk to Roger Goodman. He's the AR National Director."

"Yeh, I've heard the name," Brady said without a hint of sarcasm. "Thanks."

"Good luck. Hope to see your byline somewhere. Who did you say you're writing for?"

"I didn't," Brady said, dramatically lifting his picture ID, "but it's the Post."

"The *Washington* Post?" the Times guy asked incredulously.

"Is there any other?" Brady said as he turned to walk away. "Have a good convention."

He left the Times guy standing in the middle of the floor looking completely confounded.

From the sign-in line Brady headed to the press room, where he made the rounds looking for old acquaintances he could tap for any insights or contacts that might get him into the AR inner circle. He was appalled to realize that 90 per cent of the working journalists were young enough to be his son – maybe even his grandson. But he did bump into an old buddy who had been the New York Times guy in DC for 20 years. He had done a recent interview with Ned Blackburn, and gave Brady the contact numbers for his handlers.

Feeling that he'd made a pretty good start, James decided to go back up to his room and rest for an hour or two, until more of the principals (or at least their contacts) checked in. The door to the elevator was just closing when a commotion erupted at the front door. Brady stuck out his foot to stop the sliding door.

A large black man pushed a handful of gawkers back from the doorway, allowing a small group of self-important dignitaries to stride into the lobby with barely a look at the autograph seekers and photo takers. Brady recognized Adam Hoch immediately, walking side by side with a middle-aged man who might have been Roger Goodman. Trailing behind was a slick, tough-looking guy who from Derek's description was almost certainly Earl Henson, schmoozing with media and bystanders alike. For some reason he couldn't quite identify, Brady drew back instinctively from the elevator door and let the car resume its rise. He knew that none of the men close to Hoch had ever met him, but he didn't want to chance an unexpected meeting so early in his visit. He knew that they would eventually find out he was there, but a day or two of incognito research and interviewing would go a long way toward getting him the information he hoped to uncover to shut down Hoch's little plot.

Once upstairs he checked his phone for messages. He recognized Derek's number before he heard the voice.

"Brady. Hope you got down there ok. I'm sticking to the kid like stink to a wild pig, but so far, nothing of any importance since the drives. But watch out for those s.o.b's. The big man's driver, the black guy I told you about, flew down to Tampa this morning. He might already be there. I'm not sure why the kid is still up here, unless maybe he's holding the fort and won't be going, but I'll keep an eye on him as long as he's here. Give me a call when you get the time."

James considered returning the call but decided against it. He didn't really have much to share at this point. And he wanted to get to Ned Blackburn, the AR Presidential candidate, before Hoch could cut him off from the AR people. He called the presumed candidate's chief of staff and received a remarkably warm reception. They agreed on an interview at 4 pm that afternoon in the AR suite at the Hilton, just a short cab ride away. Brady spent the intervening time online, researching Blackburn's background and strategizing his approach to the questioning.

At 3:45 he pulled on an old herringbone sports jacket and made his way down to the lobby. He hesitated a moment in the elevator, quickly scanning the area in front of the check-in desk to be sure none of Hoch's people were loitering where they might see him leave. When he was reasonably confident they were not to be found, he walked out the front door and down the sidewalk toward the Hilton.

He arrived at the AR suite a few minutes before 4. Andrew Whiting, Blackburn's COS, met him at the door.

"Mr. James?" he asked, holding out his hand with a broad, welcoming smile.

"It is. Mr. Whiting, I presume?"

"Sounds like we should be meeting at Victoria Falls," Whiting joked. Brady smiled. He liked people who could pull off extremely arcane references without cue cards. He was starting to think the country would be much better off if the political handlers ran for office instead of the candidates.

"It's a jungle out there," Brady continued along the same lines.

"Not much better in Tampa this week. But we'll try to treat you gently. And may we expect the same from you?"

Brady held both hands in the air and turned them back and forth for inspection. "Nothing up my sleeve," he said.

From inside the suite a deep, commanding voice responded. "A journalist with nothing up his sleeve? I've got to see this."

Brady peered around the staffer to see a familiar face: Ned Blackburn - billionaire industrialist, advocate of unfettered capitalism, AR darling, and soon to be Republican VP nominee, if Hoch's machinations were successful. He motioned from a sofa, where he looked to be reviewing some notes, for Brady to come in.

"Come on in, Mr. James. I don't bite, despite what our friends on the Liberal side of the divide might say."

"You're in luck – he's in a good mood," Whiting whispered as Brady stepped past him.

"What, no pat-down, wand sweep or cavity probe?" Brady joked as he walked toward Blackburn with hand extended.

"We in AR believe in protecting civil liberties, Mr. James. And besides, I'm not an official candidate just yet so I don't have Secret Service protection. But don't be mistaken, my guys have their eyes on you. Any wrong move and…"

"Poof – I turn into a pumpkin?"

"Something like that," the billionaire said agreeably as he shook Brady's hand. His grip was strong, confident, without overdoing it.

"Can I get you anything – water, juice, or since you're a journalist, perhaps a whiskey?"

"Stereotypes die hard," Brady said. "Make it a beer."

"Beer it is. Jackie, could you get Mr. James a beer please?"

As his attractive black assistant made her way to the fridge to fish out a beer, Brady studied the AR candidate-in-waiting. If Hollywood was going to typecast a billionaire conservative, Blackburn would be it: close-cropped silver hair, blue eyes, the kind of manly man that women sigh over. Brady glanced at his own reflection in the window and sighed himself. *'Life is not fair,'* he mused.

"Have a seat, have a seat," Blackburn directed, patting the sofa next to him to ensure that Brady knew he wouldn't be invading his space.

"Mind if I record our little chat?" he asked as he pulled his recorder from his pocket.

"Of course not! Open and above board – that's our motto and our modus operandi."

"And you're running for office?" Brady quipped.

Blackburn chuckled. "Always was a bit of a maverick – if I may use that word without paying royalties…"

"I think it's public domain this campaign. Anyway, just for the record, how about a quick bio – where born, when, what colleges, how'd you make all that money…?" Brady already knew all that, but he wanted to get the interview rolling on a neutral footing.

"You've only got 30 minutes," the candidate warned, and Brady could tell he was only half-joking.

"You can be brief."

He smiled. "Ok. Born in a little town in eastern Oklahoma named Stilwell – closer to Fayetteville than Tulsa. 1948. One of the first of the Baby Boomers. Grew up there. My Dad was a driller, my Mom stayed at home until we were all grown and gone. Went to OSU, was a fair to middling student, graduated in 1970 with a degree in economics. Was all set to go to grad school to get my MBA when a friend offered me a partnership in a wildcat operation he was starting-up with his dad. They were both hands-on, roughneck engineer types, and they wanted someone to look after the business side. I figured, what the heck, if the wells come up dry I can always go to grad school then. They didn't, and I never went back."

"This friend, that was Jerry Kelly?"

"Ah, so you already know my story."

"I only know what I've read. And we both know that you can't trust everything you read, right?"

"You said it, not me."

"But you were thinking it. Anyway, so you got into the oil biz, and then in…" Brady glanced at the few notes he'd jotted on his notepad, "1974 you bought out the Kellys. Then what?" Brady always wanted the person he was interviewing to think he knew more than he did. A few choice tidbits of info usually did the trick.

"Then I was lucky enough to buy-up some government leases that turned out to be worth more than the sweat we put into them, and then we bought out a few of our competitors, diversified a bit, and here we are."

"And what got you into politics?"

Blackburn took a deep breath. "This nation is at war," he began, his expression suddenly dead serious. "A war between the people who understand that the country has gotten to where it is due to hard work by people who weren't afraid to take chances, and the people who think that 9-5 is a full day's work and taking a chance means playing a slot machine in Vegas. Now don't get me wrong. I'm not saying that the federal government shouldn't help out people who have a real need for help: people with severe handicaps, people who've run into a tornado, or hurricane, or earthquake or fire. And the government is the best vehicle for providing national defense. But beyond that, each person should take responsibility for him, or her-self, and for their family. And anything else we need as a community should come from the states.

"As you well know, Mr. James, this philosophy is not held by every citizen of this great country. There are those who think that all the money that the government spends comes from the welfare fairy, and that the government should be responsible for wiping our collective butts. I do not subscribe to that way of thinking. I think that way of thinking will eventually destroy our nation. In fact, it has already begun to do so. Someone needs to lead us back to the path of exceptionalism. Someone needs to have the courage to buck 80 years of decay otherwise known as the welfare state. I didn't see anyone doing much more than talking about our problems, so I decided to find some people who think like I do and take back this country. And that's why I'm in politics."

It was all Brady could do to not stand and applaud. *This guy is good.*

"A great story. I'm impressed," he said.

"In spite of yourself. Right?"

"I'm a journalist, Mr. Blackburn. Impartial. Just the facts."

"Mr. James, do I look simple? You're a human being, and your personal beliefs and philosophies leach into your writing, just as mine do."

"Point taken."

"Thank you for at least admitting it. Many of your colleagues do not. You know, we conservatives are portrayed as unthinking ideologues in the vast majority of media outlets in this country. And there's a reason for that."

'Because you are?' Brady thought, but held his tongue.

"Except for Rush and a couple of the guys at Fox, almost all you guys lean left. Am I wrong?"

"If you feel that way, why am I here? Why did you grant me this interview?"

The AR candidate leaned forward, no trace of levity in his expression. *"Keep your friends close, but keep your enemies closer.* Ever hear that one?"

"I think I got a fortune cookie once with that advice," Brady joked, but Blackburn wasn't laughing. Brady knew he had to bring the relationship back to neutral quickly or the interview would soon be over. "I'm not your enemy, Mr. Blackburn, but I'm not your friend either. I'm just trying to give the electorate enough information to make an informed decision. You're not opposed to that, are you?"

The stern expression on Blackburn's face slowly softened into a near-smile. "You've been doing this for a long time, haven't you?"

Brady had to admit that this guy was on the ball. He'd seen through his strategy at once. "Over thirty years," he answered.

"I thought so. And to answer your question, no, I'm not opposed to providing balanced, complete information to the voting public. In fact, I applaud you for doing so. If, that is, your interview accurately reflects who I am."

"Can't promise that. Only that it will reflect what you say. It's up to you to give me the information that keeps the story balanced."

"Touché."

"So, are we still talking here?"

The smile widened. "Yes, Mr. James, we are still talking here. What's your next question?"

For nearly an hour the interview continued as Brady attempted to dance around the questions he really wanted to ask. The only time the conversation turned prickly was when he got too close to the real point of the interview.

"So, I'm sure you've heard the rumors going around that your candidacy is just a Trojan horse, if you will, a way to get you inside the Republican ticket – perhaps as VP?"

The stony stare returned. "Haven't heard that one. Sounds like something your liberal media buddies have cooked up."

"So it's not true?"

"Mr. James," the candidate began, and Brady knew he was on thin ice, "if the American Rights party nominates me to be their Presidential candidate, it will be the proudest moment of my life."

The clock in Brady's head told him the interview was nearly over. He decided to go for it. "So do you categorically deny that there are negotiations currently underway to swing your support to one of the leading Republican candidates in return for putting you on the ticket as their Vice Presidential candidate?"

Blackburn glanced at his Chief of Staff and in the blink of an eye Whiting was on his feet.

"I'm afraid that we're going to have to call it a day for now," he announced as he walked over to stand beside his boss. "Mr. Blackburn has another appointment in just a few minutes and he needs a second to change gears."

Ignoring the staffer, Brady held the candidate's gaze. To his credit, Blackburn did not blink. "Of course," James said, trying to sound sincere. "I understand. Thank you for your time."

"My pleasure, Mr. James. I look forward to seeing your fair and unbiased transcription of our little discussion."

Brady collected his recorder and stood to shake Blackburn's hand. "Best of luck with your candidacy." He turned as if to leave.

"Oh, just one other thing," he said, turning back to the AR candidate. "If circumstances should…change, would you be willing to talk to me again?"

"I wouldn't hold my breath on that one, Mr. James," Blackburn answered coolly.

"The interview, or the change of circumstance?"

Blackburn's smile was icy. "Take your pick."

Brady nodded and headed for the door. His hand was just inches from the knob when the door swung open and he found himself face to face with a large black man, and behind him, Adam Hoch. His initial reaction was to introduce himself and cover his tracks by trying to set up an interview with the billionaire. But he caught himself before he opened his mouth, deciding it would be better if Hoch learned about his presence in Tampa from Blackburn. Might shake him up a bit to hear about the interview from *his* candidate.

He glanced at Hoch as he entered. He looked much the same as the many photos he'd seen of the man, but seemed smaller, harder. His mouth was set in a tight-lipped grimace. He stared straight ahead, not even deigning to acknowledge Brady's existence. *'Fine. You'll know me soon enough,'* Brady thought as he slipped out behind the great man.

*****

"Goddamn it!"

Adam Hoch was angry, and when he was angry there was never any doubt about it. His flushed cheeks and bulging eyes were nothing new to Tommy; he'd seen it many times before, and he was sure he'd see it many times in the future. They'd just left his meeting with the AR Presidential hopeful, which had been all sugar and light until Blackburn had casually mentioned that he'd just been interviewed for a story in the Post by some guy named Brady James. Tommy had seen the vein bulge in the old man's temple when he heard the name. But he had to give it to him, the old man hid his reaction beautifully.

"What was he asking about?" was his only question.

He listened with controlled interest as Blackburn ran through the interview, but visibly stiffened when the AR candidate mentioned the question about switching his support to a Republican Presidential nominee in exchange for the VP slot on his ticket.

"I told him to go pound sand," Blackburn answered.

"What, exactly, did you say?" Hoch pressed in the cool, hard voice that his driver/ bodyguard recognized all too well.

"I told him that if the AR faithful nominate me as their Presidential candidate it will be the proudest moment of my life."

"And he left it at that?"

Blackburn's eyes had narrowed. "No, he asked if there were negotiations underway to put me on the Republican ticket. Why do you ask?"

Hoch ignored the question. "And your response?"

"I signaled my Chief of Staff, Andy Whiting, to inform Mr. James that the interview was over. He wished me good luck and left."

"Just like that?"

"Well, he had the balls to ask me if he could come back and ask more questions 'if circumstances were to change.' Can you imagine the gall of that guy?"

Hoch sighed heavily. "Yeh, I think I can. Do me a favor," he'd said to Blackburn, "if anyone else asks to interview you, for any reason, let my people know before you agree – okay?"

"Well certainly, of course. But what's going on here? I mean, I didn't tell him anything that could hurt us." Blackburn sounded defensive, almost hurt.

"No, no, of course not," Hoch shifted into damage control mode. "You did just fine. It's just that we need to know who you're talking to and what about – to keep our PR campaign on the straight and narrow. You understand."

"Oh yeh, certainly," the candidate said, all the while his eyes suggesting he didn't have a clue what Hoch was talking about. But he'd do as he was told. That was his most endearing quality, from what Tommy had overheard in discussions back in Billings. When the old man had participated in a secure video conference with a handful of other AR supporters a few months earlier, Blackburn's 'malleability' had tipped the scales in his favor when some of the others had argued for Jacob Elias, another AR big shot. "Elias is too much his own man," Hoch had said, and it was clear he saw that as a negative.

Now, riding down in the elevator to a waiting limo, Tommy could see that he was rethinking his decision.

"Goddamn idiot," he muttered, seemingly uncaring that the tall black man was standing right behind him and could hear everything he said. "You'd think he'd know better."

Just before the doors slid open, Hoch turned to Tommy. "Call Jeffrey. Tell him to get his ass moving and take care of things, as we discussed."

By the time the elevator doors opened, his face was an inscrutable blank canvas once again as he strode out of the hotel.

CHAPTER 20

Derek had been following the grandson for nearly three days but hadn't learned much more than he'd discovered in the first few hours of the tail. The PI kept expecting the kid to head down to Tampa, but he showed no such inclination. He kept to his usual schedule, albeit with numerous side trips to see his 'girlfriend' or grab a beer at the local sports bar. If Derek hadn't known he was an egomaniacal supergeek, he'd think he was just another self-absorbed twenty-something with more money than good sense.

He talked to Brady after his meeting with Blackburn, and agreed with his friend that the interview would likely stir the AR pot significantly. He reminded James to be on his guard, that Hoch and his people had a lot riding on their little scam, not the least of which was a long stretch in federal prison if they got caught. Brady returned the advice.

The little man pocketed his cellphone and settled into the well-padded seats of the Oldsmobile, turning up the music. He decided that he'd have to switch-out the Olds for another model if the surveillance continued for more than another day or two. A big old pig like that one would be sure to draw attention sooner or later. But for now, it was the closest thing to a mattress on wheels, even if he could just barely see over the steering wheel without his two phone books.

The usual lights burned brightly in the kid's house. He could picture the sniveling little weasel eating his takeout Thai, sipping a beer, watching sports on that huge LCD TV of his. In another half-hour or so he'd probably drive over to the girlfriend's, where he'd stay until midnight or so before returning to his own place. So far he hadn't slept at her apartment; Derek wondered if that would cost him extra.

He was just settling in for a piano concerto when the front door of the kid's house swung open and he emerged toting a small carry-on bag.

'What is this?' Derek wondered as he slouched down in his seat to avoid detection. *'Finally staying over?'* It made sense. Maybe they only shacked-up on the weekends. He waited for the SUV to roar past before he swung a fast u-turn and followed at a safe distance. He had already mapped the route to the working girl's apartment in his mind when Jeffrey jumped on route 3 headed east.

'The airport?' Derek wondered as he accelerated to match the SUV's speed. Sure enough, the kid pulled into the Logan airport facility. But instead of parking in the commercial lot, the SUV cruised over to the charter side of the complex.

"Damn!" the PI swore as he pounded the steering wheel with the flat of his hand. The elder Hoch had flown to Tampa on the company jet, so Derek had assumed that the kid would fly commercial. He'd underestimated the company's resources and the kid's sense of self-importance. *'Why fly first class when you can fly your own jet?'*

Derek had to drive halfway back around the airfield to park the Olds in the commercial lot. As soon as he was situated, he grabbed the carry-on that he always kept packed in the back seat of the car for just such eventualities. He hurried as fast as he stubby little legs could carry him into the private flight lounge.

"Hey, how ya' doin'?" he asked the attractive young woman standing behind the reception desk. "I'm supposed to be meeting Jeffrey here, Jeff Hoch. We're supposed to fly out tonight."

He tried to sound just harried enough to cut off any inquiries.

"Oh my, you just missed him," the girl explained.

"Darn! Can I still catch him?"

"I believe so… I know the plane was already fueled and just waiting for him to get here. Should I contact the pilot?"

"No, no that isn't necessary. Don't want everyone and his brother to know I was late. And they'd kill me if I delayed the take-off. Where's the plane now?"

She stared out the large plate glass window at the inky blackness dotted by spotlights and support vehicle headlights. "I think that's them right over there by the Hoch hanger," she advised. "But you'd better hurry – looks like they're getting set to get underway."

"Thank you!" he half-yelled as he fast-waddled through the nearest exit door and headed toward the Gulfstream G550 jet. He wasn't sure exactly what he would do when he got to the plane, but the decision was taken out of his hands when the pitch of the turbine whine accelerated and the plane taxied toward the runway.

Derek pulled up just a few hundred feet from the jet and watched it roll away into the darkness. He waited until the ground crew had finished their work and intercepted one of the young men as he walked back toward the main building.

"Heading to Florida again?" he asked jovially, pointing with his chin at the rapidly disappearing plane.

"Nah, the old man's down there," the crewman answered. "Jeffrey's off to DC."

Derek tried to hide his surprise. "DC? Are you sure?"

"That's what the flight papers said," the orange-vested staffer said sullenly. Without waiting for further discussion, he left the midget PI standing in the middle of the taxiway.

Derek took only a few seconds to collect his wits and head toward the main terminal. It was less than ten minutes later when he learned that the last flight of the night had departed just minutes earlier.

'Coincidence?' he wondered absently.

He bought a ticket for the first flight out to DC in the morning and then took a deep breath before calling Brady to let him know that the kid had slipped away. It might not mean a thing, but then again…

*****

Even before he'd gone to bed the night before, Derek had called ahead to DC to arrange for a PI friend to locate Hoch's jet and be there when it landed. It wasn't all that hard to find the destination of a plane, if you knew the tail numbers and the right people to contact. Derek knew all the right people.

As the United jet climbed to cruising altitude, he stretched his legs and resumed the analysis that had kept him awake most of the night. What was Jeffrey doing in DC? What would Hoch do if he thought Brady was getting too close to his plan? How could they get around the billionaire's power and influence? The answers were slow in coming.

He was still mulling over the problems that confronted them when the flight attendant announced they were beginning their descent into Ronald Reagan National Airport. He didn't particularly like flying into Reagan – the runway was too short, there was too much traffic in the skies. But it was the closest airport to the Arlington hotel where he knew Jeffrey had spent the night. To his relief, the landing was smooth and uneventful.

He had to restrain himself from popping open his cellphone and checking in with the friend who was keeping an eye on Jeffrey as soon as the attendant announced that phones could be used. He doubted that any of Hoch's people had followed him, but he couldn't be certain. So he made his way into the terminal as though he hadn't a care in the world and sought out the nearest handicapped bathroom. Although he had no handicap, or physical challenge, or whatever they were calling it these days, most people took one look at his stature and decided that he deserved to use the single-seater. For Derek, it was merely a question of finding a place where his phone conversation couldn't be overheard.

He reconfirmed that Jeffrey had gone straight from the airport to the Arlington Hilton, (*'Probably trying to keep a low profile,'* he thought), and directed his associate to "stick to that little asshole like superglue" before grabbing a cab out in front of the terminal. It took him less than twenty minutes to go the five or six miles from the airport to the hotel.

He was lost in thought, running through a plan to institute rotating shifts to keep a closer eye on Jeffrey, when he noticed the flashing red and blue lights just ahead. As the cab pulled up to the Hilton he already knew in his heart what had happened. He directed the cab driver to pull into the entrance and park behind the ambulance. Two police cars with lights flashing and motors running were parked akimbo at the curb. He hadn't walked six feet when two attendants rolled a gurney out of the lobby and began fast-wheeling it to the parked ambulance. Even with an oxygen mask obscuring his face, Derek recognized his PI friend, Eddie.

"What's going on?" he asked as the two attendants struggled to load the gurney into the back of the ambulance.

"Guy fell," one attendant spit distractedly.

"Or jumped," the other chimed in as he jumped in with the gurney. The first guy slammed the doors shut and trotted up to the driver's door.

"Is he going to be okay?" Derek shouted after him.

"No saying," came the clipped response, just an instant before the ambulance siren began to wail and the vehicle screeched out of the hotel driveway, leaving the diminutive PI standing on the sidewalk in front of the Hilton entrance, a look of simmering anger painted across his features.

"So that's how it's gonna be," he muttered to himself, turning back toward the waiting cab. "You s.o.b's want war, you got it."

*****

Brady knew that Blackburn would almost certainly mention his interview to Hoch; it was only a matter of time before the billionaire, or one of his minions, paid James a visit. Or would they? Maybe they intended to act as if nothing were out of the ordinary. Act as if they knew nothing about his 'story', or about the vote rigging scandal. In any case, he'd have to be careful and keep to well-lit, populated streets and buildings until their approach was clear. Or until he could find enough info to take it to Chesley, and through him to the Feds. As long as Hoch didn't know just how close Brady was to bringing the whole outrageous story to the cops, he was probably safe. Maybe.

Through his buddies in the press corps, he'd managed to finagle an interview with Charles van der Meer, the presumed Republican nominee for VP. Brady was pretty confident that van der Meer had no knowledge of the plot to replace him, but he wanted to cross every T before taking his findings public. And if the interview ruffled Hoch's feathers? So much the better.

Van der Meer was staying at the Intercontinental, the kind of expensive, five-star business hotel that James would expect a Republican candidate to choose. The glass and steel high-rise looked a little like a scaled-down version of the GM headquarters in Detroit, but classier. Security was tight, a schizophrenic hybrid of Florida friendliness and Republican no-nonsense police state. In real terms, that meant that the greeters smiled and the scanners didn't. Apparently Brady didn't fit any of their profiles, or 'targeted identification' in current Redspeak, because after a cursory search of his notebook and recorder, and the ever-present wanding, he was waved through without so much as a second look. An Intercontinental staffer on the safe side of the screeners even asked Brady politely if he could help him. James demurred.

When the door to van der Meer's suite swung open, it was as if Brady was experiencing déjà vu. A flunky about the same age as Blackburn's Chief of Staff greeted him, and showed him into a room where the candidate sat on a sofa facing the bay. Van der Meer could have been Blackburn's fraternal twin: same square jaw and coiffed greying hair, same $1000 suit, same plastic 'who are you again?' smile.

"Mr. Van der Meer, thank you again for agreeing to talk with me," Brady said as he shook the great man's hand. He was pretty much what Brady had expected. He'd Googled the guy to learn something more than the absolute barebones sketch that the campaign had released. He already knew that Van der Meer had been elected to the Senate 11 years earlier, and that his money came from a famous computer manufacturing company that he had co-founded. But a half hour online had also revealed that he'd dumped his wife of 18 years not long after the company had made it big, replacing her with a trophy wife 15 years her junior. A few years later a union made a stink that Van der Meer had been responsible for shipping thousands of good-paying jobs offshore, and another popped up when the IRS suggested he'd forgotten to pay taxes on roughly $38 million in stock options. But he had good lawyers and even better public relations people, and it had all blown over years earlier. At this point, he looked to Brady like just about every other big player in the Grand Old Party these days – rich, conservative, and completely removed from the everyday life of most Americans.

Brady stayed away from the personal dirt he'd uncovered, sticking to questions about the Republican platform, Van der Meer's contribution to the ticket – all the usual politico babble. It didn't take Brady long to realize that Van der Meer still thought he was going to be the VP on the Republican ticket.

"I can help us with the Mountain states and several of the southern states," he'd said proudly in a moment of unexpected candor. "If our numbers are right, we should have a very good chance of winning this thing."

"Will your candidacy help with the far-right faction of your party?" Brady asked. "The folks just this side of AR?"

He didn't blink. "I think so. My conservative credentials are second to none. And since it doesn't look like anybody is going to bring AR back into the Republican fold, I think I will be as effective as anyone in winning-over the undecided."

"Speaking of AR," Brady began, uncomfortably conscious of the fact that Van der Meer's COS was now staring at him with a wary look, "does that mean you haven't heard any of the rumors about a supposed deal with AR?"

"What kind of a deal?" The candidate's tone hardened.

Brady almost felt sorry for the guy.

"Well, what I've heard is that the AR powers-that-be have read the tea leaves and have decided that they don't have a chance on the national stage, so they're holding out until the last minute to try to get the maximum concessions from you Republicans. I was wondering just what those concessions might be."

Van der Meer's icy stare gradually melted into a classic politician smile.

"Speculation, nothing but speculation," he said disarmingly. "If AR has such a plan, they certainly wouldn't share it with us – would they? I don't know if you've covered other elections, but rumors are the fool's gold of political life, and for the next week they will run rampant. Same for the Democrats. It's just the way it is in this game."

Brady watched the VP candidate closely, looking for any signs of stress or dissembling. He saw none. From what he could tell, Van der Meer didn't even know that his Grand Old Party was already negotiating for his ouster, let alone that AR's Blackburn would get the slot. Brady wondered what they'd offer the poor guy to try to keep him happy.

On the positive side, Brady was relieved that the conspiracy seemed to be limited to Hoch and his immediate cohorts, and a few key AR operatives. He'd been half-afraid that he'd find signs of a wider conspiracy, a revelation that would undermine the public's confidence in their political system even more than would already be the case. But if Van der Meer didn't know, and he'd stake his 30-odd years in the news biz on that premise, then it might be the case that only a very small group of conspirators was involved.

He was still hoping that the spooks would crack the encryption on Jeffrey's hard drives, but he couldn't count on it. He'd have to come up with another way to incriminate Hoch and company. And he'd better do it soon.

CHAPTER 21

Derek put in a call to Chesley as soon as he got inside the hotel.

"Chez, Derek here. I think we may have problems." He went on to quickly explain what had transpired, and then described the car his associate had reported the kid driving before he'd taken the fall. "My buddy is on the way to the hospital, and Jeffrey Hoch has disappeared. Any chance you can give me a hand locating the little prick?"

The cop paused for a short instant. "You know we're not supposed to snoop on citizens without probable cause."

"Yeh, and people aren't supposed to throw or push other people off of balconies. Looks like everyone might have to go to confession this week. Well?"

The pause was longer this time. "Yeh, alright. I can probably run it through our plate detection system, see what the cameras around town have picked up. But if anyone asks, I'll have to tell them something."

"Tell them a similar car was reported involved in a hit and run. Tell them you're checking up on your wife's young stud. Tell them anything. Just find the bastard."

"I'll see what I can do," Chesley answered non-committally. He would try, but he wasn't going to promise anything. "Have you heard from James?"

"Not since we touched base last night. He had a couple of interviews scheduled for today."

"He does understand that when a mouse runs around among cats, he's likely to get eaten, doesn't he?"

"He knows that people get worried when newsmen ask tough questions. And they do stupid things when they get worried. He's hoping to cause some smart people to do stupid things."

"Sometimes they do dangerous things, not just stupid."

Derek didn't have a comeback for that one.

*****

The PI had dropped off his bag at the apartment and was on his way down to his car to get something for lunch, when his cellphone rang.

"Hey, just got your voicemail," Brady's voice boomed. "How's Eddie?"

"I just spoke to the hospital. They say he's got a broken arm and hip, and a pretty bad concussion, but he'll live."

"Christ. Find out if he has health insurance. Tell him we'll help if he doesn't. And say hi when you see him." The PI heard his friend exhale deeply. "What about our little friend, Jeffrey?"

"I've got Chez trying to locate him using their plate detection system. Lucky Eddie got the basics on the kid's car before he 'tripped.'"

"Then he'll show up, sooner or later. You know, I've been trying to figure out why the kid's in DC and not down here helping his grandfather persuade the Republicans to accept an AR VP. Any thoughts?"

"I don't know. I've been wondering the same thing myself. I'm hoping he hasn't discovered my little tour of his hard drives. If he did, he might be after Danny again. Whatever it is he's doing here, I'm pretty sure it's not anything good. The kid's as arrogant as his grandfather, but doesn't seem to have the old man's common sense. When he gets off his computer and into the real world he has all the finesse of a sledgehammer."

"Maybe you'd better give Danny a call. Let him know that his evil twin is in town. And while you're at it, give Anne a buzz too. See if she's heard anything about anything – and tell her I miss her."

"Since when did I become the concierge at the Love Palace?"

"Since you agreed to work with this old broken down excuse for a reporter. You must have missed the part in our agreement that says 'other duties as required.'"

"I think I missed the whole damn agreement."

"Better for all concerned," Brady said. "Gotta run. Let me know as soon as you hear anything."

"Will do. And Brady, take care," the PI said, his tone suddenly serious. "Even without the kid, Hoch's still got his bodyguard with him, and I can tell you from personal experience the guy's got a heavy foot, especially when he tries to ram it up your ass."

"Since when did you become my wet-nurse?"

"Since I found out you were old and broken down."

"Fair enough. You do the same."

Derek hung up and stood for a moment in the apartment parking garage. Brady's words bounced around his head like echoes in the concrete garage. Why *was* Jeffrey running around DC when all the action seemed to be taking place down south? What was he up to? He decided to call Danny right then and there. The phone rang four times and Derek was on the verge of hanging up when Danny finally answered. The young geek wanted to hear about everything that was going on with the investigation, and seemed disappointed when the PI evaded his questions and cut straight to his warning. The geek took the info in stride, flippantly telling Derek that he'd be on is guard. The PI cringed but didn't tell the kid that he thought he was seriously overmatched by his Billings counterpart. He did make a few suggestions how the kid could keep from getting his ass kicked again, and when he was sure that Danny had at least heard him, he let him get back to his computers. He was about to call Anne to see how she was doing when his stomach growled. *'I'll call her from the restaurant,'* he decided, and hopping in his Caddy he headed for Dupont Circle to grab a bite.

Parking was terrible, as usual for midday, but the PI finally found a meter on a side street just blocks from the Iraqi Embassy. He walked the two blocks from P Street out to Mass Ave, glorying in the warm fall day. Old, twisted trees lined the streets. Most of their leaves had already fallen, but enough burgundy and gold remained to decorate the street in colors that would make any Redskins fan glad. Several of his favorite lunch places were located in a half-mile stretch on either side of the Circle, and he picked an Irish pub that he hadn't frequented in months. If anyone was looking for him, they'd have to know his habits pretty thoroughly to find him there.

They seated him without much of a wait and he ordered his usual fare without even glancing at the menu: pastrami on rye with cole slaw and a pickle. They had made fun of his choice the first few times he'd visited the place. After all, almost all the tourists ordered corned beef and cabbage, or one of the other traditional Irish meals. But not Derek. He knew what he liked, and that's what he was going to order, no matter what the sign out front said.

'The Jewish Leprechaun,' was what some of the servers called him, though not to his face.

As the young freckle-faced waitress walked away with his order, he spent a few moments watching the curves of her backside sway beneath her shimmering green skirt. He had to pull himself back to reality to pull out his cellphone and dial Anne's number. The phone rang 8 times and a voicemail answered: "Hi, this is Anne Waznewski in Senator Jessup's office. I'm either on another line or away from my desk just now, but if you'll leave a message…"

"Anne, Derek DiLaurain here. Brady asked me to check in to see if anything has come up on your end, and just to send his regards. As you know, he's quite the romantic fellow. Right out of Wuthering Heights. Or was it Animal House? Whatever. Give me a call when you get this." And he left his cellphone number.

He was still smiling when the waitress brought his sandwich. He winked at her and raised one eyebrow, a talent that had wowed the women for 20 years. Sure enough, the young lass smiled shyly and blushed. She hurried away without saying a word, but he saw her glance back at him before she disappeared around the corner to the kitchen.

'Still got it,' he thought as he dove into the thick pastrami creation.

It was nearly an hour later, after coffee, a piece of apple pie, and another half-dozen flirtatious looks and comments, that Derek glanced at his watch. 1:40. He knew from Brady that Anne usually ate from 12 to 1, and so should be back in the office. He dialed her number again. Same eight rings. Same voicemail.

He was about to pack it in and head back to his apartment to await Chesley's call, when a nagging disquiet in the back of his mind moved him to call Danny.

"Hey, I'm probably just turning into an old woman," he told the young computer whiz, "but would you do me a favor and run up to Anne's office and tell her to give me a call? I've left a couple of voicemails, but haven't heard back."

The kid agreed that Derek was becoming a worrying nag, but deigned to run the errand. Five minutes later the PI's phone rang.

"She's not there," he told the PI. "So I asked the other secretaries in the office and they said she received a call about 10 and left the office soon after that."

"Did she tell them where she was going?"

"Nope. Just that she'd be back for lunch."

"And she hasn't come back?"

"Her lunch bag is still sitting on her desk."

"Hmmm." Derek didn't like the sound of that. Not one little bit.

"What?" Danny asked, his voice a shade higher with concern. "You think something happened to her? Like what?"

"I don't know. Maybe nothing. But with all that's going on with Hoch and his pals, I don't like the feel of it."

"Should we call the cops?"

"Not yet. She might just be at the dentist, or getting her hair done. Who knows? But how about if you go back up there around...3 and see if she's back. Okay?"

"Yeh, sure. No problem."

"Thanks. Call me."

He hung up the phone with an unshakeable sensation that he knew now why Jeffrey had come to DC.

*****

Brady was on his way to meet with an operative from the National Republican Party when his phone rang.

"Brady, I'm so sorry…" Anne's voice began before he could even say hello. She sounded stressed, nervous.

"Anne, what's the matter? Did Derek talk to you?"

But the person who answered him was not Anne.

"Mr. James, I really think you should come back here to DC," a man's voice run through a voice synthesizer announced. "Your girlfriend misses you. *We* miss you."

"Who is this?! What do you want? Put Anne back on the phone." He barked orders, knowing they carried no weight. Sure enough, they elicited only a short, barked laugh on the other end of the line.

"You're done asking questions for a while, Mr. James. Like I said, I think you'd better get back here to DC, ASAP. Otherwise, who knows what might befall Ms. Waznewski." The threat was ill-disguised.

"Listen, you little piece of crap, you touch one hair on her head…"

"And you'll do what? Bring flowers to her grave?" The voice was cold, uncompromising. "We'll expect you back here by tonight. We'll call you at 10 pm sharp at the midget's apartment. If you want to see your friend again, I suggest you answer that call."

The hum of the dial tone replaced the hated voice.

Brady took a deep breath and ran through his options. It didn't take long. He hit the speed dial and waited.

*****

Derek saw Brady's number on his caller ID and knew why he was calling even before he answered.

"Is it about Anne?" he asked without saying hello.

"You know?"

"Not really, but I haven't been able to talk to her this morning and her coworkers say she went out at 10 after receiving a call and hasn't returned. Is it that little asshole Hoch?"

"Most likely. A bit too much of a coincidence that he flies to DC and the next day I get a call saying they have Anne and I need to get back to DC or else."

"That was it? No other demand?"

Brady stopped for a second. Derek was right. This was obviously just the first step in keeping him quiet until after the election – if not permanently.

"Nah. But I'm sure that's coming as soon as I'm back. We need to find her, and fast. If Hoch can stop us from releasing this story and contacting the authorities before the 6th, it'll be too late. Once they clean out the voting machines, our story will sound like just so much lunatic conspiracy theory. We've got to catch them in the act."

"Good luck. At this point, I think we need to focus on keeping Anne, and ourselves, alive. There's already a couple of stiffs who underestimated Hoch."

"Maybe…But, in any case, Anne is our focus. Call Chesley. Tell him it's life and death. We need to find Jeffrey."

"I'm on it, chief. You'll be back tonight?"

"I'll catch the first plane I can get a seat on. I'll call when I'm on the ground."

"Okay. And Brady?"

"Yeh?"

"Don't worry – we'll find her. I've got my own debt to repay that little asshole. And now it's payback time."

*****

As soon as he hung up, the PI dialed Chesley's personal cellphone number. He explained the situation with few words to spare.

"Your timing is good," the DC cop said in reply. "We just got a bite on the plate Jerry ID'd as the Hoch kid's rental. It was parked a couple of hours ago on 16th St SE."

"Anacostia? That's not exactly where I'd expect Jeffrey to hang out."

"And maybe that's exactly why he's there. Could be he's hired some gang-banger to help him out."

"Could be."

"Want me to send a black and white out that way?"

"No, thanks. We've already got a Senator and a Hoch employee dead, and we're thinking it might be the kid's doing. If we're right, he's a major loose cannon. Don't want to chance spooking him unless we absolutely need to. I'll head out there to look around."

"Derek, nothing personal but you'll stand out like a sore thumb. Why don't you let me take a look."

"Plainclothes?"

"Haven't worn a uniform in 12 years. Not going to start today."

The PI hesitated. He felt guilty that he hadn't contacted Anne earlier, but he recognized that Chesley was right. A white midget in Anacostia would probably draw some attention. "Yeh, all right," he conceded, "but let's coordinate. I'll park a block or two away, just in case you need some backup."

"Good. Give me an hour to clean things up here and get someone to cover for me. I'll call you when I get to the neighborhood."

As he hung up, Derek felt the familiar rush of adrenaline he always felt on occasions such as this. Maybe he was nuts, but going out after a bad guy was the closest thing to nirvana he could think of. And going after the little prick who'd nearly busted his balls, literally, was going to make it even sweeter.

*****

By the time Chesley called, Derek had been parked at 16th and U for twenty minutes. As opposed to the stakeout in Billings, where he'd drifted to classical music with no real sense of endangerment, here he kept his eyes open and his gun readily available. Not that he actually thought he'd need to use it, but it'd be a heavy deterrent if anyone were to hassle him. And if anyone were to try, it'd probably be in Anacostia.

DC is a beautiful city, for the most part, but Anacostia is not one of those parts. Located in the southeastern part of the District, check cashing services and corner liquor stores outnumber banks, gas stations and supermarkets. Ironically, it's located just a mile or so from Capitol Hill, but it's on the 'other side' of the river. Tourists don't go there, unless they're lost. Locals don't go there, unless they're looking for a good time. Small, aging houses in pristine condition share the narrow streets with rundown apartments scarred by boarded windows and dopers hanging out on the corners. It is not the place for a white midget driving a big Caddy.

Derek had been watching the street around him for a half-hour when his phone finally rang.

"The car's still here," Chesley reported. "I'm sitting about three houses up from where it's parked – in front of a two-story brick row house. Haven't seen anyone go in or out. What do you want me to do?"

"Can you hang there for a while? I think at this point we need more info."

"Sure. I told 'em at the precinct that I'd be gone for the rest of the afternoon. What are you gonna do?"

"I'm going to go run the address. See who owns it, try to find out who's living there. Then I'm going to try to get Brady on the phone. He's got a personal interest in this situation, so I want his input before we make any moves." Part of him wanted to rush the apartment and take their chances, but the more rational part realized that Anne's life was at stake. Better to take it slow and easy.

"Understood. And if I see anyone coming out?"

"If the kid's car moves, or any other vehicle that could have Anne inside, follow them. Otherwise, just jot down the license number and we'll trace them later."

"Got it."

"Should be back in an hour, hour and a half max."

"See you then."

The PI gunned his Caddy, headed toward the freeway. He tried to call Brady, but got his voicemail. *'Probably already in the air,'* he thought as he exited in the direction of his apartment. He left a message telling James to call him as soon as he landed and continued west.

*****

"There's been a change of plans," Adam Hoch said matter-of-factly to the small group assembled in the Tampa hotel suite.

"Oh yeh? And what is that?" answered a man nearly as old as Hoch himself, a big Republican benefactor with considerable sway over Party leaders.

"Have you seen the latest polls?" Hoch continued.

"As of a couple of days ago. Why?"

Hoch held up a two page report. "This is from today. The President is up 7 percent. Unless something changes, our man loses."

"Do you mean *our* man, or Blackburn?" another wealthy backer prodded.

Hoch forced a smile. "I mean Andrews," he said, naming the Republican candidate for President.

"That's not exactly news," a third participant argued. "The polls have been down for weeks now."

"Very true," Hoch said. "But what if I were to tell you that I could guarantee a victory by Mr. Andrews?"

The first benefactor chuckled humorlessly. "Do you also have a bridge for sale?" The other wealthy backers laughed. Hoch smiled as well.

"No bridge. Just a big white house in DC."

"Have you been drinking?"

The Montana billionaire ignored him. "Guaranteed. You give me the word, and Andrews will be our next President."

"Okay, I'll bite – how do you intend to make that happen?"

"That's my business. Your business is to make sure we all continue to make money, lots of money. Right?"

"Is this some kind of joke?" the eldest among them huffed.

"No joke," Hoch answered calmly. "But there is a catch..."

The other three men all harrumphed.

"No, no. Not so big a deal. Just a small trade."

"Stocks?" one asked.

"No, not stocks. In fact, nothing monetary. The one thing I ask to ensure that Mr. Andrews becomes President Andrews next Tuesday is that Van der Meer steps down – due to illness, or whatever, and is replaced."

"What?! By whom? You?!" the backers thundered.

Hoch calmed them with his hands. "Do I look like someone who'd want to be *Vice* President of the US? No, I want you to replace Van der Meer with Charles Blackburn."

The response was predictable. "Blackburn? Your AR man?" "Why?" "What's this all about?"

"Look, let's cut the crap. You don't really care who's in the White House, as long as we have our usual influence – right?"

The three elderly tycoons looked to each other for support. "Well, no, I suppose not," the most influential among them said.

"Good. Because I can assure you – 100 per cent – that Mr. Blackburn will support whatever policies we propose."

"That's all well and good, but what will Andrews say about all this?"

"He will say whatever the three of you tell him to say, unless I miss my guess. Or have you boys lost your vaunted 'touch'?"

Their egos bruised, they stumbled over each other to reassure Hoch that they could handle the GOP candidate.

"Just as I thought. And to make it a little easier when you talk to your guy, you can point out that he isn't going to win unless he makes this deal. Period. Not a chance in hell. You know that, I know that, and I hope to hell Andrews knows that."

"He knows it," their leader said solemnly.

"Excellent. Then, is it a deal?" Hoch's eyes danced with an excitement he hadn't felt in years.

"Hoch, we all know you're a clever guy," the youngest of the backers began, "but I don't see how even someone with your ingenuity is going to make up a difference of seven per cent in six days. I don't see how it's possible."

"You're right – I can't," Hoch answered, but before they could interrupt he went on, "but what I *can* do is ensure that the vote in a few key states goes our way. Andrews and Blackburn will still lose the popular vote, but they will eke out a bare majority in the Electoral College. It'll be Bush 2000 redux."

The GOP benefactors looked to each other, doubt etched in narrowed eyes and wrinkled foreheads.

"I know, I know, sounds outrageous. But I'm telling you, it can be done. And with your help, I will do it."

"This isn't going to land us all in jail, is it?" one of the three asked.

Hoch laughed, a sarcastic, cynical sound that would have sent shivers up the back of any normal human being. His three co-conspirators seemed immune. "Jail? The big bankers and insurance guys stole over a trillion dollars from this country a few years ago and not *one* of them went to jail. People like us don't go to jail," he said with such confidence, such malevolence, that not one of the three objected.

"More to the point," he continued, his voice remodulated to a more controlled, businesslike tone, "there is **no** possibility that anyone will even know that it happened. Without going into any details, suffice it to say that the second the polls close, it's over. No evidence, no trail, nothing." He realized that he was stretching the truth, but as Jack Nicholson once said in some military trial movie, they couldn't handle the truth.

"You understand what you're saying? You're talking about stealing the Presidential election?!"

"Good for you, Jasper. You weren't sleeping through our little discussion. So, what do you say – do we have a deal?"

"I still don't quite get it," the eldest backer admitted. "What's in it for you? I mean, an AR VP is a notch in your belt, admittedly. But still, it's only the VP slot. Why risk so much for so little?"

Hoch smiled. "That's my business. Yours is to deliver Andrews and the rest of his pathetic crew. I'll need to know by tomorrow, 5 pm. Yes, or no. A nation led by business-friendly Republicans, or by socialist-leaning Dems. Your choice, gentlemen."

There was still some grousing and attempts to get Hoch to disclose more about how he intended to install a President of his choice, but it was all half-hearted. The three elderly gentlemen knew that they had no chance of controlling the White House unless they went along with Hoch's crazy scheme, and for at least two of them, there was no saying that they'd be around for the next election. As they filed out of the suite, Hoch knew he had them. They'd talk to Andrews, and his close associates. And they'd promise Van der Meer something to make him forget he wasn't going to be the VP. It was all working out just as he'd planned.

Too bad they didn't know the real reason for getting his man into the VP slot. But, of course, if they knew they probably wouldn't support him. *They'll know soon enough,'* Hoch said to himself with a satisfied grin. Just a few more loose ends to take care of…

CHAPTER 22

Brady was finishing throwing his things into his suitcase when a knock sounded at the door. Thinking it was probably a bellman come to help him carry his bag, he opened the door without taking his usual peek through the peephole.

"Going somewhere?" Adam Hoch asked gratingly as he stepped past the stunned James into his room. His massive black driver/bodyguard stepped in right behind him, shutting the door and locking it.

Brady fought to control his temper – and his nerves. "Well, well – Mr. Hoch, if I'm not mistaken. To what do I owe this unexpected visit?" He followed Hoch into the room.

"Brady…You don't mind if I call you Brady, do you?" the oil tycoon began, sitting in the lone easy chair.

"Why not? You seem to be calling the shots here."

Hoch smiled bemeaningly. "Everyone says you're a bright guy. Why don't you have a seat? Get comfortable."

"Don't mind if I do." Brady sat, in part to hide his trembling knees.

"So, Mr. James. I understand that you've taken a sudden interest in the upcoming election. I thought crime was your area of expertise."

Brady bit back an ill-considered riposte. "Was," he said instead. "I retired a while back."

"Did you? Then why am I hearing from all sorts of associates that you've been interviewing them about the election? Just personal interest?"

"I retired, I didn't give up writing," he said simply. "This looks to be a very interesting race."

"How so?" Hoch came back immediately, making Brady wish he'd kept his reply more to the point. His mind whirled, trying to come up with something as bland and mundane as possible.

"It's not often you have a legitimate third party in the race. And AR looks to be carrying 11-12 per cent of the vote right now."

"Yes, that is quite interesting, isn't it?" the older man said, staring at Brady with the intensity of an entomologist dissecting a cockroach. "And so that's what you'll be writing about?"

"What else?" Brady asked, cocking his head and narrowing his eyes as if the very thought of writing about something else were alien to him. "Is there another story you want to bring to my attention?"

"No, no," Hoch replied, shrugging off the idea. "It's just, well, some of your questions to my friends seemed to suggest you were working on a theory about... an AR-GOP union of some sort. Is that not the case?"

"The idea crossed my mind," Brady answered cautiously.

"You see. My friends were right. You *are* a smart man." He leaned forward conspiratorially. "In fact, just such an 'arrangement' may take place any time now. How would you like to get an exclusive on that story, right from the horse's mouth, sort of speak?"

Brady tried to hide the relief that washed over him. But he held his ground. "You mean from party hacks, or the candidates themselves?"

A tiny scowl crept across Hoch's lips, but it was quickly replaced by the clearly artificial smile he used when trying to appear conciliatory.

"I think it might be possible to get one of the candidates to talk with you. Maybe by phone..."

James didn't blink. "It would be a lot better to have *both* the candidates, if, that is, the rumors I've heard about a split ticket are true."

Hoch stared impassively for just an instant. Brady judged he was deciding whether to lash out at this over-the-hill reporter, or find some way to co-opt him. He chose the latter.

"I...think that might be possible," he finally said. "Of course, scheduling will have to be flexible."

"Mr. Flexibility – that's me," Brady said with an ease he didn't feel. "Just tell me when and where, and I'll be there."

"Good, good," Hoch said, leaning back into the chair with a satisfied look. "My people will get a hold of you. By the way," he added, casting a glance at the half-packed bag on the bed, "are you going somewhere?"

"Back to DC. Nothing more to get down here. Unless," he added with an expectant look to Hoch, "you have something for me."

"No, not just yet," the oilman snapped, a bit too harshly. "Don't worry. We'll be in touch."

He began to stand.

"Give Tommy here your contact information. As soon as we can set something up, you'll hear from us."

Brady stood as well. "Great. One question though." Hoch visibly stiffened.

"And that would be?"

"Why me?" Brady asked as innocently as possible.

Hoch's body relaxed. "Because any reporter who's good enough to sniff out a big story like this one deserves to break it. Don't you agree?"

"Oh, I certainly do," Brady said with a smile twice as big as Hoch's own. "And thank you."

"My pleasure, son," Hoch said, walking over to Brady with hand extended. "And maybe we can do some other stories in the near future if this works out."

"About the election?"

"The election. Business. You name it. I have a number of interests, as you probably know all too well."

"That I do," Brady said, shaking the great man's hand. His grasp was firm, solid, belying his wrinkled face and silver-white hair.

"Good. Then that's that. We'll be in touch." Tommy opened the door and Hoch began to leave. "Oh," he said, stopping in the doorway as though struck by a last second thought. "Have a good flight. Keep safe," he said, but his words carried no warmth.

Brady gave the bodyguard his Post contact info, running everything back through Jimmy. When the door finally closed, Brady sat on the edge of the bed and sighed heavily.

'What was that all about?'

*****

Derek had just finished an online search of the tax records to see who owned the house in SE, when his phone rang. It was Brady.

"Hey, just got your message. Sorry, I had the phone off. Had a little visit from Mr. Hoch."

"The old man? What did he want, other than your head?"

"Actually he was very businesslike. Wanted to offer me the first interview of the new GOP-AR Presidential ticket."

"You're kidding."

"I'm not. But what did you find out about Anne? Did she turn up?"

"Not really. Like I said in my message, we found Jeffrey's car, parked in front of a row-house in Anacostia."

"Anacostia? Not exactly his hood."

"That's what we thought. But when I checked the tax records, surprise, surprise. The house in question is owned by a DC realty company, that is a subsidiary of a New Jersey oil refinery, whose CEO is a member of the Board of Directors of…"

"Let me guess," Brady interrupted. "Hoch Industries."

"Bingo! Hand the man a cupie doll. So, unless I'm mistaken, the sniveling little dweeb is in there, or nearby."

"And Anne?"

"That's what we want to find out. But before Chez and I do anything, we wanted to check in with you."

There was a short pause. "Hey, you two are there on the ground, and you've both got a lot more experience at this kind of thing than I do." Despite his best efforts, Derek could hear the concern in his friend's voice.

"So you're okay with us going in? Or at least setting up some close surveillance?"

"Yeh, do what you've got to do. But Derek..." The PI knew what was coming next. "Be careful, alright? I might be able to recover from the loss of one half-pint PI, but I'd feel kind of bad if I lost both of you."

Derek smiled. "Don't worry. I have no intention of letting some little snot-nosed geek mess my *do*."

Brady chuckled nervously. "Yeh. Nothing worse than a slick little man with a messed *do*."

The two men talked for a few more minutes, until Brady's boarding call was announced on the airport intercom. The PI jotted down his friend's arrival time and then called Chesley as soon as he hung up.

"Chez, it's me. Looks like the house is owned by a friend of Hoch's. Pretty much confirms what we've been thinking. See anyone go in or out?"

"Nobody. Place is quiet as a tomb."

"Bad choice of words, bro."

"Yeh, sorry about that. But nobody's gone in or out and there's been no visible movement inside. What did Brady have to say?"

"He said we should do what we have to do."

"Okay. And what is that?"

"Well, there's not much we can do until we know what's going on inside that house. I suggest we see about getting some sensors in place and go from there. Do you agree?"

"Absolutely. You got anything decent for equipment?"

"Some. You?"

"Some decent audio stuff. I'll have to go grab it. How about we meet back here in say, 45 minutes. Work for you?"

"Good by me."

As the PI hung up he wondered how long they had before they heard further demands from the kidnapper. Or before Anne's time ran out.

*****

It was getting dark by the time Chesley pulled in behind his friend's Caddy. He had not only dug up a couple of high quality acoustic contact mikes but a decent shotgun mike as well. They might not be able to get up to the house unnoticed, but they should be able to hear some of what was going on inside. Chesley checked that all the batteries were in place and fresh, and then adjusted his bullet proof vest. He'd thrown it on at the last minute. *'Never know what kind of crap you may be stepping into,'* he thought. He only wished he had one small enough for Derek. The smallest one the department stocked would fit him like an evening gown. And knowing the little guy, there's no way he'd go up against some perp looking like a candidate for Miss Midget USA. Even if it meant he was risking his life. He shook his head and got out of the car.

Derek was already fiddling with some stuff in a black gym bag. He was dressed head to toe in black.

"What did ya come up with?" the PI asked him as he drew closer.

"Some pretty sweet contact mikes and a shotgun." He stopped and surveyed the PI from head to foot. "What is this, Ninja night at the local Karaoke bar?"

"Funny. Real funny. Ever think of appearing on the World's Funniest Assholes? I understand they're auditioning right about now."

"I bet the line is pretty damn long," the cop said dismissively. "What'd you find?"

Derek held up several familiar devices. "Concussion grenades, smoke, an Uzi, cellphone jammer…"

"Jesus! Is any of that stuff legal?"

"It's all legal – somewhere. And besides, you're a cop. If you're using it, it's legal, right?"

Chesley didn't want to argue the point. "If you say so. So, how do we go about this?"

Derek thought for a moment. "Let's give a listen with that shotgun mike of yours to see what the situation is inside, and go from there."

Chesley pulled the mike and the parabolic reflector that attached to it from his satchel. When he had completed assembling the device Derek moved his Caddy, stopping just one house up the street and opposite the row house. The cop aimed the shotgun at the largish front windows of the home.

"Kill the motor for a second," Chesley ordered as he cupped the headphones to his ears. For thirty seconds they sat in silence, the Caddy nearly invisible on the unlit streetside.

"Nothing," Chesley finally said softly. "Don't hear a thing."

"Let me have a listen," the PI asked, taking the headphones and holding one to his right ear. Sure enough, there were no sounds emanating from the second floor apartment. "Come on," he said as he scrambled out his door and grabbed a collapsible extension pole and a contact mike from the black bag that sat on the back seat of the Caddy.

Chesley followed close behind the pocket-sized PI as he waddled at full-tilt across the roadway and up along the shadowed right side of the house. As soon as they'd come alongside the building, Derek extended the pole and handed it to Chesley. Then he attached the contact mike to a clip at the end of the pole and spit on the small suction cup that was attached to the mike.

"All yours," he whispered to Chesley. "I'd need a step ladder."

The DC cop delicately positioned the contact mike against a side window and pressed the suction cup against the glass. Derek pulled a lever on the side of the pole and the clip released. The PI then threw a switch on a wireless receiver he wore strapped to his belt and slipped a set of earphones over his head. Both men stood silent and motionless for what seemed like ten minutes but was probably no more than 15 seconds.

"Nothing," the PI announced. "No TV, radio, talking, snoring – nothing. I think we'd better get up there."

The two men made their way to the front door of the house, taking pains to keep to the shrubbery that covered much of the exterior. Pausing before they stepped out of their protective greenery, they drew their weapons and tip-toed up the five concrete steps; the PI was tempted to shoot out the light that illuminated the entrance of the attached home just five feet away, but he restrained himself.

"Feel like a goddamn deer in the headlights," he said, but Chesley didn't answer.

At the door Derek fumbled with a small key pick kit he kept in his inside jacket pocket. He almost had it out when Chesley reached past him and turned the doorknob. The faded red steel door swung open with a groan.

"Bad personal security," the cop whispered.

"Let's hope it continues."

With one last look behind them to make sure no one had noticed their entrance, the two men stepped into the building and closed the door behind them. They found themselves in a tiny alcove with two stained oak doors framing leaded glass inserts, through which they could see one led to a flight of stairs up to the second story, and the other into a threadbare living room on the right.

"Up," Chesley said, and he reached for the doorknob. Derek beat him to it. The door opened noiselessly.

The PI looked to his friend with concern. "Too easy," he whispered. Chesley nodded and motioned toward the stairs.

Guns cocked and safeties off, the two men crept up the old wooden stairs. With just their second step the ancient wood let out a pained scream that froze them to the spot. They waited. The sounds of their breathing seemed to echo in the darkened stairway. Long seconds ticked by. Both men strained to hear even the smallest sound from either above or below. Nothing. Derek signaled for them to continue. Several times more the stairs cried out under their combined weight, but the piercing sound elicited no response whatsoever.

"Don't like this," Chesley whispered just as they got to the top of the stairs. They found themselves facing another steel security door, this one a dull, dented black. "Not much we can do about it," Derek answered in a voice not much louder than a breath. He held up his hand to silently signal: one, two, THREE! He turned the knob and threw all his weight against the metal barrier. With a crash, he bounced off the door and back into Chesley's surprised arms. The two men recovered in an instant, aiming their weapons instinctively at whomever or whatever might come at them. After several tense seconds, it was obvious that nothing and no one was coming.

"What the hell?" the PI said aloud, his pride aching nearly as badly as his shoulder. "They don't lock the two outside doors but they lock this one?"

"Maybe there's something in there worth protecting," Chesley said hopefully, though by this time he didn't really know what to think.

"Let's find out." The PI pulled out his picks and set to work, patiently pushing and turning until at last a throw bolt clicked open on the other side of the door. With a nod of his head Derek signaled his readiness to go in. Chesley gave a thumbs-up.

This time when he turned the knob, the door opened easily. The two men cautiously stepped into the darkened room in a crouch, guns ready. They quickly scanned the small living room area illuminated by light from outside the building: a sagging, stained grey couch, an abandoned pizza box. Off to the left, a tiny galley kitchen with soda cups and crumpled paper bags dotting the counter. In front of them, a short hallway that disappeared into shadow.

Chesley signaled to Derek and then moved into the hallway with the PI covering him. To his left, a bathroom with cracked mirror and filthy sink and tub. In front, a closed door. Derek closed the distance between him and his buddy; when he was just a few feet away, Chesley signaled that he was going in. With a single waist-high kick of his heavy military-style boot, the DC cop smashed open the bedroom door with an explosive crash. Chesley dropped into a defensive posture, gun at shoulder level, scanning the room in an instant: a single bed with a stained mattress, a small desk with a laptop sitting open, the light from the LCD screen providing a faint glow in the tepid darkness.

"Clear!" he yelled back over his shoulder.

The PI moved into the room, his gun still drawn.

"What the hell is that?" he asked, indicating the computer.

"Take a look," Chesley said, motioning for him to come forward.

As soon as he stepped past the edge of the screen, his heart sank. "PUSH ANY BUTTON" scrolled across the screen in bold red letters.

"What d'ya think? IED? Some kind of beacon to let them know when we get here?"

"I don't think so," the tiny detective said resignedly. "This stinks of the grandson. He's all into computer games."

"So?"

"So, we play." With that, Derek punched the keyboard violently.

A badly-lit video began to play on the screen. In the background, the two men could clearly make-out Anne Waznewski seated on the same bed they saw before them, a gag across her mouth, her hands and feet bound with white cord. The video was good enough to see the terror in her eyes. Suddenly the rubber mask face of Jimmy Carter slid into view.

"Woa! You guys are good," a digitized voice announced triumphantly. "Only took you, what, a few hours to figure out this was all just a ruse to get you bogged down while we took a powder? Impressive. Now I know why the crooks run this country. But not for long…Sit tight. We'll be in touch."

With that the screen went dark as the hard drive whirled maniacally.

"Son of a bitch!" Chez spit angrily.

"I don't like that kid," Derek muttered through clenched teeth.

"What now?"

Derek stared out the darkened window for a few moments collecting his thoughts.

"Let's take a quick look around, see if they left any clues we can use to nail their smart-asses. And grab the laptop, although if I know the kid we won't find anything we can use on it."

Five minutes later they'd turned up nothing that put them any closer to finding Anne.

"Come on. Let's get out of here before someone calls the cops," Derek said.

As they made their way silently down the stairs, the PI rehearsed in his head how he'd explain to Brady that the little prick had outsmarted them, again. Not only was his ego feeling bruised, but he hurt for his friend. He knew Brady had a lot invested in the lady. Hell, he liked her well enough too.

They had just closed the outside security door behind them and were making their way down the concrete steps at the front of the row house, when Derek saw a movement out of the corner of his eye. He turned quickly to see a tiny black face disappear behind the curtains in the adjoining apartment.

"Hey, Chez, wait a second," he said turning back up the stairs. He knocked on the door where he'd seen the face peering out at them.

"Go away!" an elderly woman's voice cried out. "I'm gonna call the cops!"

"We are the cops!" Derek called back. And then turning to Chesley he added, "Show her your badge."

"What?"

"Hold your badge up to the peephole. Let her see it."

The cop shook his head but did as he was told.

"See? We're cops," Derek continued. "We just want to talk to you."

For a long moment there was no response. Then, ever so slowly, they heard three throw locks turn. The door opened just a crack. A small, grey-haired face stared out at them.

"Lemme see that badge," she demanded, her hand just barely sliding through the opening.

Derek signaled Chez to hand it over. The old woman studied it for several seconds.

"Look real enough," she finally muttered. "What you want from me?"

"We're looking for some people we think might have been staying upstairs, next door. Any chance you saw anyone leaving that building today?"

"I saw 'em," she said without hesitation. "Knowed sumptin' weren't right."

"What do you mean?"

"That black kid who been stayin' there and the skinny white guy had so much troubles carryin' that 'rug' down the stairs, I knowed sumptin' was wrong. Felt it in my bones."

"Did you get a good look at them?"

"My eyes ain't so good no mo'..."

"But you're sure it was a young black man and a skinny white man?"

"I can't see so good, but I can see white and black."

"I don't suppose you saw them get into a vehicle?" Chesley asked, his voice carrying the authority of the badge he'd worn for so many years.

"Matter of fact, I did," the woman said proudly. "Can't see worth a darn up close, but wit' dese I can see pretty darn good." The woman held up a pair of bird watcher's binocs.

"What kind of car was it?" Derek asked deferentially.

"Big white van. Don' know the brand."

"Anything written on the side, like an advertisement or some such?"

"Nope. Jus' white."

"Anything else? Any stickers, or dents, or...anything?"

"None 'a that stuff," the old woman answered thoughtfully. "But there is one thing..."

"What's that?" Chesley said with a tone that suggested he expected a useless discussion of some trivial element of the escape.

"I wro' down the license plate number," she said, holding up a torn piece of brown grocery bag. "I all'ays writes down license plates if they park in front'a my house."

Derek turned to Chesley, who shrugged. "I'll be damned."

*****

By the time Brady's plane landed, Chesley had alerted all local police units to be on the lookout for a white Chevy van with Maryland plates. The plate detection system was working overtime, matching the old lady's info with every license plate that passed in front of a security camera tied into the DC, VA or MD systems. That was a lot of cars.

As Brady was waiting for his suitcase to appear on the bag carousel he texted Derek, who was parked in the cellphone lot.

"In the luggage area. Be out front in 5 mins."

Just then he saw his suitcase slide down the chute from the tarmac above; he cheated down the line a bit to position himself for a quick grab. He had just hoisted his bag off carousel 3 when his cellphone rang.

What now?' he thought as he dug the phone out of his pocket, thinking that it was Derek getting back to him. "What's the problem, can't get that pig of yours to start?" he asked without saying hello.

"Mr. James?" a nervous but somehow familiar voice asked.

"Yes?" he answered tentatively, unable to quite place the caller in the noise and bustle of his current surroundings.

"It's me, Ted, Ted Wyman. From Ohio?"

"Oh sure, sure Ted. Sorry, I thought it was someone else."

"Is this a good time to talk?" He sounded tight, as if stretched thin.

"Yeh, good as any I guess. How are things in Ohio?"

"Do you remember what you asked me when you were here a week or so ago? About trying to develop something that could stop someone if they tried to interfere with an electronic machine?"

Brady stepped off to the side out of the rush and blocked his other ear to hear more clearly. "Yeh, of course I do."

"Well, I'm not sure yet, it's only a prototype," he hedged.

"But you may have something?"

"I might."

"Might? Can it stop them from changing votes?"

"No, not yet," Wyman admitted. "But I'm working on it. I've got a couple of jammers in testing. Only problem is, they tend to disrupt the entire system."

"Do you think you can get this thing to work by election day? On a scale of 1-10."

"Well, if I were being conservative, I'd say a 4. If I were betting on it, I'd say a 6. There are still some technical bugs I need to work out."

"Good work, Ted. Really good work. How long to install them?"

"Don't need to. They operate from outside the polling place. Like their software. Just have to be within a quarter mile or so."

"Great. Plan on having one ready for each of five or 6 counties I'll identify by Monday afternoon. Does that give you enough time?"

"Should."

"When will you know if they'll work?"

"Hard to say. Maybe tomorrow, the next day. It's not really something you can predict."

"Well stay on it. I'll be in touch. And Ted…"

"Yeh?"

"Thanks. This is a good thing you're doing for your country."

"Yeh, well I'm glad of that. But to be honest, it'll be enough just to stick it to the bastards who took those pictures. I hope they rot in hell."

"I don't know about hell, but if we're lucky maybe we'll get to see them rot in a federal prison."

"That'll work."

Brady closed his cellphone and exited the terminal. Sixty percent chance. He didn't like the odds. They needed a backup plan.

But first things first. Catching Hoch and his crew would be satisfying, but not unless they could find Anne and get her back in one piece. He'd seen enough of Vietnam, Iraq and Afghanistan to understand full well that victories in principle weren't really victories at all, but only excuses to allow the losers to satisfy their egos and keep their jobs. No, they needed to find Anne.

He looked up and saw his friend looking even smaller than usual as he waved from the bumper of the massive Caddy. Brady waved back, but without the broad smile that usually marked his return.

They'd find her. He'd make sure of it.

*****

Brady and Derek filled each other in on all the recent activity on the ride back to the PI's place.

"So we don't have any leads on where they might be?" Brady asked as soon as he heard the tale of Jeffrey's deception.

"Not yet. But we will, don't you worry about that," Derek answered immediately, trying to give his friend at least a hint of optimism. "Chez has got every cop within 100 miles on the look-out for the van, and the detection software is plowing through every car that's passed a video camera in the past couple of hours. It's just a matter of time."

"Anne may not have much time. The election is in two days. What do you think they'll do with her once the vote is over and they've won?"

Derek had had the same thought himself but hadn't dared express it. "We'll find her," was all he could manage to say.

The two men didn't say much more as Brady unpacked. Derek called Chesley for an update, but there was no news. The mood in the apartment was as dark as the night sky outside their windows.

As ten o'clock approached, the PI called Chesley again, this time to double-check that his people were ready to begin tracing the call they were expecting any minute. He assured them the resources were all in place.

He and Brady sat staring at their respective extensions from 9:55 on. By 10:05 they were both getting worried, but they remained stoically silent.

At 10:07 the phone finally rang. Brady swallowed heavily and lifted the receiver. Derek did the same in the bedroom, covering the mouthpiece with his hand.

"Hello?"

"What's the matter, you sound upset. Didn't think we'd call?" a metallic, digitally-altered voice began. He laughed. "Well here we are. I've got someone here I think wants to say hello."

Brady heard the phone being repositioned.

"Brady, Brady I'm so sorry," Anne began in a tearful, shaking voice. "I should've been more careful…"

With that her voice was replaced by the digitized sound of her kidnapper. Brady was certain it was Jeffrey.

"That's enough for now," the voice began. "Just wanted you to know that's she's with us, and she's doing just fine."

"Let me talk with her!" Brady demanded, knowing there was little chance.

"Trying to stretch this out so that you can trace the call – is that it? Sorry, Mr. James. We've rerouted this call so many times, even we don't know where it's been. So let's get down to brass tacks. We know you've been sticking your nose into the upcoming election, and that you think you know some big truth about the outcome. Well, Mr. James, the lady sitting here next to me says that you're wrong. That there's no story here. That you were mistaken. I think that's a very perceptive viewpoint, don't you?"

The gloating tone sent a chill up Brady's spine. "I suppose," he growled.

"You *suppose!?*" the voice on the other end exploded. "I think you'd better do a lot better than that, Mr. James. If, that is, you expect to see your little friend here again. We can be very accommodating to our friends. But we can also be *very* unpleasant to our enemies."

"She's not your enemy. I am. How about a trade? Me for her?"

"How gallant!" the voice answered playfully. "But not realistic. We've got what we want, and we've got you where we want you. Don't make us take steps we'd both regret. Do you understand me, Mr. James?"

"Yeh, yeh I understand." Brady's voice quaked as he struggled to hold his temper.

"Good. Then perhaps this story will have a happy ending after all. For all of us." In the background Brady could hear a timer suddenly begin beeping.

"Uh oh," the voice announced hurriedly, "gotta go. Don't want to give your friends too much time to try to trace us, do we? We'll be in touch."

He hung up.

Brady stared at the phone for several seconds before gently lowering it back into its cradle.

"It's definitely that little prick, Jeffrey," Derek said as he came into the living room, his face flushed with anger. "He's gonna regret he ever heard our names before this is all over."

Brady couldn't help thinking that they might all regret getting involved in this mess before it was all over.

*****

As they'd expected, Chesley's cops had not been able to trace the call.

"Little bastard's smart, I'll give him that," their friend had said by way of an explanation. "We unwound maybe half his phone jumps, but didn't have enough time to get them all."

Thoroughly frustrated and more than a little worried, Brady did not sleep well at all, tossing and turning as visions of a battered Anne kept violating his dreams. He had only been asleep a couple of hours when Derek barged into his bedroom and shook his weary friend into wakefulness.

"Come on – get your ass out of bed. You need to see this."

Brady cracked one eye open a slit and peeked at the alarm clock: 9:15. He started to complain, to beg for a few hours more shuteye, but before he could get the words out the little man was gone. Brady debated rolling over and covering his head with a pillow, but the insistence of his friend piqued his interest. It wasn't like Derek to be harassing his notoriously hard-sleeping guest.

"Okay, so what's so damn important?" he asked as he shuffled out into the living room. Derek was standing in front of the TV. He motioned for Brady to join him.

"BREAKING NEWS" a banner screamed at the bottom of the frame. Above it, a man Brady recognized all too well was just coming to a podium.

"Press conference?" Brady managed to croak.

"Watch."

Charles Van der Meer looked like hell, Brady thought as the GOP's Vice-presidential candidate adjusted a microphone in front of him.

"Ladies and gentlemen, fellow Republicans, my fellow Americans," he began, his voice low, his eyes looking straight into the cameras. "Today is one of the saddest days of my life." His voice trembled as if it might crack, but he held firm. "I think you all know that I'm not a man to shy away from a fight. In fact, some say that I enjoy a tussle a bit too much for my own good." A few half-hearted chuckles answered his admission. "But today I am announcing that I will be withdrawing from the political fight of my life, in order to devote all my energy and all my focus to an even bigger fight – a fight *for* my life." There were some *oohs* and *ahhs* from the assembled host. "Today I am announcing that I am withdrawing my name from consideration as the Vice-presidential candidate of the Republican Party." The buzz that filled the room was clearly audible on the TV set. "I have been diagnosed with stage 2 lung cancer. My doctors tell me that with aggressive chemo and radiation therapy, I have a good chance of beating this thing. But there is no way that I could devote the time and energy to my candidacy, or as your Vice President, that the people of this great country deserve. So, it is with great sadness that I must withdraw from the campaign. I want to thank each and every one of you for all your help and good wishes, and I trust that you will support whoever the party chooses to take my spot with all the enthusiasm and confidence that I have seen throughout this campaign. God bless you, God bless the Republican Party, and God bless the United States of America."

His eyes glistening and rimmed with red, Van der Meer turned from the podium without waiting for questions. His wife hugged him with visible desperation, and was soon joined by their two adult children. The four of them moved awkwardly to the edge of the stage as reporters shouted questions that were ignored. With one last wave, they were gone.

"He looked like he really believed it," Derek said as he muted the volume to cut off a commentator who had begun an instant analysis of the impact of Van der Meer's move.

"I wonder if he even knows it's a load of crap."

"Do you think they'd lie to him, tell him he has cancer, just to get him out of the race?"

Brady shrugged. "Like you said, he comes across totally sincere. And I can only guess at the sympathy vote Andrews and his new running mate will get."

"Diabolical."

"You can bet that somewhere Adam Hoch is applauding. Hey, I'm going to go get ready. Have you spoken to Chesley yet?" James asked as he headed back to his bedroom.

"He'll call us when he has something."

"Call him anyway. 'A hassled cop is a vigilant cop.' I think someone said that once."

"Wasn't a cop," the PI said sourly.

Less than an hour later, as the two friends were finishing their breakfast, another news flash crossed the TV screen. The morning news anchor announced that "knowledgeable sources" were indicating that Republican bigwigs and their counterparts from American Rights had held a secret meeting the previous night to discuss ways the two parties could "work together for mutual benefit." This had, not surprisingly, caused a firestorm of discussion both inside and outside the two parties.

"You think they know about Hoch's dirty little plan?" Derek asked when the announcement finished.

"AR, maybe. I doubt the GOP guys know anything about it. They're pretty nuts, but I don't think they'd go so far as to steal an election."

"Remember Bush in 2000," the PI said, only half in gest.

"Score one for the little guy," Brady said, marking the victory in thin air with his index finger.

Despite maintaining a false front of bravado, the two men were silent and pensive as the morning dragged on. Brady called Danny to see if his Agency friends had been able to secure any additional information from Jeffrey's hard drives (they hadn't), and to warn him to keep alert to his surroundings. The end result was a thoroughly angry, highly agitated young computer geek.

"Those bastards!" he shouted when Brady confirmed that Anne had been taken. "Have you called the police?"

"The cops are working on getting her back," Brady said calmly. He went on to explain that they didn't want to endanger Anne by making her disappearance public.

"So what, then? Do we just wait?"

"Like I told you, the police are helping us track her down. They're confident that we'll find her soon."

"Soon? What does that mean? Those guys that grabbed her are obviously nuts. She could be in real danger, Brady."

"We're doing all we can to keep her safe, Danny. I want to get her back as badly as anyone."

The computer techie's tone softened. "Yeh, yeh of course, I know that, Brady. It's just that...it's so damn unfair! She hasn't done anything to those assholes."

"They don't care. All that matters to them is to keep us quiet until after the election. Then they clean up the voting machines, watch their guy become VP, and dare us to make a stink without any proof. She doesn't really matter to them at all."

"That's what I'm afraid of," Danny said quietly. "That she'll be expendable."

"We'll find her," Brady said definitively.

It was two hours later when Chesley called on Derek's cellphone.

"We think we have a lead on the van," he said. "A camera up in Silver Spring caught a partial plate number on a white Chevy van. We think it's them."

"When?"

"The camera snapped them at 12:27 last night."

"That was twelve hours ago!" Brady exploded, his temper frayed.

"I know, I know. But we've got all units on alert and extra squad cars out looking for the van. If it's anywhere within 50 miles of Silver Spring, we'll find it."

Brady knew his friend was just telling him what all cops told all friends and family of missing persons. But he had to admit, it helped. "Yeh, okay, thanks. I know you guys are doing all you can to find her. I guess I'm just getting too old for this stuff."

"It's not the same when it's someone you know," the DC cop said.

"Yeh. Not the same at all."

CHAPTER 23

Adam Hoch was smiling.

The readout from the meeting between the AR and GOP executives had been everything he'd hoped for. He'd spent weeks priming key members of the Republican National Committee to consider an alliance with AR to help ensure a November victory. He'd bought two key members of the AR national committee to guarantee their acquiescence. Now the 'unfortunate' situation with Van der Meer had given them the opportunity to move beyond party loyalties to a merger that could guarantee a victory in two days' time. And if they didn't quite have the votes to put the GOP/AR ticket over the top? Well, then Mr. Wyman in Ohio, and his counterparts in Missouri, Colorado and Florida would make sure they had enough votes, no matter what the idiot voters said.

Hoch winced from the stabbing pain in his abdomen.

'Just a few more days,' he told himself. 'Then you can let it all go. Just a few more days...'

It had only been five months since he'd begun planning for this day. But somehow it seemed much longer. As much as he hated the Democratic incumbent and all his Socialist policies, he hadn't been sure whether to even attempt such a brazen assault on the electoral process. Until he got the news from those damn doctors.

Pancreatic cancer. Six months to live. Despite all his money, and all the donations he'd made to hospitals all over the country, there wasn't a thing they could do for him. Oh, they shot him full of chemo, and put him through a series of radiation treatments, and even tried three different experimental drugs (his money did help push him to the front of the line for a couple of those), but nothing had worked. The prognosis was still the same – now just a matter of weeks.

It angered him that he couldn't beat the disease. He was used to getting his way, to accomplishing everything he wanted. Now a few lousy cells were undermining his whole empire. But they wouldn't stop him. Not with the election, at least. Before he left this earthly vale he'd make sure the country was in the hands of people who understood that money was the one true God of the United States. He'd always joked that they should pass a Constitutional amendment to establish "In money we trust" as the national motto. Of course, he never said that around his religious friends. They wouldn't see the humor in it.

'Screw 'em', he thought as another wave of pain tore through his gut. He'd told all his associates that it was just an ulcer, nothing to worry about. Couldn't have worries about his health affecting the stock price of HI. In fact, the only person who even knew it was cancer was Jeffrey, and he had no idea how little time was left. Hoch shook his head. He didn't know if the kid was ready to take over the business. Oh, he was smart enough. And Hoch had surrounded him with the best advisers that money could buy.

But there was something about his grandson, something not quite right. Maybe it was the loss of his father at such an early age. Hoch knew that his son's death had affected his own life terribly. But he was an adult. He could take it. The kid? That was something else. Hoch had tried to be a good grandfather, but he had to admit that the business had always come first. Maybe he hadn't always been there when the kid was small. Maybe he could've invested more time and less money in the kids' upbringing.

What was done was done. There was no one else to whom he would even think of leaving his controlling interest in the company, but that didn't stop him from worrying about the future.

I mean, Christ! I told him to go easy on the damn accountant. And then he turns up dead. Hit and run, the cops said. I knew better, even though he wouldn't admit that he'd done it, or ordered Tommy to do it. And Wainwright! I knew I shouldn't have brought Jeffrey along when we met. I knew he'd lose his temper if the Senator didn't go along with our plan. But how the hell was I to know that he'd slug the guy and that he'd fall into the river and get dragged down by that stupid camel hair coat of his. Maybe he hit his head. Maybe he just couldn't swim too well. Whatever, he was gone before we could even try to help him. The whole project, almost destroyed before it ever really began.'

Hoch took a deep breath as the pain subsided. *'Of course, he did hack Wainwright's computer and erase all records of our communication, and he's been pretty good at keeping an eye on that goddamn retired journalist and his half-pint assistant,'* Hoch mused. *'Besides, there's no way we could've developed the software to manipulate the voting machines without his know-how. So maybe it's a wash,'* the billionaire conceded, even as a tiny voice in the back of his mind told him that Jeffrey was a loose cannon that could very easily backfire on his beautiful plan. A plan that no one except him really understood – not that damn ex-reporter, not his AR contacts, not even Jeffrey. They all thought it ended with the election. If they only knew…

'48 hours. That's all we need. Once the election is over, no one will believe a story about vote rigging without proof, any more than they believed that Bush stole the election from Gore. And when their newly elected President dies in office and Blackburn moves into the White House? Americans want to believe their system is fair. They want to think it's unassailable. And that's the weakness in the system. If only Jeffrey can do what he's told for two more days…'

The billionaire oilman shook his head. *'Nothing I can do about that now,'* he said resignedly, and with a sigh he walked to where Tommy waited in the black limo.

*****

Brady jumped up the moment the phone in Derek's apartment rang.

"Could be Chesley," he announced to the PI, who was busy cleaning and reassembling his pistol for the third time that morning.

But the voice on the other end of the line was not his police friend.

"Good morning, Mr. James," the familiar metallic digitized voice began. Brady put his hand over the mouthpiece and furiously signaled Derek to call Chesley. "I hope you slept well."

"Actually, I slept like refried crap," Brady admitted. "Let me talk to Anne."

"Oh ho, still don't understand the situation, is that it? You see Mr. James, in this relationship, I give the orders and you jump. Not the other way around."

Brady could hear the self-satisfaction in the voice on the other end of the line. *Just what I'd expect from Jeffrey,'* he thought, but he grit his teeth and tried a more conciliatory tact.

"You're right, of course," he said with just enough attitude to make it sound real. "You hold all the cards."

"Yes, I do. I'm happy to hear that you recognize that fact, Mr. James. Our lady guest seems like a nice person. I'd hate to see anything bad happen to her just because one of her friends doesn't know how talk to us. I mean, she might fall down some stairs, or get hit while changing a tire. Might even end up at the bottom of the Potomac…"

Brady took a deep breath to calm himself. "What do you want? You've already got us where you want us. What else is there?"

"Oh, quite a bit, actually. First of all, I want you to know that we are monitoring all the police frequencies. If we get even a hint that you've contacted the cops, your friend has an accident."

"We won't, we won't!" Brady lied, hoping against hope that either Jeffrey was lying or that Chesley had kept the search under wraps.

"Good. Second, I want you to email us your notes for the story you're writing. ALL the notes. And I want them in the next ten minutes." He dictated an email address.

"My computer is in the car downstairs. I'll need a few more minutes," he lied.

"I'm an understanding guy," Jeffrey taunted. "I'll give you 15. No more."

"Okay, I'll do my best." Brady speculated that Hoch wanted to know the direction the story had taken. He was confident that he could edit out the references to stealing the election and Wainwright's death and just send a bland story about the closeness of the upcoming election and how AR and the GOP might work together. Time would be tight, but it was do-able.

"And lastly, Mr. James, I want you to call off the midget. I don't like freaks, and I don't want to see him and his ugly old Cadillac within 20 miles of my current location. I see that little asshole, and your girlfriend is toast. Got it?" The voice was no longer easy-going, but hard, nasty.

"I understand."

"Good. Then perhaps this will work out after all."

"May I talk to Anne?" Brady asked quickly, before the call ended. "Just a few words to be sure she's still...okay?" The subservience he put into his voice almost made him physically nauseous, but he swallowed the bile rising in his throat.

There was a long pause. "Sure, why not? You do as we say, and we can be accommodating. Here."

Brady heard the sounds of the phone being passed. "Brady? Brady, don't come looking for me. They've got guns!"

"Calm down, calm down," he said gently. "Are you okay? Are they treating you okay?"

"Yes, I'm okay," she said with faint enthusiasm. "I just want to go home."

"Hang in there, honey. The election is the day after tomorrow. We'll have you home by Wednesday."

"That's right, James. You tell her," the digitized voice cut in. As Brady had expected, he'd been monitoring another extension. "If the two of you, and that little pain-in-the ass PI, do what we say, in three days you'll all be back together again as if this never happened."

"That's all we want."

"Good. Then this conversation is over." The phone went dead.

Derek looked to him with questioning eyes. "So?"

"So, he told me not to call the cops and not to look for Anne."

"Right," the PI said sarcastically.

"Did you get through to Chez?"

Derek nodded. "He'll call us when he has something."

"I am going to call him back and tell him to keep the cops off the radio with any talk about Anne. The kid said they're monitoring the scanner."

"Stupid geek. Why would he tell us that? Maybe he's not so bright after all."

"He's smart, all right, but it seems like he doesn't have a lot of common sense. Let's hope so, anyway."

Just then the phone rang.

"James," Brady answered, bracing for further interaction with the kidnappers.

"Brady, Chez. That little punk is too cocky for his own good. He didn't change his phone daisy-chain and we were able to pin his location down to a neighborhood in Adelphi, Maryland."

"Where the hell is that?" Brady asked, his voice tense with excitement.

"A couple of miles northwest of Silver Spring. He didn't stay on the line long enough for us to get the house address, but we know it's within a mile or so of the intersection of Metzerott and Riggs Roads. I'm going to send a bunch of black and whites out there to see if we can flush him."

"No!" Brady barked loud enough that Derek jumped. "He says he's monitoring a scanner so he's probably watching the roads as well. Everything from this point forward has to be close hold: no marked cars, no radio chatter about Anne, nothing that could make them do something stupid."

"Ok, all right," Chesley calmed his friend. "We'll keep it low key. I'll send some of our undercover guys out there with photos of Anne and Jeffrey. If they see them, or the van, I'll have 'em sit tight and get back to us. How's that?"

"Perfect. You've got our numbers."

Derek interrupted. "Brady, give him this one…" and he read off the number of a cellphone he held in his hand. "A new disposable. No way they can track it."

As soon as Brady was convinced that Chez understood what he needed done, he thanked his friend and hung up.

"The noose is tightening," the tiny PI announced confidently, moving to Brady's side to take back the cellphone.

"I don't know. I hope so, but somewhere in the back of my mind I'm thinking this could be another one of Jeffrey's tricks. Get us running in circles again."

The assured look faded from Derek's face. "Could be, I suppose. But my gut tells me no. This kid is cocky, too cocky for his own good. He thinks his grandfather's money can fix anything. He thinks he only needs to keep us quiet for another 48 hours and they've won. He's gotten sloppy."

Brady looked out the window at the cool November sky.

"I hope so," he said softly. "I really hope so."

*****

The sun was just setting, a bloody red glow staining the underside of the dark storm clouds that marked a cold front moving into the area. Brady and Derek sat at the long formal dining table sipping coffee, silent, each lost in his own thoughts.

What do we do if we don't find her?' Brady mused as he stirred his coffee endlessly. He didn't even want to consider the possibility, but he had no choice. Even with the information the cops now possessed, he knew that there was a better than fifty per cent chance that they wouldn't find Anne until after the Tuesday election. Adelphi wasn't DC, but there were still a lot of apartments and single family homes out that way, too many to search door to door. Certainly not in little more than a day.

Just 30 hours until the polls opened in New Hampshire. Thirty hours to find Anne and somehow shut down Hoch's plan before he undercut the very bedrock of the U.S. political system. His stomach growled, whether from want of food or nerves, he wasn't sure. He damn sure wasn't hungry, even though they hadn't eaten since breakfast. *'Probably too much coffee.'* That's what Anne would tell him, if she were there. Just the thought of her sent a wave of emotion surging through his body. They *had* to find her. He hadn't stayed single all these years just to see the one woman who meant something to him disappear in Hoch's damn political game!

He felt his heart racing and took a few deep breaths to calm himself down. When he looked up, Derek was looking at him quizzically.

"Too much coffee," he half-lied.

The PI nodded. "We'll find her, bro. Don't worry."

Brady didn't bother to argue. Derek knew him too well.

It was fifteen minutes later when the cellphone rang. Brady grabbed it before the first ring had ended.

"Yeh?"

"Found 'em," Chesley's voice announced proudly. "One of the kid's sidekicks took the van out to pick up some take-out, and a plainclothes detective spotted it. Tailed him back to an apartment building just off Riggs Road. He's talking to the manager right now trying to figure out the exact apartment."

Brady almost yelped out loud. "Thank you, Chez!" he said, exercising as much self-control as he could muster. "What's next?"

"Well, I thought you two master investigators might want to hightail it up here to help us snag Hoch's grandson and however many flunkies he's got working with him. If, that is, you're interested in doing a little police work instead of just writing about it."

"We're walking out the door as we speak," Brady said, indicating to his PI friend to get up and get moving.

"Come to the fast food chicken joint just north of the intersection of Riggs and Metzerott. We'll stage out of that lot. Nobody'll notice a few unmarked cars."

"See you there in…however long it takes." Brady hung up and grabbed his jacket.

"They located the van," Brady said as he headed for the door.

"Did they see Anne, or Jeffrey?"

"Just some flunky, but they're sure it's the van."

"And where are we going?"

"We've been invited to a party crashing," Brady said, and the diminutive PI heard the barely controlled anger in his friend's voice.

'Wouldn't want to be that little asshole if Brady gets to him first,' the PI thought as he waddled full speed after his friend. *'Or if I get to him first, for that matter.'* And he smiled.

CHAPTER 24

Brady glanced over at the speedometer: 75. One thing you had to say about those old Caddies, you couldn't tell if you were going 45 or 85. The big boat rocked smoothly from side to side as they tore across the Beltway toward Adelphi. No matter how fast Derek drove, however, it couldn't be fast enough for Brady. He felt as if his heart would jump out of his chest any second.

"Can you bump it up a few more mph?" he asked, knowing full well that they were already well over the speed limit.

"We won't get there any faster if we lose twenty minutes trying to talk a cop out of a ticket," the PI answered.

Brady nodded to himself. *True enough,*' he agreed, but it didn't make it any easier.

In less than twenty minutes they turned off of 495 and headed south on New Hampshire. At Adelphi they turned left and then right on Riggs. Finally, Brady spied the sign for the chicken joint up ahead.

"There!" he pointed through the windshield.

"Got it."

When they pulled into the parking lot they saw no sign whatsoever that a dozen cops were readying a raid.

"Where *are* they?" Brady asked plaintively. "Could this be the wrong place?"

"Take it easy, bro, you're gonna give yourself a stroke! Worse, you're gonna give *me* one! They're probably inside. Low-profile, remember?"

The moment Derek put the car into 'P' Brady threw open the door and hurried across the parking lot, leaving the tiny PI to shuffle after him as best he could.

"You'd think it was the goddamn Olympics," he huffed as he chugged along in Brady's wake.

Once inside, James scanned the restaurant for any sign of Chez. He saw him at once, surrounded at four adjoining tables by a motley crew – eight men and one woman – who could only be undercover cops. He waited a few seconds as DiLaurain limped into the restaurant, his face red – whether from exertion or irritation, he couldn't tell. Then the two of them walked over to where the cops were waiting.

"Gentleman, this is Brady James, once a respected member of the Fourth Estate," Chesley stood and introduced them.

"A respected reporter?" one of the younger guys said. "Isn't that an oxymoron?"

"*You're* a goddamn ox of a moron," one of the older guys joked and they all laughed.

"And this is Derek DiLaurain, PI extraordinary," Chesley continued when the guffaws had died down.

"And you're undercover as a school kid, is that it?" another cop asked.

More laughter. Normally, Derek would've lashed out at such a put-down, but he'd been around cops so long that he'd come to understand their slash and burn sense of humor. Almost.

"And what are you dressed up as, a three-bag-a-day street corner junkie?" he shot back.

Even louder laughter.

They shook hands all around. Now that the introductory pissing match was over, they could get down to business.

"Okay, this is what we've got," Chesley began, unfolding a piece of paper on which he'd drawn a basic schematic of the apartment building and the parking lot that surrounded it on three sides. "We're 99 per cent sure they're on the third floor, number 307. We think that there's three of them, in addition to Anne. We don't know if they're armed, so we will assume that they are."

Brady listened intently, but what he heard did not engender total confidence. "99 per cent...we think...we don't know..." His stomach churned but he held his tongue. He knew Chesley was a pro, and assumed the guys he'd picked would be as well.

Chesley outlined the approach he'd chosen, assigning two groups of four men to enter at opposite ends of the building, with a third group to cover the two rear exits. Speaking in a slow, methodical tone that he had obviously used many times before, he explained minute by minute how he expected the three groups to take their positions and advance on the subject apartment.

"When we get to the front door, we listen to see if we can identify where each individual inside is located. We will wait there no longer than 30 seconds, after which you, Peterson," he directed a huge hulk of a man with shoulders nearly as wide as a doorway, "you will kick in the door and Team One comes in right behind you, low and hard. I will order the perps onto the floor. If any of them raises a firearm, you will evaluate whether the captive is in any way endangered before you return fire. If she is out of the line of fire, you are cleared to use deadly force. If she is being used as a shield, get behind furniture or whatever is available and hold your fire until given further orders. If there is no threatening response, move immediately from room to room until we identify where all the perps are located as well as the victim. At no time will we risk bodily harm to the victim. Is that understood?"

Nods all around. The light-hearted mood of just minutes earlier was long gone, replaced by the game faces Brady had seen so many times before in similar situations.

"Good. Any questions?"

No one spoke up, except Brady.

"What about Derek and me?"

"You will trail behind Team 2, keeping well back until the room is secured," Chesley explained in a voice that brooked no argument. "I will call for you as soon as we are certain that the threat is neutralized. Understood?"

Brady nodded. "Got it," Derek said.

"Good," Chesley responded without even a hint of a smile. "Not to put too fine a point on this, but any interference by you two, whether intentional or not, could endanger Anne."

"We understand," Brady reiterated. He realized that his friend was risking his badge if their presence caused any kind of screw-up.

"Then let's go get Anne back from those assholes," Chesley announced to the entire group.

The twelve cops rose as one and headed to the door without any idle chatter. Chesley fell in next to his two friends.

"Don't worry, we'll get her out safe and sound," he said, resting his hand on Brady's back. "My guys are good."

"I believe you," Brady said with more certainty than he felt. Turning to face his friend, he added, "And whatever happens, thanks."

"Time for that when all this is over," he answered. "You two come with me."

The bright lights in the parking lot made everything seem a little too intense, a little too artificial to Brady as he followed his friend out the door. It was as if he were in a dream, watching all that happened from a distance. Chesley hustled them and the sole policewoman into his unmarked car and then led a small caravan of assorted muscle cars out of the lot and down Riggs to a moderately large apartment complex not a mile from the chicken joint. The cars separated as they approached the entrance to the complex, with two cars turning right into the driveway, separated one from the other by a good 100 yards, and the third driving straight past to hang a u-turn another few hundred yards down the road. It returned to the complex about two minutes later. To anyone watching from the apartments, it would look like just another three cars-full of residents on their way home. Or so the rescue team hoped.

Once inside the complex, Chesley turned off to the right of the main building while the second car parked to the left. When the third car straggled in, it went around back to park. Fortunately, the lighting in the apartment lot was nowhere near as blinding as at the restaurant, so the odds of anyone making Brady from a distance were minimal.

Derek was another matter. To be extra-cautious, Chesley let them out at the curb by the side of the building, where a lookout would have to be stationed in the stairwell to be able see them.

"Just go inside and wait for me at the bottom of the stairs. We'll be right in," he instructed.

It took all of Brady's willpower to avoid glancing up at the third floor to see if anyone was watching them as they crossed the short distance to the side entrance. Less than a minute later, Chez and his young partner came in, the older cop carrying a brown shopping bag that he immediately tossed to one side.

"Nobody worries about an old guy coming back from the supermarket," he said with just a hint of a sly smile. "Let's go."

He began climbing the stairs quickly, taking some two at a time. Brady huffed trying to keep up, and Derek pushed and pulled himself up the stairway as fast as his undersized legs could manage. At the second floor landing the DC cop stopped to let them catch up.

"Now remember, you stay back in the stairwell until I call for you – right?"

"Yeh, yeh, we'll be waiting," Brady puffed.

"Just don't forget us, Chez," Derek jibed with a tired grin.

"I'm old, not antique," the cop said, and with a nod of his head he continued up the last flight of stairs with his two friends trailing behind.

At the doorway into the third floor corridor, Chesley pulled out his cellphone and hit the walkie-talkie function.

"Team One, in place," he said softly.

Brady couldn't quite make out the two replies, but he assumed the other teams confirmed their readiness as well.

"Well, this is it," the cop whispered matter-of-factly. "Wish us luck."

"I wish you success," Brady answered.

Chesley gave him a thumbs-up and opened the door for the policewoman. "After you, darling," he said as domestically as he could muster.

The female cop gave him a nasty sneer, but she did as she was told.

Then the door swung shut, and Brady and Derek were left alone in the stairwell.

For several seconds neither man said a word. They stared at the door as if they expected it to talk to them, to explain what was happening on the other side of the white steel slab. It remained silent.

"Mighty quiet in there," Derek finally said when the tension grew too intense.

"That's a good thing, I hope."

Not five seconds later they heard the crash of a door splintering and then the all-too-familiar blast of a handgun followed immediately by return fire from a service revolver reverberated throughout the hallway.

"Damn!" the PI said, flinching back from the explosion.

Brady didn't say a word, but looked to his friend with a blank expression of horror.

Long seconds, and then minutes passed without another sound.

"I'm going to take a look," Brady said, reaching for the door handle.

Derek grabbed his arm. "Give them a few minutes," he explained softly. "Let them do their job."

Brady exhaled deeply, but then dropped his arm.

Minutes passed. The two men stood as if rooted to the stairway. As the time slipped away it looked increasingly to the PI like his friend might jump out of his skin if they didn't learn something soon. He was about to try some words of reassurance, when the door swung open. It was Chesley.

"She's fine. Come on," he said, holding the door open for them.

Brady virtually leapt through the doorway, turning left toward the room where they'd thought Anne was being held. Derek and Chesley followed close on his heels.

The door to room 307 was cracked at the throw bolt and the hinges were sprung. The unmistakable sulfurous odor of gunpowder hung heavily in the air. As anxious as he was to enter, Brady hesitated just an instant at the threshold, half afraid to step inside despite his friend's reassurance.

"Brady!" a familiar voice called out in relief and joy.

In an instant Anne's arms were around his neck, hugging him as though she would never let go.

"Are you okay?" he asked, holding her at arm's length to take a look for himself.

"I am now," she said with a smile, and before he even had time to think about it he was kissing her and holding her close.

"Where's that little asshole grandson of Hoch's?" Derek asked from the hallway, stepping past them to move into the room.

Chesley frowned. "Gone. Looks like he'd pried open the door to the adjoining room, and when we kicked in this door he took off, using some kind of climbing gear to repel down the front of the building. By the time we got the situation here under control, he was nowhere to be found. I should have posted someone out front." His slumped shoulders and weary tone spoke of the disappointment and embarrassment he felt.

"Not your fault, Chez," one of the other cops argued. "We all missed it. Who would've thought the little jerk would've climbed down the front of the building? He looks like a geek, not a goddamn mountain climber."

"Don't worry, Chez, we'll get him," Derek chimed in. "He can run, but he can't hide. It's just a matter of time."

"Yeh, thanks you two, but even so..."

"'Even so' nothing!" Brady interrupted them. "What you guys did was heroic. I'm going to file a story with the Post so that everyone in the city knows what went down here."

"You might want to wait until we get the kid and Hoch," Derek said in a whispered aside. "It'll make for a much better ending."

"Everyone's an editor," Brady said with a smile. "Yeh, ok, we'll wait, but one way or the other the people of this city are going to know what their police force do to keep them safe day in and day out."

"Thanks. Appreciate that," Chesley said with a nod. "But for now, let's get Anne and these two losers to the hospital. We've already got an APB out for Jeffrey. He won't get far."

Chesley indicated two young men, their hands cuffed behind their backs, one of whom was bleeding from a wound in his leg that two of the officers were trying to staunch. The bleeder was a long-haired Italian-looking kid with tattoos on both arms, probably no more than 25; the other was a thin black kid, even younger, with a long scar across one cheek. Neither looked all that tough at the moment.

"We'll question them, see if we can get any leads on the grandkid," Chesley explained. "Maybe he talked about his plans while they were here together."

In the distance, the sound of an ambulance siren could be heard coming closer.

"I think we have a pretty good idea of where he'll turn up," Brady said, turning to his PI friend.

"Find Hoch, and you'll find the kid," Derek echoed.

They had less than 30 hours before the polls opened.

CHAPTER 25

Jacob Andrews and Ned Blackburn were making one last tour through key swing states before the campaigning ended with a mass rally in Andrews' home state of Tennessee on election eve. With just hours remaining before the campaign came to a close, AR headquarters in Fredericksburg was a beehive of last-minute activity – finalizing plans to get out the vote, pulling ads from decided markets and swinging them to toss-up states, analyzing last-minute polling, even praying when nothing else looked to work. At a glance the mood among the hordes of young volunteers was upbeat, even cocky. A closer look, however, revealed a considerably more sober assessment by the older professional campaigners. They knew that Andrews was lagging his Democratic opponent, even with the four per cent boost from the AR faithful he got by adding Blackburn to the ticket. Barring a miracle, the GOP would lose this election by anywhere from two to five percent.

Not every older face bore a worried scowl, however. Adam Hoch was quietly confident, moving from office to office with a word of encouragement, even the occasional smile. In just over twelve hours he would engineer the greatest fraud in the history of the country, maybe even the world. And he felt good about it. He might not be around to see the long-term results of his good work, but he was assured that Blackburn would make a solid, dependable President, once Andrews was out of the picture. His beloved country would be governed according to the principles of the Constitution, not some namby pamby do-gooder philosophy that would sacrifice the risk-takers and job creators in order to subsidize the lazy and incompetent. Immigration would be orderly, based on the needs of American business, not the dreams of uneducated third world freeloaders. States' rights would trump the federal bureaucracy. Taxes would be fair, predictable and lower. The national debt would not be pushed off on our grandchildren, but eliminated once and for all. And our young boys would not be sent to fight overseas unless our own freedoms or our closest friends were threatened. Once more the U.S. would reclaim its position as the undisputed leader of a free, capitalist world. *'We'll show those damn Chinks,'* he thought as he glanced around the AR war room, a large open office space dotted with computer stations and oversized LCD screens. He felt a physical swelling of pride as he looked at all the eager young faces, dedicated, determined. These were the people who would make America great once more.

Even as he surveyed the scene, however, he couldn't help but wonder how things were going with Jeffrey. For all his brains, the kid was still unpredictable as all hell. Hoch restrained himself from calling the emergency contact number his grandson had left him, worrying that James or his midget flunky might have some way of tracing it. Those two had caused him some serious concern. But as long as they had the secretary, James wasn't going to interfere. Hoch felt it in his bones. And once the vote was over, they'd pull the software from the voting machines, buy off Wyman and his fellow election officials, and no one would be the wiser. He knew that Jeffrey wanted to deal more 'permanently' with the election geeks, but Hoch thought a few million and the threat of less pleasant circumstances would suffice. Or at least he hoped so. He hadn't wanted anyone to get hurt. But as Jeffrey always said, you can't make an omelet without breaking a few eggs. If they needed to break some eggs, so be it.

*****

Brady stood at the apartment window and watched the red flashing lights and wailing siren of the ambulance disappear from the Adelphi apartment complex parking lot. He hoped Anne understood why he hadn't come with her to the hospital. There just wasn't enough time.

"Don't worry. They'll take good care of her," Chesley reassured him. "Let's get this over with and you can go visit her."

Brady nodded and turned away from the window. He struggled to refocus on the election.

"We need to locate Hoch," Brady began once the DC cop and Derek had flopped down on the sofa. "I'm betting Jeffrey will make a beeline to the old man."

"I can call some people out in Montana," Chez offered.

Brady shook his head. "No. We have to assume Hoch's got contacts in the police force there and we don't want him covering his tracks before we can get to him. Let me call a reporter I met out there, and Derek, why don't you call that AR contact and see if he knows what Hoch is up to. I'm guessing he won't be far from those bozos come tomorrow."

"Will do, although I doubt I can get to him before tomorrow," the PI said.

"Try him now. We're running out of time."

As the PI punched in the number, Brady turned to Chesley. "Do you have any insider friends in Virginia, someone you know and trust who has the juice to get us into AR headquarters ?"

"Might. I'd have to check around a bit."

"Do it. We may need to go there if we can't find Hoch any other way."

"You got it," the DC cop said, opening his cell phone to page through his contacts.

"He's got his voicemail on," Derek reported. "Left him a message to call us first thing. Told him we want to be there on the big day to see how the operation runs."

"You know, you're one sneaky little bastard," Brady said with a smile.

"Stop it; you'll make my head swell."

"Now there's a mental image - we could put you on the dashboard like one of those bobbleheads."

"You really are one sick puppy," Derek said with a shake of his head, but the hint of a grin snuck out from under his hurt expression.

For the next hour the three men tracked down every contact they could think of who might be able to facilitate their entry into the AR headquarters building the following morning. Just to be sure, Chesley assigned a team of detectives to cover all the entrances to the building. It was nearly eight o'clock when Derek's cell rang. It was Roger Goodman, the AR National Director.

"So, you want to come down here in the morning to see how things run on game day, huh?"

"Actually, we'd like to come down there right now. You know, set the scene, meet some of the key players. It's the payoff to our story – how it all turns out and how your team handles things."

"Okay, all right, sounds like a winner. How many of you?"

"Well, if it's not asking too much, maybe four of us?"

"Four?! NBC could cover us with less than that. What are you doing, a serialized novel?"

"Hey, we're the Post – we do it right." He glanced over at Brady, who rolled his eyes.

"Yeh, right. Okay, why not. I'll call down and leave four passes under your name with security."

"Great. Thanks. By the way, are you expecting any bigshots? Blackburn, maybe even the big guy?"

"You mean Mr. Hoch? He's already down here. From what I understand, should be here most of the day tomorrow as well, although I don't know if he'll be giving interviews. We really don't have much control over our contributors, you know."

The PI swallowed hard. "Actually, I meant Mr. Andrews. But Hoch would be good as well. And anyone else who our readers might find interesting. Can you help us get to them?"

"It's going to be a nuthouse in here tomorrow, but I'll see what I can do," the politico said.

"Thank you very much. Will we see you there as well?"

"Where else would I be? Hell, I've almost been living there the last 10 days or so."

Derek made sure he kept the Director happy by setting up an interview with him the next day; by the time he hung up he was almost vibrating with energy.

"Hoch's there now and I got Goodman to give us four passes," he announced as soon as he closed the phone.

"Christ, we need to get moving! We'll need to stop by your place to pick up some equipment," Brady said to his small friend.

"What kind of equipment?"

Brady quickly explained the raw outline of his plan. "Okay?"

"You're leaving a helluva lot up to chance," Derek said with the tilt of his head that told Brady he had real reservations.

"Do you have a better idea? In seven hours the polls open in New Hampshire, and Ohio's only a few hours later. We really don't have time for anything else. It's this, or... I don't know what."

Neither of his companions said a word.

"All right then. We can pick them up on our way. Chez, can you tell your team down there to keep an eye on all the entrances to the AR building? I've got to believe that Jeffrey will be heading that way sooner rather than later."

"You got it," the cop said, and immediately punched the walkie-talkie on his cellphone.

"And let them know that if they see the grandson, do NOT stop him. Try to follow him without being seen."

"No problem-o."

"Thanks. Now let's get moving. If we can get there before Jeffrey, I think we might be able to derail this whole thing without firing a shot."

"I sure hope you're right on this," Derek said, his tone unconvinced.

"So do I," Brady said softly as he headed for the door.

*****

In the car on the way to AR Headquarters in Fredericksburg, Brady called the hospital to see how Anne was doing.

"I'm fine, I'm fine," she answered, sounding every bit her usual self. "Just a little tired and stressed-out. What are you up to?"

"We're on our way down to Fredericksburg to visit the AR National Headquarters. Seems old Mr. Hoch is down there."

"Have the cops found Jeffrey?"

"Not yet," he said, but his voice betrayed him.

"Brady, you don't think he's on his way to see his grandfather, do you? You should leave him to the police. That's not your job. He's dangerous, Brady, and more than a little nuts – I can tell you from personal experience."

"Don't worry, honey, we've got Chez with us." He looked over at his police friend who smiled and shook his head.

"That's reassuring," Anne said, "but not very. STAY OUT OF IT! I've had enough negative excitement for a few days."

"I'll be careful. I promise."

Derek tapped him on the shoulder and leaned forward, his lips puckered in mock kisses. Brady pushed him face-first back into his seat.

"You know I'd much rather be there with you."

"You're too stubborn to ever do what you're supposed to," she complained, but only half-heartedly.

"As soon as we wrap this up, I'll be headed your way."

"Hmm. I certainly hope I'm out of here before then."

"Then I'll be headed wherever you are."

Brady could almost hear her smile on the other end of the line.

"I like the way you lie, you silver-tongued devil."

"I'm hurt."

"You're full of crap, is what you are. But seriously, Brady, be careful. That kid is screwed up."

"I'll call you when I can."

"You do that."

James clicked his cellphone closed.

"Hen-pecked and you're not even married," Derek jabbed from the back seat.

"If I have to be pecked, she's the hen I want to do it," Brady said with more seriousness that the PI would have expected. He pursed his lips but kept quiet.

They stopped at Derek's apartment just long enough for the PI to run up and grab his equipment. In less than ten minutes they were headed south on I-95. Chesley had called his team and they were already in place.

Fredericksburg is a small town of roughly 25,000, located about an hour south of Washington. It was the scene of one of the bloodiest battles of the Civil War, and the echoes of that tragic day still reverberate in the hearts and minds of a good many of the long-time residents. The battlefield is a National Park, there are tours of the battle lines, and the locals claim they have more ghosts per capita than any other town in the nation.

Perfect place for AR National Headquarters.

As Chesley pulled his unmarked police car into the strip mall just off the Blue and Gray Parkway, not far from the Jefferson Davis Highway, Derek marveled at the transformation that had come over the low-key headquarters since his last visit. For one thing, the parking area in front of the building and a large open field next door were both overflowing with vehicles, including a used car lot's worth of pickup trucks. For another, a huge banner reading "Andrews-Blackburn, Government of, by and for the People" nearly covered the entire front of the structure. Brady counted the Confederate flag decals in the back windows of trucks. He gave up at 11. *The War lives on,'* Brady thought as Chez followed the directions of a young volunteer to the dirt lot adjoining the strip mall.

"You'd think something big was going on around here," Chez joked as he rammed his car into the grassy parking space.

"There is. Just not what some of them are expecting," Brady said.

"I've got the equipment," Derek added as he got out of the car.

Chez scanned the lot until he located his team members' vehicles. Out of sight, in the shadowy periphery of the lot, he met with them in groups of twos and threes and explained the drill. All of them were keen to get ahold of the little asshole who'd escaped their sweep in Maryland.

As soon as they were sure the entire perimeter of the building was covered, Brady and his two friends made their way into the AR headquarters, pushing past dozens of gleeful supporters who had come to receive instructions for transporting voters to the polls the next morning, or just to revel in the newly-found influence of their splinter group party.

"Jesus, looks like a Charlie Daniels concert," Derek whispered at the top of the stairs. Brady looked around at the strange amalgam of long-haired bearded yokels who looked like they just stepped out of a Mathew Brady photo of the Civil War with clean-cut young lawyer types in business suits. He couldn't argue with his friend's assessment. But they had more important things to do than characterize the AR electorate.

"Chez, keep an eye out for Hoch, or his bodyguard – a big black guy named Tommy. Derek and I have some arrangements to make."

With the DC cop eyeing the crowd, Brady and Derek made their way out of the milling supporters toward a corridor where the PI had met with the AR National Director just 10 days earlier. At the entrance to the hallway a stout security guard stood with his arms crossed, looking none too friendly.

"May I help you?" he asked in a tone that sounded anything but helpful.

Brady pulled out the reporter's ID he'd secured down in Florida. "Brady James, Washington Post, and my associate," he told the skeptical guard. "We're covering the election."

"This area is closed to the public," he said bluntly.

"We're not the public," Brady said. "Like I said, we're covering the election."

"Not here. Not unless someone tells me to let you through."

"Goddamn it!" Derek suddenly exploded. "We're here for an interview with Mr. Goodman. Are you going to explain to him that we couldn't do the interview because you wouldn't let us through?"

The guard looked flustered for just an instant, but rapidly recovered his cool. "Go to the receptionist out front. She'll get ahold of Mr. Goodman, and then you can do whatever he says."

The PI looked to argue some more, but Brady put his hand on the little guy's shoulder.

"We understand," he said to the guard. "You're just doing your job. We'll be back."

He steered Derek back out to the main room.

"You're not going to let that pissant guard screw things up, are you?" the PI fumed as they pushed into the mob.

"Of course not, but we don't want to alert Goodman that we're here. For all we know he's working with Hoch. Besides, I've got a better idea."

He led the way through the crowd over to where Chesley was standing and whispered in his ear. A stern look came over his friend's face.

"Let's go have a talk with this guy," he said.

"Yes, let's," Brady said, and the three of them headed back to where the guard blocked the hallway.

Derek lagged behind so no one could approach unexpectedly, while Brady and Chesley continued to where the guard awaited.

"Look, I told you, you need to get permission from the receptionist," he began while they were still ten feet away.

Chesley reached into his jacket and pulled out his identification.

"Police. I'm afraid I'm going to have to ask you to come with me."

The guard looked closely at the badge. "I can't leave my post. I'll have to contact my supervisor," he began, pulling out a small walkie-talkie.

"Sorry, no can do," Chez said, pulling out his service revolver and holding it where only the guard could see. "You're coming with me, right now."

The guard started to raise his hands, but dropped them when Chez barked an order. The DC cop pulled the guard's pistol from his holster, and then, with a look over his shoulder to make sure no one had seen them, he spun the guard as the two of them followed Brady down the hallway.

"Which ones are unoccupied?" Brady asked, indicating the offices that lined the hall.

The guard pointed with his chin. "Most of them at this end. They've got a big meeting going on down in the last office."

Brady gently turned the knob to the first door and peaked inside. It was empty.

"In here," he said, and in an instant Chez, Derek and the flustered guard all slipped in behind him.

It was less than ten minutes later when a security guard wearing a distinctly ill-fitting uniform emerged from the office.

"Make sure your guys all know Hoch and Jeffrey by sight," Brady reminded his friend.

"Oh, they'll recognize them all right," Chesley said, adjusting his hat.

"Let me know as soon as they see either of them."

"*If* they see them."

"The kid *has* to come here. He's freaked out, he probably thinks the cops are after him. Where else would he go?" Brady recognized the desperation creeping into his voice.

"I have no idea. But it's a big state."

"But his grandfather is here."

"I'll keep my fingers crossed," the cop said as he turned to take his position in the hallway.

Brady closed the door. The security guard, wearing only his underwear, with duct tape restraining his wrists, ankles and mouth, lay in one corner of the room. Derek was fiddling with some equipment in the black gym bag he carried.

"Ready?" Brady asked.

"Showtime," the PI said with a big smile.

James opened the door to the office and peered outside. The hallway was empty except for Chesley, who gave him a thumbs-up. Brady signaled to Derek and the two of them slipped quickly across the hall to an office that was pretty much the twin of the one they'd just left.

"You assemble the equipment. I'll take a look at the other offices," Brady directed.

As the PI got to work, Brady slipped out of the office and made his way down the hallway as quickly as he could without drawing unwanted attention. He made a mental note of the layout of each office and then returned to where Derek was busy assembling the trap with which he hoped to catch Hoch. As the PI tested his handiwork, Brady paced nervously. If Jeffrey didn't show up, or if they lost contact with Hoch, they had no chance to stop the old man's plan. The election would take place, four states would swing from blue to red, and Hoch's candidate would be a heartbeat from the White House. Brady wiped his palms on his jacket. They were sweating.

*****

Adam Hoch was listening to Goodman drone on about how proud he was of all his key operatives, and how a strong finish would establish AR as a power-broker for years to come. Hoch tried to disguise his disdain.

Strong finish?' he thought. *'The son of a bitch thinks we're going to lose! Once this is all over, I've got to get rid of that bastard.'*

He was running through possible scenarios to dump the National Director, when he felt his cellphone vibrate in his pocket.

'Who the hell is that?' he wondered; very few of his associates had his private number.

"Hoch," he answered softly.

"Grandpa, it's me," Jeffrey's whispered voice came through the earpiece. Hoch flinched in spite of himself. He glanced around the room to see if any of the AR flunkies had noticed. All eyes were riveted on Goodman.

"Hold on," he said brusquely, and slipped out of the office to the empty adjoining reception room. He closed the door gently. "What the hell are you doing calling me here, now?!" he whispered vehemently. "What's the matter?" He knew his grandson well enough to understand that he only called when there was trouble.

"The cops found us. They took the woman back."

Hoch swore to himself, but kept his temper in check. "Tell me. What happened?"

Jeffrey explained everything that had happened, and how he'd escaped by repelling down the front of the building.

"Did they get the other two guys who were helping you?

"Yeh. I think they shot Jermaine."

"Great, just great," the oil tycoon muttered. "Where are you now?"

"I'm here, in Fredericksburg, at the AR headquarters."

"What?! Are you out of your mind?"

There was a long pause at the other end. "I didn't have anywhere else to go. Besides, I thought this would be the *last* place they'd expect me to come. You know, hide in plain sight?"

Hoch took a deep breath. Maybe the kid was right. Maybe the cops wouldn't expect him to come there. But whatever the case, he needed to get him out of the public eye and find someplace where he could keep him under wraps for at least 24 hours. Then they'd see about getting him out of the country. South America maybe.

"Okay, all right. Maybe this will work out after all. Where are you, exactly?"

"I'm here on the second floor, in a big waiting area crammed with people."

Hoch knew exactly where that was. "Okay. Stay there. Turn toward the wall as if you're still on the phone and stay where you are until I can get Tommy over there to bring you to me. Understand?"

"Yeh, I got it."

The petulance in his voice grated on the old man's nerves, but he knew this was no time for lectures. "Be invisible," he said. "Just another of the AR faithful."

As soon as he shut his cellphone, Hoch went back into the meeting room where Tommy waited patiently just inside the door. Hoch motioned to him with a small nod of his head. He then slipped back into the adjoining room to wait for his bodyguard to join him.

"Jeffrey is out in the main waiting room, at the top of the stairs where all the AR supporters are gathering," he explained quickly as soon as the bodyguard closed the door behind him. "Go get him, and bring him here." The large black man turned to leave. "And Tommy," Hoch added, "try to be inconspicuous."

Tommy smiled. "I'm a black man in Virginia," he said. "I'm always inconspicuous."

As the door to the hallway closed, Hoch lowered himself slowly into a black leather chair tucked behind the modern glass and steel desk of one of the AR Deputy Directors. He felt tired. Old.

'Just another 24 hours,' he thought. *'Just one more day.'*

*****

Brady was pacing nervously when his phone rang.

"I think that big black dude you were telling me about just strolled past, headed for the waiting area," Chesley said quietly.

Brady felt his heart begin to pound in his chest. "Where did he come from?"

"I didn't see him come out, but I think it was at the end of the hall, or near to it."

"Can you see him from where you are?"

"Not from here, but if I cheat forward about ten feet to where the corridor turns, I can see out into the big waiting room."

"Do it. Let me know what he's up to."

"You got it."

Brady turned back towards Derek.

"Tommy's on the move," James explained to his PI buddy, who was fiddling with some electronic equipment on the desk where he'd set up shop.

"Where to?"

"Don't know. Out into the waiting area for now."

"You think it's Jeffrey?"

Brady shrugged. "Who knows? We can only hope."

'Hope, and wait,' he thought.

Seconds became minutes. Brady's thoughts sped around and around like a dog chasing its tail: what would they do if Jeffrey didn't show? Should they confront the old man? Why hadn't he heard from Wyman? He tried to focus on the task at hand, but he couldn't help himself.

And then the phone rang again.

"I think it's the kid," Chesley whispered. "They're staying out of the lights, but I'm almost sure it's him."

"Just keep an eye on him," Brady directed. "Remember, we need to catch them dead to rights. Give Hoch any wiggle room, and his lawyers will get him out of it. If they come this way, let me know."

"They're coming this way right now," Chez said.

"Okay, let'em come."

Brady slipped his cellphone into a pocket. "Chez thinks Jeffrey's here. Tommy and he are headed this way."

"Like moths to a flame," Derek muttered as he finished checking the electronics. "Here, let's get this on you." He handed Brady a Washington Redskins cap and a small black box. The PI finished adjusting his equipment just as Brady's phone rang again.

"They'll be walking past you in ten seconds. And it *is* the grandkid. I got a good look at him as they went past."

"They didn't recognize you, did they?"

"Nah. Didn't have a clue."

"Ok, thanks."

Brady signaled to Derek that they were approaching. Then he put his ear to the office door and listened as they passed by.

"The old man's not gonna like that," he heard Tommy say through the door. He couldn't make out Jeffrey's reply.

Brady counted to five and then turned the doorknob as gently and silently as he could. The door swung open without a squeak. Down at the end of the hallway, Tommy was opening an office door on the left side of the corridor; he held it open for Jeffrey to enter. Not two seconds later he glanced back over his shoulder to see if anyone had seen them. At the last instant Brady pulled back into the office they had commandeered and held his breath.

"He didn't see me, he didn't see me," he chanted to himself like a mantra.

There was no reaction from the hallway.

"The kid went into one of the offices," Brady whispered to Derek, who stood beside him at the doorway.

"Where's Tommy?" the PI asked. "Never mind, stay put. I'll look." Squatting down until he was no more than a few inches off the floor, the midget peeked out into the hallway. Tommy stood watch outside the office, looking nonchalantly alert.

"He's right outside the door. We gotta get him outta there."

Brady nodded and thought for just a second before placing another call.

"Chez? If you take a look down the hallway, you'll see that Hoch's bodyguard is standing right outside the door that I need to get into – now. Think you can convince him to move?"

"Oh, I think that's possible," the DC cop responded, and from his tone Brady knew that it would be done.

They heard Chesley's footsteps coming toward them out in the hallway; he glanced in their direction and winked as he strode past.

"Excuse me, but may I see your ID?" they heard him ask Tommy at the end of the hallway.

"What kind of ID?" the big guard asked in a tone that suggested he wasn't about to comply with any requests made by some rent-a-cop.

"An ID that permits you to be in here standing outside that door while an important meeting is taking place," Chez said with real cop attitude.

"I'm here with Mr. Hoch," Tommy said with much less 'screw you' in his voice.

"I don't care if you're here with the Queen of England. If you don't have an ID, out you go."

"Listen, buddy, Mr. Hoch doesn't pay me to go get IDs. He pays me to be out here while he's inside having his own meeting."

"Oh? Does he pay you for *this*?" Chesley asked, pulling his service revolver and sticking the barrel into Tommy's gaping mouth. "Now move!" he ordered in a tone that suffered no reply.

Brady watched while Chez shoved the big bodyguard through an emergency exit door and down some stairs. The corridor was empty. It was time.

Brady stepped out into the hallway and took a deep breath.

"Wish me luck," he told his PI friend.

"I'll be right outside the door. As will Chez too, as soon as he deals with our buddy Tommy."

'But I'll be inside with that nut job and his grandfather,' James worried despite his best efforts to remain calm. *'Oh well, let's do it...'*

He made his way down the corridor quickly, not wanting time to think too clearly about the risk he was taking. At the door to the office the PI fiddled with the equipment one last time; when he was satisfied, he tapped Brady on the hip. James looked down at Derek and smiled.

"Showtime!"

Without hesitation he threw open the door and strolled into the office. Hoch sat behind a large executive desk, with Jeffrey standing in front of him looking none too happy. At the sound of his entrance, Jeffrey reached into the waistband of his pants and turned to face Brady – a 9mm pistol in his hand.

"Hope I'm not intruding," Brady said, his voice sounding shaky in his own ears.

"For God's sake, put the pistol down," the old man ordered brusquely.

The younger Hoch hesitated a long moment, then did as he was told, stuffing the gun back into his waistband.

"I kind of thought we hadn't seen the last of you," the elder Hoch said jovially. "Have a seat."

"I'm not here to be entertained," Brady said with every ounce of authority he could muster.

"No, I suppose not," Hoch nodded with a smile. "So why exactly *are* you here?"

"Who gives a damn," Jeffrey snapped. "Let me get rid of this asshole once and for all, Grandpa."

"Relax Jeffrey! They have nothing on us."

"Not on you perhaps, but they've got plenty on your grandson: kidnapping, assault, probably a half-dozen other charges as well. He's going away for a long, long time."

"You're freakin' dreaming!" the grandson snarled. "My grandfather won't let some two-bit local cops send me to jail."

"I'm afraid he's right, Mr. James. As much as a short stint behind bars might drive some sense into his thick skull, I really can't allow my grandson to languish in some dreary prison cell."

"And how do you plan to avoid it? The cops are already looking for him from Baltimore to Richmond."

"Let them look. I won't be around here for much longer anyhow," the young Hoch answered with a cocky smile.

"Jeffrey – keep your mouth shut!"

The grandson simmered behind angry eyes, but did as he was told. For a moment no one spoke.

"You won't get away with this, you know," Brady finally broke the tense silence in the room.

"Get away with what, Mr. James? I assume you would have made some sort of move if you had solid evidence of any wrong-doing. The fact that you haven't tells me you're still fishing."

Brady weighed his next words carefully. "I know more than you think. I know that you've rigged electronic voting machines in at least three states, and that you think you can steal the election by swinging those states over to the GOP. And the AR, of course."

He watched the elder Hoch closely as he spoke. The old man kept a pretty good poker face, but Brady thought he'd seen just a flicker of surprise – or was it alarm – when he mentioned the election.

"An interesting theory, Mr. James. But is it fact, or fiction? I would suggest the latter."

Brady decided to go for broke. "Ted Wyman doesn't think so. They have him under protective custody."

"I told you we should have gotten rid of that little weasel!" Jeffrey exploded. "*I* could have gotten us into the warehouse where they keep the voting machines if you'd just given me enough time."

"Shut up!" the older Hoch shouted. "He's just fishing. He doesn't know a thing."

"I know that you were pushing Senator Wainwright to go along with your little plan just before he died – Simon Beddecker can confirm that. I'm betting the Secret Service and the DC cops will be real interested in learning where you – and Jeffrey – were on the day Wainwright died."

Jeffrey pulled out the pistol. This time his voice was cold, hard. "I'm not going to prison, Grandpa. I don't give a damn about your stupid election. This sonofabitch has got to go."

Brady waited for the old man to countermand his grandson's rant. But he remained silent.

"I'm sorry, Mr. James, but I'm afraid that I have to agree with my grandson this time," he said after a long pause. "You know more than I thought. More than I can tolerate. You know, I didn't want anyone to get hurt in all this. I only wanted what was best for this country."

Brady felt his legs get weak. What if the kid were to shoot first and ask questions later?

"I know you did," he answered Hoch softly. "I know. And I think we can make a jury understand your reasons. But only if it stops now."

Hoch smiled and nodded sadly. "You know, Mr. James, I fought in Korea, saw friends die, killed my share of gooks. All to keep this country safe. And now? Now the liberal fringe is destroying the country. Unless people who have the will and the means do something about it, the United States is going to be nothing but a shadow of what we once were, and I don't mean in a hundred years, I mean in your lifetime. Who was it who said 'desperate times call for desperate measures'? Whoever it was, they had it right."

"People have died," Brady interrupted cautiously. "A U.S Senator, one of your own employees... this has to stop."

"Not just yet, I'm afraid," Hoch replied. "In 24 hours Jeffrey will be long gone and they can do whatever they want to me. I only have a few months to live anyway."

Brady's questioning look prompted a shrug and a quick reply.

"Cancer of the pancreas. It's shot to hell. Not that it matters. My lawyers could keep the government bureaucrats tied up until I died of old age. As Mr. Wyman has no doubt told you, with a push of a button we can eliminate all traces of our software. They won't find a hint. Even a recount won't change the outcome."

"*I* developed that software," Jeffrey chimed in with obvious pride.

"Yes, you did, Jeffrey," Hoch said, and for just an instant Brady saw the proud grandfather hidden behind the stony oil baron. "And it will change the history of this nation. I suppose you know, Mr. James, that the shifting of just a few thousand votes in a handful of states can alter the outcome of the election."

"I'm well aware."

"Yes, well in just a few hours now, we will do just that. For the first time in decades this nation will be on a sound, secure footing."

Brady couldn't help himself. "What's the old saying about building on a foundation of sand?"

Hoch wouldn't be riled. "Quite the contrary, Mr. James. We will construct a new nation on the bedrock of traditional moral values, sound economic principles and an impregnable defense."

"Impressive. I wish I could be around to see it. But since it doesn't look like this will end well for me, how about one last question?"

"Ask away."

"Why do all this, why risk everything, just to get your man the VP slot? I mean, he will have influence, admittedly, but he won't be calling the tune."

Hoch smiled with satisfaction.

"Mr. Blackburn won't be Vice President for long," he explained. "In less than a year the President will contract an unknown, incurable disease that mimics ALS and will die in office."

"I assume you already have the virus in hand?"

"Safely locked away in an ultra-secure storage area."

"It sounds like you have everything under control. I'm impressed."

"Well thank you, Mr. James. If it means anything to you, I'm impressed by your ingenuity and determination. I doubt there are more than a handful of people in this country who could have figured out what we had planned."

"How long have you been working on this idea?" Brady asked, hoping to keep them talking as long as possible. But the grandson was having none of it.

"He's just playing us, Grandpa! Let me take him downstairs and be done with it."

"Take it easy, Jeffrey, take it easy. You may be right about Mr. James' motives, but I think you will move faster without him. Let me call Tommy in here and he can entertain Mr. James while you get out of town." The elder Hoch opened his cellphone and punched a single key. He waited as the phone rang. And rang.

"Odd, he's not answering," Hoch muttered, half to himself. Brady could see the wheels turn as realization dawned on the old man. "Jeffrey, give me the gun and get out of here – now!" he shouted. "Something's not right."

His grandson backed toward him, keeping his gun trained on Brady the whole time. With one last glance at their captive, he handed the pistol gingerly to his grandfather. For a long moment the two men looked at one another, knowing this might be the last time they ever saw one another.

"Go, go!" Adam shouted.

As if jolted, Jeffrey ran past Brady to the office door. But as he threw it open, the last thing he saw was Derek's head, just an instant before the midget butted him viciously in the groin.

"Ain't payback a bitch?" Derek said as Jeffrey fell to his knees, his face a purple-red balloon looking ready to explode.

Brady turned back toward Hoch, and saw the old man holding the gun in both hands, taking dead aim.

"Don't do it, Adam," Brady said with more calm than he felt. "It's over."

"You can't prove a thing. It'll be your word against mine."

Just then Chesley stepped into the room, backed by three men and a woman wearing FBI body vests. All five of them held guns.

Brady held up an arm to block Chez from going further. "Just give me one minute," he said quietly.

"One minute. That's all you get," his friend said definitively.

Brady turned back to the oil baron. "Mr. Hoch, there's no way out. Don't make this any worse than it already is."

"Like I said before we were interrupted, you can't prove anything."

"I'm afraid you're wrong there," he said, and turning to Derek he slowly accepted a small LCD screen from the PI. He held it up to show Hoch he meant no harm.

"May I show you something?" he asked.

"Sure, why not?"

Brady walked to the glass desk and placed the screen where Hoch could see it without turning away from the horde of police at the door. He pushed a button and a familiar scene appeared on the LCD.

It was Hoch, seated behind the desk, with Jeffrey standing just in front of him.

"I'm not going to prison, Grandpa. I don't give a damn about your stupid election," Jeffrey's voice called out from the monitor. "This sonofabitch has got to go."

"I'm sorry, Mr. James, but I'm afraid that I have to agree with my grandson this time. You know more than I thought. More than I can tolerate. You know, I didn't want anyone to get hurt in all this. I only wanted what was best for this country."

Brady turned the recording off. Hoch showed no outward sign of emotion, but his eyes narrowed ever so slightly.

"I always hated all that electronic gadgetry," he began evenly. "It's turning our kids into sedentary robots."

Brady took off his Redskins cap and pointed to the tiny dark lens hidden as the dot of the "i". "Sometimes it can be useful."

Hoch leaned back in his chair, but he did not lower the gun. "Do you have any idea what you've done here? You've virtually assured that this country will continue on its downward spiral. Our grandchildren, and their kids, will live in a world where the United States is no longer its political and economic leader. Can you even imagine that?"

"You don't have much faith in the average Joe, do you Mr. Hoch?"

Hoch smiled. "Is there some reason why I should? Look who they've voted for in the past few elections. Except for Reagan they've all been bureaucrats, drunks or lefties for over 50 years. You could run a trained chimpanzee and half of the people out there would vote for him."

"Isn't that what democracy is all about?"

Hoch snorted. "Democracy?! Is that what you call this? I call it 'American Idol.' Whoever the unwashed masses take a liking to from scripted debates and endless TV spots gets elected, while the moral and ethical core of this country is rotted away from the inside. Democracy…"

Chesley tapped Brady on the shoulder. "Time's up," he whispered.

"Mr. Hoch, please, put the gun down," Brady tried one last time. "No one else needs to get hurt. It's over."

Hoch stared at Brady as if looking right through him.

"Over," he said softly. "Yes, I suppose it is at that. But you mark my words, Mr. James, you may have won a battle, but our country will lose the war. I'm just happy I won't be around to see it. Goodbye, Mr. James. Goodbye, Jeffrey."

Before Brady could say a word, Hoch lifted the pistol to the side of his head and pulled the trigger. Blood, bone and gray matter splattered against the wall behind the desk as the old man fell back in his chair. The explosion echoed in the small office. Chesley threw Brady down and knelt in a firing position. There was no need.

"Grandpa!" Jeffrey wailed from the ground where an FBI agent was busy securing his hands behind his back.

Brady stumbled to his feet, the stench of blood and gunpowder strong in his nostrils.

"Goodbye, Mr. Hoch," he said softly. "I hope to hell you were wrong."

EPILOGUE

Anne, Danny, Derek and Brady sat around the big screen TV in the PI's apartment, awaiting the first returns from the eastern states.

"Anyone hungry?" Derek asked. "I think we have some hotdogs in the freezer."

Anne groaned. "Those aren't the same ones from two months ago, are they?"

"They're frozen," the PI said by way of explanation.

"Oh, that's okay then," Brady said with a superior grin. "How about beer? Do we have any more of that?"

"You can get up off that lazy butt of yours and go find out."

Brady shook his head in mock disgust. "Can't get good help these days," he muttered.

"Speaking of good help, where's Chez? I thought he was coming down here to watch the results."

"Good question," Brady said, pulling out his cellphone and holding the power button. "Let's see what he's up to."

As soon as the phone powered up, a familiar electronic reminder sounded.

"Ah, a voicemail. It's probably him."

"Probably has some cockamamie excuse like a bank robbery or triple homicide."

"Some people just don't know how to prioritize."

Brady called up the voicemail. "You have one message, left on Monday, November 3rd at 8:27 a.m.," the digitized voice intoned. Brady pushed another button. "Mr. James, it's Ted, Ted Wyman," a familiar voice said from the phone's tiny speaker. "I think I'll have those jammers we talked about. Let me know where you want them. I'll stay by the phone." And he gave an Ohio phone number.

"I keep telling you you don't check your voicemail often enough," Anne chimed in.

"Thank you," Derek agreed. "I've only been telling him that for the better part of ten years now."

"Great, now I've got *two* of you on my back. Do the henpecks show?" Brady said with a smile.

"Oh, poor boy, so abused," Anne cooed as she hugged him tightly and kissed him on the cheek.

"You stay where you are," Brady ordered his tiny friend.

"Don't worry," Derek answered with a look of horror.

Brady called Wyman to let him know that all was well and they wouldn't need his jammers after all. "At least not for this election," he added reflexively.

"I'll keep them handy," Wyman said.

"Yeh, you do that."

Brady thanked him and hung up.

Just then the doorbell rang. It was Chesley.

"Did I miss anything?" he asked, dropping a six-pack of beer on the dining room table.

"Yeh, it's 21 to 19 in the fourth quarter, just two minutes left to play," Derek teased.

"Your timing is excellent," Anne interrupted. "The first polls close in…seven minutes."

"So, who do we think is going to win?"

"Better not be that AR jerkoff," Danny said with a look of undisguised distaste, "Or I'm moving to Costa Rica."

"Do they have computers in Costa Rica?" Derek asked.

"No, but they have some pretty nice beaches, or so I've heard. And cheap."

"Doesn't sound bad," Brady said, looking to Anne for her reaction.

"We'll see," she said. "Maybe for your birthday."

"Can I go, can I go?!" Derek joked, waving his hand as if to get Anne's attention.

"As long as you don't come within a mile of wherever we stay," Brady grumbled.

"Brady!" Anne said with a slap to his shoulder. "Be nice."

"That'd be a stretch," Chesley offered.

Brady shook his head. "With friends like these…"

"Who needs a beer?"

*****

It didn't take long for the networks to start-in with the exit polls. As expected, both Ohio and Florida looked to be razor close. With the final national opinion polls calling the race a toss-up, it looked like it would be a long night.

The lead rocked back and forth as first the traditionally Blue states, and then the Red began to count votes. It was still anyone's ballgame as the Midwest, and then the Mountain states closed their polls.

"Looks like we may be here for a while," Derek said after Kansas brought the GOP/AR alliance to a 12 vote Electoral College lead. "Do we have enough beer?"

Chesley was just returning from the kitchen with three cold ones. "Down to our last 12-pack," he said. "Should I make a run?"

"I think we can tough it out," Brady said. "Besides, you still have some Jim Beam sitting around somewhere, don't you Derek?"

"In case of emergencies. Medicinal use only."

"If those damn Republicans win I'll be sick to my stomach," Danny suggested, only half in jest.

It was after midnight, with only Hawaii still voting, when the networks called Florida: Democrats, 50.7% to 49.3. Less than an hour later, it was Ohio: Dems by 37,000 votes. Still, it was nip and tuck until both Oregon and Washington slid into the Blue column. From the whoops and hollers in that apartment, you'd have thought the Redskins had won a Super Bowl. Hugs and kisses all around.

"We did it!" Danny yelled gleefully.

"I think it was the Democrats who did most of the heavy lifting," Brady corrected. "We just made sure no one cooked the books."

"Yeh, we sure cooked their goose!" Derek joined in after one or two beers too many.

"Well, that's enough excitement for one night," Chesley said as he slipped into his jacket and headed for the door. "Anyone need a lift?"

"Are you sober enough to drive?" Danny asked.

"I'm a cop. I'm always sober enough to drive!"

Anne tilted her head appraisingly, unwilling to make the call.

"Never seen him wrap his car around anything in all the years I've known him," Brady testified. "Besides, it might be hard finding a cab this time of night."

"Yeh, okay, thanks," the young State Department geek said to Chez.

Brady walked them to the door.

"Next time you have an idea for a story, call the Staties," Chesley said as he shook Brady's hand. "I'm getting too old for this crap."

"Are you kidding?!" Danny interrupted. "This was great!"

"Hey, I'm retired," Brady smiled. "I'm just looking for some peace and quiet. And maybe a few Redskin wins."

"Good luck with that one," Chez said, and with a slap to Brady's shoulder he stepped out into the hall. "Good night all!" he called back.

Danny waved to Anne, who was picking up empty beer cans and chip bags, and Derek, who was stretched out on the sofa. "See you!" He had to hurry to catch up to his ride.

"What a week," Brady groaned as he closed the apartment door. "I think I could sleep for a month."

"Well I'm going to bed right now, if you want to join me," Anne said. "And I think Derek has already found his nesting spot for the night."

Brady looked to the couch, where his friend's open mouth and rhythmic snoring seemed to prove her point.

"I'll be there in just a few minutes," he told Anne.

"You'd better hurry if you want to catch me awake."

He watched her disappear into the kitchen as he went out onto the balcony. Taking a deep breath, he looked out over the city, mesmerized by the twinkling lights and familiar sounds. The night was cool and clear; with just a slice of moon, he could actually see a few stars overhead. He looked left toward the White House, even though he knew it was too far away to see. It didn't matter; he knew it was there, and that the person living there would be someone the American people had put there. Right or wrong, good or bad, he, or she, would be a President of the people, by the people, and perhaps even for the people.

Life was good, he decided with a smile. Not perfect, but good.

Now, if only the Redskins could win a few games...

www.ingramcontent.com/pod-product-compliance
Lightning Source LLC
Chambersburg PA
CBHW031436240626
47154CB00001B/294